02

THE WHISPERER AND OTHER VOICES

TOR BOOKS BY BRIAN LUMLEY

The Necroscope Series

Necroscope
Necroscope II: Vamphyri!
Necroscope III: The Source
Necroscope IV: Deadspeak
Necroscope V: Deadspawn
Blood Brothers
The Last Aerie
Bloodwars
Necroscope: The Lost Years
Necroscope: Resurgence
Necroscope: Invaders
Necroscope: Defilers

The Titus Crow Series

Titus Crow, Volume One: The Burrowers Beneath & Transition
Titus Crow, Volume Two: The Clock of Dreams & Spawn of the Winds
Titus Crow, Volume Three: In the Moons of Borea & Elysia

The Psychomech Trilogy

Psychomech
Psychosphere
Psychamok

Other Novels

Demogorgon
The House of Doors
Maze of Worlds

Short Story Collections

Fruiting Bodies and Other Fungi
The Whisperer and Other Voices

TOR®
A TOM DOHERTY ASSOCIATES BOOK
NEW YORK

THE WHISPERER AND OTHER VOICES

BRIAN LUMLEY

THE WHISPERER AND OTHER VOICES

Copyright © 2001 by Brian Lumley

This book is printed on acid-free paper.

Design by Heidi P. F. Eriksen

A Tor Book
Published by Tom Doherty Associates, LLC
175 Fifth Avenue
New York, NY 10010

www.tor.com

Tor® is a registered trademark of Tom Doherty Associates, LLC.

Library of Congress Cataloging-in-Publication Data

Lumley, Brian.
    The whisperer and other voices / Brian Lumley.—1st ed.
        p. cm.
    "A Tom Doherty Associates book."
    Contents: Snarker's son—Aunt Hester—The whisperer—No sharks in the Med—Vanessa's voice—The statement of Henry Worthy—The disapproval of Jeremy Cleave—The luststone—The return of the Deep Ones.
    ISBN 0-312-87695-5 (acid-free paper)
    1. Horror tales, English. I. Title: Whisperer and other voices. II. Title.

PR6062.U45 W48 2001
823'.914—dc21

                                                                    00-049624

First Edition: February 2001

Printed in the United States of America

0 9 8 7 6 5 4 3 2 1

FOR BARBARA ANN

CONTENTS

INTRODUCTION

I have been a writer now for more than a third of a century, and across the years, other than my 'series' short stories and novels (such as the Necroscope series, the Titus Crow stories, and the Hero and Primal Land series), I have written a good many stand-alone novels and short stories hitherto uncollected in mass market paperback in the USA. Here Tor Books has given me the opportunity to present some of these in two large companion volumes, *The Whisperer* and *Beneath the Moors*.

The following introductions to the stories in the present volume, *The Whisperer and Other Voices*, may give the reader some insight as to how, why, or when they were written and why they are included here.

Most SF/fantasy/horror writers can't resist the occasional foray into this or that parallel universe, in which respect I'm no different from the rest. No more may be said about *Snarker's Son*, my first selection in this volume, without giving the game away. As for the purely technical details:

This short story was written in September 1970 and first appeared in England in a collection edited by Hugh Lamb. Since then I believe it's had one small press appearance in the USA, which makes it ideal for inclusion here. I may say that there is one other story in this volume that might be said to represent the flip side of *Snarker's Son*; I'll talk about it when we get there . . .

The second selection, *Aunt Hester*, dates back to December 1971.

Inspired by the work of the late great H. P. Lovecraft, it appeared in England in a David Sutton edited paperback collection and six years later was reprinted in my Arkham House collection *The Horror at Oakdeene.* Long out of print, this will be the story's first printing in a mass market edition in the USA. Though inspired by HPL, *Aunt Hester* hasn't the feel of a Lovecraftian story. The closest it comes is in its theme or motif, which . . . But no, rather than offend any Lovecraft purists out there, I won't darken HPL's doorstep by making comparisons . . .

The title story, *The Whisperer,* is in a way the flip side to *Snarker's Son,* mentioned above. For where the latter was a trip *into* the beyond, this could well be an incursion *from* some similar strange place. It was my attempt back in 1972 to write a weird tale without reference to the standard props. There are no typical monsters here but something inexplicable. The story appeared in Kirby McCauley's ground-breaking and award-winning *Frights,* and at the time (oh, a long time ago!) Kirby remarked I'd 'created a character for the supernatural gallery who bids well to be long remembered.' His words, at least, have been a long time remembered . . .

As for *No Sharks in the Med,* written in 1987 for the new *Weird Tales:*

It could only be some perverse *thing* in my nature that inspired the title of this one, for of course there *are* sharks in the Mediterranean, especially around Naples and in the Adriatic, and between Israel and Port Said, etc. And not 'merely' sharks but Great Whites, too! During my three years in Cyprus I found a dead baby Great White washed up on a beach. No more than two foot long, tip to tail, still the jaws and teeth of this infant were already formidable. It's safe to say, however, that around the Greek Islands of the holiday brochures, sharks are relatively scarce.

The ones with gills are, anyway . . .

Vanessa's Voice dates back to 1973 and saw print in *Whispers,* Stuart Schiff's excellent, long-remembered (and mourned) 'little' (and occasionally not so little) magazine, since then it has been out of print. The idea for the story came to me as a serving soldier in Germany, when for a period I was a 'drill-pig,' an instructor in the not-so-delicate art of what British soldiers call 'square-bashing.' For a whole week I *lost* my own voice, and a drill-pig without a voice is like . . . hell, a singer without a song! Or vice versa . . .

The Statement of Henry Worthy is from an *Arkham* collection of my tales published in 1977 and out of print for several years. This is its first mass market printing in the USA. It's scarcely surprising that this story is blatantly Lovecraftian; written in 1967, it was one of the first handful of stories I ever attempted, and I was heavily under the influence of HPL.

I was in Berlin at the time, and the infamous Wall was a relatively new feature. The city was dreary in the winter months, and the whole place felt like a giant goldfish bowl; only travel five or six miles in any direction, you would bump into the Wall or the Wire. So I suppose that really this story was my personal escape route—a piece of genuine escapism—and I was fortunate that I could write my way to a kind of temporary freedom. Well, good for me . . . but no such luck for Henry Worthy . . .

Next, something of a change of style and pace. *The Disapproval of Jeremy Cleave* was written for a 'Lumley Special Edition' of *Weird Tales* and is in its way a small homage to Mr Ronald Chetwynd-Hayes, a dear old Brit friend of mine who has often been "accused" of introducing humour into horror. But if we can't have a laugh at ourselves, then who can we laugh at?

After I had written this story (it was mid-August 1988, and late at night), and after I had read it back to myself, I found myself chuckling . . . until somewhere in the distance an old church clock chimed out. My back was to a misty, nighted garden—and damn me if I wasn't tempted to turn and have a look! It may have been a kind of discord in the chiming of the clock that struck me as wrong—or maybe something in the story that was right?

I remember a recent convention (World Horror Con?) where Richard Matheson read an aftermath-cum-mutant story of his to a fascinated audience. The thing was grim as can be yet at the same time funny as hell. I suppose it all depends on how you see funny, or perhaps on your concept of hell . . .

The penultimate tale, *The Luststone,* is a meeting of ancient and modern horrors. It was written in five weeks in 1981, and if you think that's a long time to write a short story, or even a long one, perhaps I had better explain that in its original form it was a novel of 60,000 words—and it was pornographic. I just wanted to see if I could do it—and did it well enough that after submitting it only once I scrapped it! I didn't want my name associated with it. But I did keep parts of it which I believed might be cannibalized later.

Seven or eight years went by; the editors of *Weird Tales* asked me if I had any new stories; that was my cue to do something with *The Luststone.* By then enough time had passed that I could see a new direction for the story and was able to turn a minus into a plus.

I find *The Luststone* very visual. It's funny, but of all the stories and novels I've written, this one is probably the most filmable. And if they gave it an 'adults only' rating, it wouldn't any longer be for the sex . . .

Which leaves us with *The Return of the Deep Ones.*

Impossible to deny Lovecraft's influence on this one even if I wanted to, which I don't. For HPL's Deep Ones—those batrachian dwellers in fathomless ocean employed so effectively in *The Shadow Over Innsmouth,* and hinted at in others of his stories—have always fascinated me. And not only me but an entire generation of authors most of whom weren't even born until long after Lovecraft's tragically early death. A recent book, *Shadows Over Innsmouth,* from Fedogan and Bremer, containing stories by Neil Gaiman, Kim Newman, Ramsey Campbell, Basil Copper and a host of others, is more than adequate proof of this. Indeed the lure was so great that in 1978 I wrote this full-length novel, *The Return of the Deep Ones,* on the same theme. It has appeared only once before in the USA—and then fifteen years ago, as a three-parter in the now extinct *Fantasy Book*—and I'm indebted to Tor Books for this opportunity to bring it to a wider American audience in the current volume . . .

Brian Lumley,
Devon, England.
May 2000.

SNARKER'S
SON

'All right, all right!' Sergeant Scott noisily submitted. 'So you're lost.
You're staying with your dad here in the city at a hotel—you went
sightseeing and you got separated—I accept all that. But look, son, we've
had lost kids in here before, often, and they didn't try on all this silly
stuff about names and spellings and all!'

Sergeant Scott had known—had been instinctively 'aware' all day—
that this was going to be one of *those* shifts. Right up until ten minutes
ago his intuition had seemed for once to have let him down. But now . . .

'It's true,' the pallid, red-eyed nine-year-old insisted, hysteria in his
voice. 'It's all true, everything I've said. This town *looks* like Mondon—
but it's not! And . . . and before I came in here I passed a store called
Woolworths—but it should have been "Wolwords"!'

'All right, let's not start that again.' The policeman put up quieting
hands. 'Now: you say you came down with your father from . . . from
Sunderpool? That's in England?'

'No, I've *told* you,' the kid started to cry again. 'It's "Eenland!" We
came down on holiday from Sunderpool by longcar, and—'

'Longcar?' Sergeant Scott cut in, frowning. 'Is that some place on
the north-east coast?'

'No, it's not a place! A longcar is . . . well, a *longcar*! Like a buzz but
longer, and it goes on the longcar lanes. You know . . . ?' The boy looked
as puzzled as Sergeant Scott, to say nothing of accusing.

'No, I don't know!' The policeman shook his head, trying to control his frown. 'A "buzz"?' Scott could feel the first twinges of one of his bilious headaches coming on, and so decided to change the subject.

'What does your father do, son? He's a science-fiction writer, eh?—And you're next in a long line?'

'Dad's a snarker,' the answer came quite spontaneously, without any visible attempt at deceit or even flippancy. In any case, the boy was obviously far too worried to be flippant. A 'nut,' Scott decided—but nevertheless a nut in trouble.

Now the kid had an inquisitive look on his face. 'What's science fiction?' he asked.

'Science fiction,' the big sergeant answered with feeling, 'is that part of a policeman's lot called "desk-duty"—when crazy lost kids walk into the station in tears to mess up said policeman's life!'

His answer set the youngster off worse than before.

Sighing, Scott passed his handkerchief across the desk and stood up. He called out to a constable in an adjacent room:

'Hey, Bob, come and look after the desk until Sergeant Healey gets in, will you? He's due on duty in the next ten minutes or so. I'll take the kid and see if I can find his father. If I can't—well, I'll bring the boy back here and the job can go through the usual channels.'

'All right, Sergeant, I'll watch the shop,' the constable agreed as he came into the duty-room and took his place at the desk. 'I've been listening to your conversation! Right rum 'un that,' he grinned, nodding towards the tearful boy. 'What an imagination!'

Imagination, yes. And yet Scott was not quite sure. There was 'something in the air,' a feeling of impending—*strangeness*—hard to define.

'Come on, son,' he said, shaking off his mood. 'Let's go.'

He took the boy's hand. 'Let's see if we can find your dad. He's probably rushing about right now wondering what's become of you.' He shook his head in feigned defeat and said: 'I don't know—ten o'clock at night, just going off duty—and *you* have to walk in on me!'

'Ten o'clock—*already*?' The boy looked up into Scott's face with eyes wider and more frightened than ever. 'Then we only have half an hour!'

'Eh?' the policeman frowned again as they passed out into the London street (or was it 'Mondon,' Scott wondered with a mental grin). 'Half an hour? What happens at half past ten, son? Do you turn into a pumpkin or something?' His humour was lost on his small charge.

'I mean the *lights*!' the boy answered, in what Scott took to be exasperation. 'That's when the lights go out. At half past ten they put the lights out.'

'They do?' the sergeant had given up trying to penetrate the boy's fertile but decidedly warped imagination. 'Why's that, I wonder?' (Let the kid ramble on; it was better than tears at any rate.)

'Don't you know *anything*?' the youngster seemed half-astonished, half-unbelieving, almost as if he thought Scott was pulling his leg.

'No,' the sergeant returned, 'I'm just a stupid copper! But come on—where did you give your father the slip? You said you passed Woolworths getting to the police station. Well, Woolworths is down this way, near the tube.' He looked at the boy sharply in mistaken understanding. 'You didn't get lost on the tube, did you? Lots of kids do when it's busy.'

'The Tube?' Scott sensed that the youngster spoke the words in capitals—and yet it was only a whisper. He had to hold on tight as the boy strained away from him in something akin to horror. 'No one goes down in the Tube any more, except—' He shuddered.

'Yes?' Scott pressed, interested in this particular part of the boy's fantasy despite himself and the need, now, to have done with what would normally be a routine job. 'Except who?'

'Not *who*,' the boy told him, clutching his hand tighter. 'Not who, but—'

'But?' again, patiently, Scott prompted him.

'Not who but *what*!'

'Well, go on,' said the sergeant, sighing, leading the way down the quiet, half-deserted street towards Woolworths. '*What*, er, goes down in the tube?'

'Why, Tubers, of course!' Again there was astonishment in the youngster's voice, amazement at Scott's obvious deficiency in general knowledge. 'Aren't you Mondoners thick!' It was a statement of fact, not a question.

'Right,' said Scott, not bothering to pursue the matter further, seeing the pointlessness of questioning an idiot. 'We've passed Woolworths—now where?'

'Over there, I think, down that street. Yes!—that's where I lost my father—down there!'

'Come on,' Scott said, leading the boy across the road, empty now of all but the occasional car, down into the entrance of the indicated street. In fact it was little more than an alley, dirty and unlighted. 'What on earth were you doing down here in the first place?'

'We weren't down here,' the youngster answered with a logic that made the sergeant's head spin. 'We were in a bright street, with lots of lights. Then I felt a funny buzzing feeling, and . . . and then I was here! I got frightened and ran.'

At that moment, their footsteps echoing hollowly on the cobbles of the alley, the sergeant felt a weird vibration that began in his feet and travelled up his body to his head, causing a burst of bright, painfully bilious stars to flash across his vision—and simultaneous with this peculiar sensation the two turned a corner to emerge with startling abruptness into a much brighter side street.

'That was the buzzing I told you about,' the boy stated unnecessarily.

Scott was not listening. He was looking behind him for the broken electric cable he felt sure must be lying there just inside the alley (the sensation must surely have been caused by a mild electric shock), but he couldn't see one. Nor could he see anything else that might have explained that tingling, nerve-rasping sensation he had known. For that matter, where was the entrance (or exit) from which he and the boy had just this second emerged?

Where was the alley?

'Dad!' the kid yelled, suddenly tugging himself free to go racing off down the street.

Scott stood and watched, his head starting to throb and the street lights flaring garishly before his eyes. At the boy's cry a lone man had turned, started to run, and now Scott saw him sweep the lad up in his arms and wildly hug him, intense and obvious relief showing in his face.

The policeman forgot the problem of the vanishing alley and walked up to them, hands behind his back in the approved fashion, smiling benignly. 'Cute lad you've got there, sir—but I should curb his imagination if I were you. Why, he's been telling me a story fit to—'

Then the benign smile slid from his face. '*Here!*' he cried, his jaw dropping in astonishment.

But despite his exclamation, Scott was nevertheless left standing on his own. For without a word of thanks both man and boy had made off down the street, hands linked, running as if the devil himself was after them!

'Here!' the policeman called again, louder. 'Hold on a bit—'

For a moment the pair stopped and turned, then the man glanced at his watch (reminding Scott curiously of the White Rabbit in *Alice in Wonderland*) before picking up the boy again and holding him close. 'Get off the street!' he yelled back at Scott as he once more started to run. 'Get off the streets, man.' His white face glanced back and up at the street lights as he ran, and Scott saw absolute fear shining in his eyes. 'It'll soon be half past ten!'

The policeman was still in the same position, his jaw hanging slack, some seconds later when the figure of the unknown man, again hugging the boy to him, vanished round a distant corner. Then he shrugged his shoulders and tried to pull himself together, setting his helmet more firmly on his aching head.

'Well I'll be—' He grinned nervously through the throb of his headache. 'Snarker's son, indeed!'

Alone, now, Scott's feeling of impending—*something*—returned, and he noticed suddenly just how deserted the street was. He had never known London so quiet before. Why, there wasn't a single soul in sight!

And a funny thing, but here he was, only a stone's throw from his station, where he'd worked for the last fifteen years of his life, and yet—damned if he could recognise the street! Well, he knew he'd brought the boy down a dark, cobbled alley from the right, and so . . .

He took the first street on the right, walking quickly down it until he hit another street he knew somewhat better—

—Or did he?

Yes, yes, of course he did. The street was deserted now, quite empty, but just over there was good old . . .

Good old Wolwords!

Lights blazed and burst into multicoloured sparks before Scott's bilious eyes. His mind spun wildly. He grabbed hold of a lamp-post to steady himself and tried to think the thing out properly.

It must be a new building, that place—yes, that had to be the answer. He'd been doing a lot of desk-duties lately, after all. It was quite possible, what with new techniques and the speed of modern building, that the store had been put up in just a few weeks.

The place didn't *look* any too new, though . . .

Scott's condition rapidly grew worse—understandably in the circumstances, he believed—but there was a tube station, nearby. He decided to take a train home. He usually walked the mile or so to his flat, the exercise did him good; but tonight he would take a train, give himself a rest.

He went dizzily down one flight of steps, barely noticing the absence of posters and the unkempt, dirty condition of the underground. Then, as he turned a corner, he came face-to-face with a strange legend, dripping in red paint on the tiled wall:

ROT THE TUBERS!

Deep creases furrowed the sergeant's forehead as he walked on, his footsteps ringing hollowly in the grimy, empty corridors, but his headache just wouldn't let him think clearly.

Tubers, indeed! What the hell—Tubers . . . ?

Down another flight of steps he went, to the deserted ticket booths, where he paused to stare in disbelief at the naked walls of the place and the dirt- and refuse-littered floor. For the first time he really saw the *condition* of the place. What had happened here? Where was everyone?

From beyond the turnstiles he heard the rumble of a distant train and the spell lifted a little. He hurried forward then, past the empty booths and through the unguarded turnstiles, dizzily down one more flight of concrete steps, under an arch and out on to an empty platform.

Not even a drunk or a tramp shared the place with him. The neons flared hideously, and he put out a hand against the naked wall for support.

Again, through the blinding flashes of light in his head, he noticed the absence of posters: the employment agencies, the pretty girls in lingerie, the film and play adverts, spectacular films and *avant-garde* productions—where in hell were they all?

Then, as for the first time he truly felt upon his spine the chill fingers of a slithering horror, there came the rumble and blast of air that announced the imminent arrival of a train—and he smelled the rushing reek of that which most certainly was *not* a train!

Even as he staggered to and fro on the unkempt platform, reeling under the fetid blast that engulfed him, the Tuber rushed from out its black hole—a *Thing* of crimson viscosity and rhythmically flickering cilia.

Sergeant Scott gave a wild shriek as a rushing feeler swept him from the platform and into the soft, hurtling plasticity of the thing—another shriek as he was whisked away into the deep tunnel and down into the bowels of the earth. And seconds later the minute hand of the clock above the empty, shuddering platform clicked down into the vertical position.

Ten-thirty—and all over Mondon, indeed throughout the length and breadth of Eenland, the lights went out.

AUNT
HESTER

I suppose my Aunt Hester Lang might be best described as the 'black sheep' of the family. Certainly no one ever spoke to her, or of her—none of the elders of the family, that is—and if my own little friendship with my aunt had been known, I am sure that would have been stamped on too, but of course that friendship was many years ago.

I remember it well: how I used to sneak round to Aunt Hester's house in hoary Castle-Ilden, not far from Harden on the coast, after school when my folks thought I was at Scouts, and Aunt Hester would make me cups of cocoa and we would talk about newts ('efts,' she called them), frogs, conkers and other things—things of interest to small boys—until the local Scouts' meeting was due to end, and then I would hurry home.

We (father, mother and myself) left Harden when I was just twelve years old, moving down to London where the Old Man had got himself a good job. I was twenty years old before I got to see my aunt again. In the intervening years I had not sent her so much as a postcard (I've never been much of a letter-writer) and I knew that during the same period of time my parents had neither written nor heard from her, but still that did not stop my mother warning me before I set out for Harden not to 'drop in' on Aunt Hester Lang.

No doubt about it, they were frightened of her, my parents—well, if not frightened, certainly they were apprehensive.

Now to me a warning has always been something of a challenge. I had arranged to stay with a friend for a week, a school pal from the good old days, but long before the northbound train stopped at Harden my mind was made up to spend at least a fraction of my time at my aunt's place. Why shouldn't I? Hadn't we always got on famously? Whatever it was she had done to my parents in the past, I could see no good reason why *I* should shun her.

She would be getting on in years a bit now. How old, I wondered? Older than my mother, her sister, by a couple of years—the same age (obviously) as her twin brother, George, in Australia—but of course I was also ignorant of his age. In the end, making what calculations I could, I worked it out that Aunt Hester and her distant brother must have seen at least one hundred and eight summers between them. Yes, my aunt must be about fifty-four years old. It was about time someone took an interest in her.

It was a bright Friday night, the first after my arrival in Harden, when the ideal opportunity presented itself for visiting Aunt Hester. My school friend, Albert, had a date—one he did not really want to put off—and though he had tried his best during the day, it had early been apparent that his luck was out regards finding, on short notice, a second girl for me. It had been left too late. But in any case, I'm not much on blind dates—and most dates are 'blind' unless you really know the girl—and I go even less on doubles; the truth of the matter was that I had wanted the night for my own purposes. And so, when the time came for Albert to set out to meet his girl, I walked off in the opposite direction, across the autumn fences and fields to ancient Castle-Ilden.

I arrived at the little old village at about eight, just as dusk was making its hesitant decision whether or not to allow night's onset, and went straight to Aunt Hester's thatch-roofed bungalow. The place stood (just as I remembered it) at the Blackhill end of cobbled Main Street, in a neat garden framed by cherry trees with the fruit heavy in their branches. As I approached the gate the door opened and out of the house wandered the oddest quartet of strangers I could ever have wished to see.

There was a humped-up, frenetically mobile and babbling old chap, ninety if he was a day; a frumpish fat woman with many quivering chins;

a skeletally thin, incredibly tall, ridiculously wrapped-up man in scarf, pencil-slim overcoat, and fur gloves; and finally, a perfectly delicate old lady with a walking-stick and ear-trumpet. They were shepherded by my Aunt Hester, no different it seemed than when I had last seen her, to the gate and out into the street. There followed a piped and grunted hubbub of thanks and general genialities before the four were gone— in the direction of the leaning village pub—leaving my aunt at the gate finally to spot me where I stood in the shadow of one of her cherry trees. She knew me almost at once, despite the interval of nearly a decade.

'Peter?'

'Hello, Aunt Hester.'

'Why, Peter Norton! My favourite young man—and tall as a tree! Come in, come in!'

'It's bad of me to drop in on you like this,' I answered, taking the arm she offered, 'all unannounced and after so long away, but I—'

'No excuses required.' She waved an airy hand before us and smiled up at me, laughter lines showing at the corners of her eyes and in her unpretty face. 'And you came at just the right time—my group has just left me all alone.'

'Your "group"?'

'My séance group! I've had it for a long time now, many a year. Didn't you know I was a bit on the psychic side? No, I suppose not; your parents wouldn't have told you about *that*, now would they? That's what started it all originally—the trouble in the family, I mean.' We went on into the house.

'Now I had meant to ask you about that,' I told her. 'You mean my parents don't like you messing about with spiritualism? I can see that they wouldn't, of course—not at all the Old Man's cup of tea—but still, I don't really see what it could have to do with them.'

'Not *your* parents, Love,' (she had always called me 'Love'), 'mine— and yours later; but especially George, your uncle in Australia. And not just spiritualism, though that has since become part of it. Did you know that my brother left home and settled in Australia because of me?' A distant look came into her eyes. 'No, of course you didn't, and I don't suppose anyone else would ever have become aware of my power if George hadn't walked me through a window...'

'Eh?' I said, believing my hearing to be out of order. 'Power? Walked you through a window?'

'Yes,' she answered, nodding her head, 'he walked me through a window! Listen, I'll tell you the story from the beginning.'

By that time we had settled ourselves down in front of the fire in Aunt Hester's living-room and I was able to scan, as she talked, the paraphernalia her 'group' had left behind. There were old leather-bound tomes and treatises, tarot cards, a ouija board shiny brown with age, oh, and several other items beloved of the spiritualist. I was fascinated, as ever I had been as a boy, by the many obscure curiosities in Aunt Hester's cottage.

'The first I knew of the link between George and myself,' she began, breaking in on my thoughts, 'as apart from the obvious link that exists between all twins, was when we were twelve years old. Your grandparents had taken us, along with your mother, down to the beach at Seaton Carew. It was July and marvellously hot. Well, to cut a long story short, your mother got into trouble in the water.

'She was quite a long way out and the only one anything like close to her was George—who couldn't swim! He'd waded out up to his neck, but he didn't dare go any deeper. Now, you can wade a long way out at Seaton. The bottom shelves off very slowly. George was at least fifty yards out when we heard him yelling that Sis was in trouble...

'At first I panicked and started to run out through the shallow water, shouting to George that he should swim to Sis, which of course he couldn't—*but he did*! Or at least, *I did*! Somehow I'd swapped places with him, do you see? Not physically but mentally. I'd left him behind me in the shallow water, in my body, and I was swimming for all I was worth for Sis in his! I got her back to the shallows with very little trouble—she was only a few inches out of her depth—and then, as soon as the danger was past, I found my consciousness floating back into my own body.

'Well, everyone made a big fuss of George; he was the hero of the day, you see? How had he done it?—they all wanted to know; and all he was able to say was that he'd just seemed to stand there watching himself save Sis. And of course he *had* stood there watching it all—through my eyes!

'I didn't try to explain it; no one would have believed or listened to me anyway, and I didn't really understand it myself—but George was always a bit wary of me from then on. He said nothing, mind you, but I think that even as early as that first time he had an idea . . .'

Suddenly she looked at me closely, frowning. 'You're not finding all this a bit too hard to swallow, Love?'

'No.' I shook my head. 'Not really. I remember reading somewhere of a similar thing between twins—a sort of Corsican Brothers situation.'

'Oh, but I've heard of many such!' she quickly answered. 'I don't suppose you've read Joachim Feery on the *Necronomicon*?'

'No,' I answered. 'I don't think so.'

'Well, Feery was the illegitimate son of Baron Kant, the German "witch-hunter." He died quite mysteriously in 1934 while still a comparatively young man. He wrote a number of occult limited editions—mostly published at his own expense—the vast majority of which religious and other authorities bought up and destroyed as fast as they appeared. Unquestionably—though it has never been discovered where he saw or read them—Feery's source books were very rare and sinister volumes; among them the *Cthaat Aquadingen*, the *Necronomicon*, von Junzt's *Unspeakable Cults*, Prinn's *De Vermis Mysteriis* and others of that sort. Often Feery's knowledge in respect of such books has seemed almost beyond belief. His quotes, while apparently genuine and authoritative, often differ substantially when compared with the works from which they were supposedly culled. Regarding such discrepancies, Feery claimed that most of his occult knowledge came to him "in dreams"!' She paused, then asked: 'Am I boring you?'

'Not a bit of it,' I answered. 'I'm fascinated.'

'Well, anyhow,' she continued, 'as I've said, Feery must somewhere have seen one of the very rare copies of Abdul Alhazred's *Necronomicon*, in one translation or another, for he published a slim volume of notes concerning that book's contents. I don't own a copy myself, but I've read one belonging to a friend of mine, an old member of my group.

Alhazred, while being reckoned by many to have been a madman, was without doubt the world's foremost authority on black magic and the horrors of alien dimensions, and he was vastly interested in every facet of freakish phenomena, physical and metaphysical.'

She stood up, went to her bookshelf and opened a large modern volume of Aubrey Beardsley's fascinating drawings, taking out a number of loose white sheets bearing lines of her own neat handwriting.

'I've copied some of Feery's quotes, supposedly from Alhazred. Listen to this one:

' 'Tis a veritable & attestable Fact, that between certain related Persons there exists a Bond more powerful than the strongest Ties of Flesh & Family, whereby one such Person may be *aware* of all the Trials & Pleasures of the other, yea, even to experiencing the Pains or Passions of one far distant; & further, there are those whose Skills in such Matters are aided by forbidden Knowledge or Intercourse through dark Magic with Spirits & Beings of outside Spheres. Of the latter: I have sought them out, both Men & Women, & upon Examination have in all Cases discovered them to be Users of Divination, Observers of Times, Enchanters, Witches, Charmers, or Necromancers. All claimed to work their Wonders through Intercourse with dead & departed Spirits, but I fear that often such Spirits were evil Angels, the Messengers of the Dark One & yet more ancient Evils. Indeed, among them were some whose Powers were prodigious, who might at Will *inhabit* the Body of another even at a great Distance & against the Will & often unbeknown to the Sufferer of such Outrage . . .'

She put down the papers, sat back and looked at me quizzically.

'That's all very interesting,' I said after a moment, 'but hardly applicable to yourself.'

'Oh, but it is, Love,' she protested. 'I'm George's twin, for one thing, and for another—'

'But you're no witch or necromancer!'

'No, I wouldn't say so—but I am a "User of Divinations," and I do "work my Wonders through Intercourse with dead & departed Spirits." That's what spiritualism is all about.'

'You mean you actually take this, er, Alhazred and spiritualism and all seriously?' I deprecated.

She frowned. 'No, not Alhazred, not really,' she answered after a moment's thought. 'But he is interesting, as you said. As for spiritualism: yes, I *do* take it seriously. Why, you'd be amazed at some of the vibrations I've been getting these last three weeks or so. *Very* disturbing, but so far rather incoherent; frantic, in fact. I'll track him down eventually, though—the spirit, I mean . . .'

We sat quietly then, contemplatively for a minute or two. Frankly, I didn't quite know what to say, but then she went on: 'Anyway, we were talking about George and how I believed that even after that first occasion he had a bit of an idea that I was at the root of the thing. Yes, I really think he did. He said nothing, and yet . . .

'And that's not all, either. It was some time after that day on the beach before Sis could be convinced that she hadn't been saved by me. She was sure it had been me, not George, who pulled her out of the deep water.

'Well, a year or two went by, and school-leaving exams came up. I was all right, a reasonable scholar—I had always been a bookish kid—but poor old George . . .' She shook her head sadly. My uncle, it appeared, had not been too bright.

After a moment she continued. 'Dates were set for the exams and two sets of papers were prepared, one for the boys, another for the girls. I had no trouble with my paper, I knew even before the results were announced that I was through easily—but before that came George's turn. He'd been worrying and chewing, cramming for all he was worth, biting his nails down to the elbows . . . and getting nowhere. I was in bed with flu when the day of his exams came round, and I remember how I just lay there fretting over him. He was my brother, after all.

'I must have been thinking of him just a bit too hard, though, for before I knew it there I was, staring down hard at an exam paper, sitting in a class full of boys in the old school!

'. . . An hour later I had the papers all finished, and then I concentrated myself back home again. This time it was a definite effort for me to find my way back to my own body.

'The house was in an uproar. I was downstairs in my dressing-gown; Mother had an arm round me and was trying to console me; Father was yelling and waving his arms about like a lunatic. "The girl's gone *mad*!" I remember him exploding, red faced and a bit frightened.

'Apparently I had rushed downstairs about an hour earlier. I had been shouting and screaming tearfully that I'd miss the exam, and I had wanted to know what I was doing home. And when they had called me *Hester* instead of *George*! Well, then I had seemed to go completely out of my mind!

'Of course, I had been feverish with flu for a couple of days. That was obviously the answer: I had suddenly reached the height of a hitherto unrecognized delirious fever, and now the fever had broken I was going to be all right. That was what they said . . .

'George eventually came home with his eyes all wide and staring, frightened-looking, and he stayed that way for a couple of days. He avoided me like the plague! But the next week—when it came out about how good his marks were, how easily he had passed his examination papers—well . . .'

'But surely he must have known,' I broke in. What few doubts I had entertained were now gone forever. She was plainly not making all of this up.

'But why should he have known, Love? He knew he'd had two pretty nightmarish experiences, sure enough, and that somehow they had been connected with me, but he couldn't possibly know that they had their origin in me—that I formed their focus.'

'He did find out, though?'

'Oh, yes, he did,' she slowly answered, her eyes seeming to glisten just a little in the homely evening glow of the room. 'And as I've said, that's why he left home in the end. It happened like this:

'I had never been a pretty girl—no, don't say anything, Love. You weren't even a twinkle in your father's eye then, he was only a boy himself, and so you wouldn't know. But at a time of life when most girls only have to pout to set the boys on fire, well, I was only very plain—and I'm probably giving myself the benefit of the doubt at that.

'Anyway, when George was out nights—walking his latest girl, dancing, or whatever—I was always at home on my own with my books. Quite simply, I came to be terribly jealous of my brother. Of course, you don't know him, he had already been gone something like fifteen years when you were born, but George was a handsome lad. Not strong, mind you, but long and lean and a natural for the girls.

'Eventually he found himself a special girlfriend and came to spend all his time with her. I remember being furious because he wouldn't tell me anything about her . . .'

She paused and looked at me and after a while I said: 'Uhhuh?' inviting her to go on.

'It was one Saturday night in the spring, I remember, not long after our nineteenth birthday, and George had spent the better part of an hour dandying himself up for this unknown girl. That night he seemed to take a sort of stupid, well, *delight* in spiting me; he refused to answer my questions about his girl or even mention her name. Finally, after he had set his tie straight and slicked his hair down for what seemed like the thousandth time, he dared to wink at me—maliciously, I thought, in my jealousy—as he went out into the night.

'That did it. Something *snapped*! I stamped my foot and rushed upstairs to my room for a good cry. And in the middle of crying I had my idea—'

'You decided to, er, swap identities with your brother, to have a look at his girl for yourself,' I broke in. 'Am I right?'

She nodded in answer, staring at the fire, ashamed of herself, I thought, after all this time. 'Yes, I did,' she said. 'For the first time I used my power for my own ends. And mean and despicable ends they were.

'But this time it wasn't like before. There was no instantaneous, involuntary flowing of my psyche, as it were. No immediate change of personality. I had to force it, to concentrate and concentrate and *push* myself. But in a short period of time, before I even knew it, well, there I was.'

'There you were? In Uncle George's body?'

'Yes, in his body, looking out through his eyes, holding in his hand the cool, slender hand of a very pretty girl. I had expected the girl, of course, and yet . . .

'Confused and blustering, letting go of her hand, I jumped back and bumped into a man standing behind me. The girl was saying: "George, what's wrong?" in a whisper, and people were staring. We were in a second-show picture-house queue. Finally I managed to mumble an answer, in a horribly hoarse, unfamiliar, frightened voice—George's voice, obviously, and my fear—and then the girl moved closer and kissed me gently on the cheek!

'She did! But of course she would, wouldn't she, if I were George? "Why, you jumped then like you'd been stung—" she started to say, but I wasn't listening, Peter, for I had jumped again, even more violently, shrinking away from her in a kind of horror. I must have gone crimson, standing there in that queue, with all those unfamiliar people looking at me—*and I had just been kissed by a girl!*

'You see, I wasn't thinking like George at all! I just wished with all my heart that I hadn't interfered, and before I knew it I had George's body in motion and was running down the road, the picture-house queue behind me and the voice of this sweet little girl echoing after me in pained and astonished disbelief.

'Altogether my spiteful adventure had taken only a few minutes, and, when at last I was able to do so, I controlled myself—or rather, George's self—and hid in a shop doorway. It took another minute or two before I was composed sufficiently to manage a, well, a "return trip," but at last I made it and there I was back in my room.

'I had been gone no more than seven or eight minutes all told, but I wasn't back to *exactly* where I started out from. Oh, George hadn't gone rushing downstairs again in a hysterical fit, like that time when I sat his exam for him—though of course the period of *transition* had been a much longer one on that occasion—but he had at least moved off the bed. I found myself standing beside the window . . .' She paused.

'And afterwards?' I prompted her, fascinated.

'Afterwards?' she echoed me, considering it. 'Well, George was very quiet about it . . . No, that's not quite true. It's not that he was quiet, rather that he avoided me more than ever, to such an extent that I hardly ever saw him—no more than a glimpse at a time as he came and went. Mother and Father didn't notice George's increased coolness towards me, but I certainly did. I'm pretty sure it was then that he had finally recognised the source of this thing that came at odd times like some short-lived insanity to plague him. Yes, and looking back, I can see how I might easily have driven George completely insane! But of course, from that time on he was forewarned . . .'

'Forewarned?' I repeated her. 'And the next time he—'

'The next time?' She turned her face so that I could see the fine scars on her otherwise smooth left cheek. I had always wondered about those scars. 'I don't remember a great deal about the next time—shock, I suppose, a "mental block," you might call it—but anyway, the next time was the *last* time! . . .

'There was a boy who took me out once or twice, and I remember that when he stopped calling for me it was because of something George had said to him. Six months had gone by since my shameful and abortive experiment, and now I deliberately put it out of my mind as I determined to teach George a lesson. You must understand, Love, that this boy I mentioned, well . . . he meant a great deal to me.

'Anyway, I was out to get my own back. I didn't know how George had managed to make it up with his girl, but he had. I was going to put an end to their little romance once and for all.

'It was a fairly warm, early October, I remember, when my chance eventually came. A Sunday afternoon, and George was out walking with his girl. I had it planned minutely. I knew exactly what I must say, how I must act, what I must do. I could do it in two minutes flat, and be back in my own body before George knew what was going on. For the first time my intentions were *deliberately* malicious . . .'

I waited for my aunt to continue, and after a while again prompted her: 'And? Was this when—'

'Yes, this was when he walked me through the window. Well, he didn't exactly walk me through it—I believe I leapt, or rather, he leapt me, if you see what I mean. One minute I was sitting on a grassy bank with the same sweet little girl, and the next there was this awful pain— My whole body hurt, and it was *my* body, for my consciousness was suddenly back where it belonged. Instantaneously, inadvertently, I was— myself!

'*But I was lying crumpled on the lawn in front of the house!* I remember seeing splinters of broken glass and bits of yellow-painted wood from my shattered bedroom window, and then I went into a faint with the pain.

'George came to see me in the hospital—once. He sneered when my parents had their backs turned. He leaned over my bed and said: "*Got* you, Hester!" Just that, nothing more.

'I had a broken leg and collarbone. It was three weeks before they let me go home. By then George had joined the Merchant Navy and my parents knew that somehow I was to blame. They were never the same to me from that time on. George had been the Apple of the Family Eye, if you know what I mean. They knew that his going away, in some unknown way, had been my fault. I did have a letter from George— well, a note. It simply warned me "never to do it again," that there were worse things than falling through windows!'

'And you never did, er, do it again?'

'No, I didn't dare; I haven't dared since. There *are* worse things, Love, than being walked through a window! And if George hates me still as much as he might . . .

'But I've often *wanted* to do it again. George has two children, you know?'

I nodded an affirmation: 'Yes, I've heard mother mention them. Joe and Doreen?'

'That's right.' She nodded. 'They're hardly children any more, but I think of them that way. They'll be in their twenties now, your cousins. George's wife wrote to me once many years ago. I've no idea how she got my address. She did it behind George's back, I imagine. Said how sorry she was that there was "trouble in the family." She sent me photographs of the kids. They were beautiful. For all I know there may have been other children later—even grandchildren.'

'I don't think so,' I told her. 'I think I would have known. They're still pretty reserved, my folks, but I would have learned that much, I'm sure. But tell me: how is it that you and Mother aren't closer? I mean, she never talks about you, my mother, and yet you are her sister.'

'Your mother is two years younger than George and me,' my aunt informed me. 'She went to live with her grandparents down South when she was thirteen. Sis, you see, was the brilliant one. George was a bit dim; I was clever enough; but Sis, she was really clever. Our parents sent Sis off to live with Granny, where she could attend a school worthy of her intelligence. She stayed with Gran from then on. We simply drifted apart . . .

'Mind you, we'd never been what you might call close, not for sisters. Anyhow, we didn't come together again until she married and came back up here to live, by which time George must have written to her and told her one or two things. I don't know what or how much he told her, but—well, she never bothered with me—and anyway I was working by then and had a flat of my own.

'Years passed, I hardly ever saw Sis, her little boy came along—you, Love—I fell in with a spiritualist group, making real friends for the first time in my life and, well, that was that. My interest in spiritualism, various other ways of mine that didn't quite fit the accepted pattern, the unspoken thing I had done to George . . . we drifted apart. You understand?'

I nodded. I felt sorry for her, but of course I could not say so. Instead I laughed awkwardly and shrugged my shoulders. 'Who needs people?'

She looked shocked. 'We all do, Love!' Then for a while she was quiet, staring into the fire.

'I'll make a brew of tea,' she suddenly said, then looked at me and smiled in a fashion I well remembered. 'Or should we have cocoa?'

'Cocoa!' I instinctively laughed, relieved at the change of subject.

She went into the kitchen and I lit a cigarette. Idle, for the moment,

I looked about me, taking up the loose sheets of paper that Aunt Hester had left on her occasional table. I saw at once that many of her jottings were concerned with extracts from exotic books. I passed over the piece she had read out to me and glanced at another sheet. Immediately my interest was caught; the three passages were all from the Holy Bible:

'Regard not them that have familiar spirits, neither seek after wizards, to be defiled by them.' Lev. 19:31.

'Then said Saul unto his servants, Seek me a woman that hath a familiar spirit, that I may go to her and enquire of her. And his servants said to him, Behold, there is a woman that hath a familiar spirit at En-dor.' 1 Sam. 28:6,7.

'Many of them also which used curious arts brought their books together, and burned them before all men.' Acts 19: 19.

The third sheet contained a quote from *Today's Christian:*

'To dabble in matters such as these is to reach within de-moniac circles, and it is by no means rare to discover scorn and scepticism transformed to hysterical possession in per-sons whose curiosity has led them merely to attend so-called "spiritual séances." These things of which I speak are of a nature as serious as any in the world today, and I am only one among many to utter a solemn warning against any intercourse with "spirit forces" or the like, whereby the un-utterable evil of demonic possession could well be the hor-rific outcome.'

Finally, before she returned with a steaming jug of cocoa and two mugs, I read another of Aunt Hester's extracts, this one again from Feery's *Notes on the Necronomicon:*

'Yea, & I discovered how one might, be he an Adept & his familiar Spirits powerful enough, control the Wanderings or Migration of his Essence into all 'manner of Beings & Persons—even from beyond the Grave of Sod or the Door of the Stone Sepulchre . . .'

I was still pondering this last extract an hour later, as I walked Harden's night streets towards my lodgings at the home of my friend.

Three evenings later, when by arrangement I returned to my aunt's cottage in old Castle-Ilden, she was nervously waiting for me at the gate and whisked me breathlessly inside. She sat me down, seated herself opposite and clasped her hands in her lap almost in the attitude of an excited young girl.

'Peter, Love, I've had an idea—such a simple idea that it amazes me I never thought of it before.'

'An idea? How do you mean, Aunt Hester—what sort of idea? Does it involve me?'

'Yes, I'd rather it were you than any other. After all, you know the story now . . .'

I frowned as an oddly foreboding shadow darkened latent areas of my consciousness. Her words had been innocuous enough as of yet, and there seemed no reason why I should suddenly feel so—*uncomfortable*, but—

'The story?' I finally repeated her. 'You mean this idea of yours concerns—Uncle George?'

'Yes, I do!' she answered. 'Oh, Love, I can *see* them, if only for a brief moment or two, I can see my nephew and niece. You'll help me? I know you will.'

The shadow thickened darkly, growing in me, spreading from hidden to more truly conscious regions of my mind. 'Help you? You mean you intend to—' I paused, then started to speak again as I saw for sure what she was getting at and realized that she meant it: 'But haven't you said that this stuff was too dangerous? The last time you—'

'Oh, yes, I know,' she impatiently argued, cutting me off. 'But now, well, it's different. I won't stay more than a moment or two—just long enough to see the children—and then I'll get straight back . . . *here*. And there'll be precautions. It can't fail, you'll see.'

'Precautions?' Despite myself I was interested.

'Yes,' she began to talk faster, growing more excited with each passing moment. 'The way I've worked it out, it's perfectly safe. To start with, George will be asleep—he won't know anything about it. When his sleeping mind moves into my body, why, it will simply stay asleep! On the other hand, when *my* mind moves into *his* body, then I'll be able to move about and—'

'And use your brother as a keyhole!' I blurted, surprising even myself. She frowned, then turned her face away. What she planned was wrong. I knew it and so did she, but if my outburst had shamed her, it certainly had not deterred her—not for long.

When she looked at me again her eyes were almost pleading. 'I know how it must look to you, Love, but it's not so. And I know that I must seem to be a selfish woman, but that's not quite true either. Isn't it natural that I should want to see my family? They are mine, you know. George, my brother; his wife, my sister-in-law; their children, my nephew and niece. Just a—yes—a "peep," if that's the way you see it. But, Love, I *need* that peep. I'll only have a few moments, and I'll have to make them last me for the rest of my life.'

I began to weaken. 'How will you go about it?'

'First, a glance,' she eagerly answered, again reminding me of a young girl. 'Nothing more, a mere glance. Even if he's awake he won't ever know I was there; he'll think his mind wandered for the merest second. If he *is* asleep, though, then I'll be able to, well, "wake him up," see his wife—and, if the children are still at home, why, I'll be able to see them, too. Just a glance.'

'But suppose something does go wrong?' I asked bluntly, coming back to earth. 'Why, you might come back and find your head in the gas oven! What's to stop him from slashing your wrists? That only takes a second, you know.'

'That's where you come in, Love.' She stood up and patted me on the cheek, smiling cleverly. 'You'll be right here to see that nothing goes wrong.'

'But—'

'And to be doubly sure,' she cut me off, 'why, *I'll be tied in my chair!* You can't walk through windows when you're tied down, now can you?'

Half an hour later, still suffering inwardly from that as yet unspecified foreboding, I had done as Aunt Hester directed me to do, tying her wrists to the arms of her cane chair with soft but fairly strong bandages from her medicine cabinet in the bathroom.

She had it all worked out, reasoning that it would be very early morning in Australia and that her brother would still be sleeping. As soon as she was comfortable, without another word, she closed her eyes and let her head fall slowly forward onto her chest. Outside, the sun still had some way to go to setting; inside, the room was still warm— yet I shuddered oddly with a deep, nervous chilling of my blood.

It was then that I tried to bring the thing to a halt, calling her name and shaking her shoulder, but she only brushed my hand away and hushed me. I went back to my chair and watched her anxiously.

As the shadows seemed visibly to lengthen in the room and my skin cooled, her head sank even deeper onto her chest, so that I began to think she had fallen asleep. Then she settled herself more comfortably yet and I saw that she was still awake, merely preparing her body for her brother's slumbering mind.

In another moment I knew that something had changed. Her position was as it had been; the shadows crept slowly still; the ancient clock on the wall ticked its regular chronological message; but I had grown inexplicably colder, and there was this feeling that *something* had changed . . .

Suddenly there flashed before my mind's eye certain of those warning jottings I had read only a few nights earlier, and there and then I was determined that this thing should go no further. Oh, she had warned me not to do anything to frighten or disturb her, but this was different. Somehow I knew that if I didn't act now—

'Hester! Aunt Hester!' I jumped up and moved towards her, my throat dry and my words cracked and unnatural-sounding. And she lifted her head and opened her eyes.

For a moment I thought that everything was all right—then . . .

She cried out and stood up, ripped bandages falling in tatters from strangely strong wrists. She mouthed again, staggering and patently disorientated. I fell back in dumb horror, knowing that something was very wrong and yet unable to put my finger on the trouble.

My aunt's eyes were wide now and bulging, and for the first time she seemed to see me, stumbling towards me with slack jaw and tongue protruding horribly between long teeth and drawnback lips. It was then that I knew what was wrong, that this frightful *thing* before me was not my aunt, and I was driven backward before its stumbling approach, warding it off with waving arms and barely articulate cries.

Finally, stumbling more frenziedly now, clawing at empty air inches in front of my face, she—it—spoke: 'No!' the awful voice gurgled over its wriggling tongue. 'No, Hester, you . . . you *fool*! I warned you . . .'

And in that same instant I saw not an old woman, but the horribly alien figure of *a man in a woman's form*!

More grotesque than any drag artist, the thing pirouetted in grim, constricting agony, its strange eyes glazing even as I stared in a paralysis of horror. Then it was all over and the frail scarecrow of flesh, purple tongue still protruding from frothing lips, fell in a crumpled heap to the floor.

That's it, that's the story—not a tale I've told before, for there would have been too many questions, and it's more than possible that my version would not be believed. Let's face it, who *would* believe me? No, I realized this as soon as the thing was done, and so I simply got rid of the torn bandages and called in a doctor. Aunt Hester died of a heart attack, or so I'm told, and perhaps she did—straining to do that which, even with her powers, should never have been possible.

During this last fortnight or so since it happened, I've been trying to convince myself that the doctor was right (which I was quite willing enough to believe at the time), but I've been telling myself lies. I think I've known the real truth ever since my parents got the letter from Australia. And lately, reinforcing that truth, there have been the dreams and the daydreams—*or are they?*

This morning I woke up to a lightless void—a numb, black, silent void—wherein I was incapable of even the smallest movement, and I was horribly, hideously frightened. It lasted for only a moment, that's all, but in that moment it seemed to me that I was dead—or that the living ME inhabited a dead body!

Again and again I find myself thinking back on the mad Arab's words as reported by Joachim Feery: ' . . . even from beyond the Grave of Sod . . .' And in the end I know that this is indeed the answer.

That is why I'm flying tomorrow to Australia. Ostensibly I'm visiting my uncle's wife, my Australian aunt, but really I'm only interested in him, in Uncle George himself. I don't know what I'll be able to do, or even if there is anything I *can* do. My efforts may well be completely useless, and yet I must try to do something.

I *must* try, for I know now that it's that or find myself once again, perhaps permanently, locked in that hellish, nighted—place?—of black oblivion and insensate silence. In the dead and rotting body of my Uncle George, already buried three weeks when Aunt Hester put her mind in his body—*the body she's now trying to vacate in favour of mine!*

THE
WHISPERER

The first time Miles Benton saw the little fellow was on the train. Benton was commuting to his office job in the city and he sat alone in a second-class compartment. The 'little fellow'—a very *ugly* little man, from what Benton could see of him out of the corner of his eye, with a lopsided hump and dark or dirty features, like a gnomish gypsy— entered the compartment and took a seat in the far corner. He was dressed in a floppy black wide-brimmed hat that fell half over his face and a black overcoat longer than himself that trailed to the floor.

Benton was immediately aware of the smell, a rank stench which quite literally would have done credit to the lowliest farmyard, and correctly deduced its source. Despite the dry acrid smell of stale tobacco from the ashtrays and the lingering odour of grimy stations, the com- partment had seemed positively perfumed prior to the advent of the hunchback. The day was quite chill outside, but Benton nevertheless stood up and opened the window, pulling it down until the draft forced back the fumes from his fellow passenger. He was then obliged to put away his flapping newspaper and sit back, his collar upturned against the sudden cold blast, mentally cursing the smelly little chap for fouling 'his' compartment.

A further five minutes saw Benton's mind made up to change com- partments. That way he would be removed from the source of the odor- ous irritation, and he would no longer need to suffer this intolerable blast of icy air. But no sooner was his course of action determined than the ticket collector arrived, sliding open the door and sticking his well-known and friendly face inside the compartment.

'Mornin', sir,' he said briskly to Benton, merely glancing at the other traveller. 'Tickets, please.'

Benton got out his ticket and passed it to be examined. He noticed with satisfaction as he did so that the ticket collector wrinkled his nose and sniffed suspiciously at the air, eyeing the hunchback curiously. Benton retrieved his ticket and the collector turned to the little man in the far corner. 'Yer ticket . . . *sir* . . . if yer don't mind.' He looked the little chap up and down disapprovingly.

The hunchback looked up from under his black floppy hat and grinned. His eyes were jet and bright as a bird's. He winked and indicated that the ticket collector should bend down, expressing an obvious desire to say something in confidence. He made no effort to produce a ticket.

The ticket collector frowned in annoyance, but nevertheless bent his ear to the little man's face. He listened for a moment or two to a chuckling, throaty whisper. It actually appeared to Benton that the hunchback was *chortling* as he whispered his obscene secret into the other's ear, and the traveller could almost hear him saying: 'Feelthy postcards! Vairy dairty pictures!'

The look on the face of the ticket collector changed immediately; his expression went stony hard.

'Aye, aye!' Benton said to himself. 'The little blighter's got no ticket! He's for it now.'

But no, the ticket collector said nothing to the obnoxious midget, but straightened and turned to Benton. 'Sorry, sir,' he said, 'but this compartment's private. I'll 'ave ter arsk yer ter leave.'

'But,' Benton gasped incredulously, 'I've been travelling in this compartment for years. It's never been a, well, a "private" compartment before!'

'No, sir, p'raps not,' said the ticket collector undismayed. 'But it is now. There's a compartment next door; jus' a couple of gents in there; I'm sure it'll do jus' as well.' He held the door open for Benton, daring him to argue the point further. 'Sir?'

'Ah, well,' Benton thought, resignedly, 'I was wanting to move.' Nevertheless, he looked down aggressively as he passed the hunchback, staring hard at the top of the floppy hat. The little man seemed to know. He looked up and grinned, cocking his head on one side and grinning.

Benton stepped quickly out into the corridor and took a deep breath. 'Damn!' he swore out loud.

'Yer pardon, sir?' inquired the ticket collector, already swaying off down the corridor.

'Nothing!' Benton snapped in reply, letting himself into the smoky, crowded compartment to which he had been directed.

The very next morning Benton plucked up his courage (he had never been a *very* brave man), stopped the ticket collector, and asked him what it had all been about. Who had the little chap been. What privileges did he have that an entire compartment had been reserved especially for him, the grim little gargoyle?

To which the ticket collector replied: 'Eh? An 'unchback? Are yer sure it was *this* train, sir? Why, we haint 'ad no private or reserved compartments on this 'ere train since it became a commuter special! And as fer a 'unchback—well!'

'But surely you remember asking me to leave my compartment— *this* compartment?' Benton insisted.

' 'Ere, yer pullin' me leg, haint yer, sir?' laughed the ticket collector good-naturedly. He slammed shut the compartment door behind him and smilingly strode away without waiting for an answer, leaving Benton alone with his jumbled and whirling thoughts.

'Well, I never!' the commuter muttered worriedly to himself. He scratched his head and then, philosophically, began to quote a mental line or two from a ditty his mother had used to say to him when he was a child:

> *The other day upon the stair*
> *I saw a man who wasn't there . . .*

Benton had almost forgotten about the little man with the hump and sewer-like smell by the time their paths crossed again. It happened one day some three months later, with spring just coming on, when, in acknowledgement of the bright sunshine, Benton decided to forego his usual sandwich lunch at the office for a noonday pint at the Bull & Bush.

The entire pub, except for one corner of the bar, appeared to be quite crowded, but it was not until Benton had elbowed his way to the corner in question that he saw why it was unoccupied, or rather, why it had only one occupant. The *smell* hit him at precisely the same time as he saw, sitting on a bar stool with his oddly humped back to the regular patrons, the little man in black with his floppy broad-brimmed hat.

That the other customers were aware of the cesspool stench was obvious—Benton watched in fascination the wrinkling all about him of at least a dozen pairs of nostrils—and yet not a man complained. And more amazing yet, no one even attempted to encroach upon the little fellow's territory in the bar corner. No one, that is, except Benton . . .

Holding his breath, Benton stepped forward and rapped sharply with his knuckles on the bar just to the left of where the hunchback sat. 'Beer, barman. A pint of best, please.'

The barman smiled chubbily and stepped forward, reaching out for a beer pump and slipping a glass beneath the tap. But even as he did so the hunchback made a small gesture with his head, indicating that he wanted to say something . . .

Benton had seen all this before, and all the many sounds of the pub—the chattering of people, the clink of coins, and the clatter of glasses—seemed to fade to silence about him as he focussed his full concentration upon the barman and the little man in the floppy hat. In slow motion, it seemed, the barman bent his head down towards the hunchback, and again Benton heard strangely chuckled whispers as the odious dwarf passed his secret instructions.

Curiously, fearfully, in something very akin to dread, Benton watched the portly barman's face undergo its change, heard the *hissss* of the beer pump, saw the full glass come out from beneath the bar . . .

to plump down in front of the hunchback! Hard-eyed, the barman stuck his hand out in front of Benton's nose. 'That's half a dollar to you, sir.'

'But . . .' Benton gasped, incredulously opening and closing his mouth. He already had a coin in his hand, with which he had intended to pay for his drink, but now he pulled his hand back.

'Half a dollar, sir,' the barman repeated ominously, snatching the coin from Benton's retreating fingers, 'and would you mind moving down the bar, please? It's a bit crowded this end.'

In utter disbelief Benton jerked his eyes from the barman's face to his now empty hand, and from his hand to the seated hunchback, and as he did so the little man turned his head towards him and grinned. Benton was aware only of the bright, bird-like eyes beneath the wide brim of the hat—not of the darkness surrounding them. One of those eyes closed suddenly in a wink, and then the little man turned back to his beer.

'But,' Benton again croaked his protest at the publican, 'that's *my* beer he's got!' He reached out and caught the barman's rolled-up sleeve, following him down the bar until forced by the press of patrons to let go. The barman finally turned.

'Beer, sir?' The smile was back on his chubby face. 'Certainly—half a dollar to you, sir.'

Abruptly the bar sounds crashed in again upon Benton's awareness as he turned to elbow his way frantically, almost hysterically, through the crowded room to the door. Out of the corner of his eye he noticed that the little man, too, had left. A crush of thirsty people had already moved into the space he had occupied in the bar corner.

Outside in the fresh air Benton glared wild-eyed up and down the busy street, and yet he was half afraid of seeing the figure his eyes sought. The little man, however, had apparently disappeared into thin air.

'God damn him!' Benton cried in sudden rage, and a passing policeman looked at him very curiously indeed.

He was annoyed to notice that the policeman followed him all the way back to the office.

————

At noon the next day Benton was out of the office as if at the crack of a starting pistol. He almost ran the four blocks to the Bull & Bush, pausing only to straighten his tie and tilt his bowler a trifle more aggressively in the mirror of a shop window. The place was quite crowded, as before, but he made his way determinedly to the bar, having first checked that the air was quite clean—ergo, that the little man with the hump was quite definitely *not* there.

He immediately caught the barman's eye. 'Bartender, a beer, please. And—' He lowered his voice. '—a word, if you don't mind.'

The publican leaned over the bar confidentially, and Benton lowered his tone still further to whisper: 'Er, who *is* he—the, er, the little chap? Is he, perhaps, the boss of the place? Quite a little, er, *eccentric*, isn't he?'

'Eh?' said the barman, looking puzzledly about. 'Who d'you mean, sir?'

The genuinely puzzled expression on the portly man's face ought to have told Benton all he needed to know, but Benton simply could not accept that, not a second time. 'I mean the hunchback,' he raised his voice in desperation. 'The little chap in the floppy black hat who sat in the corner of the bar only yesterday—who stank to high heaven and drank *my* beer! Surely you remember him?'

The barman slowly shook his head and frowned, then called out to a group of standing men: 'Joe, here a minute.' A stocky chap in a cloth cap and tweed jacket detached himself from the general hubbub and moved to the bar. 'Joe,' said the barman, 'you were in here yesterday lunch; did you see a—well, a—how was it, sir?' He turned back to Benton.

'A little chap with a floppy black hat and a hump,' Benton patiently, worriedly repeated himself. 'He was sitting in the bar corner. Had a pong like a dead rat.'

Joe thought about it for a second, then said: 'Yer sure yer got the right pub, guv'? I mean, we gets no tramps or weirdos in 'ere. 'Arry won't 'ave 'em, will yer, 'Arry?' He directed his question at the barman.

'No, he's right, sir. I get upset with weirdos. Won't have them.'

'But . . . this *is* the Bull & Bush, isn't it?' Benton almost stammered, gazing wildly about, finding unaccustomed difficulty in speaking.

'That's right, sir,' answered Harry the barman, frowning heavily now and watching Benton sideways.

'But—'

'Sorry, chief,' the stocky Joe said with an air of finality. 'Yer've got the wrong place. Must 'ave been some other pub.' Both the speaker and the barman turned away a trifle awkwardly, Benton thought, and he could feel their eyes upon him as he moved dazedly away from the bar towards the door. Again lines remembered of old repeated themselves in his head:

> *He wasn't there again today—*
> *Oh how I wish he'd go away!*

'Here, sir!' cried the barman, suddenly, remembering. 'Do you want a beer or not, then?'

'*No!*' Benton snarled. Then, on impulse: 'Give it to—to *him!*— when next he comes in . . .'

Over the next month or so certain changes took place in Benton, changes which would have seemed quite startling to anyone knowing him of old. To begin with, he had apparently broken two habits of very long standing. One: instead of remaining in his compartment aboard the morning train and reading his newspaper—as had been his wont for close on nine years—he was now given to spending the first half hour of his journey peering into the many compartments while wandering up and down the long corridor, all the while wearing an odd, part puzzled, part apologetic expression. Two: he rarely took his lunch at the office any more, but went out walking in the city instead, stopping for a drink and a sandwich at any handy local pub. (But never the Bull & Bush, though he always ensured that his strolling took him close by the latter house, and had anyone been particularly interested, then Benton might have been noticed to keep a very wary eye on the pub, almost as if he had it under observation.)

But then, as summer came on and no new manifestations of Benton's—*problem*—came to light, he began to forget all about it, to relegate it to that category of mental phenomena known as 'daydreams,' even though he had known no such phenomena before. And as the summer waxed, so the nagging worry at the back of his mind waned, until finally he convinced himself that his daydreams were gone for good.

But he was wrong . . .

And if those two previous visitations had been dreams, then the third could only be classified as—nightmare!

July saw the approach of the holiday period, and Benton had long had places booked for himself and his wife at a sumptuously expensive and rather exclusive coastal resort, far from the small Midlands town he called home. They went there every year. This annual 'spree' allowed Benton to indulge his normally repressed escapism, when for a whole fortnight he could pretend that he was other than a mere clerk among people who usually accepted his fantasies as fact, thereby reinforcing them for Benton.

He could hardly wait for it to come round, that last Friday evening before the holidays, and when it did he rode home in the commuter special in a state of high excitement. Tomorrow would see him off to the sea and the sun; the cases were packed, the tickets arranged. A good night's rest now—and then, in the morning . . .

He was whistling as he let himself in through his front door, but the tone of his whistle soon went off key as he stepped into the hall. Dismayed, he paused and sniffed, his nose wrinkling. Out loud, he said: 'Huh! The drains must be off again.' But there was something rather special about that poisonous smell, something ominously familiar; and all of a sudden, without fully realising why, Benton felt the short hairs at the back of his neck begin to rise. An icy chill struck at him from nowhere.

He passed quickly from the hall into the living room, where the air seemed even more offensive, and there he paused again as it came to him in a flash of fearful memory just *what* the awful stench of ordure was, and *where* and *when* he had known it before.

The room seemed suddenly to whirl about him as he saw, thrown carelessly across the back of his own easy chair, a monstrously familiar hat—a floppy hat, black and wide-brimmed!

The hat grew beneath his hypnotized gaze, expanding until it threatened to fill the whole house, his whole mind, but then he tore his eyes away and broke the spell. From the upstairs bedroom came a low, muted sound: a moan of pain—or pleasure? And as an incredibly obscene and now well-remembered chuckling whisper finally invaded Benton's horrified ears, he threw off shock's invisible shackles to fling himself breakneck up the stairs.

'Ellen!' he cried, throwing open the bedroom door just as a second moan sounded—*and then he staggered, clutching at the wall for support, as the scene beyond the door struck him an almost physical blow!*

The hunchback lay sprawled naked upon Benton's bed, his malformed back blue-veined and grimy. The matted hair of his head fell forward onto Ellen's white breasts and his filthy hands moved like crabs over her arched body. Her eyes were closed, her mouth open and panting; her whole attitude was one of complete abandon. Her slender hands clawed spastically at the hunchback's writhing, scurvy thighs . . .

Benton screamed hoarsely, clutching wildly at his hair, his eyes threatening to pop from his head, and for an instant time stood still. Then he lunged forward and grabbed at the man, a great power bursting inside him, the strength of both God and the devil in his crooked fingers—but in that same instant the hunchback slipped from the far side of the bed and out of reach. At an almost impossible speed the little man dressed and, as Benton lurched drunkenly about the room, he flitted like a grey bat back across the bed. As he went his face passed close to Ellen's, and Benton was aware once again of that filthy whispered chuckle as the hunchback sprang to the floor and fled the room.

Mad with steadily mounting rage, Benton hardly noticed the sudden slitting of his wife's eyes, the film that came down over them like a silky shutter. But as he lunged after the hunchback, Ellen reached out a naked leg, deliberately tripping him and sending him flying out onto the landing.

By the time he regained his feet, to lean panting against the landing rail, the little man was at the hall door, his hat once more drooping about grotesque shoulders. He looked up with eyes like malignant jewels in the shadow of that hat, and the last thing that the tormented householder saw as the hunchback closed the door softly behind him was that abhorrent, omniscient wink!

When he reached the garden gate some twoscore seconds later, Benton was not surprised to note the little man's complete disappearance ...

Often, during the space of the next fortnight, Benton tried to think back on the scene which followed immediately upon the hunchback's departure from his house, but he was never able to resolve it to his satisfaction. He remembered the blind accusations he had thrown, the venomous bile of his words, his wife's patent amazement which had only served to enrage him all the more, the shock on Ellen's reddening face as he had slapped her mercilessly from room to room. He remembered her denial and the words she had screamed after locking herself in the bathroom: 'Madman, madman!' she had screamed. And then she had left, taking her already packed suitcase with her.

He had waited until Monday—mainly in a vacant state of shock— before going out to a local ironmonger's shop to buy himself a sharp, long-bladed Italian knife ...

It was now the fourteenth day, and still Benton walked the streets. He was grimy, unshaven, hungry, but his resolution was firm. Somewhere, *somewhere*, he would find the little man in the outsize overcoat and black floppy hat, and when he did he would stick his knife to its hilt in the hunchback's slimy belly and he would cut out the vile little swine's brains through his loathsomely winking eyes! In his mind's eye, even as walked the night streets, Benton could *see* those eyes gleaming like jewels, quick and bright and liquid, and faintly in his nostrils there seemed to linger the morbid stench of the hybrid creature that wore those eyes in its face.

And always his mother's ditty rang in his head:

> *The other day upon the stair*
> *I saw a man who wasn't there.*
> *He wasn't there again today—*
> *Oh, how I wish . . .*

But no, Benton did *not* wish the little man away; on the contrary, he desperately wanted to find him!

Fourteen days, fourteen days of madness and delirium, but through all the madness a burning purpose had shone out like a beacon. Who, what, why? Benton knew not, and he no longer wanted to know. But somewhere, *somewhere . . .*

Starting the first Tuesday after that evening of waking nightmare, each morning he had caught the commuter special as of old, to prowl its snake-like corridor and peer in poisonously through the compartment windows; every lunchtime he had waited in a shop doorway across the street from the Bull & Bush until closing time, and in between times he had walked the streets in all the villages between home and the city. Because somewhere, *somewhere!*

'Home.' He tasted the word bitterly. 'Home'—hah! That was a laugh! And all this after eleven years of reasonably harmonious married life. He thought again, suddenly, of Ellen, then of the hunchback, then of the two of them together . . . and in the next instant his mind was lit by a bright flash of inspiration.

Fourteen days—*fourteen days including today*—and this was Saturday night! Where would he be now if this whole nightmare had never happened? Why, he would be on the train with his wife, going home from their holiday!

Could it possibly be that—

Benton checked his watch, his hands shaking uncontrollably. Ten to nine; the nine o'clock train would be pulling into the station in only ten more minutes!

He looked wildly about him, reality crashing down again as he found himself in the back alleys of his home town. Slowly the wild light went out of his eyes, to be replaced by a strangely warped smile as he realised that he stood in an alley only a few blocks away from the railway station . . .

They didn't see him as they left the station, Ellen in high heels and a chic outfit, the hunchback as usual in his ridiculous overcoat and floppy black hat. But Benton saw them. They were (it still seemed completely unbelievable) arm in arm, Ellen radiant as a young bride, the little man reeking and filthy; and as Benton heard again that obscene chuckle, he choked and reeled with rage in the darkness of his shop doorway.

Instantly the little man paused and peered into the shadows where Benton crouched. Benton cursed himself and shrank back; although the street was almost deserted, he had not wanted his presence known just yet.

But his presence *was* known!

The hunchback lifted up Ellen's hand to his lips in grotesque chivalry and kissed it. He whispered something loathsomely, and then, as Ellen made off without a word down the street, he turned again to peer with firefly eyes into Benton's doorway. The hiding man waited no longer. He leapt out into view, his knife bright and upraised, and the hunchback turned without ceremony to scurry down the cobbled street, his coat fluttering behind him like the wings of a great crippled moth.

Benton ran, too, and quickly the gap between them closed as he drove his legs in a vengeful fury. Faster and faster his breath rasped as he drew closer to the fugitive hunchback, his hand lifting the knife for the fatal stroke.

Then the little man darted round a corner into an alleyway. No more than a second later Benton, too, rushed wildly into the darkness of the same alley. He skidded to a halt, his shoes sliding on the cobbles. He stilled his panting forcibly.

Silence . . .

The little devil had vanished again! He—

No, *there* he was—cringing like a cornered rat in the shadow of the wall.

Benton lunged, his knife making a crescent of light as it sped toward the hunchback's breast, but like quicksilver the target shifted as the little man ducked under his pursuer's arm to race out again into the street, leaving the echo of his hideous chuckle behind him.

That whispered chuckle drove Benton to new heights of raging bloodlust and, heedless now of all but the chase, he raced hot on the hunchback's trail. He failed to see the taxi's lights as he ran into the street, failed to hear its blaring horn—indeed, he was only dimly aware of the scream of brakes and tortured tyres—so that the darkness of oblivion as it rushed in upon him came as a complete surprise . . .

The darkness did not last. Quickly Benton swam up out of unconsciousness to find himself crumpled in the gutter. There was blood on his face, a roaring in his ears. The street swam round and round.

'Oh, God!' he groaned, but the words came out broken, like his body, and faint. Then the street found its level and steadied. An awful dull ache spread upwards from Benton's waist until it reached his neck. He tried to move, but couldn't. He heard running footsteps and managed to turn his head, lifting it out of the gutter in an agony of effort. Blood dripped from a torn ear. He moved an arm just a fraction, fingers twitching.

'God mister what were you doing what were you *doing?*' the taxi driver gabbled. 'Oh Jesus Jesus you're hurt you're hurt. It wasn't my fault it wasn't me!'

'Never, uh . . . mind.' Benton gasped, pain threatening to pull him under again as the ache in his lower body exploded into fresh agony. 'Just . . . get me, uh, into . . . your car and . . . hospital or . . . doctor.'

'Sure, yes!' the man cried, quickly kneeling.

If Benton's nose had not been clogged with mucus and drying blood he would have known of the hunchback's presence even before he heard the terrible chuckling from the pavement. As it was, the sound made him jerk his damaged head round into a fresh wave of incredible pain. He turned his eyes upwards. Twin points of light stared down at him from the darkness beneath the floppy hat.

'Uh . . . I suppose, uh, you're satisfied . . . now?' he painfully inquired, his hand groping uselessly, longingly for the knife which now lay halfway across the street.

And then he froze. Tortured and racked though his body was— desperate as his pain and injuries were—Benton's entire being *froze* as, in answer to his choked question, *the hunchback slowly, negatively shook his shadowed head!*

Dumbfounded, amazed, and horrified, Benton could only gape, even his agony forgotten as he helplessly watched from the gutter a repeat performance of those well-known gestures, those scenes remembered of old and now indelibly imprinted upon his mind: the filthy whispering in the taxi driver's ear; the winking of bright, bird eyes; the mazed look spreading like pale mud on the frightened man's face. Again the street began to revolve about Benton as the taxi driver walked as if in a dream back to his taxi.

Benton tried to scream but managed only a shuddering cough. Spastically his hand found the hunchback's grimy ankle and he gripped it tight. The little man stood like an anchor, and once more the street steadied about them as Benton fought his mangled body in a futile attempt to push it to its feet. He could not. There was something wrong with his back, something broken. He coughed, then groaned and relaxed his grip, turning his eyes upwards again to meet the steady gaze of the hunchback.

'Please . . .' he said. But his words were drowned out by the sudden sound of a revving engine, by the shriek of skidding tyres savagely reversing; and the last thing Benton saw, other than the black bulk of the taxi looming and the red rear lights, was the shuttering of one of those evil eyes in a grim farewell wink . . .

———

Some few minutes later the police arrived at the scene of the most inexplicable killing it had ever been their lot to have to attend. They had been attracted by the crazed shrieking of a white-haired, utterly lunatic taxi driver.

NO SHARKS IN
THE MED

Customs was nonexistent; people bring duty-frees *out* of Greece, not in. As for passport control: a pair of tanned, hairy, bored-looking characters in stained, too-tight uniforms and peaked caps were in charge. One to take your passport, find the page to be franked, scan photograph and bearer both with a blank gaze that took in absolutely nothing unless you happened to be female and stacked (in which case it took in everything and more), then pass the passport on. Geoff Hammond thought: *I wonder if that's why they call them passports?* The second one took the little black book from the first and hammered down on it with his stamp, impressing several pages but no one else, then handed the important document back to its owner—but grudgingly, as if he didn't believe you could be trusted with it.

This second one, the one with the rubber stamp, had a brother. They could be, probably were, twins. Five-eightish, late twenties, lots of shoulders and no hips; raven hair shiny with grease, so tightly curled it looked permed; brown eyes utterly vacant of expression. The only difference was the uniform: the fact that the brother on the home-and-dry side of the barrier didn't have one. Leaning on the barrier, he twirled cheap, yellow-framed, dark-lensed glasses like glinting propellers, observed almost speculatively the incoming holidaymakers. He wore shorts, frayed where they hugged his thick thighs, barely long enough to be decent. *Hung like a bull!* Geoff thought. It was almost embarrassing. Dressed for the benefit of the single girls, obviously. He'd be hoping they were taking notes for later. His chances might improve if he were two inches taller and had a face. But he didn't; the face was as vacant as the eyes.

Then Geoff saw what it was that was wrong with those eyes: beyond the barrier, the specimen in the bulging shorts was wall-eyed. Likewise his twin punching the passports. Their right eyes had white pupils that stared like dead fish. The one in the booth wore lightly-tinted glasses, so that you didn't notice until he looked up and stared directly at you. Which in Geoff's case he hadn't, but he was certainly looking at Gwen. Then he glanced at Geoff, patiently waiting, and said: 'Together, you?' His voice was a shade too loud, making it almost an accusation.

Different names on the passports, obviously! But Geoff wasn't going to stand here and explain how they were just married and Gwen hadn't had time to make the required alterations. That really *would* be embarrassing! In fact (and come to think of it), it might not even be legal. Maybe she should have changed it right away, or got something done with it, anyway, in London. The honeymoon holiday they'd chosen was one of those get-it-while-it's-going deals, a last-minute half-price seat-filler, a gift horse; and they'd been pushed for time. But what the hell—this was 1987, wasn't it?

'Yes,' Geoff finally answered. 'Together.'

'Ah!' The other nodded, grinned, appraised Gwen again with a raised eyebrow, before stamping her passport and handing it over.

Wall-eyed bastard! Geoff thought.

When they passed through the gate in the barrier, the other wall-eyed bastard had disappeared . . .

Stepping through the automatic glass doors from the shade of the airport building into the sunlight of the coach terminus was like opening the door of a furnace; it was a replay of the moment when the plane's air-conditioned passengers trooped out across the tarmac to board the buses waiting to convey them to passport control. You came out into the sun fairly crisp, but by the time you'd trundled your luggage to the kerbside and lifted it off the trolley your armpits were already sticky.

One o'clock, and the temperature must have been hovering around eighty-five for hours. It not only beat down on you but, trapped in the concrete, beat up as well. Hammerblows of heat.

A mini-skirted courier, English as a rose and harassed as hell—her white blouse soggy while her blue-and-white hat still sat jaunty on her head—came fluttering, clutching her millboard with its bulldog clip and thin sheaf of notes. 'Mr Hammond and Miss—' she glanced at her notes '—Pinter?'

'Mr and Mrs Hammond,' Geoff answered. He lowered his voice and continued confidentially: 'We're all proper, legitimate, and true. Only our identities have been altered in order to protect our passports.'

'Um?' she said.

Too deep for her, Geoff thought, sighing inwardly.

'Yes,' said Gwen, sweetly. 'We're the Hammonds.'

'Oh!' the girl looked a little confused. 'It's just that—'

'I haven't changed my passport yet,' said Gwen, smiling.

'Ah!' Understanding finally dawned. The courier smiled nervously at Geoff, turned again to Gwen. 'Is it too late for congratulations?'

'Four days,' Gwen answered.

'Well, congratulations anyway.'

Geoff was eager to be out of the sun. 'Which is our coach?' he wanted to know. 'Is it—could it possibly be—air-conditioned?' There were several coaches parked in an untidy cluster a little farther up the kerb.

Again the courier's confusion, also something of embarrassment showing in her bright blue eyes. 'You're going to—Achladi?'

Geoff sighed again, this time audibly. It was her business to know where they were going. It wasn't a very good start.

'Yes,' she cut in quickly, before he or Gwen could comment. 'Achladi—but not by coach! You see, your plane was an hour late; the coach for Achladi couldn't be held up for just one couple; but it's okay—you'll have the privacy of your own taxi, and of course Skymed will foot the bill.'

She went off to whistle up a taxi and Geoff and Gwen glanced at each other, shrugged, sat down on their cases. But in a moment the courier was back, and behind her a taxi came rolling, nosing into the kerb. Its driver jumped out, whirled about opening doors, the boot, stashing cases while Geoff and Gwen got into the back of the car. Then, throwing his straw hat down beside him as he climbed into the driving seat and slammed his door, the young Greek looked back at his passengers and smiled. A single gold tooth flashed in a bar of white. But the smile was quite dead, like the grin of a shark before he bites, and the voice when it came was phlegmy, like pebbles colliding in mud. 'Achladi, yes?'

'Ye—' Geoff began, paused, and finished: '—es! Er, Achladi, right!' Their driver was the wall-eyed passport-stamper's wall-eyed brother.

'I Spiros,' he declared, turning the taxi out of the airport. 'And you?'

Something warned Geoff against any sort of familiarity with this one. In all this heat, the warning was like a breath of cold air on the back of his neck. 'I'm Mr Hammond,' he answered, stiffly. 'This is my wife.' Gwen turned her head a little and frowned at him.

'I'm—' she began.

'My *wife*!' Geoff said again. She looked surprised but kept her peace.

Spiros was watching the road where it narrowed and wound. Already out of the airport, he skirted the island's main town and raced for foothills rising to a spine of half-clad mountains. Achladi was maybe half an hour away, on the other side of the central range. The road soon became a track, a thick layer of dust over pot-holed tarmac and cobbles; in short, a typical Greek road. They slowed down a little through a village where white-walled houses lined the way, with lemon groves set back between and behind the dwellings, and were left with bright flashes of bougainvillea-framed balconies burning like after-images on their retinas. Then Spiros gave it the gun again.

Behind them, all was dust kicked up by the spinning wheels and the suction of the car's passing. Geoff glanced out of the fly-specked rear window. The cloud of brown dust, chasing after them, seemed ominous in the way it obscured the so-recent past. And turning front again, Geoff saw that Spiros kept his strange eye mainly on the road ahead, and the good one on his rearview. But watching what? The dust? No, he was looking at . . .

At Gwen! The interior mirror was angled directly into her cleavage.

They had been married only a very short time. The day when he'd take pride in the jealousy of other men—in their coveting his wife—was still years in the future. Even then, look but don't touch would be the order of the day. Right now it was watch where you're looking, and possession was ninety-nine point nine percent of the law. As for the other point one percent: well, there was nothing much you could do about what the lecherous bastards were thinking!

Geoff took Gwen's elbow, pulled her close and whispered: 'Have you noticed how tight he takes the bends? He does it so we'll bounce about a bit. He's watching how your tits jiggle!'

She'd been delighting in the scenery, hadn't even noticed Spiros, his eyes or anything. For a beautiful girl of twenty-three, she was remarkably naïve, and it wasn't just an act. It was one of the things Geoff loved best about her. Only eighteen months her senior, Geoff hardly considered himself a man of the world, but he did know a rat when he smelled one. In Spiros's case he could smell several sorts.

'He . . . what—?' Gwen said out loud, glancing down at herself. One button too many had come open in her blouse, showing the edges of her cups. Green eyes widening, she looked up and spotted Spiros's rearview. He grinned at her through the mirror and licked his lips, but without deliberation. He was naïve, too, in his way. In his different sort of way.

'Sit over here,' said Geoff out loud, as she did up the offending button *and* the one above it. 'The view is much better on this side.' He half stood, let her slide along the seat behind him. Both of Spiros's eyes were now back on the road. . . .

Ten minutes later they were up into a pass through gorgeous pine-clad slopes so steep they came close to sheer. Here and there scree slides showed through the greenery, or a thrusting outcrop of rock. 'Mountains,' Spiros grunted, without looking back.

'You have an eye for detail,' Geoff answered.

Gwen gave his arm a gentle nip, and he knew she was thinking *sarcasm is the lowest form of wit—and it doesn't become you!* Nor cruelty, apparently. Geoff had meant nothing special by his 'eye' remark, but Spiros was sensitive. He groped in the glove compartment for his yellow-rimmed sunshades, put them on. And drove in a stony silence for what looked like being the rest of the journey.

Through the mountains they sped, and the west coast of the island opened up like a gigantic travel brochure. The mountains seemed to go right down to the sea, rocks merging with that incredible, aching blue. And they could see the village down there, Achladi, like something out of a dazzling dream perched on both sides of a spur that gentled into the ocean.

'Beautiful!' Gwen breathed.

'Yes.' Spiros nodded. 'Beautiful, thee village.' Like many Greeks speaking English, his definite articles all sounded like *thee.* 'For fish, for thee swims, thee sun—is beautiful.'

After that it was all downhill, winding, at times precipitous, but the view was never less than stunning. For Geoff, it brought back memories of Cyprus. Good ones, most of them, but one bad one that always made him catch his breath, clench his fists. The reason he hadn't been too keen on coming back to the Med in the first place. He closed his eyes in an attempt to force the memory out of mind, but that only made it worse, the picture springing up that much clearer.

He was a kid again, just five years old, late in the summer of '67. His father was a Staff-Sergeant Medic, his mother with the QARANCs; both of them were stationed at Dhekelia, a Sovereign Base Area garrison just up the coast from Larnaca where they had a married quarter. They'd met and married in Berlin, spent three years there, then got posted out to Cyprus together. With two years done in Cyprus, Geoff's father had a year to go to complete his twenty-two. After that last year in the sun . . . there was a place waiting for him in the ambulance pool of one of London's big hospitals. Geoff's mother had hoped to get on the nursing staff of the same hospital. But before any of that . . .

Geoff had started school in Dhekelia, but on those rare weekends when both of his parents were free of duty, they'd all go off to the beach together. And that had been his favourite thing in all the world: the beach with its golden sand and crystal-clear, safe, shallow water. But sometimes, seeking privacy, they'd take a picnic basket and drive east along the coast until the road became a track, then find a way down the cliffs and swim from the rocks up around Cape Greco. That's where it had happened.

'Geoff!' Gwen tugged at his arm, breaking the spell. He was grateful to be dragged back to reality. 'Were you sleeping?'

'Daydreaming,' he answered.

'Me, too!' she said. 'I think I must be. I mean, just *look* at it!'

They were winding down a steep ribbon of road cut into the mountain's flank, and Achladi was directly below them. A coach coming up squeezed by, its windows full of brown, browned-off faces. Holidaymakers going off to the airport, going home. Their holidays were over, but Geoff's and Gwen's was just beginning, and the village they had come to *was* truly beautiful. Especially beautiful because it was unspoiled. This was only Achladi's second season; before they'd built the airport you could only get here by boat. Very few had bothered.

Geoff's vision of Cyprus and his bad time quickly receded; while he didn't consider himself a romantic like Gwen, still he recognized Achladi's magic. And now he supposed he'd have to admit that they'd made the right choice.

White-walled gardens; red tiles, green-framed windows, some flat roofs and some with a gentle pitch; bougainvillea cascading over white, arched balconies; a tiny white church on the point of the spur where broken rocks finally tumbled into the sea; massive ancient olive trees in walled plots at every street junction, and grapevines on trellises giving a little shade and dappling every garden and patio. That, at a glance, was Achladi. A high wall kept the sea at bay, not that it could ever be a real threat, for the entire front of the village fell within the harbour's crab's-claw moles. Steps went down here and there from the sea wall to the rocks; a half-dozen towels were spread wherever there was a flat or gently-inclined surface to take them, and the sea bobbed with a half-dozen heads, snorkels and face-masks. Deep water here, but a quarter-mile to the south, beyond the harbour wall, a shingle beach stretched like the webbing between the toes of some great beast for maybe a hundred yards to where a second claw-like spur came down from the mountains. As for the rest of this western coastline: as far as the eye could see both north and south, it looked like sky, cliff and sea to Geoff. Cape Greco all over again. But before he could go back to that:

'Is Villa Eleni, yes?' Spiros's gurgling voice intruded. 'Him have no road. No can drive. I carry thee bags.'

The road went right down the ridge of the spur to the little church. Halfway, it was crossed at right angles by a second motor road which contained and serviced a handful of shops. The rest of the place was made up of streets too narrow or too perpendicular for cars. A few ancient scooters put-putted and sputtered about, donkeys clip-clopped here and there, but that was all. Spiros turned his vehicle about at the main junction (the *only* real road junction) and parked in the shade of a giant olive tree. He went to get the luggage. There were two large cases, two small ones. Geoff would have shared the load equally, but found himself brushed aside; Spiros took the elephant's share and left him with the small-fry. He wouldn't have minded, but it was obviously the Greek's chance to show off his strength.

Leading the way up a steep cobbled ramp of a street, Spiros's muscular buttocks kept threatening to burst through the thin stuff of his cut-down jeans. And because the holidaymakers followed on a little way behind, Geoff was aware of Gwen's eyes on Spiros's tanned, gleaming thews. There wasn't much of anywhere else to look. 'Him Tarzan, you Jane,' he commented, but his grin was a shade too dry.

'Who you?' she answered, her nose going up in the air. 'Cheetah?'

'*Uph, uph!*' said Geoff.

'Anyway,' she relented. 'Your bottom's nicer. More compact.'

He saved his breath, made no further comment. Even the light cases seemed heavy. If he was Cheetah, that must make Spiros Kong! The Greek glanced back once, grinned in his fashion, and kept going. Breathing heavily, Geoff and Gwen made an effort to catch up, failed miserably. Then, toward the top of the way Spiros turned right into an arched alcove, climbed three stone steps, put down his cases and paused at a varnished pine door. He pulled on a string to free the latch, shoved the door open and took up his cases again. As the English couple came round the corner he was stepping inside. 'Thee Villa Eleni,' he said, as they followed him in.

Beyond the door was a high-walled courtyard of black and white pebbles laid out in octopus and dolphin designs. A split-level patio fronted the 'villa,' a square box of a house whose one redeeming feature had to be a retractable sun-awning shading the windows and most of the patio. It also made an admirable refuge from the dazzling white of everything.

There were whitewashed concrete steps climbing the side of the building to the upper floor, with a landing that opened onto a wooden-railed balcony with its own striped awning. Beach towels and an out-sized lady's bathing costume were hanging over the rail, drying, and all the windows were open. Someone was home, maybe. Or maybe sitting in a shady taverna sipping on iced drinks. Downstairs, a key with a label had been left in the keyhole of a louvred, fly-screened door. Geoff read the label, which said simply: MR HAMMOND. The booking had been made in his name.

'This is us,' he said to Gwen, turning the key.

They went in, Spiros following with the large cases. Inside, the cool air was a blessing. Now they would like to explore the place on their own, but the Greek was there to do it for them. And he knew his way around. He put the cases down, opened his arms to indicate the central room. 'For sit, talk, thee resting.' He pointed to a tiled area in one corner, with a refrigerator, sink unit and two-ring electric cooker. 'For thee toast, coffee—thee fish and chips, eh?' He shoved open the door of a tiny room tiled top to bottom, containing a shower, wash basin and WC. 'And this one,' he said, without further explanation. Then five strides back across the floor took him to another room, low-ceilinged, pine-beamed, with a Lindean double bed built in under louvred windows. He cocked his head on one side. 'And thee bed—just one . . .'

'That's all we'll need,' Geoff answered, his annoyance building.

'Yes,' Gwen said. 'Well, thank you, er, Spiros—you're very kind. And we'll be fine now.'

Spiros scratched his chin, went back into the main room and sprawled in an easy chair. 'Outside is hot,' he said. 'Here she is cool—*chrio*, you know?'

Geoff went to him. 'It's *very* hot,' he agreed, 'and we're sticky. Now we want to shower, put our things away, look around. Thanks for your help. You can go now.'

Spiros stood up and his face went slack, his expression more blank than before. His wall-eye looked strange through its tinted lens. 'Go now?' he repeated.

Geoff sighed. 'Yes, go!'

The corner of Spiros's mouth twitched, drew back a little to show his gold tooth. 'I fetch from airport, carry cases.'

'Ah!' said Geoff, getting out his wallet. 'What do I owe you?' He'd bought drachmas at the bank in London.

Spiros sniffed, looked scornful, half turned away. 'One thousand,' he finally answered, bluntly.

'That's about four pounds and fifty pence,' Gwen said from the bedroom doorway. 'Sounds reasonable.'

'Except it was supposed to be on Skymed.' Geoff scowled. He paid up anyway and saw Spiros to the door. The Greek departed, sauntered indifferently across the patio to pause in the arched doorway and look back across the courtyard. Gwen had come to stand beside Geoff in the double doorway under the awning.

The Greek looked straight at her and licked his fleshy lips. The vacant grin was back on his face. 'I see you,' he said, nodding with a sort of slow deliberation.

As he closed the door behind him, Gwen muttered, 'Not if I see you first! *Ugh!*'

'I am with you,' Geoff agreed. '*Not* my favourite local character!'

'Spiros,' she said. 'Well, and it suits him to a tee. It's about as close as you can get to spider! And that one *is* about as close as you can get!'

They showered, fell exhausted on the bed—but not so exhausted that they could just lie there without making love.

Later—with suitcases emptied and small valuables stashed out of sight, and spare clothes all hung up or tucked away—dressed in light, loose gear, sandals, sunglasses, it was time to explore the village. 'And afterwards,' Gwen insisted, 'we're swimming!' She'd packed their towels and swimwear in a plastic beach bag. She loved to swim, and Geoff might have, too, except . . .

But as they left their rooms and stepped out across the patio, the varnished door in the courtyard wall opened to admit their upstairs neighbours, and for the next hour all thoughts of exploration and a dip in the sea were swept aside. The elderly couple who now introduced themselves gushed, there was no other way to describe it. He was George and she was Petula.

'My *dear*,' said George, taking Gwen's hand and kissing it, 'such a *stunning* young lady, and how sad that I've only two days left in which to enjoy you!' He was maybe sixty-four or five, ex-handsome but sagging a bit now, tall if a little bent, and brown as a native. With a small grey moustache and faded blue eyes, he looked as if he'd—no, in all probability he *had*—piloted Spitfires in World War II! Alas, he wore the most blindingly colourful shorts and shirt that Gwen had ever seen.

Petula was very large, about as tall as George but two of him in girth. She was just as brown, though (and so presumably didn't mind exposing it all), seemed equally if not more energetic, and was never at a loss for words. They were a strange, paradoxical pair: very upper-crust, but at the same time very much down to earth. If Petula tended to speak with plums in her mouth, certainly they were of a very tangy variety.

'He'll flatter you to death, my dear,' she told Gwen, ushering the newcomers up the steps at the side of the house and onto the high balcony. 'But you must *never* take your eyes off his hands! Stage magicians have nothing on George. Forty years ago he magicked himself into my bedroom, and he's been there ever since!'

'She seduced me!' said George, bustling indoors.

'I did not!' Petula was petulant. 'What? Why he's quite simply a wolf in . . . in a Joseph suit!'

'A Joseph suit?' George repeated her. He came back out onto the balcony with brandy-sours in a frosted jug, a clattering tray of ice-cubes, slices of sugared lemon and an eggcup of salt for the sours. He put the lot down on a plastic table, said: 'Ah!—glasses!' and ducked back inside again.

'Yes,' his wife called after him, pointing at his Bermudas and Hawaiian shirt. 'Your clothes of many colours!'

It was all good fun and Geoff and Gwen enjoyed it. They sat round the table on plastic chairs, and George and Petula entertained them. It made for a very nice welcome to Achladi indeed.

'Of course,' said George after a while, when they'd settled down a little, 'we first came here eight years ago, when there were no flights, just boats. Now that people are flying in—' he shrugged '—two more seasons and there'll be belly-dancers and hotdog stands! But for now it's . . . just perfect. Will you look at that view?'

The view from the balcony was very fetching. 'From up here we can see the entire village,' said Gwen. 'You must point out the best shops, the bank or exchange or whatever, all the places we'll need to know about.'

George and Petula looked at each other, smiled knowingly.

'Oh?' said Gwen.

Geoff checked their expressions, nodded, made a guess: 'There are no places we need to know about.'

'Well, three, actually,' said Petula. 'Four if you count Dimi's—the taverna. Oh, there are other places to eat, but Dimi's is *the* place. Except I feel I've spoilt it for you now. I mean, that really is something you should have discovered for yourself. It's half the fun, finding the best place to eat!'

'What about the other three places we should know about?' Gwen inquired. 'Will knowing those spoil it for us, too? Knowing them in advance, I mean?'

'Good Lord, no!' George shook his head. 'Vital knowledge, young lady!'

'The baker's,' said Petula. 'For fresh rolls—daily.' She pointed it out, blue smoke rising from a cluster of chimneypots. 'Also the booze shop, for booze—'

'—Also daily,' said George, pointing. 'Right there on that corner—where the bottles glint. D'you know, they have an *ancient* Metaxa so cheap you wouldn't—'

'*And*,' Petula continued, 'the path down to the beach. Which is . . . over there.'

'But tell us,' said George, changing the subject, 'are you married, you two? Or is that too personal?'

'Oh, of *course* they're married!' Petula told him. 'But very recently, because they still sit so close together. Touching. You see?'

'Ah!' said George. 'Then we shan't have another elopement.'

'You know, my dear, you really are an old idiot,' said Petula, sighing. 'I mean, elopements are for lovers to be together. And these two already *are* together!'

Geoff and Gwen raised their eyebrows. 'An elopement?' Gwen said. 'Here? When did this happen?'

'Right here, yes,' said Petula. 'Ten days ago. On our first night we had a young man downstairs, Gordon. On his own. He was supposed to be here with his fiancée, but she's jilted him. He went out with us, had a few too many in Dimi's and told us all about it. A Swedish girl—very lovely, blonde creature—was also on her own. She helped steer him back here and, I suppose, tucked him in. She had her own place, mind you, and didn't stay.'

'But the next night she did!' George enthused.

'And then they ran off,' said Petula, brightly. 'Eloped! As simple as that. We saw them once, on the beach, the next morning. Following which—'

'—Gone!' said George.

'Maybe their holidays were over and they just went home,' said Gwen, reasonably.

'No.' George shook his head. 'Gordon had come out on our plane, his holiday was just starting. She'd been here about a week and a half, was due to fly out the day after they made off together.'

'They paid for their holidays and then deserted them?' Geoff frowned. 'Doesn't make any sense.'

'Does anything, when you're in love?' Petula sighed.

'The way I see it,' said George, 'they fell in love with each other, and with Greece, and went off to explore all the options.'

'Love?' Gwen was doubtful. 'On the rebound?'

'If she'd been a mousey little thing, I'd quite agree,' said Petula. 'But no, she really was a beautiful girl.'

'And him a nice lad,' said George. 'A bit sparse but clean, good-looking.'

'Indeed, they were much like you two,' his wife added. 'I mean, not *like* you, but like you.'

'Cheers,' said Geoff, wryly. 'I mean, I know I'm not Mr Universe, but—'

'Tight in the bottom!' said Petula. 'That's what the girls like these days. You'll do all right.'

'See,' said Gwen, nudging him. 'Told you so!'

But Geoff was still frowning. 'Didn't anyone look for them? What if they'd been involved in an accident or something?'

'No,' said Petula. 'They were seen boarding a ferry in the main town. Indeed, one of the local taxi drivers took them there. Spiros.'

Gwen and Geoff's turn to look at each other. 'A strange fish, that one,' said Geoff.

George shrugged. 'Oh, I don't know. You know him, do you? It's that eye of his which makes him seem a bit sinister . . .'

Maybe he's right, Geoff thought.

Shortly after that, their drinks finished, they went off to start their explorations . . .

The village was a maze of cobbled, white-washed alleys. Even as tiny as it was you could get lost in it, but never for longer than the length of a street. Going downhill, no matter the direction, you'd come to the sea. Uphill you'd come to the main road, or if you didn't, then turn the next corner and *continue* uphill, and then you would. The most well-trodden alley, with the shiniest cobbles, was the one that led to the hard-packed path, which in turn led to the beach. Pass the 'booze shop' on the corner twice, and you'd know where it was always. The window was plastered with labels, some familiar and others entirely conjectural; inside, steel shelving went floor to ceiling, stacked with every conceivable brand; even the more exotic and (back home) wildly expensive stuffs were on view, often in ridiculously cheap, three-litre, duty-free bottles with their own chrome taps and display stands.

'Courvoisier!' said Gwen, appreciatively.

'Grand Marnier, surely!' Geoff protested. 'What, five pints of Grand Marnier? At that price? Can you believe it? But that's to take home. What about while we're here?'

'Coconut liqueur,' she said. 'Or better still, mint chocolate—to compliment our midnight coffees.'

They found several small tavernas, too, with people seated outdoors at tiny tables under the vines. Chicken portions and slabs of lamb sputtering on spits; small fishes sizzling over charcoal; *moussaka* steaming in long trays . . .

Dimi's was down on the harbour, where a wide, low wall kept you safe from falling in the sea. They had a Greek salad which they divided two ways, tiny cubes of lamb roasted on wooden slivers, a half-bottle of local white wine costing pennies. As they ate and sipped the wine, so they began to relax; the hot sunlight was tempered by an almost imperceptible breeze off the sea.

Geoff said: 'Do you really feel energetic? Damned if I do.'

She didn't feel full of boundless energy, no, but she wasn't going down without a fight. 'If it was up to you,' she said, 'we'd just sit here and watch the fishing nets dry, right?'

'Nothing wrong with taking it easy,' he answered. 'We're on holiday, remember?'

'Your idea of taking it easy means being bone idle!' she answered. '*I* say we're going for a dip, then back to the villa for siesta and you know, and—'

'Can we have the you know before the siesta?' He kept a straight face.

'—And then we'll be all settled in, recovered from the journey, ready for tonight. Insatiable!'

'Okay.' He shrugged. 'Anything you say. But we swim from the beach, not from the rocks.'

Gwen looked at him suspiciously. 'That was almost too easy.'

Now he grinned. 'It was the thought of, well, you know, that did it,' he told her . . .

Lying on the beach, panting from their exertions in the sea, with the sun lifting the moisture off their still-pale bodies, Gwen said: 'I don't understand.'

'Hmm?'

'You swim very well. I've always thought so. So what is this fear of the water you complain about?'

'First,' Geoff answered, 'I don't swim very well. Oh, for a hundred yards I'll swim like a dolphin—any more than that and I do it like a brick! I can't float. If I stop swimming I sink.'

'So don't stop.'

'When you get tired, you stop.'

'What was it that made you frightened of the water?'

He told her:

'I was a kid in Cyprus. A little kid. My father had taught me how to swim. I used to watch him diving off the rocks, oh, maybe twenty or thirty feet high, into the sea. I thought I could do it, too. So one day when my folks weren't watching, I tried. I must have hit my head on something on the way down. Or maybe I simply struck the water all wrong. When they spotted me floating in the sea, I was just about done for. My father dragged me out. He was a medic—the kiss of life and all that. So now I'm not much for swimming, and I'm absolutely *nothing* for diving! I will swim—for a splash, in shallow water, like today—but that's my limit. And I'll only go in from a beach. I can't stand cliffs, height. It's as simple as that. You married a coward. So there.'

'No I didn't,' she said. 'I married someone with a great bottom. Why didn't you tell me all this before?'

'You didn't ask me. I don't like to talk about it because I don't much care to remember it. I was just a kid, and yet I knew I was going to die. And I knew it wouldn't be nice. I still haven't got it out of my system, not completely. And so the less said about it the better.'

A beach ball landed close by, bounced, rolled to a stand-still against Gwen's thigh. They looked up. A brown, burly figure came striding. They recognized the frayed, bulging shorts. Spiros.

'Hallo,' he said, going down into a crouch close by, forearms resting on his knees. 'Thee beach. Thee ball. I swim, play. You swim?' (This to Geoff.) 'You come swim, throwing thee ball?'

Geoff sat up. There were half a dozen other couples on the beach; why couldn't this jerk pick on them? Geoff thought to himself: *I'm about to get sand kicked in my face!* 'No,' he said out loud, shaking his head. 'I don't swim much.'

'No swim? You frighting thee big fish? Thee sharks?'

'Sharks?' Now Gwen sat up. From behind their dark lenses she could feel Spiros's eyes crawling over her.

Geoff shook his head. 'There are no sharks in the Med,' he said.

'Him right.' Spiros laughed high-pitched, like a woman, without his customary gurgling. A weird sound. 'No sharks. I make thee jokes!' He stopped laughing and looked straight at Gwen. She couldn't decide if he was looking at her face or her breasts. Those damned sunglasses of his! 'You come swim, lady, with Spiros? Play in thee water?'

'My . . . *God!*' Gwen sputtered, glowering at him. She pulled her dress on over her still-damp, very skimpy swimming costume, packed her towel away, picked up her sandals. When she was annoyed, she really *was* annoyed.

Geoff stood up as she made off, turned to Spiros. 'Now listen—' he began.

'Ah, you go now! Is okay. I see you.' He took his ball, raced with it down the beach, hurled it out over the sea. Before it splashed down he was diving, low and flat, striking the water like a knife. Unlike Geoff, he swam very well indeed . . .

When Geoff caught up with his wife she was stiff with anger. Mainly angry with herself. 'That was *so* rude of me!' she exploded.

'No it wasn't,' he said. 'I feel exactly the same about it.'

'But he's so damned ... persistent! I mean, he knows we're to-gether, man and wife ... "thee bed—just one." How *dare* he intrude?'

Geoff tried to make light of it. 'You're imagining it,' he said.

'And you? Doesn't he get on your nerves?'

'Maybe I'm imagining it too. Look, he's Greek—and not an espe-cially attractive specimen. Look at it from his point of view. All of a sudden there's a gaggle of dolly-birds on the beach, dressed in stuff his sister wouldn't wear for undies! So he tries to get closer—for a better view, as it were—so that he can get a wall-eyeful. He's no different to other blokes. Not quite as smooth, that's all.'

'Smooth!' she almost spat the word out. 'He's about as smooth as a badger's—'

'—bottom,' said Geoff. 'Yes, I know. If I'd known you were such a bum-fancier I mightn't have married you.'

And at last she laughed, but shakily.

They stopped at the booze shop and bought brandy and a large bottle of Coca-Cola. And mint chocolate liqueur, of course, for their midnight coffees ...

That night Gwen put on a blue-and-white dress, very Greek if cut a little low in the front, and silver sandals. Tucking a handkerchief into the breast pocket of his white jacket, Geoff thought: *She's beautiful!* With her heart-shaped face and the way her hair framed it, cut in a page-boy style that suited its shiny black sheen—and her green, green eyes—he'd always thought she looked French. But tonight she was definitely Greek. And he was so glad that she was English, and his.

Dimi's was doing a roaring trade. George and Petula had a table in the corner, overlooking the sea. They had spread themselves out in order to occupy all four seats, but when Geoff and Gwen appeared they waved, called them over. 'We thought you'd drop in,' George said, as they sat down. And to Gwen: 'You look charming, my dear.'

'Now I feel I'm really on my holidays,' Gwen smiled.

'Honeymoon, surely,' said Petula.

'*Shh!*' Geoff cautioned her. 'In England they throw confetti. Over here it's plates!'

'Your secret is safe with us,' said George.

'Holiday, honeymoon, whatever,' said Gwen. 'Compliments from handsome gentlemen; the stars reflected in the sea; a full moon rising and bouzouki music floating in the air. And—'

'—The mouth-watering smells of good Greek grub!' Geoff cut in. 'Have you ordered?' He looked at George and Petula.

'A moment ago,' Petula told him. 'If you go into the kitchen there, Dimi will show you his menu—live, as it were. Tell him you're with us and he'll make an effort to serve us together. Starter, main course, a pudding—the lot.'

'Good!' Geoff said, standing up. 'I could eat the saddle off a donkey!'

'Eat the whole donkey,' George told him. 'The one who's going to wake you up with his racket at six-thirty tomorrow morning.'

'You don't know Geoff,' said Gwen. 'He'd sleep through a Rolling Stones concert.'

'And *you* don't know Achladi donkeys!' said Petula.

In the kitchen, the huge, bearded proprietor was busy, fussing over his harassed-looking cooks. As Geoff entered he came over. 'Good evenings, sir. You are new in Achladi?'

'Just today.' Geoff smiled. 'We came here for lunch but missed you.'

'Ah!' Dimitrios gasped, shrugged apologetically. 'I was sleeps! Every day, for two hours, I sleeps. Where you stay, eh?'

'The Villa Eleni.'

'Eleni? Is me!' Dimitrios beamed. '*I* am Villa Eleni. I mean, I owns it. Eleni is thee name my wifes.'

'It's a beautiful name,' said Geoff, beginning to feel trapped in the conversation. 'Er, we're with George and Petula.'

'You are eating? Good, good. I show you.' Geoff was given a guided tour of the ovens and the sweets trolley. He ordered, keeping it light for Gwen.

'And here,' said Dimitrios. 'For your lady!' He produced a filigreed silver-metal brooch in the shape of a butterfly, with 'Dimi's' worked into the metal of the body. Gwen wouldn't like it especially, but politic to accept it. Geoff had noticed several female patrons wearing them, Petula included.

'That's very kind of you,' he said.

Making his way back to their table, he saw Spiros was there before him.

Now where the hell had he sprung from? And what the hell was he playing at?

Spiros wore tight blue jeans, (his image, obviously), and a white T-shirt stained down the front. He was standing over the corner table, one hand on the wall where it overlooked the sea, the other on the table itself. Propped up, still he swayed. He was leaning over Gwen. George and Petula had frozen smiles on their faces, looked frankly astonished. Geoff couldn't quite see all of Gwen, for Spiros's bulk was in the way.

What he could see, of the entire mini-tableau, printed itself on his eyes as he drew closer. Adrenaline surged in him and he began to breathe faster. He barely noticed George standing up and sliding out of view. Then as the bouzouki tape came to an end and the taverna's low babble of sound seemed to grow that much louder, Gwen's outraged voice suddenly rose over everything else:

'Get . . . your . . . filthy . . . paws . . . *off* me!' she cried.

Geoff was there. Petula had drawn as far back as possible; no longer smiling, her hand was at her throat, her eyes staring in disbelief. Spiros's left hand had caught up the V of Gwen's dress. His fingers were inside the dress and his thumb outside. In his right hand he clutched a pin like the one Dimitrios had given to Geoff. He was protesting:

'But I giving it! I putting it on your dress! Is nice, this one. We friends. Why you shout? You no like Spiros?' His throaty, gurgling voice was slurred: waves of ouzo fumes literally wafted off him like the stench of a dead fish. Geoff moved in, knocked Spiros's elbow away where it leaned on the wall. Spiros must release Gwen to maintain his balance. He did so, but still crashed half-over the wall. For a moment Geoff thought he would go completely over, into the sea. But he just lolled there, shaking his head, and finally turned it to look back at Geoff. There was a look on his face which Geoff couldn't quite describe. Drunken stupidity slowly turning to rage, maybe. Then he pushed himself upright, stood swaying against the wall, his fists knotting and the muscles in his arms bunching.

Hit him now, Geoff's inner man told him. *Do it, and he'll go clean over into the sea. It's not high, seven or eight feet, that's all. It'll sober the bastard up, and after that he won't trouble you again.*

But what if he couldn't swim? *You know he swims like a fish—like a bloody shark!*

'You think you better than Spiros, eh?' The Greek wobbled dangerously, steadied up and took a step in Geoff's direction.

'No!' the voice of the bearded Dimitrios was shattering in Geoff's ear. Massive, he stepped between them, grabbed Spiros by the hair, half-dragged, half-pushed him towards the exist. 'No, *everybody* thinks he's better!' he cried. 'Because everybody *is* better! Out—' He heaved Spiros yelping into the harbour's shadows. 'I tell you before, Spiros: drink all the ouzo in Achladi. Is your business. But not let it ruin *my* business. Then comes thee *real* troubles!'

Gwen was naturally upset. It spoiled something of the evening for her. But by the time they had finished eating, things were about back to normal. No one else in the place, other than George and Petula, had seemed especially interested in the incident anyway.

At around eleven, when the taverna had cleared a little, the girl from Skymed came in. She came over.

'Hello, Julie!' said George, finding her a chair. And, flatterer born, he added: 'How lovely you're looking tonight—but of course you look lovely all the time.'

Petula tut-tutted. 'George, if you hadn't met me, you'd be a gigolo by now, I'm sure!'

'Mr Hammond,' Julie said. 'I'm terribly sorry. I should have explained to Spiros that he'd recover the fare for your ride from me. Actually, I believed he understood that, but apparently he didn't. I've just seen him in one of the bars and asked him how much I owed him. He was a little upset, wouldn't accept the money, told me I should see you.'

'Was he sober yet?' Geoff asked, sourly.

'Er, not very, I'm afraid. Has he been a nuisance?'

Geoff coughed. 'Only a *bit* of a one.'

'It was a thousand drachmas,' said Gwen.

The courier looked a little taken aback. 'Well it should only have been seven hundred.'

'He did carry our bags, though,' said Geoff.

'Ah! Maybe that explains it. Anyway, I'm authorized to pay you seven hundred.'

'All donations are welcome,' Gwen said, opening her purse and accepting the money. 'But if I were you, in future I'd use someone else. This Spiros isn't a particularly pleasant fellow.'

'Well he does seem to have a problem with the ouzo,' Julie answered. 'On the other hand—'

'He has *several* problems!' Geoff was sharper than he meant to be. After all, it wasn't her fault.

'—He also has the best beach,' Julie finished.

'Beach?' Geoff raised an eyebrow. 'He has a beach?'

'Didn't we tell you?' Petula spoke up. 'Two or three of the locals have small boats in the harbour. For a few hundred drachmas they'll take you to one of a handful of private beaches along the coast. They're private because no one lives there, and there's no way in except by boat. The boatmen have their favorite places, which they guard jealously and call "their" beaches, so that the others don't poach on them. They take you in the morning or whenever, collect you in the evening. Absolutely private . . . ideal for picnics . . . romance!' She sighed.

'What a lovely idea,' said Gwen. 'To have a beach of your own for the day!'

'Well, as far as I'm concerned,' Geoff told her, 'Spiros can keep his beach.'

'Oh-oh!' said George. 'Speak of the devil . . .'

Spiros had returned. He averted his face and made straight for the kitchens in the back. He was noticeably steadier on his feet now. Dimitrios came bowling out to meet him and a few low-muttered words passed between them. Their conversation quickly grew more heated, becoming rapid-fire Greek in moments, and Spiros appeared to be pleading his case. Finally Dimitrios shrugged, came lumbering towards the corner table with Spiros in tow.

'Spiros, he sorry,' Dimitrios said. 'For tonight. Too much ouzo. He just want be friendly.'

'Is right,' said Spiros, lifting his head. He shrugged helplessly. 'Thee ouzo.'

Geoff nodded. 'Okay, forget it,' he said, but coldly.

'Is . . . okay?' Spiros lifted his head a little more. He looked at Gwen.

Gwen forced herself to nod. 'It's okay.'

Now Spiros beamed, or as close as he was likely to get to it. But still Geoff had this feeling that there was something cold and calculating in his manner.

'I make it good!' Spiros declared, nodding. 'One day, I take you thee *best* beach! For thee picnic. Very private. Two peoples, no more. I no take thee money, nothing. Is good?'

'Fine,' said Geoff. 'That'll be fine.'

'Okay.' Spiros smiled his unsmile, nodded, turned away. Going out, he looked back. 'I sorry,' he said again, and again his shrug. 'Thee ouzo . . .'

'Hardly eloquent,' said Petula, when he'd disappeared.

'But better than nothing,' said George.

'Things are looking up!' Gwen was happier now.

Geoff was still unsure how he felt. He said nothing . . .

'Breakfast is on us,' George announced the next morning. He smiled down on Geoff and Gwen where they drank coffee and tested the early morning sunlight at a garden table on the patio. They were still in their dressing-gowns, eyes bleary, hair tousled.

Geoff looked up, squinting his eyes against the hurtful blue of the sky, and said: 'I see what you mean about that donkey! What the hell time is it, anyway?'

'Eight-fifteen,' said George. 'You're lucky. Normally he's at it, oh, an hour earlier than this!' From somewhere down in the maze of alleys, as if summoned by their conversation, the hideous braying echoed yet again as the village gradually came awake.

Just before nine they set out, George and Petula guiding them to a little place bearing the paint-daubed legend: 'Brekfas Bar.' They climbed steps to a pine-railed patio set with pine tables and chairs, under a varnished pine frame supporting a canopy of split bamboo. Service was good; the 'English' food hot, tasty, and very cheap; the coffee dreadful!

'*Yechh!*' Gwen commented, understanding now why George and Petula had ordered tea. 'Take a note, Mr Hammond,' she said. 'Tomorrow, no coffee. Just fruit juice.'

'We thought maybe it was us being fussy,' said Petula. 'Else we'd have warned you.'

'Anyway,' George sighed. 'Here's where we have to leave you. For tomorrow we fly—literally. So today we're shopping, picking up our duty-frees, gifts, the postcards we never sent, some Greek cigarettes.'

'But we'll see you tonight, if you'd care to?' said Petula.

'Delighted!' Geoff answered. 'What, Zorba's Dance, moussaka, and a couple or three of those giant Metaxas that Dimi serves? Who could refuse?'

'Not to mention the company,' said Gwen.

'About eight-thirty, then,' said Petula. And off they went.

'I shall miss them,' said Gwen.

'But it will be nice to be on our own for once,' Geoff leaned over to kiss her.

'Hallo!' came a now familiar, gurgling voice from below. Spiros stood in the street beyond the rail, looking up at them, the sun striking sparks from the lenses of his sunglasses. Their faces fell and he couldn't fail to notice it. 'Is okay,' he quickly held up a hand. 'I no stay. I busy. Today I make thee taxi. Later, thee boat.'

Gwen gave a little gasp of excitement, clutched Geoff's arm. 'The private beach!' she said. 'Now that's what I'd call being on our own!' And to Spiros: 'If we're ready at one o'clock, will you take us to your beach?'

'Of course!' he answered. 'At one o'clock, I near Dimi's. My boat, him called *Spiros* like me. You see him.'

Gwen nodded. 'We'll see you then.'

'Good!' Spiros nodded. He looked up at them a moment longer, and Geoff wished he could fathom where the man's eyes were. Probably up Gwen's dress. But then he turned and went on his way.

'Now we shop!' Gwen said.

They shopped for picnic items. Nothing gigantic, mainly small things. Slices of salami, hard cheese, two fat tomatoes, fresh bread, a bottle of light white wine, some feta, eggs for boiling, and a liter of crystal-clear bottled water. And as an afterthought: half a dozen small pats of butter, a small jar of honey, a sharp knife and a packet of doilies. No wicker basket; their little plastic coolbox would have to do. And one of their pieces of shoulder luggage for the blanket, towels, and swim things. Geoff was no good for details; Gwen's head, to the contrary, was only happy buzzing with them. He let her get on with it, acted as beast of burden. In fact there was no burden to mention. After all, she was shopping for just the two of them, and it was as good a way as any to explore the village stores and see what was on offer. While she examined this and that, Geoff spent the time comparing the prices of various spirits with those already noted in the booze shop. So the morning passed.

At eleven-thirty they went back to the Villa Eleni for you know and a shower, and afterwards Gwen prepared the foodstuffs while Geoff lazed under the awning. No sign of George and Petula; eighty-four degrees of heat as they idled their way down to the harbour; the village had closed itself down through the hottest part of the day, and they saw no one they knew. Spiros's boat lolled like a mirrored blot on the stirless ocean, and Geoff thought: *Even the fish will be finding this a bit much!* Also: *I hope there's some shade on this blasted beach!*

Spiros appeared from behind a tangle of nets. He stood up, yawned, adjusted his straw hat like a sunshade on his head. 'Thee boat,' he said, in his entirely unnecessary fashion, as he helped them climb aboard. *Spiros* 'thee boat' was hardly a hundred percent seaworthy, Geoff saw that immediately. In fact, in any other ocean in the world she'd be condemned. But this was the Mediterranean in July.

Barely big enough for three adults, the boat rocked a little as Spiros yanked futilely on the starter. Water seeped through boards, rotten and long since sprung, black with constant damp and badly caulked. Spiros saw Geoff's expression where he sat with his sandals in half an inch of water. He shrugged. 'Is nothings,' he said.

Finally the engine coughed into life, began to purr, and they were off. Spiros had the tiller; Geoff and Gwen faced him from the prow, which now lifted up a little as they left the harbour and cut straight out to sea. It was then, for the first time, that Geoff noticed Spiros's furtiveness: the way he kept glancing back toward Achladi, as if anxious not to be observed. Unlikely that they would be, for the village seemed fast asleep. Or perhaps he was just checking landmarks, avoiding rocks or reefs or what have you. Geoff looked overboard. The water seemed deep enough to him. Indeed, it seemed much *too* deep! But at least there were no sharks . . .

Well out to sea, Spiros swung the boat south and followed the coastline for maybe two and a half to three miles. The highest of Achladi's houses and apartments had slipped entirely from view by the time he turned in towards land again and sought a bight in the seemingly unbroken march of cliffs. The place was landmarked: a fang of rock had weathered free, shaping a stack that reared up from the water to form a narrow, deep channel between itself and the cliffs proper. In former times a second, greater stack had crashed oceanward and now lay like a reef just under the water across the entire frontage. In effect, this made the place a lagoon: a sandy beach to the rear, safe water, and the reef of shattered, softly matted rocks where the small waves broke.

There was only one way in. Spiros gentled his boat through the deep water between the crooked outcrop and the over-hanging cliff. Clear of the channel, he nosed her into the beach and cut the motor; as the keel grated on grit he stepped nimbly between his passengers and jumped ashore, dragging the boat a few inches up onto the sand. Geoff

passed him the picnic things, then steadied the boat while Gwen took
off her sandals and made to step down where the water met the sand.
But Spiros was quick off the mark.

He stepped forward, caught her up, carried her two paces up the
beach and set her down. His left arm had been under her thighs, his
right under her back, cradling her. But when he set her upon her own
feet his right hand had momentarily cupped her breast, which he'd quite
deliberately squeezed.

Gwen opened her mouth, stood gasping her outrage, unable to give
it words. Geoff had got out of the boat and was picking up their things
to bring them higher up the sand. Spiros, slapping him on the back,
stepped round him and shoved the boat off, splashed in shallow water
a moment before leaping nimbly aboard. Gwen controlled herself, said
nothing. She could feel the blood in her cheeks but hoped Geoff
wouldn't notice. Not here, miles from anywhere. Not in this lonely
place. No, there must be no trouble here.

For suddenly it had dawned on her just how very lonely it was.
Beautiful, unspoiled, a lovers' idyll—but oh so very lonely . . .

'You alright, love?' said Geoff, taking her elbow. She was looking at
Spiros standing silent in his boat. Their eyes seemed locked, it was as if
she didn't see him but the mind behind the sunglasses, behind those
disparate, dispassionate eyes. A message had passed between them.
Geoff sensed it but couldn't fathom it. He had almost seemed to hear
Spiros say 'yes,' and Gwen answer 'no.'

'Gwen?' he said again.

'I see you,' Spiros called, grinning. It broke the spell. Gwen looked
away, and Geoff called out:

'Six-thirty, right?'

Spiros waggled a hand this way and that palm-down, as if unde-
cided. 'Six, six-thirty—something,' he said, shrugging. He started his
motor, waved once, chugged out of the bay between the jutting sentinel
rock and the cliffs. As he passed out of sight the boat's engine roared
with life, its throaty growl rapidly fading into the distance . . .

———

Gwen said nothing about the incident; she felt sure that if she did, then Geoff would make something of it. Their entire holiday could so easily be spoiled. It was bad enough that for her the day had already been ruined. So she kept quiet, and perhaps a little too quiet. When Geoff asked her again if anything was wrong, she told him she had a headache. Then, feeling a little unclean, she stripped herself quite naked and swam while he explored the beach.

Not that there was a great deal to explore. He walked the damp sand at the water's rim to the southern extreme and came up against the cliffs where they curved out into the sea. They were quite unscalable, towering maybe eighty or ninety feet to their jagged rim. Walking the hundred or so yards back the other way, the thought came to Geoff that if Spiros didn't come back for them—that is, if anything untoward should happen to him—they'd just have to sit it out until they were found. Which, since Spiros was the only one who knew they were here, might well be a long time. Having thought it, Geoff tried to shake the idea off, but it wouldn't go away. The place was quite literally a trap. Even a decent swimmer would have to have at least a couple of miles in him before considering swimming out of here.

Once lodged in Geoff's brain, the concept rapidly expanded itself. Before . . . he had looked at the faded yellow and bone-white facade of the cliffs against the incredible blue of the sky with admiration; the beach had been every man's dream of tranquility, privacy, Eden with its own Eve; the softly lapping ocean had seemed like a warm, soothing bath reaching from horizon to horizon. But now . . . the place was so like Cape Greco. Except at Greco there had always been a way down to the sea—and up from it . . .

The northern end of the beach was much like the southern, the only difference being the great fang of rock protruding from the sea. Geoff stripped, swam out to it, was aware that the water here was a great deal deeper than back along the beach. But the distance was only thirty feet or so, nothing to worry about. And there were hand- and footholds galore around the base of the pillar of upthrusting rock. He hauled himself up onto a tiny ledge, climbed higher (not too high), sat on a projecting fist of rock with his feet dangling and called to Gwen.

His voice surprised him, for it seemed strangely small and panting. The cliffs took it up, however, amplified and passed it on. His shout reached Gwen where she splashed; she spotted him, stopped swimming and stood up. She waved, and he marvelled at her body, her tip-tilted breasts displayed where she stood like some lovely Mediterranean nymph, all unashamed. *Venus rising from the waves.* Except that here the waves were little more than ripples.

He glanced down at the water and was at once dizzy: the way it lapped at the rock and flowed so gently in the worn hollows of the stone, all fluid and glinting motion; and Geoff's stomach following the same routine, seeming to slosh loosely inside him. *Damn* this terror of his! What was he but eight, nine feet above the sea? God, he might as well feel sick standing on a thick carpet!

He stood up, shouted, jumped outward, toward Gwen.

Down he plunged into cool, liquid blue, and fought his way to the surface, and swam furiously to the beach. There he lay, half-in, half-out of the water, his heart and lungs hammering, blood coursing through his body. It had been such a little thing—something any ten-year-old child could have done—but to him it had been such an effort. And an achievement!

Elated, he stood up, sprinted down the beach, threw himself into the warm, shallow water just as Gwen was emerging. Carried back by him she laughed, splashed him, finally submitted to his hug. They rolled in twelve inches of water and her legs went round him; and there where the water met the sand they grew gentle, then fierce, and when it was done the sea laved their heat and rocked them gently, slowly dispersing their passion . . .

About four o'clock they ate, but very little. They weren't hungry; the sun was too hot; the silence, at first enchanting, had turned to a droning, sun-scorched monotony that beat on the ears worse than a city's roar. And there was a smell. When the light breeze off the sea swung in a certain direction, it brought something unpleasant with it.

To provide shade, Geoff had rigged up his shirt, slacks, and a large beach towel on a frame of drifted bamboo between the brittle, sand-papered branches of an old tree washed halfway up the sand. There in this tatty, makeshift teepee they'd spread their blanket, retreated from the pounding sun. But as the smell came again, Geoff crept out of the cramped shade, stood up and shielded his eyes to look along the wall of the cliffs. 'It comes . . . from over there,' he said, pointing.

Gwen joined him. 'I thought you'd explored?' she said.

'Along the tideline,' he answered, nodding slowly. 'Not along the base of the cliffs. Actually, they don't look too safe, and they overhang a fair bit in places. But if you'll look where I'm pointing—there, where the cliffs are cut back—is that water glinting?'

'A spring?' she looked at him. 'A waterfall?'

'Hardly a waterfall,' he said. 'More a dribble. But what is it that's dribbling? I mean, springs don't stink, do they?'

Gwen wrinkled her nose. 'Sewage, do you think?'

'Yecchh!' he said. 'But at least it would explain why there's no one else here. I'm going to have a look.'

She followed him to the place where the cliffs were notched in a V. Out of the sunlight, they both shivered a little. They'd put on swimwear for simple decency's sake, in case a boat should pass by, but now they hugged themselves as the chill of damp stone drew off their stored heat and brought goose-pimples to flesh which sun and sea had already roughened. And there, beneath the overhanging cliff, they found in the shingle a pool formed of a steady flow from on high. Without a shadow of a doubt, the pool was the source of the carrion stench; but here in the shade its water was dark, muddied, rippled, quite opaque. If there was anything in it, then it couldn't be seen.

As for the waterfall: it forked high up in the cliff, fell in twin streams, one of which was a trickle. Leaning out over the pool at its narrowest, shallowest point, Geoff cupped his hand to catch a few droplets. He held them to his nose, shook his head. 'Just water,' he said. 'It's the pool itself that stinks.'

'Or something back there?' Gwen looked beyond the pool, into the darkness of the cave formed of the V and the overhang.

Geoff took up a stone, hurled it into the darkness and silence. Clattering echoes sounded, and a moment later—

Flies! A swarm of them, disturbed where they'd been sitting on cool, damp ledges. They came in a cloud out of the cave, sent Geoff and Gwen yelping, fleeing for the sea. Geoff was stung twice, Gwen escaped injury; the ocean was their refuge, shielding them while the flies dispersed or returned to their vile-smelling breeding ground.

After the murky, poisonous pool the sea felt cool and refreshing. Muttering curses, Geoff stood in the shallows while Gwen squeezed the craters of the stings in his right shoulder and bathed them with salt water. When she was done he said, bitterly: 'I've *had* it with this place! The sooner the Greek gets back the better.'

His words were like an invocation. Towelling themselves dry, they heard the roar of Spiros's motor, heard it throttle back, and a moment later his boat came nosing in through the gap between the rock and the cliffs. But instead of landing he stood off in the shallow water. 'Hallo,' he called, in his totally unnecessary fashion.

'You're early,' Geoff called back. And under his breath: *Thank God!*

'Early, yes,' Spiros answered. 'But I have thee troubles.' He shrugged.

Gwen had pulled her dress on, packed the last of their things away. She walked down to the water's edge with Geoff. 'Troubles?' she said, her voice a shade unsteady.

'Thee boat,' he said, and pointed into the open, lolling belly of the craft, where they couldn't see. 'I hitting thee rock when I leave Achladi. Is okay, but—' And he made his fifty-fifty sign, waggling his hand with the fingers open and the palm down. His face remained impassive, however.

Geoff looked at Gwen, then back to Spiros. 'You mean it's unsafe?'

'For three peoples, unsafe—maybe.' Again the Greek's shrug. 'I thinks, I take thee lady first. Is okay, I come back. Is bad, I find other boat.'

'You can't take both of us?' Geoff's face fell.

Spiros shook his head. 'Maybe big problems,' he said.

Geoff nodded. 'Okay,' he said to Gwen. 'Go just as you are. Leave all this stuff here and keep the boat light.' And to Spiros: 'Can you come in a bit more?'

The Greek made a clicking sound with his tongue, shrugged apologetically. 'Thee boat is broked. I not want thee more breakings. You swim?' He looked at Gwen, leaned over the side and held out his hand. Keeping her dress on, she waded into the water, made her way to the side of the boat. The water only came up to her breasts, but it turned her dress to a transparent, clinging film. She grasped the upper strake with one hand and made to drag herself aboard. Spiros, leaning backwards, took her free hand.

Watching, Geoff saw her come half out of the water—then saw her freeze. She gasped loudly and twisted her wet hand in Spiros's grasp, tugged free of his grip, flopped back down into the water. And while the Greek regained his balance, she quickly swam back ashore. Geoff helped her from the sea. 'Gwen?' he said.

Spiros worked his starter, got the motor going. He commenced a slow, deliberate circling of the small bay.

'Gwen?' Geoff said again. 'What is it? What's wrong?' She was pale, shivering.

'He . . .' she finally started to speak. 'He . . . had an erection! Geoff, I could see it bulging in his shorts, throbbing. My God—and I know it was for me! And the boat . . .'

'What about the boat?' Anger was building in Geoff's heart and head, starting to run cold in his blood.

'There was no damage—none that I could see, anyway. He . . . he just wanted to get me into that boat, on my own!'

Spiros could see them talking together. He came angling close into the beach, called out: 'I bring thee better boat. Half an hour. Is safer. I see you.' He headed for the channel between the rock and the cliff and in another moment passed from sight . . .

'Geoff, we're in trouble,' Gwen said, as soon as Spiros had left. 'We're in serious trouble.'

'I know it,' he said. 'I think I've known it ever since we got here. That bloke's as sinister as they come.'

'And it's not just his eye, it's his mind,' said Gwen. 'He's sick.' Finally, she told her husband about the incident when Spiros had carried her ashore from the boat.

'So that's what that was all about,' he growled. 'Well, something has to be done about him. We'll have to report him.'

She clutched his arm. 'We have to get back to Achladi before we can do that,' she said quietly. 'Geoff, I don't think he intends to let us get back!'

That thought had been in his mind, too, but he hadn't wanted her to know it. He felt suddenly helpless. The trap seemed sprung and they were in it. But what did Spiros intend, and how could he possibly hope to get away with it—whatever 'it' was? Gwen broke into his thoughts:

'No one knows we're here, just Spiros.'

'I know,' said Geoff. 'And what about that couple who . . .' He let it tail off. It had just slipped from his tongue. It was the last thing he'd wanted to say.

'Do you think I haven't thought of that?' Gwen hissed, gripping his arm more tightly yet. 'He was the last one to see them—getting on a ferry, he said. But did they?' She stripped off her dress.

'What are you doing?' he asked, breathlessly.

'We came in from the north,' she answered, wading out again into the water. 'There were no beaches between here and Achladi. What about to the south? There are other beaches than this one, we know that. Maybe there's one just half a mile away. Maybe even less. If I can find one where there's a path up the cliffs . . .'

'Gwen,' he said. 'Gwen!' Panic was rising in him to match his impotence, his rage and terror.

She turned and looked at him, looked helpless in her skimpy bikini—and yet determined, too. And to think he'd considered her naïve! Well, maybe she had been. But no more. She managed a small smile, said, 'I love you.'

'What if you exhaust yourself?' He could think of nothing else to say.

'I'll know when to turn back,' she said. Even in the hot sunlight he felt cold, and knew she must, too. He started towards her, but she was already into a controlled crawl, heading south, out across the submerged rocks. He watched her out of sight round the southern extreme of the jutting cliffs, stood knotting and unknotting his fists at the edge of the sea . . .

For long moments Geoff stood there, cold inside and hot out. And at the same time cold all over. Then the sense of time fleeting by overcame him. He ground his teeth, felt his frustration overflow. He wanted to shout but feared Gwen would hear him and turn back. But there must be something he could do. With his bare hands? Like what? A weapon—he needed a weapon.

There was the knife they'd bought just for their picnic. He went to their things and found it. Only a three-inch blade, but sharp! Hand-to-hand it must give him something of an advantage. But what if Spiros had a bigger knife? He seemed to have a bigger or better everything else.

One of the drifted tree's branches was long, straight, slender. It pointed like a mocking, sandpapered wooden finger at the unscalable cliffs. Geoff applied his weight close to the main branch. As he lifted his feet from the ground the branch broke, sending him to his knees in the sand. Now he needed some binding material. Taking his unfinished spear with him, he ran to the base of the cliffs. Various odds and ends had been driven back there by past storms. Plastic Coke bottles, fragments of driftwood, pieces of cork . . . a nylon fishing net tangled round a broken barrel!

Geoff cut lengths of tough nylon line from the net, bound the knife in position at the end of his spear. Now he felt he had a *real* advantage. He looked around. The sun was sinking leisurely towards the sea, casting his long shadow on the sand. How long since Spiros left? How much time left till he got back? Geoff glanced at the frowning needle of the sentinel rock. A sentinel, yes. A watcher. Or a watchtower!

He put down his spear, ran to the northern point and sprang into the sea. Moments later he was clawing at the rock, dragging himself from the water, climbing. And scarcely a thought of danger, not from the sea or the climb, not from the deep water or the height. At thirty feet the rock narrowed down; he could lean to left or right and scan the sea to the north, in the direction of Achladi. Way out on the blue, sails gleamed white in the brilliant sunlight. On the far horizon, a smudge of smoke. Nothing else.

For a moment—the merest moment—Geoff's old nausea returned. He closed his eyes and flattened himself to the rock, gripped tightly where his fingers were bedded in cracks in the weathered stone. A mass of stone shifted slightly under the pressure of his right hand, almost causing him to lose his balance. He teetered for a second, remembered Gwen . . . the nausea passed, and with it all fear. He stepped a little lower, examined the great slab of rock which his hand had tugged loose. And suddenly an idea burned bright in his brain.

Which was when he heard Gwen's cry, thin as a keening wind, shrilling into his bones from along the beach. He jerked his head round, saw her there in the water inside the reef, wearily striking for the shore. She looked all in. His heart leaped into his mouth, and without pause he launched himself from the rock, striking the water feet first and sinking deep. No fear or effort to it this time; no time for any of that; surfacing, he struck for the shore. Then back along the beach, panting his heart out, flinging himself down in the small waves where she kneeled, sobbing, her face covered by her hands.

'Gwen, are you all right? What is it, love? What's happened? I *knew* you'd exhaust yourself!'

She tried to stand up, collapsed into his arms and shivered there; he cradled her where earlier they'd made love. And at last she could tell it.

'I . . . I stayed close to the shore,' she gasped, gradually getting her breath. 'Or rather, close to the cliffs. I was looking . . . looking for a way up. I'd gone about a third of a mile, I think. Then there was a spot where the water was very deep and the cliffs sheer. Something touched my legs and it was like an electric shock—I mean, it was so unexpected there in that deep water. To feel something slimy touching my legs like that. *Ugh!*' She drew a deep breath.

'I thought: *God, sharks!* But then I remembered: there are no sharks in the Med. Still, I wanted to be sure. So . . . so I turned, made a shallow dive and looked to see what . . . what . . .' She broke down into sobbing again.

Geoff could do nothing but warm her, hug her tighter yet.

'Oh, but there *are* sharks in the Med, Geoff,' she finally went on. 'One shark, anyway. His name is Spiros! A spider? No, he's a shark! Under the sea there, I saw . . . a girl, naked, tethered to the bottom with a rope round her ankle. And down in the deeps, a stone holding her there.'

'My God!' Geoff breathed.

'Her thighs, belly, were covered in those little green swimming crabs. She was all bloated, puffy, floating upright on her own internal gasses. Fish nibbled at her. Her nipples were gone . . .'

'The fish!' Geoff gasped. But Gwen shook her head.

'Not the fish,' she rasped. 'Her arms and breasts were black with bruises. Her nipples had been bitten through—*right* through! Oh, Geoff, Geoff!' She hugged him harder than ever, shivering hard enough to shake him. 'I *know* what happened to her. It was him, Spiros.' She paused, tried to control her shivering, which wasn't only the after-effect of the water.

And finally she continued: 'After that I had no strength. But somehow I made it back.'

'Get dressed,' he told her then, his voice colder than she'd ever heard it. 'Quickly! No, not your dress—my trousers, shirt. The slacks will be too long for you. Roll up the bottoms. But get dressed, get warm.'

She did as he said. The sun, sinking, was still hot. Soon she was warm again, and calmer. Then Geoff gave her the spear he'd made and told her what he was going to do . . .

There were two of them, as like as peas in a pod. Geoff saw them, and the pieces fell into place. Spiros and his brother. The island's codes were tight. These two looked for loose women; loose in their narrow eyes, anyway. And from the passports of the honeymooners it had been plain that they weren't married. Which had made Gwen a whore, in their eyes. Like the Swedish girl, who'd met a man and gone to bed with him. As easy as that. So Spiros had tried it on, the easy way at first. By making it plain that he was on offer. Now that that hadn't worked, now it was time for the hard way.

Geoff saw them coming in the boat and stopped gouging at the rock. His fingernails were cracked and starting to bleed, but the job was as complete as he could wish. He ducked back out of sight, hugged the sentinel rock and thought only of Gwen. He had one chance and mustn't miss it.

He glanced back, over his shoulder. Gwen had heard the boat's engine. She stood halfway between the sea and the waterfall with its foul pool. Her spear was grasped tightly in her hands. *Like a young Amazon*, Geoff thought. But then he heard the boat's motor cut back and concentrated on what he was doing.

The *put-put-put* of the boat's exhaust came closer. Geoff took a chance, glanced round the rim of the rock. Here they came, gentling into the channel between the rock and the cliffs. Spiros's brother wore slacks; both men were naked from the waist up; Spiros had the tiller. And his brother had a shotgun!

One chance. *Only one chance.*

The boat's nose came inching forward, began to pass directly below. Geoff gave a mad yell, heaved at the loose wedge of rock. For a moment he thought it would stick and put all his weight into it. But then it shifted, toppled.

Below, the two Greeks had looked up, eyes huge in tanned, startled faces. The one with the shotgun was on his feet. He saw the falling rock in the instant before it smashed down on him and drove him through the bottom of the boat. His gun went off, both barrels, and the shimmering air near Geoff's head buzzed like a nest of wasps. Then, while all below was still in a turmoil, he aimed himself at Spiros and jumped.

Thrown about in the stern of his sinking boat, Spiros was making ready to dive overboard when Geoff's feet hit him. He was hurled into the water, Geoff narrowly missing the swamped boat as he, too, crashed down into the sea. And then a mad flurry of water as they both struck out for the shore.

Spiros was there first. Crying out, wild, outraged, frightened, he dragged himself from the sea. He looked round and saw Geoff coming through the water—saw his boat disappear with only ripples to mark its passing, and no sign of his brother—and started at a lop-sided run up the beach. Towards Gwen. Geoff swam for all he was worth, flew from the sea up onto the land.

Gwen was running, heading for the V in the cliff under the waterfall. Spiros was right behind her, arms reaching. Geoff came last, the air rasping in his lungs, hell's fires blazing in his heart. He'd drawn blood and found it to his liking. But he stumbled, fell, and when he was up again he saw Spiros closing on his quarry. Gwen was backed up against the cliff, her feet in the water at the shallow end of the vile pool. The Greek made a low, apish lunge at her and she struck at him with her spear.

She gashed his face even as he grabbed her. His hand caught in the loose material of Geoff's shirt, tearing it from her so that her breasts lolled free. Then she stabbed at him again, slicing him across the neck. His hands flew to his face and neck; he staggered back from her, tripped, and sat down in chest-deep water; Geoff arrived panting at the pool and Gwen flew into his arms. He took the spear from her, turned it towards Spiros.

But the Greek was finished. He shrieked and splashed in the pool like the madman he was, seemed incapable of getting to his feet. His wounds weren't bad, but the blood was everywhere. That wasn't the worst of it: the thing he'd tripped on had floated to the surface. It was beginning to rot, but it was—or had been—a young man. Rubbery arms and legs tangled with Spiros's limbs; a ghastly, gaping face tossed with his frantic threshing; a great black hole showed where the bloated corpse had taken a shotgun blast to the chest, the shot that had killed him.

For a little while longer Spiros fought to be rid of the thing—screamed aloud as its gaping, accusing mouth screamed horribly, silently at him—then gave up and flopped back half-in, half-out of the water. One of the corpse's arms was draped across his heaving, shuddering chest. He lay there with his hands over his face and cried, and the flies came swarming like a black, hostile cloud from the cave to settle on him.

Geoff held Gwen close, guided her away from the horror down the beach to a sea which was a deeper blue now. 'It's okay,' he kept saying, as much for himself as for her. 'It's okay. They'll come looking for us, sooner or later.'

As it happened, it was sooner . . .

VANESSA'S VOICE

I still can't believe that it happened *that* way. I get this feeling that I must have missed something, that I was mistaken; an earthquake, perhaps, or some other perfectly normal and explicable *physical* phenomenon, as opposed to—

And yet—well, I have Jim's letter, and I have the evidence of my own five senses, which I've always believed to be sound enough.

The letter (more a note, really) is quite a simple thing, delivered to me by a solicitor—afterwards. Jim knew what was coming, I think. Certainly he had a good idea. But of course he had lived with it, with the growing manifestations which only he recognized, with the guilt. Perhaps, (I keep trying to convince myself) that's all it was: a guilt complex that got out of control, that took over. But that hardly explains the end of it all, what I saw and heard—or rather, *didn't* hear—and the medical evidence . . .

I've known Jim always; he was the type of person you seem always to have known. He was there at school; clever enough but nothing outstanding, played the recorder and two-finger piano. He was there in town—at the dances, a good-looker, in the pubs, a witty conversationalist. He never had a lot of money, but sufficient. Charm, for want of a better word, was Jim's forte. If he'd been Italian, then Jim would have made a damn good gigolo (but he was English and usually the soul of sincerity); if he'd been a politician, then you'd vote for him. He was 'a nice person.' No teacher ever caned him at school; no girl ever refused him a dance; no one ever interrupted one of his funny stories; and not even the bums tried to impose upon him. Yes, he certainly had something. A combination of Prince Charming without a princedom, and young Frank Sinatra without a voice. But—

—Vanessa had the voice.

I didn't know Vanessa when first they took up with each other. Jim had a flat in town, sufficient for a bachelor, always upside down but clean; the type of place you could take a friend for coffee (or a last drink after they'd called time) without feeling embarrassed. Jim didn't pay much for the place; he got on well with his landlord and there hadn't been a lot of trouble in the five years he'd been there.

The first I knew of Vanessa was when I noticed how *much* neater Jim's place was. Immaculate?—not quite that, no, it was just a flat all said and done, but what a woman does for a house Vanessa had done for Jim's flat. I said nothing (at that time I knew nothing) but I guessed there was a woman somewhere. Why not? He'd had girlfriends before, though none had ever made her presence so plainly known as this one.

Then one evening Jim 'phoned and asked me out for a drink. He wanted me to meet Vanessa. I went, I saw, I didn't like! They say opposites attract: well then things were as they should be, for this girl was surely Jim's opposite.

She was blonde, blue-eyed and beautiful, and she knew it. She could sing, and she knew that too. That first night I got filled up to here with it; with her singing, I mean.

Now I don't know opera from rock-'n'-roll—I might just be able to tell you the difference between Gigli and Chuck Berry, or Ray Charles and Chopin—but that night I learned things, or at least I *should* have learned things if I'd been at all interested and if it hadn't all been layered on so thick and sticky.

Vanessa was excited, Jim explained, because she'd just been 'sent for' by 'someone big' in the 'music world' down in London. Which was as far as he got, for that was where Vanessa took over. Her voice needed 'exposure,' she told me. She'd had enough of these 'one night stands' at local dance halls. She needed 'a manager,' a well-organized 'tour,' or even better, a 'recording contract.' After all, well, 'ballads' were okay, and the occasional sentimental 'pop number,' but she had a 'near-opera voice' and she didn't want to ruin it. And so on for three solid hours, with every musical term or name in the business thrown in for good measure.

What amazed me was that Jim seemed to lap it all up like so much spilled honey; he savoured every word of it, every beautifully formed word from Vanessa's beautifully formed mouth. If he wasn't in love with her, he was in love with her love of her! And . . . I don't know (perhaps it was because he was such a good listener) but whenever she stopped to sip her drink or light a cigarette Vanessa seemed to find Jim almost as fascinating as she found herself! He had plainly 'charmed' her, but it was patent he was no less charmed himself. She was a year or two older than his twenty-five, possibly more mature, too, despite her blatant vanity.

I asked myself if this affair could last: and I answered that it couldn't. A girl so very much in love with herself needed no such love from a man, certainly not from Jim. I knew he didn't have sufficient drive anyway to keep up with her demands. For Vanessa would require more than love. She would require admiration for breakfast, dinner and supper; and while love's young flame burns brightly, still it invariably burns down the candle. There would be others, I guessed, with longer candles than Jim, who could wait him out until his love and admiration might seem to Vanessa to be on the wane, and then step in armed with refreshing flattery to drive him out.

All this from a first drink with a girl, one I had never met before? I have always prided myself on being able to read characters. But I could never have foreseen the end of it . . .

Next spring they were married. In between I hadn't seen much of them. I knew, though, that before they married they had been hard pressed to find any time to spend together; Vanessa's singing had been taking her all over the country. That was why Jim had quit his job to become her manager proper. It had worked quite well, it seemed, and their engagement had followed quickly.

It was only after the wedding that Vanessa decided she needed a manager with a bit more acumen, someone with a real 'in' in the business. And of course being Jim, her husband stepped aside and agreed; and they went on, with success following success for Vanessa and Jim being ever the more pushed back, out of things and, I guessed, beginning to feel just a bit sorry for himself.

I hadn't known, however, that he'd taken seriously to booze. The first I knew of it was when I heard how Vanessa had missed out on what had looked like being a good contract with a small but established recording company.

Jim had apparently been to blame. He hadn't liked the way one of the company's executives had seemed to have more than a merely speculative eye on his wife. After a late-night party, at which Jim had consumed far more than his fair share of alcoholic refreshments, there had been an argument and the said executive had lost some teeth. Later it came out that Jim's apprehensions had been quite without foundation; the man he had hit was queer as a nine-bob-note, quite harmless. His manner towards Vanessa had meant nothing; he was 'that way' with every girl who worked for him—and with the men too, only with them he meant it!

Vanessa had been furious, but Jim had managed to win her over by telling her that she would only be wasting her talents with such a piddling little company anyway. And of course, knowing how good she was and that therefore he must be perfectly correct, she had forgiven him.

A year went by; Jim's drinking got worse as he was pushed more and more into the background; their quarrels grew more frequent. And yet at better times they still seemed to find a mutual fascination, though such times were now few and far between.

Came the time, about fifteen months after their marriage, when Vanessa appeared to have reached her musical ceiling and was on a rapid decline. She had grown, too, to morbidly bewailing her fate and to blame all failures on Jim. After all, hadn't he been responsible that time for ruining what could have been her big chance? And didn't he live off her, like a leech, following her all over the country and drinking what few pounds she picked up just as fast as she made them?

Truth to tell, Jim had lost a lot of his charm. In just a year his drinking had taken a heavy toll. Vanessa, on the other hand (though she had also started to argue with her manager) was still very beautiful and her voice was better than ever. With the right breaks—

Those breaks finally came one night on a stage in a dance hall in the Midlands. For some time (it later came out) an agent from one of the big companies had been following her about, just listening. In the dressing-room he finally approached and asked Vanessa if she could talk to him. He was going to a party, would she come along? He wanted to talk business. Vanessa agreed. She was delighted. She knew that her voice had been in very good form that night. Moreover she had argued again with her manager—something to do with Jim's drinking—and he had promptly ripped up her contract and walked out on her.

At the party, held at a large private house on the outskirts of Nottingham, Jim had tinkled the piano and thrown back the gin while Vanessa sang blues and ballads to the delight of the guests and in particular the handsome agent, Tony Hanks, whose eyes never left her.

Perhaps it was the way Hanks watched her, his open admiration—and not only for her voice—and certainly the drink had much to do with it, but Jim soon began to sour, and his piano-playing, too. The trouble started when Hanks went over to the piano and laid a hand on Jim's shoulder.

No one heard what he said for sure; something like: 'Okay, move over, son, I'm still sober. Perhaps Vanessa can follow me—she certainly couldn't be expected to follow you!'

At least, that's what Jim told me Hanks said when I met him later. Of course he had flared up, tried to land one on the agent's nose, and Hanks had spread him all over the piano!

When Jim came to he found himself lying on his back in the shallow water of the fish pond in the garden. The party was over and the last guests were straggling home. A cartoon drunk with a balloon told him that Vanessa had gone off in tears with Hanks right after the 'fight.'

And though they later patched it up between them, that was really the beginning of the end. Jim came back to his flat in town here, where eventually I heard all his troubles out, and he stayed for a week nursing his injured pride. But at the end of that first week he wrote Vanessa a letter which she answered, and within a month he went off again after her.

By that time, though, she had signed a touring contract with Tony Hanks and the agent had become her manager and closest companion. There was no funny business between them, you understand; but now, though the money was starting to roll in thick and fast, Jim seemed to find himself in the background even more than before. It seemed as though he was never able to spend a minute alone with his wife, and always he lived with the knowledge that her money was buying his booze.

And so, after a time, it was decided that he should come back to the Midlands to live. Jim and Vanessa, they had made a sort of 'pact' between them. I met him a few weeks after he got back. He was a very different man to the one I had known only a few years earlier. Gaunt and haggard, with all the symptoms of a seasoned alcoholic, Jim nevertheless was at last making a try of it. He had found work, forced himself to cut down on his drinking; he was saving his money and gradually drawing about himself the trappings of former pride and strength— what little he ever had.

He told me about the 'arrangement' that he and Vanessa had come to. They would give themselves time to think things over. Jim would come back to his flat; she would follow her career; at the end of a year they would see what was to be done about things, they would see how things stood between them . . .

No, all was not over between them, not yet, not quite, and Jim's working and self-imposed sobriety was his way of showing Vanessa that he could still make a go of life, and that therefore they could make a go of their marriage despite differences of ambition, character and personality.

It was not very long after this that Vanessa bought the house between Leicester and Loughborough, a lonely old place not far out of

Woodhouse. From then on, whenever she had a weekend to play with, she'd spend her time there with Jim. Plainly she, too, was trying hard to make a go of it. But of course her career, her voice, always came first.

And always, sooner or later, the time would come around when she must be off chasing her career. Hanks would pick her up in his big car and her husband would be left alone once more in the rambling old-fashioned house, for he had again given up his flat to move in there. When she was with him at the house things were good for Jim, and I visited once or twice. At such times Vanessa's personality and ego dominated all, but Jim seemed happy, even if he was back to his drinking—and anyway, who was I to complain or comment?

All too soon came the time when Vanessa had to be away for what looked like being the better part of a year, and that hit Jim badly. Plainly he was very much in love with her. Nevertheless the year went by, and towards the end of it Vanessa's first record boosted her to stardom overnight. Within a few days of the record's release she was appearing on popular television shows as regular as clockwork; her beautiful voice could be heard on every juke box in the country. And then Jim was invited to her big success party.

You would think he'd long have been warned off parties, wouldn't you?

The celebration was to be at the home of Vanessa's parents in Harden on the Northeast coast, a small town perched upon the cliffs and overlooking the North Sea. This (if things worked out) was to be their venue for the reunion proper as they had planned it more than a year earlier. In all that time, though their letters had been pretty regular, the pair had spent no more than a dozen or so weekends together, and in the last four months they had not been together at all.

The big day came round at last and Jim caught a train for the Northeast, but he missed his evening connection in York and so got into Harden more than an hour late that night. Vanessa's parents were quite well-to-do, of old Harden stock, and it looked to Jim as though the whole town was in attendance at their big house on the cliffs. Music played, guests laughed and chattered about the gardens and in and out of the many rooms, lights blazed and accentuated the gaiety.

A summer breeze brought the tang of ocean to Jim as he got out of his taxi and walked down the lighted path to the house—and it brought the sound of Vanessa's voice.

Never had he heard her sing so beautifully, a soul-rending ballad of unrequited love, and as she came to the end of her song on a high sustained note, Jim paused in the door of that room where the guests of honour were gathered to hear Vanessa sing. Tony Hanks was at the piano, and Vanessa sat beside him looking as lovely as Jim had ever seen her.

And just as she looked up to see him standing there, so her handsome manager leaned over to kiss her on the cheek.

I suspect that it was more a feeling of hurt in his heart than anger—though certainly there must have been a lot of frustration there too—but whatever it was it sent Jim striding across the room to yank the agent from his seat at the piano and smack him soundly all about the room. Jim was sober this time, and now the memory of the indignities he had suffered at the hands of this man, real and imagined, rose up in his mind to sting him again. Too, the element of surprise was on his side. Hanks stood no chance but bounced from wall to wall in the disarrayed room, until Jim ended it with a beautiful punch to the agent's jaw.

It was only then, when the scene was over all bar the recriminations and the clearing up, that Jim noticed Vanessa, shocked and weeping, standing alone in a corner of the room and tenderly holding her throat. During the fight she had tried to separate the two men, and a wild blow from her husband had caught her in the throat.

Some reunion. What could Jim say?—what could he do? He had won this round of his own little personal battle with Tony Hanks but had completely lost the last round of his fight for compatibility; Vanessa could see now, quite clearly, that they could never hit it off—not while she had her career, her voice . . .

He came back yet again to the Midlands, this time to pine his heart out and write letter after letter—with no response, no answer, and eventually no hope. It seemed that Vanessa just did not want to know.

Then he found out about her voice. Jim found out?—the whole

country found out!—through the medium of the daily newspapers. To Vanessa's credit she managed to keep the true story quiet. The public only heard about her 'accident'; how she had somehow hurt her throat, the fact that her voice might never be the same again.

And it never was.

Within the space of another month Tony Hanks had her to the best specialists in Europe, to no avail. Her vocal chords were irreparably damaged; she would never sing again. And from then on the end came very quickly.

The final phase began when Vanessa's parents wrote Jim at the old place near Woodhouse. He was still living there, hoping against hope that Vanessa would show up there sooner or later. The letter begged him to go up to Harden and talk to Vanessa. She was suffering terribly from depression—acting and talking wildly, threatening suicide—continually restless, living on her nerves. Hanks, cutting his losses, had finally walked out on her. Her parents believed that if only Jim could get her to come back to the Midlands with him that everything could be smoothed over. She often mentioned his name in her troubled dreams. Jim *must* come up to Harden! The way Vanessa was going, well, she would probably end up in a home!

And so off Jim went again to the Northeast—and to tragedy. He was with her when it happened.

Again the newspapers carried the story—of a woman tormented by the collapse of her career, a collapse incidental upon a personal, tragic accident—how she had been 'Unable to bear the thought of a life without song,' how she had taken that life in a wild leap from the cliffs at Harden-on-the-Coast.

After the funeral Jim came back to the Midlands to stay, this time for good. He was the very epitome of heartbreak, and it seemed to me that in only a very short time he became the merest ghost of a man. The house was his, now, and an expensive affair it would prove to be. Vanessa had left no will, and her money (what little was left following her tour of the finest European throat specialists) was tied up with the recording company.

Money or none, Jim made no attempt to return to work but spent his time wandering about the large, lonely house and through the ancient streets of nearby Woodhouse.

Occasionally he would come to see me in town. On those very rare occasions I would get the impression that he wanted to tell me something, but he never did. He did ask me something once, though, something which, looking back now that it's all over, I find very relevant. At the time I thought nothing of it.

'What do you think,' (he'd asked me) 'about the next world?'

'Eh? You mean life after death? Well, you know me, Jim. So far as I'm concerned it's all worms and dust. No life after death because there's simply nothing left for life to exist in—and no reason why it should. No, when we shake off this mortal coil we shake off life past, present and future. The world goes on . . . but the dead are gone!'

He seemed strangely relieved. 'Who said that—that last?'

'I did!'

He laughed, but I thought his laughter was awfully dry and strained. In fact that was the last time I ever heard Jim laugh.

I saw him in town only once more after that, and he looked so ill on that occasion—so haunted—that from then on I hardly let a day pass without I would talk to him on the telephone just to be sure he was all right.

I have said that he was ill, that he looked haunted, but in addition he seemed to have developed a nervous tic, a diseased twitch that pulled the flesh spasmodically at the corner of his mouth; and he seemed always to be listening for something, something no one else could hear. I began to hear it put about by people we both knew that old Jim was pretty weird these days, '*funny*, you know?'

I didn't agree, but I couldn't disagree either. For that last time I saw him in town—in a cafe in broad daylight, over coffee and in the middle of a perfectly ordinary, routine conversation—he had suddenly silenced me with a raised finger to whisper: 'Listen!—*Shhh!*—You hear that?' But other than the chatter of people conversing over coffee and biscuits, the clinking of cups, and the traffic noises from outside—there had been nothing.

Then came the day of his telephone call. He was hysterical on the other end of the line, screaming into the 'phone, pleading with me to go up to Woodhouse, to the old place at once. 'It's getting worse!' he screamed. 'Can't you *hear* it—even over the 'phone? Dave—Dave, I think I'm going to go out of my mind!'

I told him to hang on, stay right where he was, I would be over immediately. And then I drove out of town like I've never driven before or since. The god of motorists must surely have been on my side that day, for the wonder is that I didn't get picked up for speeding or jumping red lights in town; but whether the gods were with me or not I was soon out on the country roads, and then I really put my foot down.

Why I should have been in such a panic personally, I still don't know—unless it was his voice, Jim's plainly terrified, trembling voice when he asked: 'Can't you *hear* it—even over the 'phone?' All I had heard was his hoarse, panicked breathing and, in the tinny distance, a crackling of faraway static . . .

After skidding to a halt in a spray of gravel chips, vaulting the garden gate and rushing up the path to the house, I discovered the door to the old place to be open. Not bothering to knock or announce my arrival in any way, I quickly let myself in.

The place was as I had previously known it. A little unlived-in, perhaps (as well it might seem in the absence of Vanessa's great energy and aura); and at first I thought it was empty, that Jim had managed to get a grip on himself and had gone out. Then I heard the wind—at least, it *sounded* like the wind!

Or the ghost of a wind—a keening, eerie wail that went on and on monotonously—a sound which finally I traced to the library. It was Jim, kneeling on the carpeted floor by the old piano, head in hands, eyes glaring in a dead white face, rocking to and fro, to and fro in a lunatic rhythm. He saw me and keened all the louder, froth dribbling from drawn back lips.

I crossed the room and took him by the shoulder. 'Jim, what—'

'*Now!*' he screamed, shaking off my hand. 'Now d'you hear it?' His glaring eyes burned into mine for a moment before he returned to his wailing and rocking.

I felt the hair on my neck abruptly stiffen and glanced over my shoulder in spontaneous apprehension. Empty, the room was empty of life except for myself and my poor friend—and yet . . .

Could I hear something, a distant voice, lifted high in a malevolent, magnificently sustained note? No, of course not, my alert imagination and nothing more; but then a tremulous tinkling drew my disbelieving eyes to the ornate chandelier depending in glittering glass tiers from the centre of the ceiling.

The chandelier was vibrating, its multifaceted baubles thrumming visibly, resonating in sympathy with—what? And wine glasses, too, in their rosewood cabinet across the room, humming and moving, dancing to some unheard rhythm, giving testimony to an unseen presence.

The chandelier, the wine glasses—my eyes moved jerkily from one to the other and back again, comprehending and yet refusing to believe. A sharp splintering sound yanked my head round to the windows. A diagonal crack had appeared in one of the panes, and even as I stared an adjacent window shivered to fragments in its frame. A succession of sharp explosions sounded from the cabinet of glasses, but these were almost drowned out as Jim's keening became a high-pitched scream of purest agony.

'The singing!' he screamed. 'For God's sake—can't you hear her voice?—*Her beautiful, awful voice!*' Sweat burst out in glistening globules on his parchment forehead and face, and he pressed his hands even tighter to his head. Still I could hear nothing but the continuous disintegration of protesting glass, and now glass fragments were flying in all directions from the wildly gyrating chandelier.

Jim drew back his hands from his head and clapped at his ears, clapped so hard I thought he must crush his head between his palms. He did this three or four times, an expression of indescribable pain etched in acid lines upon his wetly gleaming features, and then, as the chandelier finally shook itself free from the ceiling to crash down onto the carpet, his eyes popped almost from their sockets and he toppled over like a felled tree to lie motionless at my feet. His eyes continued to stare madly, but they were quickly glazing over.

The house was suddenly, dreadfully still, and, whimpering, I fled at last, leaving Jim's lifeless body behind me where it lay.

A week or so later his letter came from his solicitor, telling how on impulse he'd *pushed* Vanessa from the cliffs that night when she'd asked for a divorce, asking me to let the world know that she hadn't taken her own life. Her parents had been completely mistaken; she hadn't needed Jim at all, hadn't wanted him. In fact she had grown to loathe him. Her mind had finally focussed upon him, and had identified him as the cause of all her disappointments, and (not unreasonably) the personified destruction of all her dreams. Certainly she had called his name in her sleep—but her parents had not heard the curses that accompanied those cries for Jim in the night.

Personally, well, I still refuse to believe in life after death, but if the will is strong enough, and if there is a purpose . . . perhaps *something* lingers on, for a while at least.

But that it should have happened *that* way . . .

I haven't been to the police yet, and this is the first time I ever refused Jim anything. It couldn't do anyone any good to know the whole story—it could only serve to blacken a dead man's name—and in any case I know that he's been punished enough. The autopsy showed Jim's death to have been caused by a bursting of the brain. His eardrums were little more than tatters, and every membrane of his body had been ruptured.

THE STATEMENT OF
HENRY WORTHY

I

Difficult as it is to find a way in which to tell the truth of the hideous affair, I know that if I am to avoid later implication in the events leading up to and relevant to the disappearance of my poor nephew, Matthew Worthy, it is imperative that the tale be told. And yet . . .

The very nature of that alien and foulest of afflictions which contaminated Matthew is sufficient, merely thinking back on it in the light of what I know now, to cause me to look over my shoulder in apprehension and to shudder in an involuntary spasm—this in spite of the fact that it is far from chilly here in my study, and despite the effects of the large draft of whisky I have just taken, a habit rapidly grown on me over the last few days.

Better, I suppose, to start at the very beginning, at that time in early July of this Year of Our Lord, 1931, when Matthew came down from Edinburgh to visit. He was a fine young man: tall, with a strong, straight back and a good, wide-browed, handsome face. He had a shock of jet hair which took him straight to the hearts of the more eligible young ladies of Eeley-on-the-Moor, and of the neighbouring village of High-Marske, which also fell within the boundaries of my practice; but strangely, at only twenty-one years of age, Matthew had little interest in the young women of the two villages. His stay, he calculated, would be too short to acquire any but the remotest friendships; he was far too busy with his studies to allow himself to be anything but mildly interested in the opposite sex.

Indeed, Matthew's professors had written to inform me of the brilliance of their pupil, predicting a great future for him. In the words of one of these learned gentlemen: 'It is more apparent every day, from the intensity of his studies, the freshness with which he views every aspect of his work, and the hitherto untried methods which he employs in many of his tasks and experiments, that the day will come when he will be—for he surely has the potential—one of the greatest scientists in his field in the country and perhaps the whole world. Already he emulates many of the great men who, not so very long ago, were his idols, and the time draws ever nearer when he will have the capacity to exceed even the greatest of them.'

And now Matthew is gone. I do not say 'dead'—no, he is, as I myself may well soon be, *departed* . . . And yet it is my hope that I might still be able to release him from the hell which at present is his prison.

When Matthew came down to Yorkshire it was not without a purpose. He had read of how, twenty-five years ago, the German genius Horst Graumer found two completely unknown botanical specimens on the moors. This was shortly before that fatal ramble from which Graumer never returned. Since the German's disappearance—despite frequent visits to the moors by various scientific bodies—no further evidence of the *Graumer Specimens* had been found. Now that the original plants, at the University of Cologne, were nothing more than mummified fragments, in spite of all precautions taken to preserve them, Matthew had decided that it was time someone else explored the moors. For unless they had been faked, the *Graumer Specimens* were unique in botany, and before his disappearance Graumer himself had described them as being 'sehr sonderbare, mysteriöse Unkräuter!'—very strange and mysterious weeds . . .

So it was that shortly before noon on the seventh day of July Matthew set out over the moors, taking with him a rucksack, some food, and a rope. The latter was to ensure, in the event of his finding what he sought on some steep incline, that he would experience no difficulty in collecting specimens. With the fall of night he still had not returned, and although a search party was organized early the next morning no trace of him could be found. Just as Horst Graumer had disappeared a quarter of a century earlier, so now had my nephew apparently vanished from the face of the earth.

I was ready to give Matthew up for dead when, on the morning of the fourteenth, he stumbled into my study with twigs and bits of bracken sticking to the material of his rough climbing clothes. His hair was awry; he was bearded; the lower legs of his trousers were strangely slimed and discoloured, yet apart from his obvious weariness and grimy aspect he seemed perfectly sound and well nourished.

Seeing this, my first joy at having him back turned to a rage in which I demanded to know 'what the devil the young skelp meant by worrying people half to death?—And where in the name of heaven had he *been* this last week?—And did he not know that the entire country-side had been in an uproar over him?'—and so on.

Matthew apologized profusely for everything and condemned himself for his own stupidity, but when his story was told I did not have it in me to blame him for what had happened, and rightly so. It seemed that he had climbed a particularly steep knoll somewhere on the moors. Upon reaching the summit a mist had set in which prevented his exploration of the peak. Before the mist settled, however, he had been overjoyed to find a single misshapen weed that he did not recognize and which, so far as he knew, was as yet unclassified. He believed it to be similar to the much sought after *Graumer Specimens*!

Intending first to study the plant in its natural surroundings, he did not uproot it but left it as it was. He merely sat down, marked his rough position on a map he had taken with him, and waited for the mist to clear. After about an hour, by which time he was thoroughly drenched, he gave up all hope of the mist clearing before nightfall and set about making the descent.

He found that in the opaque greyness of the mist the downward route he had chosen was considerably more difficult to manoeuvre than the one by which he had climbed. Indeed, the knoll's steepness—plus the fact that he was wet and uncomfortable—caused him to slip and slither for a short distance down the wild slope. Suddenly, as his slide was coming to an end, he bumped over the edge of a narrow crack in the earth, broke through the bracken which partly covered it, and shot into space with his arms wildly flailing. He fell some distance before landing on his back on a dry ledge at the bottom of the crevice.

When he somewhat dazedly had a look around, he was surprised that he had not suffered a serious injury. He had fallen some twenty feet onto a bank of sandy shingle. The place was a sort of pothole, with walls which were so sheer that in places they overhung. It was plainly impossible to climb out unaided. At his feet was a motionless, slimy-green pool that narrowed to a mere channel at a point where it vanished under a low archway of limestone at one end of the defile.

The true horror of his situation dawned on him fully when he realized that he had lost his rucksack, and further that his rope was useless to him as he had no grappling hook. It fully appeared that unless a miracle occurred and he could somehow devise a means of getting out, he would be forced to spend the rest of his days in this dank and cheerless place; and those days would not be too many with nothing but the evil-looking water of the scummy pool as sustenance. He did have a small pocket first-aid kit that I had given to him in case of emergencies, and this he used as best he could to clean up his few bruises and abrasions.

After sitting thus occupied, recovering himself, and regaining a little of his composure, Matthew took to exploring his prison. The place had a perceptibly foreboding aura about it, and hanging in the air was a sickly-sweet smell so heavy it seemed almost a taste rather than an odour. All was silent except for a distant *drip, drip, drip* of water. Little light entered the hole from above, but Matthew was not too disheartened for the stone walls were covered with a grey, semiluminescent moss that gave off a dim light.

He had left Eeley-on-the-Moor before noon, and he calculated that by now it must be about seven in the evening. He knew that in another hour or so I would begin to worry about him—but what could he do about it? He was virtually a prisoner, and try as he might he could think of no practical way out. Upon examining his rope he saw that it was badly frayed in two places. He cursed himself for not having checked it before setting out, then hung it over a projecting rock and swung on it to test its capacity to take his weight. The rope broke twice before he was finally left with a serviceable length of no more than twenty feet or so.

He tied one end of this remaining piece of rope to a fairly large stone but upon tossing it upwards was dismayed to find that it only reached a point a good two or three feet short of the lip of the crevice. All he could do now, he decided, was sit it out and hope that some search party would find him. He realized that no such search party would exist until early morning at the soonest, and so knew that it was pointless to try calling for help.

It did not become noticeably darker, though he knew it must fast be approaching night, and he put this down to the fact that the moss on the walls was supplementing the natural light. He knew his fancy to be correct when, a short while later, he saw twinkling through the crack above him the first stars in the night sky.

Thoroughly tired now, he sat down in the driest place he could find and fell asleep, but his sleep was troubled by nightmare visions of weird events and strange creatures. He awoke several times, stifled by the unnatural and oppressive warmth of the place, to find the echoes of his own cries of terror still ringing in the hole's foul atmosphere. Even when wide awake the next morning the dreams persisted in his memory. In them he had seemed to understand all of the horrible and strangely threatening occurrences.

In one of these dreams there had been a misty landscape of queer rock formations, unfamiliar trees, and giant ferns; plants which, to the best of Matthew's knowledge, had not existed on Earth since the dawn of time. He had been one of a crowd of loathsome ape-like beings, ugly, with flat faces and sloping foreheads. They had approached a forbidden place, a hole in the earth from which nameless vapours poured out a ghastly stench.

They had captives, these ape men, creatures like themselves—yet monstrously different—who had defied the Laws. These prisoners had lately trespassed upon this holy ground unbidden by the priests, and they had also dared to spy upon the God-things conjured in horrible rituals by those same hierophants. Because of the horror of what they saw they had practiced sedition, calling for the overthrow of the priests and the expulsion of those Gods from Outside. Fearing that this call might *somewhere* be heard, the God-things had paused momentarily in their horrific pleasures to order their priests to punish the offenders— whom they would make recognizable through growing physiological differences!

And indeed those captives were different . . . They were slimy to the touch and seemed to exude a dreadful moisture which stank evilly. They stumbled rather than walked, apparently afflicted with some nervous disorder which caused their steps to be short and jerky.

But when in his dream Matthew had looked closer at those prisoners of the ape men, then he had seen that he was wrong. They suffered from no nervous disorder—the trouble was all physical. Their legs appeared to be joined from knee to groin by some ghastly fungoid growth, and their arms were similarly fastened to their sides. Their eyes were almost completely scaled over, and their mouths were gone, closed forever by strips of the horrid, scaly substance which was apparently growing over their whole bodies. Matthew knew somehow that this terrible leper-growth was the first phase of their punishment for what they had dared to do—and that the balance was still to be paid.

The entire unholy procession had been led by three creatures different again from the rest. Their foreheads were not so sloped, giving them a position somewhat higher on the evolutionary scale, and they were taller by a head than the others. These were the priests, and they wore the only clothing of the entire assembly: coarse, dark cloaks thrown about their shoulders.

The priests had carried flaring torches, intoning some weird chant which—while Matthew was unable to remember why—he had known in his dream to be immemorially significant. It had been in the form of an invocation to certain 'Gods' of an ancient myth cycle. How he understood anything of the dream was a mystery to him; he remembered that on the few occasions when the beings talked to one another, the tongue they used was not one he should normally have been conversant with. Indeed, he said he believed it to be a language dead and vanished from the face of the Earth for some hundreds of thousands, if not millions, of years.

Soon the group arrived at the malodorous pit, and at its very rim the priests stood with their torches held high over the hole while their chanting grew in volume and fervour. The evil-smelling vapours swirled up around them, occasionally enveloping them completely from the view of their followers; and then, suddenly, as the chanting reached a fever pitch, the unfortunate ones were thrust forward and one after the other were thrown bodily into that eldritch chasm. They were incapable of screaming for their mouths were scaled over, but even had that not been so they would not have screamed. No, they seemed somehow to *welcome* being thrown into the dreadful abyss.

As the bodies of the unfortunates vanished in reeking darkness, the priests slowly turned towards Matthew, approaching him with alien and horribly sly smiles upon their faces. Not knowing why he, personally, should suddenly feel so horrified, Matthew nevertheless turned to run—*but could only stumble!*—and in an instant the whole crowd was around him. The evil implication of the looks upon their faces was now all too clear, and he opened his mouth to reject their unspoken accusation, but . . .

. . . Horror upon horror—*he could barely move his jaws!*

He tried to raise his arms to protect himself but could not do so. It was as though his limbs were pinned to his body and, half-knowing what he would see, he glanced down at himself. Even this simple movement seemed to be too great an effort for him, but somehow he accomplished it and saw . . . and saw—

He, too, was one of—*Them!*

His arms were webbed to his sides and his legs were partly joined. His skin was green and foul and he stank of an unholy, sickly-sweetness.

But he was hardly given time to examine these abnormalities, for the horde had already lifted him into the air and borne him to the edge of the pit!

That, mercifully, was when he awoke.

||

If my memory serves me correctly, that is the way Matthew related to me the contents of his dream in the hole. There were more dreams later, but I have told of this first one in some detail for I believe that in an inexplicable way its events are related to the rest of my story. It is my belief that in his slumbers Matthew had seen actual occurrences from the abysmal prehistory of his terrifying prison . . .

On his second day in the hole he waded into the pool and found it unpleasantly warm and greasy, as though composed of thick vegetable secretions rather than water. A great thirst was on him, but he could not bring himself to drink that foul muck.

Finding that the pool was quite shallow, he waded to the archway and stooped beneath and beyond it. The water—if such it could be called—beyond the arch was only slightly deeper, and the living walls gave off sufficient light for him to see that the same sandy shelf continued in this secondary cave. Wet and slimy, he climbed out onto the shelf and looked about him. There were long, sharp stalactites hanging from above—for here there was no crack in the ceiling—but though these eon-formed stone daggers were fascinating enough in themselves, it was the *other* things which primarily claimed Matthew's astounded attention.

This primeval cavern contained wonders to fill to bursting point the heart of any man of science—and especially a botanist. Protruding from the walls were plants unlike any existing upon the surface of the Earth—huge pod-like things, standing on end all around the walls with their lower roots trailing in the slimy water. Each plant seemed to be growing out of, or depending from, the wall of the cave; or perhaps they had grown up out of the water, later to fasten upon the walls in the manner of certain other climbing, clinging plants.

The things were between five and six feet long top to bottom, as green as the evil mutations in my nephew's dreams. They were also slimy and exuded a vile fluid which dripped off them into the pool. Matthew wondered if this constant dripping of vegetable secretions was the reason the pool was so odious.

Later in that secret cave, after he had recovered from his first amazement at this terrific find, he also discovered some water which was at least cleaner than that of the pool. It dripped from the tips of those dagger-like, depending rock formations, and although it had an unpleasant taste—an unwholesome acidity—it went far towards quenching his by now burning thirst. Yet he drank falteringly, as though his whole body instinctively drew back from having anything to do with that unknown hole in the earth.

But now he was filled with anger. What a find! A discovery so immense that he was 'made' for life, his future assured, if he could but get out of that accursed pit. It was then that he first saw the means of his salvation. In the gravel of the shelf were many half-buried flat stones. If he could get a sufficient number of these stones to the other side of the natural archway, he could perhaps build them up to form a platform from which to throw his weighted rope over the lip of the crevice.

His difficulties were many. There was the unpleasant feel of the water (for which he had developed a morbid dread); the great weight of the large stones; the fact that he quickly exhausted the supply of readily available stones on the surface and had to dig in the sandy shingle for others.

It was when he was moving the first of these stones that he noticed, in the dim light, the intricate, runic designs cut into their surfaces. Strange cabalistic signs literally covered them, and although he had no knowledge of their meaning, still they filled him with dread. They reminded him of similar glyphs once glimpsed in the university's rare books department—in the pages of a book by von Junzt—and again he experienced that reluctance of soul encountered upon drinking the dripping water. Nonetheless, he progressed with his work until he had a platform of stones almost three feet high against the wall of his prison.

This took him halfway through his third miserable day in the hole. Though he could now almost reach the lip of the crevice with his weighted rope, he had exhausted his supply of stones and was too weak from hunger and exhaustion to dig for more. He knew that soon he would be starving and that if he was ever to complete his task and get out of the place he must have food . . . But what to eat?

For all he knew the plants in the inner cave may well be poisonous, but they were his only hope, and so he took his first bite from one of them. That first bite, while it made him feel sick, was nevertheless strangely satisfying. Later he was able completely to fill himself from the plant and the strength he gained from this singular food source was prodigious. After a while the sickly taste no longer made him feel ill; indeed, he began to enjoy a narcotic sense of well-being.

Just how true this was—the fact that he had deeply drugged himself—was not realized until another evil dream released him from his torpor. He had been in the hole almost seven days when his own screaming roused him from the throes of nightmare. He could fairly well gauge just how much time had passed by the heavy stubble grown on his chin.

In his new dream the priest-creatures had sealed off the sacrificial cavern with holy, inscribed stones—the very stones for which he now dug so frantically in the floor of the pit—but there had been much more than that to the dream; Matthew admitted so much but would tell me no more of that final nightmare, merely stating that it 'did not bear relating.'

With his new-found strength and in his frantic haste, it took him only a few hours to complete the platform. At last he was able to fling his stone-laden rope up out of the defile and, amazingly, with his very first attempt came success! The rough stone wedged, and held, and without a great deal of effort he was able to haul himself out. Elated, he scrambled down the knoll and hurried back across the moors to Eeley.

In just a few days Eeley and High-Marske got over the upset that Matthew had caused; the groups which had gathered in the village pubs to chat and wonder about his disappearance themselves dispersed. Then, after Matthew had assured police Sergeant Mellor that the pit was so out of the way as to create no menace to village children, he was able to get down to his studies again.

He had unintentionally brought back with him a portion of the plant from which he had eaten; he assured me that in his haste to escape from the pit he would never consciously have thought of it. In fact his sample was one that he had torn from the plant to eat later and which he found, upon his return, still in his pocket where he had put it. Though the fragment was rapidly deteriorating, it was still firm enough to permit him to study it.

And Matthew's studies occupied him completely for the next few days. The hybrid weed he had found atop the knoll was all but forgotten and the possibility that more such fascinating specimens existed in that area was matterless to him. For the moment all his energies were concentrated on his as yet unidentified sample.

One afternoon three or four days after his return, I was sitting in my study checking through some notes on the ailments, real or imagined, of some of my elder patients, when Matthew burst unbidden upon me from the corridor. His eyes were quite wild and he seemed somehow to have aged years. There was a look of absolute puzzlement—or shock—on his face, and his jaw hung slack in undisguised amazement.

'Uncle,' he blurted, 'perhaps you can help me. Goodness knows I *need* help. I just can't understand it . . . or don't want to. It's not natural. Natural?—why, it's *impossible*—and yet there it is . . .' He shook his head in defeat.

'Oh?' I said. 'What's impossible, Matthew?'

For a moment he was silent, then: 'Why, that plant—or *thing!* It has no right to exist. None of them has. At first I thought I must be mistaken, but then I checked and double-checked and checked again— and I know I'm right. They just can't do it!'

As patiently as I could, I asked: 'Who, exactly, are "they," and what is it that "they" can't do?'

'The plants,' he told me in an exasperated tone of voice. 'They can't reproduce! Or if they can I've no idea how they do it. And that's only a part of it. In attempting to classify the things I've tried tricks that would get me locked up if any conventional botanist knew of them. Why!—I can't even say for sure that they're plants—in fact I'm almost certain that they're not. And that leads on to something else—'

He leaned forward in his chair and stared at me. 'Seeing as how I've decided they're not plants, I thought perhaps they might be some obscure animal form—like those sea animals which were mistaken for plants for such a long time—I mean, anemones and the like. I've checked it all out, and . . . no such thing! I've got a whole library of books up there,' he indicated with a toss of his head to the upstairs room, 'but nothing that's any good to me.'

'So you're baffled,' I said. 'But surely you've made some mistake? It's obvious that whatever they are they must be one or the other, plants or animals. Call in a second opinion.'

'Never!—Certainly not until I've done a lot more work on my own,' Matthew cried. 'This thing is big, fantastic. A new form of life! But you must excuse me, uncle. I have to get back to work. There's so much I've got to understand . . .'

Suddenly he paused, seeming uneasy; his manner became somehow, well, furtive. 'I've especially got to understand that other thing— the structure of the cells, I mean. It's quite uncanny. How can it be explained? The cell structure is almost—it's almost human!' And with that he hurried out of my room.

For a moment I laughed to myself. Everything is fantastic to the young. Matthew had made a mistake, of course, for if those things were neither animals nor plants—then what in heaven's name were they?

III

The ghastly thing started the next morning, showing first of all in small greenish patches of flaky yet slimy substance on Matthew's arms and chest. Just a few patches at first, but they refused to submit to the application of antiseptic swabs or the recently introduced fungicidal creams, and within the course of the day a loathsome green network had spread over the boy's entire frame so that I was forced to confine him to his bed.

I did all I could to reassure and comfort him, and later in the evening hung a notice on my waiting-room door informing my patients, mercifully few and with only trivial complaints, that due to alterations in my work schedule I was forced to holiday early and only very urgent calls would be answered. I added to this the address of a friend of mine in Hawthorpe, a consulting doctor whom I contacted with a similar story of altered work schedules and who willingly accepted my plan for any of my flock who might require medical attention.

All this done I attempted to fathom the horror that had overtaken my nephew, and in this I could only be doomed to failure through the completely alien nature of the thing. The only definite statement of fact I could make about it was that I knew certain of its symptoms: Matthew had hardly eaten at all since his adventure in the pit, neither had I seen him take any sort of drink, and yet he had shown no signs of hunger. I was not to know it, but the metamorphosis taking place in his body was one which did not yet require to be fed. A new way of feeding was developing . . .

Dazedly, desperately attempting to understand this monstrous thing come so suddenly upon my house, I worked all through the night and into the next morning; but having done everything I could think of to check the vile *acceleration* of Matthew's affliction, and failing, I suggested calling in a specialist. It was the worst thing I could have done. Matthew reacted like a wild thing, screaming that there was nothing anyone could do for him and that 'knowledge of those *things* in the pit must spread no further!' Plainly he believed that the disease had come back with him from the pit on the moors, that he had poisoned his system by eating of those obscene plants—and in all truth I was hardly able to dispute it.

Sobbing and shrieking, swearing that he would soon cease to be a bother to me, he made me promise not to tell anyone of the horror or bring in anyone to see him. I thought I knew his meaning about ceasing to be a bother: in all my textbooks I could find nothing like my nephew's disease; only leprosy could be said even to approximate it, and leprosy did not have its fantastic acceleration. Reluctantly I calculated that the virulence of Matthew's disease would kill him within a fortnight, and for this reason I agreed to his every request.

The next night, out for a breath of badly needed fresh air, I managed to catch Ginger, my cat. Since first Matthew returned from his prolonged ramble Ginger had refused to enter the house, preferring to howl horribly on the step outside for hours on end. I brought him in and left him in a very agitated state downstairs with a bowl of milk. The next morning—the fourth morning, I think, of the manifestation of the horror—I found Ginger's fearful, death-stiffened corpse on the dispensary floor. One of the room's small windowpanes was cracked where the unfortunate and terrified animal had tried to escape. But from what? Animals can sense things too deep for the blunted human mind to grasp—and what Ginger had sensed had frightened him to death.

Other animals, too, had noticed something strange about my house, and dogs in particular would come nowhere near the place. Even my pony, tied in a warm lean-to behind the house, had danced nervously in his stall all through those long nights . . .

On the same morning that I found Ginger dead, when I carefully slipped back the sheets from Matthew's sleeping form, doctor though I am and despite the fact that my experience has included every type of illness and ailment, I recoiled in terror from that which lay upon the bed. Three hours later, at about eleven in the morning, when I was satisfied that I had done everything I possibly could, I laid down my tools. I had worked with surgical swabs and scrapers, sponges and acids, and my nephew's body beneath the dressings was not a pretty sight. But at least it was clean—for the moment.

When the anesthetic wore off and Matthew awoke, though he was obviously in great pain, he managed to tell me of the new dream which had disturbed his sleep. He had seemed to be in a misty place where there was only a voice, continually repeating a phrase in an alien tongue, which as before he had somehow been able to understand. The voice had called:

'Ye shall not *associate* with them. Ye shall not *know* them or walk *among* them or *near* them . . .' And Matthew had been afraid for his very soul.

That afternoon we slept. Both of us were near exhaustion and it was only later in the evening, when I was disturbed by his cries, that I awoke. He was having yet another nightmare and I listened intently by his bedside in case he said something new in connection with the horror. Had I roused him then I might have saved his mind, but I am glad now that I did nothing, being satisfied to sit listening while he rambled in his sleep. It seemed to me that he was better asleep; whatever dreams he experienced, they could in no way be worse than the reality.

I was deeply shocked by the poisonous odour that drifted up from his restless form, for only a few hours earlier I had cleansed him completely of every sign of the horror. I had hoped that my extreme surgical efforts might be sufficient to halt the rapid encroachment of the dread growth, but I had been grasping at straws. That smell made it all too obvious that my hopes had been in vain. Then, as I continued watching, Matthew began to writhe and gibber dementedly.

'No, no,' he gasped, 'I will *not* stand like this, as though I were part of the place, with the muck dripping off me. *I will not!*' For a long moment his chest rose and fell spasmodically. Then, in a calmer voice, he continued:

'No one must learn of the pit . . . Sinned . . . Committed the ultimate abomination, and soon I must answer the call . . . No priests, no ceremony for me . . . Dead before the dinosaurs . . . And no one must see me . . . Too many inquisitive minds, curious delvers in mysteries . . . Spread the thing across the whole world . . . God knows . . . Tell no one . . . No one must know . . . Ultimate sin . . . *Heaven help me!*'

There was a long pause here, and in Matthew's sleeping attitude I could suddenly detect an air of listening. Finally he began to talk again: 'But these voices! Who are they? I don't know these names. John Jamieson Hustam . . . Gint Rillson . . . Feth Bandr? And the others—what of them? Ganhfl Degrahms? Sgyss-Twell? Neblozt? Ungl? Uh'ang?'

At this point he grew even quieter. His lips drew back from his teeth and the cords of his neck stood out grotesquely. Cold sweat appeared on his brow and his low moaning became coarser, merely a cracked whisper. 'That other, weak, dying voice! *Who's that? What's that? . . .* Whisperer—who are you? Your name sounds famil . . . No—no, it's not so!' Now his voice fell so low it became a mere hiss of breath:

'You . . . *can't* . . . be!'

Suddenly, with one hoarsely screamed word—or name—he sat rigidly upright, wide awake. Eyes bugging he gazed terrified, unseeing, about the room. For a moment I was at a loss to understand—but then I saw the foam gathering at the corner of his mouth and the way his eyes were beginning to roll vacantly in his poisoned, suddenly grinning face. I sat by him then, cradling him in my arms as, sobbing, he rocked back and forth, completely robbed of his sanity.

At the time I did not understand that name he screamed, but now I understand everything. Especially I know what it was that finally proved too much for my nephew's severely overtaxed mind and body. That which he had—dreamed?

Matthew did not recover, and from that moment on I had to care for him like a newborn babe; he was incapable of even the most basic rationalization. Yet in a way I believe that this was the best thing that could have happened. There was little I could do to help him, physically or mentally, and I had completely given up my brief idea of calling in a specialist. No doctor would ever have dreamed, while the chance remained of the horror being communicable, of risking passing that loathsomeness on to another human being—which was, of course, the main reason I had stopped practising. No, I was on my own with Matthew, and all I could do was wait and see what form the advancing terror would take.

Up to this time I myself had shown no sign of having contracted the disease, and after every session with my nephew I made sure that I bathed, cleansing myself thoroughly. True, lately I had shown a loss of appetite (but surely, in retrospect, that was only to be expected?) which at the time was an additional worry for I recognized the symptom. Still, I told myself, in all probability my fears were purely psychological.

Early the following morning, while he slept, I gave Matthew a further anaesthetic and removed his dressings. By now I was almost inured to shock and the sight of that dreadful green network growing *in* the wounds—in his very flesh—only verified what I had expected. The smell from the uncovered areas was terrible, and I saw that far from being beneficial my cutting and burning had probably worsened the boy's condition. Indeed, by midday I knew that there was no hope left for him at all. His arms were webbing to his sides and his thighs already clung together; the growth was spreading so rapidly over and through him that I knew he had only a day or so left.

It is not my intention to tell the way in which the horror increased in Matthew from that time onwards. Suffice to say that I began to lace the baths I was taking with ever increasing frequency with carbolic—a little more each time—until, when I last bathed just yesterday, the percentage of acid in the water was sufficient to raise small blisters on my legs. Yet my efforts seemed worthwhile, for even after Matthew—got away—and shuffled off to the moors two days ago, my body was still clean, though my appetite was nonexistent. I had hoped, indeed prayed, that this inability of mine to eat was psychological—but again all my hopes were in vain.

There, I have admitted it: yes, I too am infected! Shortly after I started to write this, yesterday evening after returning from the moors, I noticed the first discoloured, scaly spot on the back of my hand . . .

But in my hurry to get done with this I have jumped ahead of myself. I must go back two nights, to the evening Matthew vanished into the mist, for the worst is yet to be told.

IV

Believing that he only had a few more hours left at the most, and wanting to be near him in case he regained his sanity shortly before passing away—as has happened in less outré cases—I had been sitting by Matthew's bed. There I had dropped off to sleep, only to be roused later by the frantic tremblings and quakings from the now totally changed creature before me. By this time my nephew's only resemblance to anything human was his general outline. His eyes burned with a horrific intensity through the thin slits in the green mask which his face had become.

As I came fully awake I saw the . . . *Thing*—I can barely bring myself to think of it as Matthew—moving. Slowly it bent upward from the waist, trembling and straining in every part, until finally it sat upright. The awful head turned slowly in my direction, and then I heard the last words my nephew was ever to speak:

'W-water . . . B-bath . . . Get—me—to—the—b-bath . . .'

The thing had swung the green web which passed for the lower part of its body over the edge of the bed and somehow had managed to stand. In shuffling steps—still attired in the dressing-gown I had loaned to Matthew in compensation for quartering him in a drafty room—it made for the door. In a moment or two I recovered myself and went quickly to the aid of my . . . my nephew, only to discover that his mutation, whatever human attributes might have been lost, did not lack strength. Matthew's movements were only obstructed by his covering of rapidly stiffening green growth; I had merely to steady him while he grew accustomed to this new, shuffling locomotive system. Exactly how I managed I do not recall, but eventually I got the shuffler into the bath where he sat, propped up and shuddering, until I could half-fill the tub with warm water.

It was then, after running to and fro half a dozen times with my huge iron kettle, that I noticed something happening in the bath—something which so terrified me that I only just managed to stagger away, out of the bathroom, before I fainted dead away on the floor . . .

Darkness had fallen by the time I regained consciousness. Remembering what had caused me to faint, I started violently; then, feeling the stone of the floor against my cheek, I got to my feet. When I had last seen my nephew—or rather the thing which he had become—he had been *secreting* greenish droplets of some unnameable ichor into the bath. But now, except for that—liquid—the bath was empty.

Galvanized into frantic haste I followed the thing's tracks, green droplets which glistened damply on the floor, until I eventually discovered the note on my writing desk. And its message told me that the Matthew-thing was still crazed, for its contents were undeniably the ramblings of madness. Numb with shock, horror, and disbelief I deciphered the almost illegible writing upon a now odious sheet of damp, green-spattered notepaper, and made it out to read:

'Water not right . . . Hungry . . . Must go to pit . . . Pool . . . Don't try to find me . . . I am all right . . . Not diseased . . .

' "M" '

It was after I followed those evil droplets from my desk to the back door, and found it swinging open—after I realized that the entire house could be contaminated and after I shudderingly, more closely studied the contents of the bath—that I heard the sudden scream from outside. I ran back to the door and threw it open. Staggering towards my house from the moors and moving in the direction of the village, gasping and panting, was the mist-wreathed figure of Ben Carter, the village poacher.

'Lock your doors, doctor!' he hoarsely yelled as he saw me. 'There's something horrible loose on the moors—something *horrible!*' Without pausing in his stumbling run, he went by my gate and gradually vanished into the mist. To an extent I was relieved; he would not be reporting the nature of what he had seen to the police. Not immediately at any rate—not with that brace of fine hares swinging round his neck. I watched Ben until the mist had completely swallowed him up, and then I rapidly donned a raincoat and plunged out into the darkness.

My task was hopeless. With night already settled on the moors and a thickening mist to contend with, I stood no chance of finding him. Indeed I was fortunate in the end, over an hour later, even to find the road back to Eeley. Nonetheless I knew that with the dawn I would have to go out on the moors and try again. I could not leave him out there in that state. What if someone else were to find him?

Obviously Matthew had headed for the pit—his scrawled note had made that much at least clear—but how was I ever to find that terrible place without a clue as to its whereabouts? It was then that I remembered the map upon which Matthew said he had marked his location on the knoll. The map—of course!

I found it in his room . . .

I hardly slept at all that night—my dreams would not permit sleep—and early morning found me setting out over the moors. I will not describe the route I took for reasons which must be perfectly obvious. Heaven forbid it, but in the event of my final plan not working it is best that no one else knows of that place on the moors.

Eventually, in mid-morning, I found the terrible hole in the ground where all of this evil had begun. Even to my untrained eyes it was all too plain that there was something hideously wrong with the vegetation around the mouth of that pit. The plants, even those which were common and recognizable, were all strangely withered and mutated. *Sehr sonderbare, mysteriöse Unkräuter!*

I knew that if I was ever to be sure of what I had started to suspect, if I was ever to have definite proof, then I would have to climb down into the hole. All along I had foreseen this, but now the very thought of it was more than sufficient to cause me to shudder horribly . . . And my flesh was still creeping as I hammered my stake into the earth and made fast my rope, for even up there in the misty morning sunlight the air was tainted with an all too familiar smell.

Hurriedly now, for I feared my courage would soon desert me, I lowered myself into the hole. Climbing down into dimness, I was immediately aware of the poisonous quality of the atmosphere; but I was given little chance to dwell on the thought for soon my feet found the platform of stones which Matthew had built.

In the feeble light I could see that part of the platform had tumbled down, and close by there was a monstrously suggestive depression in the sandy shingle of the shelf. As I studied this hollow it suddenly, shockingly dawned on me that in his condition Matthew would never have been able to *climb* down here, even though his rope was still hanging where he had left it. The difficulties he must have faced even in the climbing of the knoll seemed insurmountable; yet I was certain that he had managed it and was even now somewhere nearby in the dimness. I was certain because of that depression in the shingle . . .

For while there were other marks in the sand—the signs of my nephew's previous visit—this one was plainly deeper, fresher, and *different*. It was exactly the kind of hollow one would expect a falling body to make in wet sand! . . . I turned my mind hurriedly away from the thought.

Matthew had described the glowing moss on the walls of the place, and sure enough it was there, but I was unwilling to explore any further in its light alone. I took out my pocket-torch and switched it on. The torch must have received a bang in my climbing for its beam was now weak and intermittent. Nor did the mist, which was thickening up above, help any; it only served to shut out the dim light filtering down from the crack.

First I shone the beam of my torch around the pallid walls and over the surface of the soupy water; then I sought out the natural archway where the pool passed out of sight. Feeling my courage ebbing again I quickly waded into the pool. The way that slime *oozed* around my legs made me tremble violently and I was vastly relieved that the foul muck did not reach the tops of my waders.

I went straight to the archway, lowering my head and bending my back to pass beyond it. There, in the dingy confines of the cave, the first things that showed in the flickering light of my torch were the hanging daggers of stone depending from the vaulted ceiling. Then, as I turned to my left, the beam passed over something else—a shape slumped against the wall.

Not daring to move I stood there, shaking feverishly, a cold sweat upon my brow. The only sound other than my pounding heart was the slow drip, drip, drip of falling droplets of God-only knows what evil moisture.

The hair of my neck bristled in a fearful dread, but as my fear gradually subsided I began slowly to move again, swinging my torch around to the right. This time when my beam picked out the thing against the wall I gripped my torch firmly and moved closer. It was one of the plants—but not quite as Matthew had described them. This one hung soggily from the wall of the cave and there was no firmness about it. I concluded that it was either dead or dying and saw that I must be correct when I swung my beam down the length of the thing. A great portion of it had been stripped away. I guessed that this had been the specimen from which my nephew had eaten.

Then something else caught my eye, something which very dully reflected the light from my torch. Reaching out with my free hand I touched the hard object which seemed to be imbedded in the plant about halfway up its length. Whatever it was, possibly a metallic crystal of some sort, it came away in my hand and I put it in my pocket for future reference.

More daring now, I moved further into the cave, examining more of the green pods as I came upon them, still finding them frightful in some strange way but unable to account completely for my fear. And then I stopped dead. I had almost forgotten just what I was looking for—but now I remembered . . .

In a dark corner one of the plant-things stood all alone with its lower roots trailing in the soupy pool. It would have been just like all the other specimens except for one shocking difference . . . *It was wearing the dressing-gown I had loaned to Matthew!*

And more: as I swung my torch beam in disbelief up and down the length of the thing, *it blinked at me!* It blinked—thin slits opened and closed where eyes should be, and in that moment of madness, in that instant of utter insanity, as my very mind buckled—I looked into the agonized eyes of Matthew Worthy!

How to describe the rest.

Oh, I was transformed in one mind-shattering moment. My torch fell from nerveless fingers and I heard myself scream a hoarse, babbling scream of horror. I threw up my hands and staggered back, away from what I had seen, away from the brainblasting abnormality against the wall. Then I turned to flee full tilt—shrieking, splashing through the vileness of the pool—through a maze of dripping stalactites, past a host of green, insinuously oozing *things*—bumping in my haste from wall to wall, sometimes coming into contact with slimy obscenities which had no right to exist. And all the time I screamed and babbled shamelessly, even as I clawed my way up the dangling rope and hauled myself out into the daylight, even as I plummeted headlong down the steep slope heedless of life or limb, until I tripped and flew forward into merciful oblivion . . .

Merciful oblivion, I say, and it is the truth, for had I not knocked myself unconscious I have no doubt that I would have remained permanently mindless. What I had *seen* had been terrible enough without the other. That other which I had *heard* had been, if anything, worse. For even as the torch fell from my fingers and I screamed, other voices had screamed with me! Voices which could not be 'heard' physically—for their owners were incapable of physical speech—voices I heard with my mind alone, which were utterly horrible and alien to me and full of eternal misery . . .

When I came to my senses I was lying at the foot of the knoll. I refrained from an immediate mental examination of what I knew now to be the horrible truth, for therein lay a return to madness. Instead I brushed myself off and hurried back as quickly as my throbbing head would allow to Eeley. My house and practice lay at the extreme edge of the village, but nonetheless I approached it from the fields and let myself in at the back door. I burnt my waders immediately, noting especially that the slime upon them blazed fiercely with a sulphurous brightness. Later, after I had scrubbed myself from head to toe, examining each limb minutely and finding no trace of the horror, I remembered the rock crystal I had put in my pocket.

In the clear daylight it was obviously not a crystal; it appeared to be more like a bracelet of some sort, and yet this fact did not properly surprise me. The soft metal links must have long since oxidized, for as I examined the rotted thing, all of it—with the exception of a small flat circle or disc—crumbled away in my hands. Even this solid, circular portion, about an inch and one half across, was mostly slimy and green. I placed it in a flask of dilute acid to clean it; by which time, of course, I knew what it was.

As I watched the acid doing its work I began, involuntarily, to tremble. My mind was a turmoil of terrible thoughts. I knew what my nephew had become, and presumably the partly eaten thing which had provided this metal clue had also once been human. Certainly it had been some sort of being from any one of many periods of time. I could not help but ask myself: in the latter stages of change or after the change was complete, *could the pit-creatures feel anything?*

Watching the seething mass in the flask I suddenly began to babble idiotically and had to battle consciously with myself to stop it. No wonder Matthew had been baffled with regard to the reproductory system of these pitiful horrors. How does a magnet cause a pin to become magnetic? Why will one rotten apple in a barrel ruin all the other fruit? Oh, yes—eating from one of the things had helped Matthew contract the change, but that was not what had started the thing. *Proximity* was sufficient! Nor was the horror truly a disease, as Matthew had tried to tell me in his awful note, but a *devolution*—a gestalt of human being and thing—both living, if such could be called life, and dependent one upon the other.

This was the sort of thing I was babbling to myself as the acid completed its work, and I shook so that I had to steady myself before I was able to draw out from the acid the flat, now shiny disc.

What was it Matthew had dreamed? 'They had walked this holy ground unbidden . . .' Had that been sufficient in the old days—in pre-history, when the area about the pit must have been far more poisonous than it was now—to bring about the change? I think that even at the beginning Matthew must have partly guessed the truth, for had he himself not told me that he found the cell structure to be 'almost human'?

Poor Matthew—that name he screamed before going mad. At last I understood it all. There it all was before me: the final, leaping horror. My own nephew, an unwilling, though perhaps not completely *un-knowing* anthropophagite. A cannibal!

For the shiny thing I held in my shuddering hand was a German watch of fairly modern appearance, and on the back was an inscription in German. An inscription so simple that even I, unversed in that language, could translate it to read:

'WITH LOVE, FROM GERDA TO HORST' . . .

Since then it has taken long hours to pull myself together sufficiently to formulate my plan, that plan I have already mentioned and yet which even now I hardly dare think about. I had fervently hoped that I would never have to use it, but now, with the spread of the poison through my body, it appears that I must . . .

When the ashes of my house have cooled the police will find this manuscript locked in a safe in the deep, damp cellar, but long before the flames have died down I shall have returned to the pit. I will take with me as much petrol as I can carry. My plan is simple really, and I shall know no pain. Nor will the *inhabitants* of that place know pain, not if a powerful drug may yet affect them. As the anaesthetic takes hold and while I am still able, I shall pour the petrol on the surface of that evil pool.

My statement is at an end—

—Perhaps tonight puzzled observers will wonder at the pillar of sulphurous fire rising over the moors . . .

THE DISAPPROVAL OF
JEREMY CLEAVE

'My husband's eye,' she said quite suddenly, peering over my shoulder in something of morbid fascination. 'Watching us!' She was very calm about it, which ought to say quite a lot about her character. A very cool lady, Angela Cleave. But in view of the circumstances, a rather odd statement; for the fact was that I was making love to her at the time, and somewhat more alarming, her husband had been dead for six and a half weeks!

'*What!?*' I gasped, flopping over onto my back, my eyes following the direction of her pointing finger. She seemed to be aiming it at the dresser. But there was nothing to be seen, not anywhere in that huge, entirely extravagant bedroom. Or perhaps I anticipated too much, for while it's true that she had specified an 'eye,' for some reason *I* was looking for a complete person. This is perhaps readily understandable— the shock, and what all. But no such one was there. Thank God!

Then there came a rolling sound, like a marble down a gentle slope, and again I looked where she was pointing. Atop the dresser, a shape wobbled into view from the back to the front, being brought up short by the fancy gilt beading around the dresser's top. And she was right, it was an eye—a glass eye—its deep green pupil staring at us somehow morosely.

'Arthur,' she said, in the same breathless, colourless voice, 'this really makes me feel very peculiar.' And truth to tell it made me feel that way, too. Certainly it ruined my night.

But I got up, went to the dresser and brought the eye down. It was damp, or rather sticky, and several pieces of fluff had attached themselves to it. Also, I fancied it smelled rather, but in a bedroom perfumed as Angela Cleave's that was hard to say. And not something one *would* say, anyway.

'My dear, it's an eye,' I said, 'only a glass eye!' And I took it to the vanity basin and rinsed it thoroughly in cold water. 'Jeremy's, of course. The . . . vibrations must have started it rolling.'

She sat up in bed, covering herself modestly with the silk sheet (as if we weren't sufficiently acquainted) and brushed back a lock of damp, golden hair from her beautiful brow. And: 'Arthur,' she said, 'Jeremy's eye was buried with him. He desired to be put to rest looking as perfectly natural as possible—*not* with a patch over that hideous hole in his face!'

'Then it's a spare,' I reasoned, going back to the bed and handing it to her. She took it—an entirely unconscious act—and immediately snatched back her hand, so that the thing fell to the floor and rolled under the bed. And:

'*Ugh!*' she said. 'But I didn't *want* it, Arthur! And anyway, I never knew he had a spare.'

'Well, he obviously did,' I sighed, trying to get back into bed with her. But she held the covers close and wouldn't have me.

'This has quite put me off,' she said. 'I'm afraid I shall have a headache.' And suddenly, for all that she was a cool one, it dawned on me how badly this silly episode had jolted her. I sat on the bed and patted her hand, and said: 'Why don't you tell me about it, my dear?'

'It?' She looked at me curiously, frowning.

'Well, it has to be something more than just a silly old glass eye, now doesn't it? I mean, I've never seen you so shaken.' And so she told me.

'It's just something he said to me,' she explained, 'one night when I was late home after the opera. In fact, I believe I'd spent a little time with you that night? Anyway, in that perfectly *vulgar* way of his, he said: "Angela, you must be more discreet. Discretion, my girl! I mean, I know we don't have it off as often as you'd possibly like—but you can't accuse me of holding too tight a rein, now can you? I mean—har! har!—I don't keep too close an eye on you—eh? Eh? Not *both* of 'em anyway, har! har!"

'So I asked him what on earth he meant? And he answered, "Well, those damned *boyfriends*, my dear! Only right you should have an escort, me being incapacitated and all, but I've a position to maintain and scandal's something I won't hear of. So you just watch your step!" '

'Is that all?' I said, when it appeared she'd finished. 'But I've always understood that Jeremy was perfectly reasonable about . . . well, your *affairs* in general.' I shrugged. 'It strikes me he was simply trying to protect his good name—and yours!'

'Sometimes, Arthur,' she pouted then, 'you sound just like him! I'd hate to think you were going to turn out just like *him!*'

'Not at all!' I answered at once. 'Why, I'm not at all like him! I do . . . everything he didn't do, don't I? And I'm, well, entire? I just can't understand why a fairly civil warning should upset you so—especially now that he's dead. And I certainly can't see the connection between that and . . . and this,' and I kicked the eye back under the bed, for at that moment it had chosen to trundle out again.

'A civil warning?' She looked at me, slowly nodding her agreement. 'Well, I suppose it was, really.' But then, with a degree more animation: 'But he wasn't very civil the next time!'

'He caught you out again?'

'No,' she lifted her chin and tossed back her hair, peevishly, I thought, 'in fact it was you who caught me out!'

'Me?' I was astonished.

'Yes,' she was pouting again, 'because it was that night after the ball, when you drove me home and we stopped off at your place for a drink and . . . and slept late.'

'Ah!' I said. 'I suspected there might be trouble that time. But you never *told* me!'

'Because I didn't want to put you off; us being so good together, and you being his closest friend and all. Anyway, when I got in he was waiting up for me, stamping round the place on that pot leg of his, blinking his one good eye furiously at me. I mean he really was raging! "Half past three in the morning?" he snorted. "What? *What?* By God, but if the neighbours saw you coming in, I'll . . . I'll—" '

'Yes,' I prompted her. ' "I'll—?" '

'And then he threatened me,' she said.

'Angela, darling, I'd already guessed that!' I told her. 'But *how* did he threaten you—and what has it to do with this damned eye?'

'Arthur, you know how I dislike language.' Her tone was disapproving. But on the other hand she could see that I was getting a bit ruffled and impatient. 'Well, he reminded me how much older he was than I, and how he probably only had a few years left, and that when he was gone everything would be mine. *But*, he also pointed out how it wouldn't be very difficult to change his will—which he would if there should be any sort of scandal. Well of course there wasn't a scandal and he didn't change his will. He didn't get the chance, for it was . . . all so very sudden!' And likewise, she was suddenly sniffling into the hankie she keeps under the pillow. 'Poor Jeremy,' she sobbed, 'over the cliff like that.' And just as quickly she dried up and put the hankie away again. It helps to have a little cry now and then.

'But there you go!' I said, triumphantly. 'You've said it yourself: he *didn't* change the will! So . . . not much of a threat in that!'

'But that's not all,' she said, looking at me straight in the eye now. 'I mean, you know how Jeremy had spent all of that time with those *awful* people up those *awful* rivers? Well, and he told me he'd learned something of their jojo.'

'Their juju,' I felt obliged to correct her.

'Oh, jojo, juju!' She tossed her hair. 'He said that they set spells when they're about to die, and that if their last wishes aren't carried out to the letter, then that they send, well, *parts* of themselves back to punish the ones they held to trust!'

'Parts of them—?' I began to repeat her, then tilted my head on one side and frowned at her very seriously. 'Angela, I—'

But off she went, sobbing again, face down in the pillows. And this time doing it properly. Well, obviously the night was ruined. Getting dressed, I told her: 'But of course that silly glass eye *isn't* one of Jeremy's parts; it's artificial, so I'm sure it wouldn't count—*if* we believed in such rubbish in the first place. Which we don't. But I do understand how you must have felt, my darling, when you saw it wobbling about up there on the dresser.'

She looked up and brushed away her tears. 'Will I see you tomorrow night?' And she was anxious, poor thing.

'Of course you will,' I told her, 'tomorrow and every night! But I've a busy day in the morning, and so it's best if I go home now. As for you: you're to take a sleeping draught and get a good night's sleep. And meanwhile—' I got down on my knees and fished about under the bed for the eye, '—did Jeremy have the box that this came in?'

'In that drawer over there.' She pointed. 'What on earth do you want with that?'

'I'm simply putting it away,' I told her, 'so that it won't bother us again.' But as I placed the eye in its velvet-lined box I glanced at the name of the suppliers—Brackett and Sanders, Jewellers, Brighton—and committed their telephone number to memory . . .

The next day in the City, I gave Brackett and Sanders a ring and asked a question or two, and finished by saying: 'Are you absolutely sure? No mistake? Just the one? I see. Well . . . thank you very much. And I'm sorry to have troubled you . . .' But that night I didn't tell Angela about it. I mean, so what? So he'd used two different jewellers. Well, nothing strange about that; he got about a fair bit in his time, old Jeremy Cleave.

I took her flowers and chocolates, as usual, and she was looking quite her old self again. We dined by candlelight, with a background of soft music and the moon coming up over the garden, and eventually it was time for bed.

Taking the open, somewhat depleted box of chocolates with us, we climbed the stairs and commenced a ritual which was ever fresh and exciting despite its growing familiarity. The romantic preliminaries, sweet prelude to boy and girl togetherness. These were broken only once when she said:

'Arthur, darling, just before I took my draught last night I tried to open the windows a little. It had got very hot and sticky in here. But that one—' and she pointed to one of a pair of large, pivot windows, '—wouldn't open. It's jammed or something. Do be a dear and do something with it, will you?'

I tried but couldn't; the thing was immovable. And fearing that it might very well become hot and sticky again, I then tried the other window which grudgingly pivoted. 'We shall have them seen to,' I promised.

Then I went to her where she lay; and in the next moment, as I held her in my arms and bent my head to kiss the very tip of a brown, delicious . . .

Bump!

It was perfectly audible—a dull thud from within the wardrobe—and both of us had heard it. Angela looked at me, her darling eyes startled, and mine no less; we both jerked bolt upright in the bed. And:

'What . . . ?' she said, her mouth staying open a very little, breathing lightly and quickly.

'A garment, falling from its hanger,' I told her.

'Nevertheless, go and see,' she said, very breathlessly. 'I'll not be at ease if I think there's something trapped in there.'

Trapped in there? In a wardrobe in her bedroom? What could possibly be trapped in there? She kept no cats. But I got out of bed and went to see anyway.

The thing fell out into view as soon as I opened the door. Part of a mannequin? A limb from some window-dresser's storeroom? An anatomical specimen from some poor unfortunate's murdered, dismembered torso? At first glance it might have been any of these things. And indeed, with the latter in mind, I jumped a foot—before I saw that it was none of those things. By which time Angela was out of bed, into her dressing-gown and haring for the door—which wouldn't open. For she had seen it, too, and unlike me she'd known exactly what it was.

'His leg!' she cried, battering furiously at the door and fighting with its ornate, gold-plated handle. 'His bloody *awful* leg!'

And of course it was: Jeremy Cleave's pot left leg, leather straps and hinged kneejoint and all. It had been standing in there on its foot, and a shoe carton had gradually tilted against it, and finally the force of gravity had won. But at such an inopportune moment. 'Darling,' I said, turning to her with the thing under my arm, 'but it's only Jeremy's pot leg!'

'Oh, of *course* it is!' she sobbed, finally wrenching the door open and rushing out onto the landing. 'But what's it doing there? It should be buried with him in the cemetery in Denholme!' And then she rushed downstairs.

Well, I scratched my head a little, then sat down on the bed with the limb in my hands. I worked its joint to and fro for a while, and peered down into its hollow interior. Pot, of one sort or another, but tough, quite heavy, and utterly inanimate. A bit smelly, though, but not unnaturally. I mean, it probably smelled of Jeremy's thigh. And there was a smear of mud in the arch of the foot and on the heel, too . . .

By the time I'd given it a thorough bath in the vanity basin Angela was back, swaying in the doorway, a glass of bubbly in her trembling little hands. And she looked like she'd consumed a fair old bit of the rest of the bottle, too. But at least she'd recovered something of her former control. 'His leg,' she said, not entering the room while I dried the thing with a fluffy towel.

'Certainly,' I said, 'Jeremy's *spare* pot leg.' And seeing her mouth about to form words: 'Now don't say it, Angela. Of *course* he had a spare, and this is it. I mean, can you imagine if he'd somehow broken one? What then? Do you have spare reading glasses? Do I have spare car keys? Naturally Jeremy had spare . . . things. It's just that he was sensitive enough not to let you see them, that's all.'

'Jeremy, sensitive!' She laughed, albeit hysterically. 'But very well— you must be right. And anyway, I've never been in that wardrobe in a donkey's years. Now do put it away—no, not there, but in the cupboard under the stairs—and come to bed and love me.'

And so I did. Champagne has that effect on her.

But afterwards—sitting up in bed in the darkness, while she lay huddled close, asleep, breathing across my chest—I thought about him, the 'Old Boy,' Jeremy.

Adventurer, explorer, wanderer in distant lands. That was him. Jeremy Johnson Cleave, who might have been a Sir, a Lord, a Minister, but chose to be himself. Cantankerous old (old-*fashioned*) bugger! And yet in many ways quite modern, too. Naïve about certain things—the way he'd always trusted me, for instance, to push his chair along the airy heights of the cliff tops when he didn't much feel like hobbling—but in others shrewd as a fox, and nobody's fool. Never for very long, anyway.

He'd lost his eye to an N'haqui dart somewhere up the Orinoco or some such, and his leg to a croc in the Amazon. But he'd always made it back home, and healed himself up, and then let his wanderlust take him off again. As for juju: well, a man is liable to see and hear and touch upon some funny things in the far-flung places of the world, and almost certainly he's like to go a bit native, too . . .

The next day (today, in fact, or yesterday, since it's now past midnight) was Friday, and I had business which took me past Denholme. Now don't ask me why, but I bought a mixed posy from the florist's in the village and stopped off at the old graveyard, and made my way to Jeremy's simple grave. Perhaps the flowers were for his memory; there again they could have been an alibi, a reason for my being there. As if I needed one. I mean I had been his friend, after all! Everyone said so. But it's also a fact that murderers do, occasionally, visit their victims.

The marble headstone gave his name and dates, and a little of the Cleave history, then said:

> *Distant lands ever called him;*
> *he ever ventured,*
> *and ever returned.*
> *Rest in Peace.*

Or pieces? I couldn't resist a wry chuckle as I placed my flowers on his hollow plot.

But . . . hollow?

'Subsidence, sir,' said a voice directly behind me as a hand fell on my arm. Lord, how I jumped!

'What?' I turned my head to see a gaunt, ragged man leaning on his shovel: the local gravedigger.

'Subsidence,' he said again, his voice full of dialect and undisguised disgust, gravelly as the path he stood on. 'Oh, they likes to blame me for it—saying as 'ow I don't pack 'em down tight enough, an' all—but the fact is it's the subsidence. One in every 'alf-dozen or so sinks a little, just like Old J. J's 'ere. This was 'is family seat, y'know: Denholme. Last of the line, 'e were—*and* a rum un'! But I suppose you knows all that.'

'Er, yes,' I said. 'Quite.' And, looking at the concave plot: 'Er, a little more soil, d'you think? Before they start blaming it on you again?'

He winked and said, 'I'll see to 'er right this minute, sir, so I will! Good day to you.' And I left him scratching his head and frowning at the grave, and finally trundling his barrow away, doubtless to fetch a little soil.

And all of this was the second thing I wasn't going to report to Angela, but as it happens I don't suppose it would have made much difference anyway . . .

So tonight at fall of dark I arrived here at their (hers, now) country home, and from the moment I let myself in I knew that things weren't right. So would anyone have known, the way her shriek came knifing down the stairs:

'Arthur! *Arthur!*' her voice was piercing, penetrating, very nearly unhinged. 'Is that you? Oh, for *God's sake* say it's you!'

'But of course it's me, darling, who else would it be?' I shouted up to her. 'Now what on earth's the matter?'

'The matter? The matter?' She came flying down the stairs in a towelling robe, rushed straight into my arms. 'I'll tell you what's the matter . . .' But out of breath, she couldn't. Her hair was wet and a mess, and her face wasn't done yet, and . . . well, she looked rather floppy all over.

So that after a moment or so, rather brusquely, I said: 'So tell me!'

'It's *him!*' she gasped then, a shudder in her voice. 'Oh, it's him!'

And bursting into tears she collapsed against me, so that I had to drop my chocolates and flowers in order to hold her up.

'Him?' I repeated her, rather stupidly, for by then I believe I'd begun to suspect that it might indeed be 'him' after all—or at least something of his doing.

'Him!' she cried aloud, beating on my chest. 'Him, you fool—*Jeremy!*'

Well, 'let reason prevail' has always been my family motto, and I think it's to my merit that I didn't break down and start gibbering right there and then, along with Angela ... Or on the other hand, perhaps I'm simply stupid. Anyway I didn't, but picked up my flowers and chocolates—yes, and Angela, too—and carried them all upstairs. I put her down on the bed, but she jumped up at once, and commenced striding to and fro, to and fro, wringing her hands.

'Now what *is* it?' I said, determined to be reasonable.

'*Not* in that tone of voice!' she snarled at me, coming to a halt in front of me with her hands clenched into tight little knots and her face all twisted up. 'Not in that "oh, Angela's being a silly again" voice! I said it's him, and I *mean* it's him!'

But now I was angry, too. 'You mean he's here?' I scowled at her.

'I mean he's *near*, certainly!' she answered, wide- , wild-eyed. 'His bloody bits, anyway!' But then, a moment later, she was sobbing again, those deep racking sobs I just can't put up with; and so once more I carried her to the bed.

'Darling,' I said, 'just tell me all about it and I'll sort it out from there. And that's a promise.'

'Is it, Arthur? Is it? Oh, I do hope so!'

So I gave her a kiss and tried one last time, urging: 'Now come on, do tell me about it.'

'I ... I was in the bath,' she started, 'making myself nice for you, hoping that for once we could have a lovely quiet evening and night together. So there I am soaping myself down, and all of a sudden I feel that someone is watching me. And he was, he was! Sitting there on the end of the bath! Jeremy!'

'Jeremy,' I said, flatly, concentrating my frown on her. 'Jeremy . . . the man?'

'No, you fool—*the bloody eye!*' And she ripped the wrapper from the chocolates (her favourite liqueurs, as it happens) and distractedly began stuffing her mouth full of them. Which was when the thought first struck me: *maybe she's cracked up!*

But: 'Very well,' I said, standing up, striding over to the chest of drawers and yanking open the one with the velvet-lined box, 'in that case—'

The box lay there, open and quite empty, gaping at me. And at that very moment there came a well-remembered rolling sound, and I'll be damned if the hideous thing didn't come bowling out of the bathroom and onto the pile of the carpet, coming to a halt there with its malefic gaze directed right at me!

And: *Bump!—bump!* from the wardrobe, and *BUMP!* again: a final kick so hard that it slammed the door back on its hinges. And there was Jeremy's pot leg, jerking about on the carpet like a claw freshly wrenched from a live crab! I mean not just lying there but . . . active! Lashing about on its knee-hinge like a wild thing!

Disbelieving, jaw hanging slack, I backed away from it—backed right into the bed and sat down there, with all the wind flown right out of me. Angela had seen everything and her eyes were threatening to pop out of her head; she dribbled chocolate and juice from one corner of her twitching mouth, but still her hand automatically picked up another liqueur. Except it wasn't a liqueur.

I waved a fluttery hand, croaked something unintelligible, tried to warn her. But my tongue was stuck to the roof of my mouth and the words wouldn't come. '*Gurk!*' was the only thing I managed to get out. And that too late for already she'd popped the thing into her mouth. Jeremy's eye—but *not* his glass eye!

Oh, and what a horror and a madness and an asylum then as she bit into it! Her throat full of chocolate, face turning blue, eyes bulging as she clawed at the bedclothes going 'Ak—ak—*ak!*' And me trying to massage her throat, and the damned pot leg kicking its way across the

floor towards me, and that bloody nightmare glass eye wobbling there
for all the world as if its owner were laughing!

Then . . . Angela clawed at me one last time and tore my shirt right
down the front as she toppled off the bed. Her eyes were standing out
like organ stops and her face was purple, and her dragging nails opened
up the shallow skin of my chest in five long red bleeding lines, but I
scarcely noticed. For Jeremy's leg was still crashing about on the floor
and his eye was still laughing.

I started laughing, too, as I kicked the leg into the wardrobe and
locked it, and chased the eye across the floor and under Angela's
dressing-table. I laughed and I laughed—laughed until I cried—and
perhaps wouldn't have sobered yet, except . . .

What was that?

That bumping, out there on the landing!

And it—he—Jeremy, is still out there, bumping about even now.
He's jammed the windows again so that I can't get out, but I've barri-
caded the door so that *he* can't get in; and now we're both stuck. I've
a slight advantage, though, for I can see, while he's quite blind! I mean,
I *know* he's blind for his glass eye is in here with me and his real eye is
in Angela! And his leg will come right through the panelling of the
wardrobe eventually I suppose, but when it does I'll jump on it and
pound the thing to pieces.

And he's out there blind as a bat hopping around on the landing,
going *gurgle, gurgle, gurgle* and stinking like all Hell! Well, sod you Jeremy Johnson Cleave for I'm not coming out. I'm just going to stay here
always. I won't come out for you or for the maid when she comes in
the morning or for the cook or the police or anybody.

I'll just stay here with my pillows and my blankets and my thumb
where it's nice and safe and warm. Here under the bed.

Do you hear me, Jeremy?

Do you hear me?

I'm—not—coming—out!

THE
LUSTSTONE

I

The ice was only a memory now, a racial memory whose legends had come down the years, whose evidence was graven in the land in hollow glacial tracts. Of the latter: time would weather the valley eventually, soften its contours however slowly. But the memories would stay, and each winter the snows would replenish them.

That was why the men of the tribes would paint themselves yellow in imitation of the sun-god, and stretch themselves in a line across the land east to west and facing north, and beat back the snow and ice with their clubs. And *frighten* it back with their screams and their leapings. With their magic they defeated winter and conjured spring, summer, and autumn, and thus were the seasons perpetuated.

The tribes, too, were perpetuated; each spring the tribal wizards—the witch-doctors—would perform those fertility rites deemed necessary to life, by means of which the grass was made to grow, the beasts to mate, and Man the weapon-maker to increase and prosper upon the face of the earth. It was the time of the sabretooth and the mammoth, and it was the springtime of Man, the thinking animal whose destiny is the stars. And even in those far dim primal times there were visionaries.

Chylos of the mighty Southern Tribe was one such: Chylos the Chief, the great wizard and seer whose word was law in the mid-South. And in that spring some ten thousand years ago, Chylos lay on his bed in the grandest cave of all the caves of the Southern Tribe, and dreamed his dream.

He dreamed of invaders!

Of men not greatly unlike the men of the tribes, but fiercer far and with huge appetites for ale, war, and women. Aye, and there were gross-bearded ones, too, whose dragon-prowed ships were as snakes of the sea, whose horned helmets and savage cries gave them the appearance of demons! But Chylos knew that he dreamed only of the far future and so was not made greatly fearful.

And he dreamed that in that distant future there were others who came from the east with fire and thunder, and in his dreams Chylos heard the agonized screams of the descendants of his tribe, men, women, and children; and saw visions of black war, red rape, and rivers of crimson blood. A complex dream it was, and alien these invaders: with long knives and axes which were not of stone, and again wearing horned helmets upon their heads to make them more fearsome yet. From the sea they came, building mounds and forts where they garrisoned their soldiers behind great earthworks.

And some of them carried strange banners, covered with unknown runes and wore kilts of leather and rode in horse-drawn chairs with flashing spokes in their wheels; and their armies were disciplined thousands, moving and fighting with one mind . . .

Such were Chylos's dreams, which brought him starting awake; and so often had he dreamed them that he knew they must be more than mere nightmares. Until one morning, rising from his bed of hides, he saw that it was spring again and knew what must be done. Such visions as he had dreamed must come to pass, he felt it in his old bones, but not for many years. Not for years beyond his numbering. Very well: the gods themselves had sent Chylos their warning, and now he must act. For he was old and the earth would claim him long before the first invaders came, and so he must unite the tribes now and bring them together. And they must grow strong and their men become great warriors.

And there must be that which would remain long after Chylos himself was gone: a reminder, a monument, a *Power* to fuel the loins of the men and make the tribes strong. A driving force to make his people lusty, to ensure their survival. There must be children—many children! And their children in their turn must number thousands, and theirs must number . . . such a number as Chylos could not envisage. Then when the invaders came the tribes would be ready, unconquerable, indestructible.

So Chylos took up his staff and went out into the central plain of the valley, where he found a great stone worn round by the coming and going of the ice; a stone half as tall again as a man above the earth, and as much or more of its mass still buried in the ground. And upon this mighty stone he carved his runes of fertility, powerful symbols that spelled LUST. And he carved designs which were the parts of men and women: the rampant pods and rods of seed, and the ripe breasts and bellies of dawning life. There was nothing of love in what he drew, only of lust and the need to procreate; for man was much more the animal in those dim forgotten days and love as such one of his weaknesses. But when Chylos's work was done, still he saw that it was not enough.

For what was the stone but a stone? Only a stone carved with cryptic runes and symbols of sexuality, and nothing more. It had no power. Who would remember it in a hundred seasons, let alone years? Who would know what it meant?

He called all the leaders of the tribes together, and because there was a recent peace in the land they came. And Chylos spoke to those headmen and wizards, telling them of his dreams and visions, which were seen as great omens. Together the leaders of the tribes decided what must be done; twenty days later they sent all of their young men and women to Chylos the Seer, and their own wizards went with them.

Meanwhile a pit had been dug away from the foot of the great stone, and wedged timbers held back that boulder from tumbling into the pit. And of all the young men and women of the tribes, Chylos and the Elders chose the lustiest lad and a broad-hipped lass with the breasts of a goddess; and they were proud to be chosen, though for what they knew not.

But when they saw each other, these two, they drew back snarling; for their markings were those of tribes previously opposed in war! And such had been their enmity that even now when all the people were joined, still they kept themselves apart each tribe from the other. Now that the pair had been chosen to be together—and because of their markings, origins, and tribal taboos, the greatest of which forbade intercourse between them—they spoke thus:

'What is the meaning of this?' cried the young man, his voice harsh, affronted. 'Why am I put with this woman? She is not of my tribe. She is of a tribe whose very name offends me! I am not at war with her, but neither may I know her.'

And she said: 'Do my own Elders make mock of me? Why am I insulted so? What have I done to deserve this? Take this thing which calls itself a man away from me!'

But Chylos and the Elders held up their hands, saying: 'Be at peace, be at peace with one another. All will be made plain in due time. We bestow upon you a great honour. Do not dishonour your tribes.' And the chosen ones were subdued, however grudgingly.

And the Elders whispered among each other and said: 'We chose them and the gods were our witnesses and unopposed. They are more than fit for the task. Joining them like this may also more nearly fuse their tribes, and bring about a lasting peace. It must be right.' And they were all agreed.

Then came the feasting, of meats dipped in certain spices and herbs known only to the wizards and flavoured with the crushed horn of mammoth, and the drinking of potent ales, all liberally sprinkled with the potions of the wizards. And when the celebrant horde was feasted and properly drunk, then came the oiled and perfumed and grotesquely clad dancers, whose dance was the slow-twining dance of the grossly endowed gods of fertility. And as the dance progressed so drummers took up the beat, until the pulses of the milling thousands pounded and their bodies jerked with the jerking of the male and female dancers.

Finally the dance ended, but still the drummers kept to their madly throbbing beat; while in the crowd lesser dances had commenced, not so practised but no less intense and even more lusty. And as the celebrants paired off and fell upon each other, thick pelts were tossed into the pit where the great stone balanced, and petals of spring flowers gathered with the dew upon them, making a bower in the shadow of the boulder; and this was where the chosen couple were made to lie down, while all about the young people of the tribes spent themselves in the ritual spring orgy.

But the pair in the pit—though they had been stripped naked, and while they were drunk as the rest—nevertheless held back and drew apart, and scowled at each other through slitted eyes. Chylos stood at the rim and screamed at them: 'Make love! Let the earth soak up your juices!' He prodded the young man with a spear and commanded him: 'Take her! The gods demand it! What? And would you have the trees die, and all the animals, and the ice come down again to destroy us all? *Do you defy the gods?*'

At that the young man would obey, for he feared the gods, but she would not have him. 'Let him in!' Chylos screamed at her. 'Would you be barren and have your breasts wither, and grow old before your time?' And so she wrapped her legs about the young man. But he was uncertain, and she had not accepted him; still, it seemed to Chylos that they were joined. And as the orgy climbed to its climax he cried out his triumph and signalled to a pair of well-muscled youths where they stood back behind the boulder. And coming forward they took up hammers and with mighty blows knocked away the chocks holding back the great stone from the pit.

The boulder tilted—three hundred tons of rock keeling over—and in the same moment Chylos clutched his heart, cried out and stumbled forward, and toppled into the pit!—and the rune-inscribed boulder with all its designs and great weight slammed down into the hole with a shock that shook the earth. But such was the power of the orgy that held them all in sway, that only those who coupled in the immediate vicinity of the stone knew that it had moved at all!

Now, with the drumming at a standstill, the couples parted, fell back, lay mainly exhausted. A vast field, as of battle, with steam rising as a morning mist. And the two whose task it had been to topple the boulder going amongst them, seeking still-willing, however aching flesh in which to relieve their own pent passions.

Thus was the deed done, the rite performed, the magic worked, the luststone come into being. Or thus it was intended. And old Chylos never knowing that, alas, his work was for nothing, for his propitiates had failed to couple . . .

Three winters after that the snows were heavy, meat was scarce, and the tribes warred. Then for a decade the gods and their seasonal rites were put aside, following which that great ritual orgy soon became a legend and eventually a myth. Fifty years later the luststone and its carvings were moss-covered, forgotten; another fifty saw the stone a shrine. One hundred more years passed and the domed, mossy top of the boulder was hidden in a grove of oaks: a place of the gods, taboo.

The plain grew to a forest, and the stone was buried beneath a growing mound of fertile soil; the trees were felled to build mammoth pens, and the grass grew deep, thick, and luxurious. More years saw the trees grow up again into a mighty oak forest; and these were the years of the hunter, the declining years of the mammoth. Now the people were farmers, of a sort, who protected limited crops and beasts against Nature's perils. There were years of the long-toothed cats and years of the wolf. And now and then there were wars between the tribes.

And time was the moon that waxed and waned, and the hills growing old and rounded, and forests spanning the entire land; and the tribes flourished and fought and did little else under the green canopy of these mighty forests . . .

Through all of this the stone slept, buried shallow in the earth, keeping its secret, but lovers in the forest knew where to lie when the moon was up. And men robbed by the years or by their own excesses could find a wonder there, when forgotten strength returned, however fleetingly, to fill them once more with fire.

As for old Chylos's dream: it came to pass, but his remedy was worthless. Buried beneath the sod for three thousand years the luststone lay, and felt the tramping feet of the nomad-warrior Celts on the march. Five thousand more years saw the Romans come to Britain, then the Anglo-Saxons, the Vikings, and still the luststone lay there.

There were greater wars than ever Chylos had dreamed, more of rape and murder than he ever could have imagined. War in the sea, on the land and in the air.

And at last there was peace again, of a sort. And finally—

Finally . . .

II

Garry Clemens was a human calculator at a betting shop in North London; he could figure the numbers, combinations and value of a winning ticket to within a doesn't-matter-a-damn faster than the girls could feed the figures into their machines. All the punters knew him; generally they'd accept without qualms his arbitration on vastly complicated accumulators and the like. With these sort of qualifications Garry could hold down a job any place they played the horses—which was handy because he liked to move around a lot and betting on the races was his hobby. One of his hobbies, anyway.

Another was rape.

Every time Garry took a heavy loss, then he raped. That way (according to his figuring) he won every time. If he couldn't take it out on the horse that let him down, then he'd take it out on some girl instead. But he'd suffered a spate of losses recently, and that had led to some trouble. He hated those nights when he'd go back to his flat and lie down on his bed and have nothing good to think about for that day. Only bad things, like the two hundred he'd lost on that nag that should have come in at fifteen to one, or the filly that got pipped at the post and cost him a cool grand. Which was why he'd finally figured out a way to ease his pain.

Starting now he'd take a girl for every day of the week, and that way when he took a loss—no matter which day it fell on—he'd always have something good to think about that night when he went to bed. If it was a Wednesday, why, he'd simply think about the Wednesday girl, et cetera . . .

But he'd gone through a bad patch and so the rapes had had to come thick and fast, one and sometimes two a week. His Monday girl was a redhead he'd gagged and tied to a tree in the centre of a copse in a built-up area. He'd spent a lot of time with her, smoked cigarettes in between and talked dirty and nasty to her, raped her three times. Differently each time. Tuesday was a sixteen-year-old kid down at the bottom of the railway embankment. No gag or rope or anything; she'd been so shit-scared that after he was through she didn't even start yelling for an hour. Wednesday (Garry's favourite) it had been a heavily pregnant coloured woman he'd dragged into a burned-out shop right in town! He'd made that one do everything. In the papers the next day he'd read how she lost her baby. But that hadn't bothered him too much.

Thursday had been when it started to get sticky. Garry had dragged this hooker into a street of derelict houses but hadn't even got started when along came this copper! He'd put his knife in the tart's throat—so that she wouldn't yell—and then got to hell out of there. And he'd reckoned himself lucky to get clean away. But on the other hand, it meant he had to go out the next night, too. He didn't like the tension to build up too much.

But Friday had been a near-disaster, too. There was a house-party not far from where he lived, and Garry had been invited. He'd declined, but he was there anyway—in the garden of the house opposite, whose people weren't at home. And when this really stacked piece had left the party on her own about midnight, Garry had jumped her. But just when he'd knocked her cold and was getting her out of her clothes, then the owners of the house turned up and saw him in the garden. He'd had to cut and run like the wind then, and even now it made his guts churn when he thought about it.

So he'd kept it quiet for a couple of weeks before starting again, and then he'd finally found his Thursday girl. A really shy thing getting off a late-night tube, who he'd carried into a parking lot and had for a couple of hours straight. And she hadn't said a word, just panted a lot and been sick. It turned out she was dumb—and Garry chuckled when he read that. No wonder she'd been so quiet. Maybe he should look for a blind one next time . . .

A week later, Friday, he'd gone out again, but it was a failure; he couldn't find anyone. And so the very next night he'd taken his Saturday girl—a middle-aged baglady! So what the hell!—a rape is a rape is a rape, right? He gave her a bottle of some good stuff first, which put her away nicely, then gave her a hell of a lot of bad stuff in as many ways as he knew how. She probably didn't even feel it, wouldn't even remember it, so afterwards he'd banged her face on the pavement a couple of times so that when she woke up at least she'd know *something* had happened! Except she hadn't woken up. Well, at least that way she wouldn't be talking about it. And by now he knew they'd have his semen type on record, and that they'd also have *him* if he just once slipped up. But he didn't intend to.

Sunday's girl was a lady taxi driver with a figure that was a real stopper! Garry hired her to take him out of town, directed her to a big house in the country and stopped her at the bottom of the drive. Then he hit her on the head, ripped her radio out, drove into a wood and had her in the back of the cab. He'd really made a meal of it, especially after she woke up; but as he was finishing she got a bit too active and raked his face—which was something he didn't much like. He had a nice face, Garry, and was very fond of it. So almost before he'd known that he was doing it, he'd gutted the whore!

But the next day in the papers the police were talking about skin under her fingernails, and now he knew they had his blood-group but definitely, too. *And* his face was marked; not badly, but enough. So it had been time to take a holiday.

Luckily he'd just had a big win on the gee-gees; he phoned the bookie's and said he wasn't up to it—couldn't see the numbers too clearly—he was taking time off. With an eye-patch and a bandage to cover the damage, he'd headed west and finally holed up in Chichester.

But all of that had been twelve days ago, and he was fine now, and he still had to find his girl-Friday. And today *was* Friday, so . . . Garry reckoned he'd rested up long enough.

This morning he'd read about a Friday night dance at a place called Athelsford, a hick village just a bus ride away. Well, and he had nothing against country bumpkins, did he? So Athelsford it would have to be . . .

It was the middle of the long hot summer of '76. The weather fore-
casters were all agreed for once that this one would drag on and on,
and reserves of water all over the country were already beginning to
suffer. This was that summer when there would be shock reports of the
Thames flowing backwards, when rainmakers would be called in from
the USA to dance and caper, and when a certain Government Ministry
would beg householders to put bricks in their WC cisterns and thus
consume less of precious water.

The southern beaches were choked morning to night with kids on
their school holidays, sun-blackened treasure hunters with knotted han-
kies on their heads and metal detectors in their hands, and frustrated
fishermen with their crates of beer, boxes of sandwiches, and plastic
bags of smelly bait. The pubs were filled all through opening hours with
customers trying to drown their thirsts or themselves, and the resorts
had never had it so good. The nights were balmy for lovers from Land's
End to John o' Groat's, and nowhere balmier than in the country lanes
of the Southern Counties.

Athelsford Estate in Hampshire, one of the few suburban housing
projects of the sixties to realize a measure of success (in that its houses
were good, its people relatively happy, and—after the last bulldozer had
clanked away—its countryside comparatively unspoiled) suffered or enjoyed the heatwave no more or less than anywhere else. It was just
another small centre of life and twentieth-century civilization, and apart
from the fact that Athelsford was 'rather select,' there was little as yet
to distinguish it from a hundred other estates and small villages in the
country triangle of Salisbury, Reading, and Brighton.

Tonight being Friday night, there was to be dancing at the Barn.
As its name implied, the place had been a half-brick, half-timber barn;
but the Athelsfordians being an enterprising lot, three of their more
affluent members had bought the great vault of a place, done it up with
internal balconies, tables, and chairs, built a modest car park to one
side—an extension of the village pub's car park—and now it was a
dance hall, occasionally used for weddings and other private functions.
On Wednesday nights the younger folk had it for their discotheques

(mainly teenage affairs, in return for which they kept it in good repair), but on Friday nights the Barn became the focal point of the entire estate. The Barn and the Old Stage.

The Old Stage was the village pub, its sign a coach with rearing horses confronted by a highwayman in tricorn hat. Joe McGovern, a widower, owned and ran the pub, and many of his customers jokingly associated him with the highwayman on his sign. But while Joe was and always would be a canny Scot, he was also a fair man and down to earth. So were his prices. Ten years ago when the estate was new, the steady custom of the people had saved the Old Stage and kept it a free house. Now Joe's trade was flourishing, and he had plenty to be thankful for.

So, too, Joe's somewhat surly son Gavin. Things to be thankful for, and others he could well do without. Gavin was, for example, extremely thankful for the Barn, whose bar he ran on Wednesday and Friday nights, using stock from the Old Stage. The profits very nicely supplemented the wage he earned as a county council labourer working on the new road. The wage he *had* earned, anyway, before he'd quit. That had only been this morning, but already he sort of missed the work, and he was sure he was going to miss the money. But . . . oh, he'd find other work. There was always work for good strong hands. He had that to be thankful for, too: his health and strength.

But he was *not* thankful for his kid sister, Eileen: her 'scrapes and narrow escapes' (as he saw her small handful of as yet entirely innocent friendships with the local lads), and her natural, almost astonishing beauty, which drew them like butterflies to bright flowers. It was that, in large part, which made him surly; for he knew that in fact she wasn't just a 'kid' sister any more, and that sooner or later she . . .

Oh, Gavin loved his sister, all right—indeed he had transferred to her all of his affection and protection when their mother died three years ago—but having lost his mother he wasn't going to lose Eileen, too, not if he could help it.

Gavin was twenty-two, Eileen seventeen. He was over six feet tall, narrow-hipped, wide in the shoulders: a tapering wedge of muscle with a bullet-head to top it off. Most of the village lads looked at Eileen, then looked at Gavin, and didn't look at Eileen again. But those of them who looked at her twice reckoned she was worth it.

She was blonde as her brother was dark, as sweet and slim as he was huge and surly; five-seven, with long shapely legs and a waist like a wisp, and blue eyes with lights in them that danced when she smiled; the very image of her mother. And that was Gavin's problem—for he'd loved his mother a great deal, too.

It was 5.30 P.M. and brother and sister were busy in workclothes, loading stock from the back door of the Old Stage onto a trolley and carting it across the parking lot to the Barn. Joe McGovern ticked off the items on a stock list as they worked. But when Gavin and Eileen were alone in the Barn, stacking the last of the bottles onto the shelves behind the bar, suddenly he said to her: 'Will you be here tonight?'

She looked at her brother. There was nothing surly about Gavin now. There never was when he spoke to her; indeed his voice held a note of concern, of agitation, of some inner struggle which he himself couldn't quite put his finger on. And she knew what he was thinking and that it would be the same tonight as always. Someone would dance with her, and then dance with her again—and then no more. Because Gavin would have had 'a quiet word with him.'

'Of course I'll be here, Gavin,' she sighed. 'You know I will. I wouldn't miss it. I love to dance and chat with the girls—*and* with the boys—when I get the chance! Why does it bother you so?'

'I've told you often enough why it bothers me,' he answered gruffly, breathing heavily through his nose. 'It's all those blokes. They've only one thing on their minds. They're the same with all the girls. But you're not just any girl—you're my sister.'

'Yes,' she answered, a trifle bitterly, 'and don't they just know it! You're always there, in the background, watching, somehow threatening. It's like having two fathers—only one of them's a tyrant! Do you know, I can't remember the last time a boy wanted to walk me home?'

'But . . . you *are* home!' he answered, not wanting to fight, wishing now that he'd kept his peace. If only she was capable of understanding the ways of the world. 'You live right next door.'

'Then simply *walk* me!' she blurted it out. 'Oh, anywhere! Gavin, can't you understand? It's *nice* to be courted, to have someone who wants to hold your hand!'

'That's how it starts,' he grunted, turning away. 'They want to hold your hand. But who's to say how it finishes, eh?'

'Well not much fear of that!' She sighed again. 'Not that I'm that sort of girl anyway,' and she looked at him archly. 'But even if I was, with you around—straining at the leash like . . . like a great hulking watchdog—nothing's very much likely to even get started, now is it?' And before he could answer, but less harshly now: 'Now come on,' she said, 'tell me what's brought all this on? You've been really nice to me this last couple of weeks. The hot weather may have soured some people, but you've been really sweet—like a big brother should be—until out of the blue, like this. I really don't understand what gets into you, Gavin.'

It was his turn to sigh. 'Aren't you forgetting something?' he said. 'The assault—probably with sexual motivation—just last week, Saturday night, in Lovers' Lane?'

Perhaps Eileen really ought not to pooh-pooh that, but she believed she understood it well enough. 'An assault,' she said. 'Motive: "probably" sexual—the most excitement Athelsford has known in . . . oh, as long as *I* can remember! And the "victim": Linda Anstey. Oh, my, *what* a surprise! *Hah!* Why, Linda's always been that way! Every kid in the school had fooled around with her at one time or another. From playing kids' games to . . . well, everything. It's the way she is and everyone knows it. All right, perhaps I'm being unfair to her: she might have asked for trouble and she might not, but it seems hardly surprising to me that if it was going to happen to someone, Linda would be the one!'

'But it *did* happen,' Gavin insisted. 'That kind of bloke does exist— plenty of them.' He stacked the last half-dozen cans and made for the exit; and changing the subject (as he was wont to do when an argument was going badly for him, or when he believed he'd proved his point sufficiently) said: 'Me, I'm for a pint before I get myself ready for to-night. Fancy an iced lemonade, kid?' He paused, turned back towards her, and grinned, but she suspected it was forced. If only she could gauge what went on in his mind.

But: 'Oh, all right!' She finally matched his grin. 'If you're buying.' She caught up with him and grabbed him, standing on tip-toe to give him a kiss. 'But Gavin—promise me that from now on you won't worry about me so much, okay?'

He hugged her briefly, and reluctantly submitted: 'Yeah, all right.'

But as she led the way out of the Barn and across the car park, with the hot afternoon sun shining in her hair and her sweet, innocent body moving like that inside her coveralls, he looked after her and worried all the harder; worried the way an older brother *should* worry, he thought, and yet somehow far more intensely. And the worst of it was that he *knew* he was being unreasonable and obsessive! But (and Gavin at once felt his heart hardening) . . . oh, he recognized well enough the way the village Jack-the-Lads looked at Eileen, and knew how much they'd like to get their itchy little paws on her—the grubby-minded, horny . . .

. . . But there Gavin's ireful thoughts abruptly evaporated, the scowl left his face, and he frowned as a vivid picture suddenly flashed onto the screen of his mind. It was something he'd seen just this morning, across the fields where they were laying the new road; something quite obscene which hadn't made much of an impression on him at the time, but which now . . . and astonished, he paused again. For he couldn't for the life of him see how he'd connected up a thing like that with Eileen! And it just as suddenly dawned on him that the reason he knew how the boys felt about his sister was because he sometimes felt that way too. Oh, not about *her*—no, of course not—but about . . . a boulder? Well, certainly it had been a boulder that did it to him this morning, anyway.

And: *Gavin, son,* he told himself, *sometimes I think you're maybe just a tiny wee bit sick!* And then he laughed, if only to himself.

But somehow the pictures in his mind just wouldn't go away, and as he went to his upstairs room in the Old Stage and slowly changed into his evening gear, so he allowed himself to go over again the peculiar occurrences of the morning . . .

III

That Friday morning, yes, and it had been hot as a furnace. And every member of the road gang without exception looking forward to the coming weekend, to cool beers in cool houses with all the windows thrown open; so that as the heat-shimmering day had drawn towards noon they'd wearied of the job and put a lot less muscle into it.

Also, and to make things worse, this afternoon they'd be a man short; for this was Gavin McGovern's last morning and he hadn't been replaced yet. And even when he was . . . well, it would take a long time to find someone else who could throw a bulldozer around like he could. The thing was like a toy in his hands. But . . . seeing as how he lived in Athelsford and had always considered himself something of a traitor anyway, working on the link road, he'd finally decided to seek employment elsewhere.

Foreman John Sykes wasn't an Athelsfordian, but he made it his business to know something about the people working under him—especially if they were local to the land where he was driving his road. He'd got to know Big Gavin pretty well, he reckoned, and in a way envied him. He certainly wouldn't mind it if *his* Old Man owned a country pub! But on the other hand he could sympathize with McGovern, too. He knew how torn he must feel.

This was the one part of his job that Sykes hated: when the people up top said the road goes here, and the people down here said oh no it doesn't, not in *our* back garden! Puffed up, awkward, defiant little bastards! But at the same time Sykes could sympathize with them also, even though they were making his job as unpleasant as they possibly could. And that was yet another reason why the work hadn't gone too well this morning.

Today it had been a sit-in, when a good dozen of the locals had appeared from the wood at the end of Lovers' Lane, bringing lightweight fold-down garden chairs with them to erect across the road. And there they'd sat with their placards and sandwiches on the new stretch of tarmac, heckling the road gang as they toiled and sweated into their dark-stained vests and tried to build a bloody road which wasn't wanted. And which didn't seem to want to be built! They'd stayed from maybe quarter past nine to a minute short of eleven, then got up and like a gaggle of lemmings waddled back to the village again. Their 'good deed' for the day—*Goddam!*

Christ, what a day! For right after that . . . *big* trouble, mechanical trouble! Or rather an obstruction which had caused mechanical trouble. Not the more or less passive, placard-waving obstruction of people— which was bad enough—but a rather more physical, much more tangible obstruction. Namely, a bloody great boulder!

The first they'd known of it was when the bulldozer hit it while lifting turf and muck in a wide swath two feet deep. Until then there had been only the usual stony debris—small, rounded pebbles and the occasional blunt slab of scarred rock, nothing out of the ordinary for these parts—and Sykes hadn't been expecting anything quite this big. The surveyors had been across here, hammering in their long iron spikes and testing the ground, but they'd somehow missed this thing. Black granite by its looks, it had stopped the dozer dead in its tracks and given Gavin McGovern a fair old shaking! But at least the blade had cleared the sod and clay off the top of the thing. Like the dome of a veined, bald, old head it had looked, sticking up there in the middle of the projected strip.

'See if you can dig the blade under it,' Sykes had bawled up at Gavin through clouds of blue exhaust fumes and the clatter of the engine. 'Try to lever the bastard up, or split it. We have to get down a good forty or fifty inches just here.'

Taking it personally—and with something less than an hour to go, eager to get finished now—Gavin had dragged his sleeve across his brown, perspiration-shiny brow and grimaced. Then, tilting his helmet back on his head, he'd slammed the blade of his machine deep into the earth half a dozen times until he could feel it biting against the unseen curve of the boulder. Then he'd gunned the motor, let out the clutch, shoved, and lifted all in one fluid movement. Or at least in a movement that should have been fluid. For instead of finding purchase the blade had ridden up, splitting turf and topsoil as it slid over the fairly smooth surface of the stone; the dozer had lurched forward, slewing round when the blade finally snagged on a rougher part of the surface; the offside caterpillar had parted in a shriek of hot, tortured metal.

Then Gavin had shut her off, jumped down, and stared disbelievingly at his grazed and bleeding forearm where it had scraped across the iron frame of the cab. 'Damn—*damn!*' he'd shouted then, hurling his safety helmet at the freshly turned earth and kicking the dozer's broken track.

'Easy, Gavin,' Sykes had gone up to him. 'It's not your fault, and it's not the machine's. It's mine, if anybody's. I had no idea there was anything this big here. And by the look of it this is only the tip of the iceberg.'

But Gavin wasn't listening; he'd gone down on one knee and was examining part of the boulder's surface where the blade had done a job of clearing it off. He was frowning, peering hard, breaking away small scabs of loose dirt and tracing lines or grooves with his strong, blunt fingers. The runic symbols were faint, but the carved picture was more clearly visible. There were other pictures, too, with only their edges showing as yet, mainly hidden under the curve of the boulder. The ganger got down beside Gavin and assisted him, and slowly the carvings took on clearer definition.

Sykes was frowning, too, now. What the Hell? A floral design of some sort? Very old, no doubt about it. Archaic? Prehistoric?

Unable as yet to make anything decisive of the pictures on the stone, they cleared away more dirt. But then Sykes stared harder, slowly shook his head, and began to grin. The grin spread until it almost split his face ear to ear. Perhaps not prehistoric after all. More like the work of some dirty-minded local kid. And not a bad artist, at that!

The lines of the main picture were primitive but clinically correct, however exaggerated. And its subject was completely unmistakable.

Gavin McGovern continued to stare at it, and his bottom jaw had fallen open. Finally, glancing at Sykes out of the corner of his eye, he grunted: 'Old, do you think?'

Sykes started to answer, then shut his mouth and stood up. He thought fast, scuffed some of the dirt back with his booted foot, bent to lean a large, flat flake of stone against the picture, mainly covering it from view. Sweat trickled down his back and made it itch under his wringing shirt. Made it itch like the devil, and the rest of his body with it. The boulder seemed hot as Hell, reflecting the blazing midday sunlight.

And 'Old?' the ganger finally answered. 'You mean, like ancient? Naw, I shouldn't think so . . . Hey, and Gavin, son—if I were you, I wouldn't go mentioning this to anyone. You know what I mean?'

Gavin looked up, still frowning. 'No,' he shook his head, 'what do you mean?'

'What?' said Sykes. 'You mean to say you can't see it? Why, only let this get out and there'll be people coming from all over the place to see it! Another bloody Stonehenge, it'll be! And what price your Athelsford then, eh? Flooded, the place would be, with all sorts of human debris come to see the famous dirty caveman pictures! You want that, do you?'

No, that was the last thing Gavin wanted. 'I see what you mean,' he said, slowly. 'Also, it would slow you down, right? They'd stop you running your road through here.'

'That, too, possibly,' Sykes answered. 'For a time, anyway. But just think about it. What would you rather have: a new road pure and simple—or a thousand yobs a day tramping through Athelsford and up Lovers' Lane to ogle this little lot, eh?'

That was something Gavin didn't have to think about for very long. It would do business at the Old Stage a power of good, true, but then there was Eileen. Pretty soon they'd be coming to ogle her, too. 'So what's next?' he said.

'You leave that to me,' Sykes told him. 'And just take my word for it that this time tomorrow this little beauty will be so much rubble, okay?'

Gavin nodded; he knew that the ganger was hot stuff with a drill and a couple of pounds of explosive. 'If you say so.' He spat into the dust and dirt. 'Anyway, I don't much care for the looks of the damned thing!' He scratched furiously at his forearm where his graze was already starting to scab over. 'It's not right, this dirty old thing. Sort of makes me hot and . . . itchy!'

'Itchy, yeah,' Sykes agreed. And he wondered what sort of mood his wife, Jennie, would be in tonight. If this hot summer sun had worked on her the way it was beginning to work on him, well tonight could get to be pretty interesting. Which would make a welcome change!

Deep, dark, and much disturbed now, old Chylos had felt unaccustomed tremors vibrating through his fossilized bones. The stamping of a thousand warriors on the march, roaring their songs of red death? Aye, perhaps. And:

'*Invaders!*' Chylos breathed the word, without speaking, and indeed without breathing.

'*No,*' Hengit of the Far Forest Tribe contradicted him. '*The mammoths are stampeding, the earth is sinking, trees are being felled. Any of these things, but no invaders. Is that all you dream about, old man? Why can't you simply lie still and sleep like the dead thing you are?*'

'*And even if there were invaders,*' the revenant of a female voice now joined in, Alaze of the Shrub Hill folk, '*would you really expect a man of the Far Forest Tribe to come to arms? They are notorious cowards! Better you call on me, Chylos, a woman, to rise up against these invaders—if there really were invaders, which there are not.*'

Chylos listened hard—to the earth, the sky, the distant sea—but no longer heard the thundering of booted feet, nor warcries going up into the air, nor ships with muffled oars creeping and creaking in the mist. And so he sighed and said: '*Perhaps you are right—but nevertheless we should be ready! I, at least, am ready!*'

And: '*Old fool!*' Hengit whispered of Chylos into the dirt and the dark.

And: *'Coward!'* Alaze was scathing of Hengit where all three lay
broken, under the luststone . . .

7.15 P.M.

The road gang had knocked off more than two hours ago and the light
was only just beginning to fade a little. An hour and a half to go yet to
the summer's balmy darkness, when the young people would wander
hand in hand, and occasionally pause mouth to mouth, in Lovers' Lane.
Or perhaps not until later, for tonight there was to be dancing at the
Barn. And for now . . . all should be peace and quiet out here in the
fields, where the luststone raised its veined dome of a head through
the broken soil. All *should* be quiet—but was not.

'Levver!' shouted King above the roar of the bikes, his voice full of
scorn. 'What a bleedin' player you turned out to be! What the 'ell do
yer call this, then?'

'The end o' the bleedin' road,' one of the other bikers shouted.
'That's where!'

'Is it ever!' cried someone else.

Leather grinned sheepishly and pushed his Nazi-style crash-helmet
to the back of his head. 'So I come the wrong way, di'n I? 'Ell's teef, the
sign said bleedin' Affelsford, dinnit?'

'Yers,' King shouted. 'Also NO ENTRY an' WORKS IN PRO-bleedin'-
GRESS! 'Ere, switch off, you lot. I can't 'ear meself fink!'

As the engines of the six machines clattered to a halt, King got off
his bike and stretched, stamping his feet. His real name was Kevin, but
as leader of a chapter of Hell's Angels, who needed a name like that? A
crude crown was traced in lead studs on the back of his leather jacket
and a golden sovereign glittered where it dangled from his left earlobe.
No more than twenty-five or -six years of age, King kept his head clean-
shaven under a silver helmet painted with black eye-sockets and fretted
nostrils to resemble a skull. He was hard as they come, was King, and
the rest of them knew it.

'That's the place I cased over there,' said Leather, pointing. He had
jumped up onto the dome of a huge boulder, the luststone, to spy out

the land. 'See the steeple there? That's Affelsford—and Comrades, does it have *some* crumpet!'

'Well, jolly dee!' said King. 'Wot we supposed to do, then? Ride across the bleedin' fields? Come on, Levver my son—you was the one rode out here and onced it over. 'Ow do we bleedin' *get* there?' The rest of the Angels sniggered.

Leather grinned. 'We goes up the motorway a few 'undred yards an' spins off at the next turnin', that's all. I jus' made a simple mistake, di'n I.'

'Yers,' said King, relieving himself loudly against the luststone. 'Well, let's not make no more, eh? I gets choked off pissin' about an' wastin' valuable time.'

By now the others had dismounted and stood ringed around the dome of the boulder. They stretched their legs and lit 'funny' cigarettes. 'That's right,' said King, 'light up. Let's have a break before we go in.'

'Best not leave it too late,' said Leather. 'Once the mood is on me I likes to get it off . . .'

'One copper, you said,' King reminded him, drawing deeply on a poorly constructed smoke. 'Only one bluebottle in the whole place?'

'S'right,' said Leather. 'An' 'e's at the other end of town. We can wreck the place, 'ave our fun wiv the girlies, be out again before 'e knows we was ever in!'

' 'Ere,' said one of the others. 'These birds is the real fing, eh, Levver?'

Leather grinned crookedly and nodded. 'Built for it,' he answered. 'Gawd, it's ripe, is Affelsford.'

The gang guffawed, then quietened as a dumpy figure approached from the construction shack. It was one of Sykes's men, doing night-watchman to bolster his wages. 'What's all this?' he grunted, coming up to them.

'Unmarried muvvers' convention,' said King. 'Wot's it look like?' The others laughed, willing to make a joke of it and let it be; but Leather jumped down from the boulder and stepped forward. He was eager to get things started, tingling—even itchy—with his need for violence.

'Wot's it ter you, baldy?' he snarled, pushing the little man in the chest and sending him staggering.

Baldy Dawson was one of Sykes's drivers and didn't have a lot of muscle. He did have common sense, however, and could see that things might easily get out of hand. 'Before you start any rough stuff,' he answered, backing away, 'I better tell you I took your bike numbers and phoned 'em through to the office in Portsmouth.' He had done no such thing, but it was a good bluff. 'Any trouble—my boss'll know who did it.'

Leather grabbed him by the front of his sweat-damp shirt. 'You little—'

'Let it be,' said King. ' 'E's only doin' 'is job. Besides, 'e 'as an 'ead jus' like mine!' He laughed.

'Wot?' Leather was astonished.

'Why spoil fings?' King took the other's arm. 'Now listen, Levver me lad—all you've done so far is bog everyfing up, right? So let's bugger off into bleedin' Affelsford an' 'ave ourselves some fun! You want to see some blood—okay, me too—but for Chrissakes, let's get somefing for our money, right?'

They got back on their bikes and roared off, leaving Baldy Dawson in a slowly settling cloud of dust and exhaust fumes. 'Young bastards!' He scratched his naked dome. 'Trouble for someone before the night's out, I'll wager.'

Then, crisis averted, he returned to the shack and his well-thumbed copy of *Playboy* . . .

IV

'This time,' said Chylos, with some urgency, 'I cannot be mistaken.'

The two buried with him groaned—but before they could comment:

'Are you deaf, blind—have you no feelings?' he scorned. 'No, it's simply that you do not have my magic!'

'It's your "magic" that put us here!' finally Hengit answered his charges. 'Chylos, we don't need your magic!'

'But the tribes do,' said Chylos. 'Now more than ever!'

'Tribes?' this time it was Alaze who spoke. 'The tribes were scattered, gone, blown to the four winds many lifetimes agone. What tribes do you speak of, old man?'

'The children of the tribes, then!' he blustered. 'Their children's children! What does it matter? They are the same people! They are of our blood! And I have dreamed a dream . . .'

'That again?' said Hengit. 'That dream of yours, all these thousands of years old?'

'Not the old dream,' Chylos denied, 'but a new one! Just now, lying here, I dreamed it! Oh, it was not unlike the old one, but it was vivid, fresh, new! And I cannot be mistaken.'

And now the two lying there with him were silent, for they too had felt, sensed, something. And finally: 'What did you see . . . in this dream?' Alaze was at least curious.

'I saw them as before,' said Chylos, 'with flashing spokes in the wheels of their battle-chairs; except the wheels were not set side by side but fore and aft! And helmets upon their heads, some with horns! They wore shirts of leather picked out in fearsome designs, monstrous runes; sharp knives in their belts, aye, and flails—and blood in their eyes! Invaders—I cannot be mistaken!'

And Hengit and Alaze shuddered a little in their stony bones, for Chylos had inspired them with the truth of his vision and chilled them with the knowledge of his prophecy finally come true. But . . . what could they do about it, lying here in the cold earth? It was as if the old wizard read their minds.

'You are not bound to lie here,' he told them. 'What are you now but will? And my will remains strong! So let's be up and about our work. I, Chylos, have willed it—so let it be!'

'Our work? What work?' the two cried together. 'We cannot fight!'

'You could if you willed it,' said Chylos, 'and if you have not forgotten how. But I didn't mention fighting. No, we must warn them. The children of the children of the tribes. Warn them, inspire them, cause them to lust *after the blood of these invaders!'* And before they could question him further:

'*Up, up, we've work to do!'* Chylos cried. '*Up with you and out into the night, to seek them out. The children of the children of the tribes . . . !'*

From the look of things, it was all set to be a full house at the Barn. Athelsfordians in their Friday-night best were gravitating first to the Old Stage for a warm-up drink or two, then crossing the parking lot to the Barn to secure good tables up on the balconies or around the dance floor. Another hour or two and the place would be in full swing. Normally Gavin McGovern would be pleased with the way things were shaping up, for what with tips and all it would mean a big bonus for him. And his father at the pub wouldn't complain, for what was lost on the swings would be regained on the roundabouts. And yet . . .

There seemed a funny mood on the people tonight, a sort of scratchiness about them, an abrasiveness quite out of keeping. When the disco numbers were playing the girls danced with a sexual aggressiveness Gavin hadn't noticed before, and the men of the village seemed almost to be eyeing each other up like tomcats spoiling for a fight. Pulling pints for all he was worth, Gavin hadn't so far had much of a chance to examine or analyse the thing; it was just that in the back of his mind some small dark niggling voice seemed to be urgently whispering: '*Look out! Be on your guard! Tonight's the night! And when it happens you won't believe it!* But . . . it could simply be his imagination, of course.

Or (and Gavin growled his frustration and self-annoyance as he felt that old obsession rising up again) it could simply be that Eileen had found herself a new dancing partner, and that since the newcomer had walked into the place they'd scarcely been off the floor. A fact which in itself was enough to set him imagining all sorts of things, and uppermost the sensuality of women and sexual competitiveness, readiness, and willingness of young men. And where Gavin's sister was concerned, much too willing!

But Eileen had seen Gavin watching her, and as the dance tune ended she came over to the bar with her young man in tow. This was a ploy she'd used before: a direct attack is often the best form of defence. Gavin remembered his promise, however, and in fact the man she was with seemed a very decent sort at first glance: clean and bright, smartly dressed, seriously intentioned. Now Gavin would see if his patter matched up to his looks.

'Gavin,' said Eileen, smiling warningly, 'I'd like you to meet Gordon Cleary—Gordon's a surveyor from Portsmouth.'

'How do you do, Gordon.' Gavin dried his hands, reached across the bar to shake with the other, discovered the handshake firm, dry, and no-nonsense. But before they could strike up any sort of conversation the dance floor had emptied and the bar began to crowd up. 'I'm sorry.' Gavin shrugged ruefully. 'Business. But at least you were here first and I can get you your drinks.' He looked at his sister.

'Mine's easy,' she said, smiling. 'A lemonade, please.' And Gavin was pleased to note that Cleary made no objection, didn't try to force strong drink on her.

'Oh, a shandy for me,' he said, 'and go light on the beer, please, Gavin, for I'll be driving later. And one for yourself, if you're ready.'

The drinks were served and Gavin turned to the next party of customers in line at the bar. There were four of them: Tod Baxter and Angela Meers, village sweethearts, and Allan Harper and his wife, Val. Harper was a PTI at the local school; he ordered a confusing mixture of drinks, no two alike; Gavin, caught on the hop, had a little trouble with his mental arithmetic. 'Er, that's two pounds—er—' He frowned in concentration.

'Three pounds and forty-seven pence, on the button!' said Gordon Cleary from the side. Gavin looked at him and saw his eyes flickering over the price list pinned up behind the bar.

'Pretty fast!' he commented, and carried on serving. But to himself he said: *Except I hope it's only with numbers . . .*

Gavin wasn't on his own behind the bar; at the other end, working just as hard, Bill Salmons popped corks and pulled furious pints. Salmons was ex-Army, a parachutist who'd bust himself up jumping. You wouldn't know it, though, for he was strong as a horse. As the disc jockey got his strobes going again and the music started up, and as the couples gradually gravitated back towards the dance floor, Gavin crossed quickly to Salmons and said: 'I'm going to get some of this sweat off. Two minutes?'

Salmons nodded, said: 'Hell of a night, isn't it? Too damned *hot!*'

Gavin reached under the bar for a clean towel and headed for the gents' toilet. Out of the corner of his eye he saw that Eileen and Gordon Cleary were back on the floor again. Well, if all the bloke wanted was to dance . . . that was okay.

In the washroom Gavin took off his shirt, splashed himself with cold water, and towelled it off, dressed himself again. A pointless exercise: he was just as hot and damp as before! As he finished off Allan Harper came in, also complaining of the heat.

They passed a few words; Harper was straightening his tie in a mirror when there came the sound of shattering glass from the dance hall, causing Gavin to start. 'What—?' he said.

'Just some clown dropped his drink, I expect,' said Harper. 'Or fainted for lack of air! It's about time we got some decent air-conditioning in this—'

And he paused as there sounded a second crash—which this time was loud enough to suggest a table going over. The music stopped abruptly and some girl gave a high-pitched shriek.

We warned you! said several dark little voices in the back of Gavin's mind. 'What the hell—?' He started down the corridor from the toilets with Harper hot on his heels.

Entering the hall proper the two skidded to a halt. On the other side of the room a village youth lay sprawled among the debris of a wrecked table, blood spurting from his nose. Over him stood a Hell's Angel, swinging a bike chain threateningly. In the background a young girl sobbed, backing away, her dress torn down the front. Gavin would have started forward, but Harper caught his arm. 'Look!' he said.

At a second glance the place seemed to be crawling with Angels. There was one at the entrance, blocking access; two more were on the floor, dragging Angela Meers and Tod Baxter apart. They had yanked the straps of Angela's dress down, exposing her breasts. A fifth Angel had clambered into the disco control box, was flinging records all over the place as he sought his favourites. And the sixth was at the bar.

Now it was Gavin's turn to gasp, 'Look!'

The one at the bar, King, had trapped Val Harper on her bar stool. He had his arms round her, his hands gripping the bar top. He rubbed himself grindingly against her with lewdly suggestive sensuality.

For a moment longer the two men stood frozen on the perimeter of this scene, nailed down by a numbness which, as it passed, brought rage in its wake. The Angel with the chain, Leather, had come across the floor and swaggered by them into the corridor, urinating in a semi-circle as he went, saying: 'Evenin' gents. This the bog, then?'

What the hell's happening? thought Harper, lunging towards the bar. There must be something wrong with the strobe lights: they blinded him as he ran, flashing rainbow colours in a mad kaleidoscope that flooded the entire room. The Angel at the bar was trying to get his hand down the front of Val's dress, his rutting movements exaggerated by the crazy strobes. Struggling desperately, Val screamed.

Somewhere at the back of his shocked mind, Harper noted that the Angels still wore their helmets. He also noted, in the flutter of the crazy strobes, that the helmets seemed to have grown horns! *Jesus, it's like a bloody Viking invasion!* he thought, going to Val's rescue . . .

It had looked like a piece of cake to King and his Angels. A gift. The kid selling tickets hadn't even challenged them. Too busy wetting his pants, King supposed. And from what he had seen of the Barn's clientele: pushovers! As soon as he'd spotted Val Harper at the bar, he'd known what he wanted. A toffy-nosed bird like her in a crummy place like this? She could only be here for one thing. And not a man in the place to deny him whatever he wanted to do or take.

Which is why it came as a total surprise to King when Allan Harper spun him around and butted him square in the face. Blood flew as the astonished Angel slammed back against the bar; his spine cracked against the bar's rim, knocking all the wind out of him; in another moment Bill Salmons's arm went round his neck in a strangle-hold.

There was no time for chivalry: Harper the PTI finished it with a left to King's middle and a right to his already bloody face. The final blow landed on King's chin, knocking him cold. As Bill Salmons released him he flopped forward, his death's-head helmet flying free as he landed face-down on the floor.

Gavin McGovern had meanwhile reached into the disc jockey's booth, grabbed his victim by the scruff of the neck, and hurled him out of the booth and across the dance floor. Couples hastily got out of the way as the Angel slid on his back across the polished floor. Skidding to a halt, he brought out a straight-edged razor in a silvery flash of steel. Gavin was on him in a moment; he lashed out with a foot that caught the Angel in the throat, knocking him flat on his back again. The razor spun harmlessly away across the floor as its owner writhed and clawed at his throat.

Seeing their Angel at Arms on the floor like that, the pair who tormented Angela Meers now turned their attention to Gavin McGovern. They had already knocked Tod Baxter down, kicking him where he huddled. But they hadn't got in a good shot, and as Gavin loomed large so Tod got to his feet behind them. Also, Allan Harper was dodging his way through the now strangely silent crowd where he came from the bar.

The Angel at the door, having seen something of the melee and wanting to get his share while there was still some going, also came lunging in through the wild strobe patterns. But this one reckoned without the now fully roused passions of the young warriors of the Athelsford tribe. Three of the estate's larger youths jumped him, and he went down under a hail of blows. And by then Allan Harper, Gavin McGovern and Tod Baxter had fallen on the other two. For long moments there were only the crazily flashing strobes, the dull thudding of fists into flesh, and a series of fading grunts and groans.

Five Angels were down; and the sixth, coming out of the toilets, saw only a sea of angered faces all turned in his direction. Faces hard and full of fury—*and* bloodied, crumpled shapes here and there, cluttering the dance floor. Pale now and disbelieving, Leather ran towards the exit, found himself surrounded in a moment. And now in the absolute silence there was bloodlust written on those faces that ringed him in.

They rolled over him like a wave, and his Nazi helmet flew off and skidded to a rocking halt . . . at the feet of Police Constable Charlie Bennett, Athelsford's custodian of the law, where he stood framed in the door of the tiny foyer.

Then the normal lights came up and someone cut the strobes, and as the weirdly breathless place slowly came back to life, so PC Bennett was able to take charge. And for the moment no one, not even Gavin, noticed that Eileen McGovern and her new friend were nowhere to be seen . . .

V

Chylos was jubilant. *'It's done!'* he cried in his grave. *'The invaders* defeated, beaten back!'

And: *'You were right, old man,'* finally Hengit grudgingly answered. *'They were invaders, and our warnings and urgings came just in time. But this tribe of yours—pah! Like flowers, they were, weak and waiting to be crushed—until we inspired them.'*

And now Chylos was very angry indeed. *'You two!'* he snapped like a bowstring. *'If you had heeded me at the rites, these many generations flown, then were there no requirement for our efforts this night! But . . . perhaps I may still undo your mischief, even now, and finally rest easy.'*

'That can't be, old man, and you know it,' this time Alaze spoke up. *'Would that we could put right that of which you accuse us; for if our blood still runs in these tribes, then it were only right and proper. But we cannot put it right. No, not even with all your magic. For what are we now but worm-fretted bones and dust? There's no magic can give us back our flesh . . .'*

'There is,' Chylos chuckled then. *'Oh, there is! The magic of this stone. No, not your flesh but your will. No, not your limbs but your lust. Neither your youth nor your beauty nor even your hot blood, but your spirit! Which*

is all you will need to do what must be done. For if the tribes may not be imbrued with your seed, strengthened by your blood—then it must be with your spirit. I may not do it for I was old even in those days, but it is still possible for you. If I will it—and if you will it.

'Now listen, and I shall tell you what must be done . . .'

Eileen McGovern and 'Gordon Cleary' stood outside the Barn in the deepening dusk and watched the Black Maria come and take away the battered Angels. As the police van made off down the estate's main street, Eileen leaned towards the entrance to the disco, but her companion seemed concerned for her and caught her arm. 'Better let it cool down in there,' he said. 'There's bound to be a lot of hot blood still on the boil.'

'Maybe you're right.' Eileen looked up at him. 'Certainly you were right to bundle us out of there when it started! So what do you suggest? We could go and cool off in the Old Stage. My father owns it.'

He shrugged, smiled, seemed suddenly shy, a little awkward. 'I'd rather hoped we could walk together,' he said. 'The heat of the day is off now—it's cool enough out here. Also, I'll have to be going in an hour or so. I'd hoped to be able to, well, talk to you in private. Pubs and dance halls are fine for meeting people, but they're dreadfully noisy places, too.'

It was her turn to shrug. It would be worth it if only to defy Gavin. And afterwards she'd make him see how there was no harm in her friendships. 'All right,' she said, taking Cleary's arm. 'Where shall we walk?'

He looked at her and sighed his defeat. 'Eileen, I don't know this place at all. I wouldn't know one street or lane from the next. So I suppose I'm at your mercy!'

'Well,' she laughed. 'I do know a pretty private place.' And she led him away from the Barn and into an avenue of trees. 'It's not far away, and it's *the* most private place of all.' She smiled as once more she glanced up at him in the flooding moonlight. 'That's why it's called Lovers' Lane . . .'

Half an hour later in the Barn, it finally dawned on Gavin McGovern that his sister was absent. He'd last seen her with that Gordon Cleary bloke. And what had Cleary said: something about having to drive later? Maybe he'd taken Eileen with him. They must have left during the ruckus with the Angels. Well, at least Gavin could be thankful for that!

But at eleven o'clock when the Barn closed and he had the job of checking and then shifting the stock, still she wasn't back. Or if she was she'd gone straight home to the Old Stage and so to bed. Just before twelve midnight Gavin was finished with his work. He gratefully put out the lights and locked up the Barn, then crossed to the Old Stage where his father was still checking the night's take and balancing the stock ledger.

First things first, Gavin quietly climbed the stairs and peeped into Eileen's room; the bed was still made up, undisturbed from this morning; she wasn't back. Feeling his heart speeding up a little, Gavin went back downstairs and reported her absence to his father.

Burly Joe McGovern seemed scarcely concerned. 'What?' he said, squinting up from his books. 'Eileen? Out with a young man? For a drive? So what's your concern? Come on now, Gavin! I mean, she's hardly a child!'

Gavin clenched his jaws stubbornly as his father returned to his work, went through into the large private kitchen and dining room and flopped into a chair. Very well, then he would wait up for her himself. And if he heard that bloke's car bringing her back home, well he'd have a few words to say to him, too.

It was a quarter after twelve when Gavin settled himself down to wait upon Eileen's return; but his day had been long and hard, and something in the hot summer air had sapped his usually abundant energy. The evening's excitement, maybe. By the time his father went up to bed Gavin was fast asleep and locked in troubled dreams . . .

Quite some time earlier:

. . . In the warm summer nights, Lovers' Lane wasn't meant for fast walking. It was only a mile and a half long, but almost three-quarters of an hour had gone by since Eileen and her new young man had left the Barn and started along its winding ways. Lovers' Lane: no, it wasn't the sort of walk you took at the trot. It was a holding-hands, swinging-arms-together, soft-talking walk; a kissing walk, in those places where the hedges were silvered by moonlight and lips softened by it. And it seemed strange to Eileen that her escort hadn't tried to kiss her, not once along the way . . .

But he had been full of talk: not about himself but mainly the night—how much he loved the darkness, its soft velvet, which he claimed he could feel against his skin, the *aliveness* of night—and about the moon: the secrets it knew but couldn't tell. Not terribly scary stuff but . . . strange stuff. Maybe too strange. And so, whenever she had the chance, Eileen had tried to change the subject, to talk about herself. But oddly, he hadn't seemed especially interested in her.

'Oh, there'll be plenty of time to talk about personalities later,' he'd told her, and she'd noticed how his voice was no longer soft but . . . somehow coarse? And she'd shivered and thought: *Time later? Well of course there will be . . . won't there?*

And suddenly she'd been aware of the empty fields and copses opening on all sides, time fleeting by, the fact that she was out here, in Lovers' Lane, with . . . a total stranger? What was this urgency in him, she wondered? She could feel it now in the way his hand held hers almost in a vice, the coarse, jerky tension of his breathing, the way his eyes scanned the moonlit darkness ahead and to left and right, looking for . . . what?

'Well,' she finally said, trying to lighten her tone as much as she possibly could, digging her heels in a little and drawing him to a halt, 'that's it—all of it—Lovers' Lane. From here on it goes nowhere, just open fields all the way to where they're digging the new road. And anyway it's time we were getting back. You said you only had an hour.'

He held her hand more tightly yet, and his eyes were silver in the night. He took something out of his pocket and she heard a click, and the something gleamed a little in his dark hand. 'Ah, but that was then and this is now,' Garry Clemens told her, and she snatched her breath and her mouth fell open as she saw his awful smile. And then, while her mouth was still open, suddenly he *did* kiss her—and it was a brutal kiss and very terrible. And now Eileen knew.

As if reading her mind, he throatily said: 'But if you're good and do *exactly* as you're told—then you'll live through it.' And as she filled her lungs to scream, he quickly lifted his knife to her throat, and in his now choking voice whispered, 'But if you're *not* good then I'll hurt you very, very much and you won't live through it. And one way or the other it will make no difference: I shall have you anyway, for you're my girl-Friday!'

'Gordon, I—' she finally breathed, her eyes wide in the dark, heart hammering, breasts rising and falling unevenly beneath her thin summer dress. And trying again: 'Tell me this is just some sort of game, that you're only trying to frighten me and don't mean any . . . of . . . it.' But she knew only too well that he did.

Her voice had been gradually rising, growing shrill, so that now he warningly hissed: 'Be *quiet!*' And he backed her up to a stile in the fence, pressing with his knife until she was aware of it delving the soft skin of her throat. Then, very casually, he cut her thin summer dress down the front to her waist and flicked back the two halves with the point of his knife. Her free hand fluttered like a trapped bird, to match the palpitations of her heart, but she didn't dare do anything with it. And holding that sharp blade to her left breast, he said:

'Now we're going across this stile and behind the hedge, and then I'll tell you all you're to do and how best to please me. And that's important, for if you *don't* please me—well, then it will be good night, Eileen, Eileen!'

'Oh, God! *Oh, God!*' she whispered, as he forced her over the fence and behind the tall hedge. And:

'Here!' he said. 'Here!'

And from the darkness just to one side of him, another voice, not Eileen's, answered, *'Yes, here! Here!'* But it was *such* a voice . . .

'What . . . ?' Garry Clemens gulped, his hot blood suddenly ice. 'Who . . . ?' He released Eileen's hand and whirled, scything with his knife—scything nothing!—only the dark, which now seemed to close in on him. But:

'*Here,*' said that husky, hungry, lusting voice again, and now Clemens saw that indeed there was a figure in the dark. A naked female figure, voluptuous and inviting. And, '*Here!*' she murmured yet again, her voice a promise of pleasures undreamed, drawing him down with her to the soft grass.

Out of the corner of his eye, dimly in his confused mind, the rapist saw a figure—fleeting, tripping, and staggering upright, fleeing—which he knew was Eileen McGovern where she fled wildly across the field. But he let her go. For he'd found a new and more wonderful, more exciting girl-Friday now. 'Who . . . who *are* you?' he husked as he tore at his clothes—astonished that she tore at them, too.

And: '*Alaze,*' she told him, simply. '*Alaze . . .*'

Eileen—running, crashing through a low thicket, flying under the moon—wanted to scream but had no wind for it. And in the end was too frightened to scream anyway. For she knew that someone ran with her, alongside her; a lithe, naked someone, who for the moment held off from whatever was his purpose.

But for how long?

The rattle of a crate deposited on the doorstep of the Old Stage woke Gavin McGovern up from unremembered dreams, but dreams which nevertheless left him red-eyed and rumbling inside like a volcano. Angry dreams! He woke to a new day, and in a way to a new world. He went to the door and it was dawn; the sun was balanced on the eastern horizon, reaching for the sky; Dave Gorman, the local milkman, was delivering.

'Wait,' Gavin told him, and ran upstairs. A moment later and he was down again. 'Eileen's not back,' he said. 'She was at the dance last night, went off with some bloke, an outsider. He hasn't brought her back. Tell them.'

Gorman looked at him, almost said: *Tell who?* But not quite. He knew who to tell. The Athelsford Tribe.

Gavin spied the postman, George Lee, coming along the road on his early morning rounds. He gave him the same message: his sister,

Eileen, a girl of the tribe, had been abducted. She was out there some-where now, stolen away, perhaps hurt. And by the time Gavin had thrown water in his face and roused his father, the message was already being spread abroad. People were coming out of their doors, moving into the countryside around, starting to search. The tribe looked after its own . . .

And beneath the luststone:

Alaze was back, but Hengit had not returned. It was past dawn and Chylos could feel the sun warming their mighty headstone, and he won-dered what had passed in the night: was his work now done and could he rest?

'How went it?' the old wizard inquired immediately, as Alaze settled back into her bones.

'It went . . . well. To a point,' she eventually answered.

'A point? What point?' He was alarmed. 'What went wrong? Did you not follow my instructions?'

'Yes,' she sighed, 'but—'

'But?' And now it was Chylos's turn to sigh. 'Out with it.'

'I found one who was lusty. Indeed he was with a maid, which but for my intervention he would take against her will! Ah, but when he saw me he lusted after her no longer! And I heeded your instructions and put on my previous female form for him. According to those same instructions, I would teach him the true passions and furies and ecstasies of the flesh; so that afterwards and when he was with women of the tribe, he would be untiring, a satyr, and they would always bring forth from his potent seed. But because I was their inspiration, my spirit would be in all of them! This was why I put on flesh; and it was a great magic, a gigantic effort of will. Except . . . it had been a long, long time, Chylos. And in the heat of the moment I relaxed my will; no, he relaxed it for me, such was his passion. And . . . he saw me as I was, as I am . . .'

'Ah!' said Chylos, understanding what she told him. 'And after-wards? Did you not try again? Were there no others?'

'There might have been others, aye—but as I journeyed out from this *stone, the greater the distance the less obedient my will. Until I could no longer call flesh unto myself. And now, weary, I am returned.'*

Chylos sagged down into the alveolate, crumbling relics of himself. *'Then Hengit is my last hope,'* he said.

At which moment Hengit returned—but hangdog, as Chylos at once observed. And: *'Tell me the worst,'* the old man groaned.

But Hengit was unrepentant. *'I did as you instructed,'* he commenced his story, *'went forth, found a woman, put on flesh. And she was of the tribe, I'm sure. Alas, she was a child in the ways of men, a virgin, an innocent. You had said: let her be lusty, willing—but she was not. Indeed, she was afraid.'*

Chylos could scarce believe it. *'But—were there no others?'*

'Possibly,' Hengit answered. *'But this was a girl of the tribe, lost and afraid and vulnerable. I stood close by and watched over her, until the dawn . . .'*

'Then that is the very end of it,' Chylos sighed, beaten at last. And his words were truer than even he might suspect.

But still, for the moment, the luststone exerted its immemorial influence . . .

Of all the people of Athelsford who were out searching in the fields and woods that morning, it was Gavin McGovern who found the rapist Clemens huddled beneath the hedgerow. He heard his sobbing, climbed the stile, and found him there. And in the long grass close by, he also found his knife still damp with dew. And looking at Clemens the way he was, Gavin fully believed that he had lost Eileen forever.

He cried hot, unashamed tears then, looked up at the blue skies she would never see again, and blamed himself. *My fault—my fault! If I'd not been the way I was, she wouldn't have needed to defy me!*

But then he looked again at Clemens, and his surging blood surged more yet. And as Clemens had lusted after Eileen, so now Gavin lusted after him—after his life!

He dragged him out from hiding, bunched his white hair in a hamlike hand, and stretched his neck taut across his knee. Then—three things, occurring almost simultaneously.

One: a terrific explosion from across the fields, where John Sykes had kept his word and reduced the luststone to so much rubble. Two: the bloodlust went out of Gavin like a light switched off, so that he gasped, released his victim, and thrust him away. And three, he heard the voice of his father, echoing from the near-distance and carrying far and wide in the brightening air:

'Gavin, we've found her! She's unharmed! She's all right!'

PC Bennett, coming across the field, his uniformed legs damp from the dewy grass, saw the knife in Gavin's hand and said, 'I'll take that, son.' And having taken it he also went to take charge of the gibbering, worthless, soul-shrivelled maniac thing that was Garry Clemens.

And so in a way old Chylos was right, for in the end nothing had come of all his works. But in several other ways he was quite wrong . . .

THE RETURN OF THE DEEP ONES

I

THE CONCH

My prime purpose in the time which remains to me—and I have reason to believe that there may not be a great deal of that—is to chronicle the events leading up to my present untenable situation. In so doing I intend to leave a warning and an indictment against the insidious encroachment of horrors previously undreamed of. Without a doubt the veracity of the facts I shall present will be questioned, but of one thing I am certain: that if ever the whole truth of the matter is known, Man will never again pretend to occupy his much-vaunted role as 'Master of His Own Destiny!' *He is not!*—and has he ever been?

I now find myself questioning the fundamental laws of space and time—those oh-so-long-accepted concepts of cosmogony, of heredity, and of all matters anthropological—yes, and the very basis of human existence itself. Yet the start of it all seemed so very innocuous. I look back on it now, and—

But it were best that I begin at the very beginning . . .

———

Some few short weeks ago in the late spring, I received via airmail package from America a fairly large, unusual, especially attractive conch. The shell, carefully wrapped against any possible breakage, was as big as my two fists together. It had an almost circular aperture of about two inches in diameter, and its reddish colour and spiked, tightly coiled whorl gave it the appearance almost of a huge, venomous insect. Of course, when I call the shell 'attractive,' I speak as a man who once found in all seashells the entire spectrum of Nature's beauty epitomized. In retrospect, I suppose others might well have found the shell quite repulsive.

My hitherto unknown benefactor gave an address in Innsmouth, a coastal town in America's New England, and he had penned a brief letter of introduction:

> Dear Mr Vollister,
> Please forgive this unsolicited intrusion, but having read your recent articles in *Oceans,* I know you to be a conchologist of note and a well-known marine biologist. To show my appreciation of your work (I myself was always deeply interested in conchology but never had a professional's aptitude for the work), I herewith enclose a conch from local waters. I am told that the shell is not at all common on your own Atlantic coastline, and since this is an especially beautiful specimen I thought you might like to own it. In the event of your already having one in your collection, then please forgive the frivolous impulse which alone prompted me to do this and accept the shell anyway as a token of my admiration.
>
> Yours very sincerely
William P. Marsh

To say that I was delighted with this completely unexpected gift would be to understate my feelings severely. And as for Mr Marsh's comment about the relative scarcity of his shell on my side of the Atlantic: that, too, was an understatement of no small magnitude.

While I am fairly conversant with all manner of conches on a world-wide scale, my particular speciality concerns those molluscs indigenous to British waters. I could therefore state with some certainty that no such shell was ever taken from the sea off Britain's coast, and I had not previously known of its existence on any coast! The thing was completely new to me; in all my wide experience I had never before come across its like.

To complicate matters and astound me even further, after my initial surprise had worn off and when I sat down to study the shell in greater detail, I discovered one more fact whose singularity would normally have been immediately apparent to me: namely that the shell was sinistral. Looked at from the pointed end, its spiral wound anti-clockwise, towards the left. I knew of only half a dozen shells like this in the whole world, all in private collections and all, in the eyes of their owners, quite priceless.

In short, this shell appeared quite unique; but despite its sinistrality I saw nothing actually 'sinister' about it. Not then.

It was not long, however, before I came to realize that the new conch had somehow . . . changed things? Yes, I think that is perhaps the best way to put it: to say that the shell had wrought a change in me, in my perceptions. And the first manifestation of the change took place that very night.

I live alone, have done so since my wife died of cancer four years ago, and since then my lovely home has always seemed an extremely sparse and lonely place. Yet that night it was different. There seemed to be an almost tangible *presence* in the house, the feeling of a not entirely sympathetic audience to my every move and mood, so that for the first time in longer than I cared to think I felt not at all alone.

The sensation was in no way ghostly, and I certainly did not feel threatened, but at the same time I found it difficult to concentrate on my reading, and twice I actually found myself looking over my shoulder at some imagined sound or motion or whatever behind me. On both occasions my eyes turned to the new conch where I had carefully set it down upon an occasional table.

Before retiring, I wrote a letter to a friend of mine in London. He owned a marvellous collection of shells containing many thousands of specimens, and while his overall knowledge of the sciences of the seas was limited, his specialized knowledge of conches—from the shapes, colours, and sizes, to the waters in which they lived, bred, and died— was almost inexhaustible. He was perhaps the world's foremost conchologist, and therefore probably the most reliable authority. In my letter I gave a detailed description of my latest acquisition, even to the point of doing a fairly accurate sketch of the thing, and asked for information. I made no mention of its origin.

After writing the letter, suddenly tired, I poured myself my customary nightcap and went to stand on the balcony for a few minutes. I watched the sea at low tide, calm and distant, while the moon silvered the sands below the house. Soon, beginning to feel the coolness of the night breeze off the sea, I locked the balcony's windows and went to bed.

I fell asleep almost immediately and began to dream, and my dreams that night were curiously void of visions or scenes and consisted instead of sounds. But such sounds!

They began with the mildest of susurrations: the sounds of small waves breaking on a rough and rocky shore somewhere at the edge of the world. And the sound was so pure, so innocent, that I knew—the way one always 'knows' in dreams—that these were the first waves and this the first shore, the shore of a primal ocean formed of a billion years of rain, that first great rain which filled in the rocky basins of the young Earth to lie volcanically warm through all the years of the pre-Cambrian age, warm yet empty of life, sterile and dead, awaiting Nature's great awakening.

Then the watery sounds grew louder and I envisioned the primal moon—a rough sphere of partly plastic rock, alive with its own volcanic activity—wobbling uncertainly in an as yet eccentric orbit, gradually taming the tides of Earth's mighty oceans in which, at last, the first life-forms swam and spurted, or walked on jointed chitinous limbs. And the tides came and went for a quarter-billion years as gradually the ocean's sounds grew louder, until it seemed I could hear the cries of her denizens, forever locked in the eternal battle for life, for existence, in vast and mildly salty vaults of Ocean.

And always in the background, in my inner ear, there was a less certain sound, one that I sensed rather than heard, the impossible sound of sentience—of *intelligence*—however alien, in a world where the first dinosaurs had yet to emerge from the steaming fens of the Carboniferous.

But now, building rapidly from the surging sounds of tumultuous tides, there came the crash and roar of massive waves and the howling of ocean tempests. I heard the sundering of mighty volcanic cliffs as the raging sea brought them avalanching down, and the cries of great winged reptiles buffeted by winds that whipped imagined wave-crests to a white and frothing frenzy.

And behind all of this strange voices cried out in concerted . . . prayers? Prayers, yes, but to no God of Earth. This I knew, and knew also that these worshippers, whoever—whatever—they were, had pre-dated Man in this world we call our own.

Then those strangely familiar voices receded, were swept away in a resurgence of the crazed rushing and roaring, until it seemed that I myself struggled and gyrated in pounding surf and roiling whirlpools. And at last, dizzy and overwhelmed by these awesome sounds and sensations, I started awake.

Or, rather, I *seemed* to wake up. My uncertainty stems from the fact that later I was made to believe that I could not possibly have awakened. Let me explain:

I have said that I started awake. Outside, the storm raged and I could plainly hear the surf on the cliffs. My first thoughts, however dull and heavy those thoughts were, involved getting up to check the windows and doors. Then I remembered having done so the night before. A glance at my watch showed me that the time was 2.15 A.M. I put my head back on to the pillows and listened for a while to the howling of the wind and the rush of water; and finally I drifted back into a sleep which, apart from very vague and fantastic impressions of limitless deeps and weed-festooned submarine cities and shrines, was restful and trouble-free.

In the morning, with the sun blazing through my bedroom window as it climbed, already midway to the zenith, I awakened, remembered the night's storm and, clad in my dressing-gown, went through into my study and out on to the balcony. The sea was as calm as when last I saw it; the beach at the foot of the cliffs was not strewn with the driftwood and debris I had expected; there was no evidence at all to support my storm's existence!

But there *had* been a storm, surely . . . ?

I was at the door for the delivery of the morning newspaper and I casually mentioned how fresh the world looked after the storm. The youth from the village news agent's shop, Graham Lane, answered:

'What, last night, Mr Vollister?' He grinned. 'You must have been dreaming, sir. No storm last night . . .'

'About two in the morning?' I persisted, frowning. 'Certainly between two and three. Wind howling and the sea in an uproar?'

He yawned and shook his head. 'Not last night. I was walking with my girl on the beach until two-thirty. Beautiful night.'

Suddenly I knew that he was right, and I immediately changed the subject. 'On the beach until two-thirty, Graham? With a girl? Is it that serious, then?'

He laughed. 'The big day's in September,' he said. 'Would you like an invitation?'

'By all means! I'd be delighted,' I answered, and again changed the subject: 'How's Old Man Lane keeping?'

'Not too good. The shop's been too much for him for years now. Once I'm wed I think he'll take a back seat and let me run the business.'

—And we chatted for a minute or two longer before I gave him my letter to post and let him take himself off on his bicycle. But I wasn't really concentrating on the conversation; I was trying to work out what had happened. This was something entirely outside my experience. For, after all, a dream is a dream and should in no way have supernatural complications. Dreams do not carry over into the waking world—or should not—or at least mine never had. Not until now. In the end, I simply shrugged it off with a weak and rather bewildered laugh.

Then, distractedly, though my heart was hardly in it, I scanned the newspaper and read the one or two items of interest. Afterwards I washed and dressed, made breakfast, and finally went back into the study where the strange new shell awaited my attention. I picked the thing up and thoughtfully admired it, mentally attempting a comparison with other specimens in my own large collection. In its shape it was not unlike the Sicilian *Spondylus gussoni*, though of course it was many times larger than that common shell. I was completely baffled.

I took down several books on conchology from their shelves and made a most diligent search, thinking that perhaps in all the hours I had previously spent researching those very books, somehow I might have missed or forgotten or simply skipped over the New England shell. But no, the thing was given no mention, not even in my most comprehensive works. It was, it must be, a hitherto unknown species. But if this were so, then why had my American benefactor seen fit to pretend that it was fairly common? And why had he sent it to me?

I carefully composed a letter to Mr Marsh at his Innsmouth address, then spent half an hour on the telephone talking with a friend of mine in one of the larger reference libraries in London. If my own books weren't comprehensive enough, then it was perfectly obvious that the library in nearby Newquay wouldn't be able to offer much. London should have been a different matter entirely. But that as it may be, my efforts once more proved fruitless; the conch I described was nowhere to be found on record.

That afternoon I took my daily walk in the village, posted my letter to Mr Marsh, purchased one or two household items, and finally headed for home again. I had an article to finish, and worked at it for an hour or so before retiring early. Slightly apprehensive though I was about sleeping (the thought had come to me from somewhere that my problem—if indeed I had a problem—was most likely tied up with my subconscious, my sleeping mind), I nevertheless passed a completely undisturbed night and, following a light breakfast, went back to work on my manuscript.

And so life went on, once more mundane and tranquil enough, for two more days and nights until the weekend came around. By that time, while my new shell remained as enigmatic and unknowable as ever, the

edge of its mystery had become dulled for me, particularly since receiving from Ian Carling, my great conchologist colleague, a telephone call
which, while his excitement at my news was amply apparent, left me
just as unenlightened as before. He did mention, though, that he had
spoken of my discovery to a friend of his, 'a queer sort of chap but
likable enough in his own way,' who had said he might contact me. At
Ian's request I made a mental note to obtain photographs of the shell
and get them off to him as soon as possible.

But then, just before noon, when I had barely started upon the final
revision of my manuscript, my telephone rang again . . . and continued
to ring insistently, so that I was obliged to leave my work to answer it.
The caller introduced himself as one David Semple, of Mayfair in London, and he was that friend whom Ian Carling had mentioned.

'Any friend of Ian's is a friend of mine, Mr Semple. What can I do
for you?'

'David—please call me David,' he insisted. 'And it's more what I
can do for you, I think.'

'Oh?'

'Yes. Ian has mentioned this queer shell of yours, and I think I
might be able to throw some light on it.'

'You're a conchologist then, Mr, er, David?'

'No, no—but I am a collector.'

'Of shells?'

'Of books!'

'Books?'

'Indeed, Mr Vollister—or should I call you John?'

'Please do.'

'Good . . . Yes, I collect books. Old and new—first editions and
modern reprints, priceless antiques and worthless, poorly-printed pa-
perbacks. But they all have one thing in common. You see, John, I've
had a lifelong interest in the macabre, the weird, the strange, the occult!'

'Well, that's all very interesting, er, David, but I fail to see—'

'Wait, wait! About this shell of yours—let me read something to
you. One moment. Ah, here we are:

' "Even as big as a small child's head, the seashell is thickish and bears sharp spines ringed about its coils. Its mouth is not much smaller than the mouth of a man, and indeed it has the look of some animal's mouth. Reddish in hue, the shell has not a wholesome aspect, but the snail itself is as a delicacy to the tainted palates of the Deep Ones. Yet they crop the slug with care, for under their direction vast colonies of the creatures layer the pearly and subaqueous houses and temples of their cities! Thus were the mighty Pacific temples beautified in the great deeps about R'lyeh, and even Y'ha-Nthlei's columns and colossi are cemented with the grey-green nacre of the shellfish's mantle . . ." '

The voice at the other end of the line paused, then: 'Well?'

'Well, I suppose it could be my shell,' I told him, 'but where on earth did you find that passage you just read to me? It sounded extremely old—not to mention very weird!'

'Yes, it's over two hundred years old: an English translation of a passage from an even older German work, the rather ugly *Untersee Kulten* of Graf Grauberg. And there are illustrations, too—rather crude, I fear, but adequate. So that if this is your shell, why, you should easily manage to match the drawings against the real thing.'

'I'd like to see that book,' I said at once, trying but not quite managing to keep the eagerness out of my voice.

'But that's why I'm calling you,' he answered. 'It so happens I'm to be in your area for a few days early next week—some business to attend to, you know—and I thought we might meet.'

'Why, certainly: I look forward to it. You might like to stay here at the house?'

'Thank you—very hospitable—but no. I'm a founder-member of a boating club not far from Newquay. I shall stay there and not put you to any trouble. Now then, if you'll tell me when we can meet . . . ?'

'Why, any time—but can't you tell me more about the book right now? Perhaps I could obtain a copy, and—'

'Obtain a copy of the *Cthaat Aquadingen*?' He laughed. 'No, I don't think you could, John. It's one of those books—like Gantley's *Hydrophinnae* and Gaston le Fe's *Dwellers in the Depths*—which are very seldom found. Banned or burned, mostly, many years ago. Forbidden volumes, 'black books,' they're called: like the *Necronomicon* of Abdul

Alhazred, and Von Junzt's *Nameless Cults*. But we'll talk a lot more next week.'

'Fine. I'm home all week. I usually take a walk in the afternoon along the beach or in the town, but you can get me at home most of the time. Just give me a ring . . .'

'Oh, don't worry, John,' he told me, sounding suddenly strange and distant. 'I'll be in touch with you . . .' And with that he was gone.

Sunday and Monday passed very slowly. My interest in the new shell had waxed, waned a little, and was now redoubled. I would find myself pacing the floor of my study with the thing in my hands, quite without realizing that I had picked it up at all. I could not wait for Mr Semple's call. Then, Tuesday afternoon . . .

I walked along the clifftop path towards the precipitous wooden stairway that led down to the beach. There, sitting on the grass at the very edge of the cliff, a girl gazed out across the sea, her legs dangling in space one hundred and twenty feet above needle rocks, her chin cupped in her hands. She wore jeans, an oversized sweater of a towelling material, and her hair was tied back with a silken green handkerchief. Beside her on the grass lay a yellow crash-helmet with a jaunty peak; the sort young ladies wear when riding or being carried on scooters and motorcycles.

I do not much care for heights and always feel uncomfortable when others treat them with contempt. I paused, keeping well back from the rim, and called: 'Miss? Excuse me? Er—could I talk to you?'

She turned and smiled—a peculiar sort of smile, I thought—then swung her legs up and rolled clear of the edge. Picking up her crash-helmet, she climbed easily to her feet. She was no more than twenty-two, twenty-three at the outside, but there was in her face something that hinted of a rare intelligence, a wisdom belying her years. Her features were almost elfinlike, large-eyed and small-chinned, and her hair was so black and so reflected the green of the handkerchief that it seemed almost green itself, even pearly in its gloss.

She approached me with her head on one side, still half-smiling. 'Yes?'

'I'm sorry, er, Miss. Heights affect me badly. I just wanted to get you away from the edge of the cliff. Please forgive me.'

'Don't let it worry you,' she answered in an accent, however slight, which immediately gave her away for an American. 'I was just about to go down to the beach anyhow. Are you going down?'

'Yes, I am.'

'Well, would you mind if I walked with you?'

'Not at all, I—'

'It's just that the beach looks so lonely.'

'I know what you mean.'

We said no more until the wooden steps were behind us and the cliffs towered above. On the way down, she had gone before me, and I admit that I found myself attracted by her lithe, jean-clad form. Reaching the bottom first, she had turned to smile at me again, half-knowingly, I thought. But knowing what? Her look, it dawned on me, was not at all one of wide-eyed innocence. Then she laughed at my own serious expression, asking:

'You're sure you don't mind me walking with you?'

'Er, no. I mean, I'm sure!'

'You look so worried!' She laughed. She linked arms with me and we walked down towards the sea, turning north towards the village when we reached the high-water mark.

'Big, isn't it?' she said, holding my arm tightly.

'Hm? The sea? Yes, it's big.'

'My home,' she said, 'is—let's see—way over there!' She squinted out over the flat grey sea, pointing a finger west and slightly south.

'North America,' I said. 'New York, perhaps?'

'Close enough, I suppose. What's in a few hundred miles?' Then her hand flew to her mouth in mock alarm. 'There I go, giving away all of my secrets.'

'Secrets?'

'A girl with no secrets has no mystery . . . ' Then she quickly changed the subject. 'Do you swim?'

'I do. I swim very well. But the sea is still quite cold. You won't find many bathers for a month or so yet.'

'Let's swim,' she answered impulsively.

'But—what about costumes?'

At that, she laughed—as earthy a laugh as ever I heard—and began to pull her sweater up over her head. Embarrassed, I half-turned away, anxiously searching the beach with my eyes but seeing no one. Out of the corner of my eye I saw her stepping out of her jeans, and again I averted my gaze. But her laughter was wholly free and fresh, so that when I heard her feet flying seaward I turned to stare after her . . .

And then I, too, had to laugh. Her bikini, tiny though it was, was most certainly decent. Obviously she had worn it beneath her clothes; and equally obvious was the fact that she had deliberately set out to embarrass me! Oddly enough, I didn't mind at all.

She ran into the calm sea and swam maybe fifty yards out. There she played, splashed, and shouted, occasionally diving beneath the surface and staying down for what I thought to be inordinately long periods. Using my watch, I timed her on her last dive and found that she stayed down for well over two minutes; the girl swam like a fish! And yet I was in no way astonished by her performance. I myself have always found swimming a delight, and my own capacity for remaining underwater for long periods has often surprised my friends. I believed it to be simply a matter of willpower.

A few minutes later she came out of the water and ran up the beach to me. She sat at my feet where I myself sat on a flat stone and handed me her sweater of soft towelling.

'Dry my back,' she commanded, turning her back to me and letting her hair fall forward over her shoulders. However cold she felt—and indeed her skin was cold—she hardly showed it; not a goose-bump showed on her pale skin and her breathing seemed perfectly controlled. Despite the fact that I was at least fifteen to twenty years her senior (or then again, perhaps because of it), I fancied that my heart beat a little faster as I patted her back dry and gave her back her sweater.

Later, as we continued our walk along the beach and climbed the crumbling sea wall to the promenade and so into the village, she told me her name. She was Sarah Bishop, an American of an old New England family, on holiday ('vacation,' she said) with her father. They would be in England for some weeks yet while her father sorted out various property matters. Having several relatives living in Cornwall, the old gentleman—he was sixty-seven—was thinking of retiring there. When I asked where she and her father were staying, she told me they had rooms at a boat club between the village and Newquay.

At this I was reminded of what David Semple had told me when I invited him to stay at my house: that he was a 'founder-member of a boating club not far from Newquay.' I wondered if his club—presumably some exclusive sort of place for rich yachtsmen and such—could be one and the same with Sarah's, and I was on the point of questioning her about the place when we reached the village police station.

There, as if I no longer existed—or as if she had never heard of the word 'good-bye'—she turned her back on me, put on her crash-helmet, unlocked the anti-thief device on a motor-scooter which was parked at the kerb, and kicked the engine into life. As she guided the scooter into the road I was moved to call out:

'We may meet again . . . ?' And having said it, I felt unaccountably foolish.

She looked back over her shoulder and smiled that strange smile of hers. 'Oh, we surely will,' she said. 'Of course we will!' Then, in a clatter of tiny pistons, she was gone. She left behind a dispersing cloud of blue exhaust smoke.

Walking home again along the beach, I found my mind wandering. I was miles away, almost completely unaware of the passage of time or distance, and it actually came as a surprise when I found myself at the top of the wooden stairway that led to my clifftop retreat. Daydreaming, my mind had been on many things—but chiefly on the girl. She evoked something in me; a memory that seemed much more than mere memory, really; a feeling of . . . déjà vu?

Her skin, for instance. When I had dried her, I had noticed a peculiar film to it, a sort of mild oiliness, but the feeling had not been at all unpleasant. Remembering, my fingers tingled slightly. It dawned on me that I had not felt this way for . . . for a very long time.

II

THE PLACE ON THE BEACH

That night I worked until very late and retired well after midnight. I slept until mid-morning, ate a small breakfast, and was no sooner dressed than I became aware of a visitor. I heard a car approaching the house and went out on the balcony in time to see it draw to a halt below. When the driver got out, I hailed him from where I stood at the balcony rail:

'Hello, there! Can I help?'

'I'm David Semple,' came the reply. 'Have I come to the right place?'

'You certainly have. Wait just a moment and I'll be down.'

The house is built to my own specifications, with bedrooms, study, and bathroom upstairs; kitchen, small library, storage space, and garage downstairs. Since I never did learn how to drive, the garage long ago became just another storage room.

I hurried downstairs and unlocked the front door. Semple grasped my hand as soon as I appeared. His handshake was firm enough, though cool and moist. I welcomed him in and saw him upstairs and into my study; and there, as unobtrusively as I might while pouring drinks, I carefully scrutinized him.

He was slim, rather pale, and I would have guessed that he wore a toupee. His skin was uncommonly rough and seemed large-pored. His walk was almost that of a sailor; and why not, since on his own word he was a founder-member of his boating club? For no justifiable reason, I found myself disliking him. There was something odd about him, something I could not quite pin down, insubstantial, but something which nevertheless set my teeth on edge.

No sooner had Semple made himself comfortable than he spotted the conch where it lay upon the occasional table. 'Ah!' he exclaimed.

'Yes, most certainly!' He crossed the room and picked up the object of his interest. 'Without a doubt this is the shell—the shell from the book!'

'You're absolutely sure?'

'As sure as I can be without actually having the book here with me to make a positive comparison.'

'You didn't bring it?' My voice showed my disappointment.

'No, I'm sorry. Fool that I am, I left it at the club. But we can have a look at it later . . .'

By now, however, and despite my consuming interest in his subject, I had taken the opportunity of studying my visitor more closely. In so doing I had discovered several more peculiar idiosyncrasies none of which, however petty they might seem normally, had improved my liking for the man.

There was, for instance, an odd gasping quality in his voice, a suggestion of fighting for air that made me wonder if perhaps he was asthmatic. But if so, why did he wear his silken scarf so high on his neck and so well wrapped about his throat? Indeed, why wear a scarf at all on this unusually warm day? Also, now that we were together in the close confines of my study, I found myself very nearly offended by the heavy odour of his aftershave—if that was what it was—and even more disturbed by an underlying smell of . . . of what?

Perhaps the sun was at fault, warming the beach to send the taint of rotting seaweed wafting up to my balcony. But the balcony doors were closed, and what slight breeze there was came off the land . . .

I was aware suddenly of his strange gaze. He was looking at me most oddly, eyes large and round behind modern, heavy-rimmed spectacles—and it was a look which, inexplicable as my feelings were, chilled and quickly unnerved me.

I half started to my feet, causing him quickly to enquire: 'Is there . . . something?'

'Do forgive me,' I fumbled. 'It's the room—so stuffy—forgive me for bringing you into an unaired room—I worked late last night.'

'My goodness! Don't concern yourself,' he answered at once. 'I'm perfectly comfortable.'

'I'll open the French windows anyway,' I said, getting hold of myself at last.

'Please do, if it will make you happy. Probably a good idea. I should hate to pass on to you my cold and sore throat.'

So that was it, and doubtless the smell I had noticed was an embrocation of some sort or other. Nevertheless, my initial dislike for Semple remained. Still, he was not here for my approval but to offer his assistance. For that, at least, I should be grateful. I decided to put my unnatural apprehensions behind me and try to be as pleasant as I could in Semple's presence.

'How did you find your way to the house, er, David? It's not the easiest place to find, and the road between here and the main road is barely a track.'

'Oh, I—' He looked momentarily lost for words, then quickly went on: 'I obtained directions in the village. Of course, I don't know the locals, but they seemed to know you well enough.'

'Yes, they do, though I suppose I must seem a bit reclusive to them.'

'This is an excellent whisky,' he said after a while, changing the subject.

'Thank you. I pamper myself a little. But I've been thinking, David, what an odd coincidence this is.'

'Coincidence?' he sounded wary.

'Yes. That this ridiculous enigma of a seashell came into my possession in the first place, and that you should then find reference to it in some strange old book. Even better—that we should discover two facets of the same mystery and bring them together through a mutual friend. That in itself seems something of a coincidence.'

'I suppose so,' he said after a moment, again favouring me with that weird look. 'But listen—you can't possibly have had lunch yet— why not come back with me to the club? We can eat there and you can look at my books to your heart's content.'

'Books?'

'Oh, yes. I brought more than just the one. Well, what do you say? Later I'll drive you back here.'

I agreed to his suggestion without further discussion, and not entirely because of my interest in the American shell. Sarah Bishop had been in the back of my mind since last I had seen her riding off on her motor-scooter. If Sarah and her father were staying at Semple's club, then perhaps I would meet her again this very day, and—

—But in any case, she was very much secondary to my obsession with tracking down the new shell (or so I told myself). This might be my last chance to discover whether or not the conch was indeed a brand-new species, hitherto unknown to science—though apparently, if Semple were correct, it had not been unknown to the author or authors of his book.

I wanted to change into more suitable clothing, but Semple said that was completely unnecessary. No one at the club worried greatly about dress. Comfort was thought to be more desirable; and in any case I was already perfectly well attired. I consented to remain just as I was, and we went down to the car.

During the journey, which took little more than twenty-five minutes, we remained for the most part silent. Semple concentrated on the road and I cradled the shell in my lap and eagerly looked forward to reading of the thing and seeing its representation in his book. For the first half-mile the ride was bumpy and slow, but then we turned left on to the main road and the car shot forward. We passed through the village in a matter of minutes and several miles later turned left again on to a third-class road or track that led seaward, toward shrub and bramble-grown cliff-tops.

Where human habitation was concerned, this area of the coast was only very sparsely settled; one or two farms, yes, but not even a hamlet outside of Seaham, 'the village,' as I have always referred to it. The next town of any size or importance was Newquay, half an hour's drive up the coast. If privacy were a prerequisite, then this must surely be the perfect place for an exclusive club. The coast was very wild, however, and so for a place of any size to be built a large amount of money would have to be spent. Well, there were still plenty of people who could afford that sort of money.

Soon, tall shrubs and tangled undergrowth sprang up to border the track. Semple drove carefully through this shaded region for a hundred yards or more, over a rise and then down to where the horizon showed a mating of sea and sky. There, where shrubs, trees, and brambles had been cleared away to allow gravel to be laid, he turned under a large, low, open-fronted structure to park alongside a dozen or more cars of various makes. Several were of the large American variety, one of which was just pulling away.

Turning in my seat to stare after the car as it drove off, I caught a glimpse of dark, lumpish figures with pale faces in the passenger seats. Strangely round eyes peered back at me for a split second, then were gone. What it was about those faces I couldn't say, but at the sight of them—the merest glimpse—it was as if someone walked over my grave . . .

We left the car and walked to the edge of the cliffs. Below us, like a bite taken out of the coastline, a small bay enclosed a crescent-shaped beach. One of the rocky bay arms had been extended to form a jetty and breakwater that curved inward and protected the calm waters of the tiny bay. A variety of boats—even a small, very expensive-looking yacht—were moored in the bay, though there appeared to be little sign of life. The patio which fronted the club itself was deserted.

Right where we stood, the cliffs had tumbled down years ago, leaving massive blocks of stone that formed an uneven and precipitous slope down to grassy banks, but the debris of the fallen cliff was grassed over now and trees and shrubs had sprung up along the length of the fault. A wide wooden stairway with a handrail fell steeply from our position, losing itself in the trees, becoming visible again at the bottom. There it merged with a path of concrete paving-slabs which in turn led to the club sprawling on the beach.

The clubhouse seemed deserted to me, and as Semple and I descended the stairway I examined the place whenever I sighted it between the trees. Grey and blue, it was of modern design and spacious. Its front was raised up on piles driven deep into the bed of a kidney-shaped depression scooped out of the beach well above the tideline; its sides and rear area were shaded by fangs of rock weathered from the cliffs, and by trees grown in the lee of those same jagged boulders. It looked for all the world like the retreat of some retired and reclusive tycoon rather than any sort of boating club I had ever seen before.

We entered the building by a side door that opened into a small lounge or reception area. Across the room was a moderately stocked bar, but no one seemed to be in attendance. A frosted glass door to our right led out on to the raised patio in front of the club. It would be pleasant, I thought, to sit out there in the summer when the tide was in. An iced drink, sunglasses, the cool breeze off the sea . . .

Semple's voice brought me back down to earth:

'My room is this way—'

We passed through a swing door to our left into a long corridor. Passing us on his way to the room we had just left, a tall, bent, peculiarly vacant-looking man of indeterminate years smiled emotionlessly at Semple, enquiring in a rough, guttural, and most unappetizing voice: 'Can I get you a drink, sir? And your friend?'

'Thank you, Sargent, yes. Whisky, I think?' Semple looked to me for my approval.

I nodded, 'Yes, that'll do fine.'

'A bottle, Sargent,' said Semple, 'and two glasses. Oh, yes—and some crushed ice.'

'Your room, sir? Or the club room?'

'My room, Sargent. Oh, and you'd better book Mr Vollister in for lunch.' He turned to me. 'It's fish today. Very good!'

Shambling by us, the man called Sargent mumbled something about only being a moment or two, then he passed out of sight through the swing door.

'This way,' said Semple, leading me down the corridor.

I was struck by the gloominess of the place. Very little light entered from outside. While the furnishings seemed sumptuous enough, still there was an aura of mustiness about them, of an unpleasant dampness. Perhaps the club was a little too close to the sea after all, or maybe the central heating was out of order. There must, of course, have been central heating . . .

Doors were set at regular intervals along the inside wall of the corridor. Reaching the last of these, Semple took out a key and opened it. He ushered me into the small room beyond, saying: 'Make yourself comfortable, John. I'll be but a moment.'

He went out, turning right into the corridor and leaving the door ajar. Out of completely uncharacteristic, almost morbid curiosity, I peered out into the corridor after him in time to see him disappearing through a second swing door at the corridor's end. As the door swung behind him, a muted babble of voices came back to me—secretive voices, I thought—from what must have been the club room. Then the door swung quietly shut, deadening all but the merest murmur of conversation. Since I could make out no single word, I moved back into Semple's room.

A moment or two after I had seated myself in an easy chair, Sargent knocked and entered. He carried a tray with bottle, glasses, and a small silver bucket full of ice. After muttering something that I found completely incoherent, in answer to which I could merely smile and nod, he left and I was able to have a look around Semple's room.

The atmosphere actually was gloomy, so much so that I put on the light, a tiny shaded bulb in the centre of the ceiling, the better to see by. The room was as small as I would expect a guestroom in a place such as this to be, with a single bed along one wall, a small table of Eastern design near the head of the bed, the easy chair in which I sat, a linen basket, a narrow cupboard, one small desk, and a straight-backed chair. Also, along the wall opposite the bed, was a three-tier bookshelf.

All disquieting thoughts and doubts, however dimly formulated, were immediately crowded to the back of my mind. I stood up and went to the bookshelf. There, among many titles previously unheard of, were several that Semple had mentioned when first he contacted me: such books as the *Cthaat Aquadingen*, Gantley's *Hydrophinnae*, and Gaston le Fe's *Dweller in the Depths*. But among the others new to me were volumes whose very titles seemed disturbing, conjuring up vague memories or pseudo-memories of youthful nightmares. I mean titles like the *Book of Dzyan*, and the *Dhol Chants*, the *Liber Ivoris*, and the *R'lyeh Text*. Volumes such as these, despite the fact that as yet I knew nothing at all about them, cast ominous shadows over my mind; and the peculiar aura that I had felt from the first in this decidedly odd building seemed to thicken, closing in upon me as I stood, wrapt in the contemplation of Semple's 'library.'

Finally, I took down one of the books—at which the door swung open behind me and my host's voice said:

'Ah, yes! The *Cthaat Aquadingen*—of the great deeps and the dark demons that inhabit them. Yes, and the spells with which to raise these demons—among other things! You are correct, John, that's the book with the description and drawing of your shell. Would you like to make a comparison now?'

He took the book from me, opened it, and began to search the pages. I picked up the New England conch from where I had laid it, and Semple indicated that I should sit at the desk. He sat beside me at the head of the bed, saying:

'All of my books deal with the weird, John—at least, with subjects considered weird by the unenlightened—and that's why I was so inter-ested in your shell. If I'm right, well, it will have been interesting to track down an actual specimen from a book considered by most to be nothing but a pack of esoteric fables, lies, and fairy stories. Ah! Here we are. Now, then, what do you think of that?'

He placed the book on the desk before me so that I could study the faded text and drawing on the chosen page. And without a doubt it was a drawing of my shell!

Holding the conch, I turned it until its angle was that at which the artist had drawn it, and it was the very duplicate of the shell on the printed page. The inks with which the drawing had been tinted were just as faded as the text, but even so the colours came through, helping in positive identification.

In a way, I was disappointed (that the shell was not the unique thing I had thought it, not even in its sinistrality, for the drawing was left-handed, too), but at the same time I found myself fascinated by the text. 'This is the section you read out to me over the telephone,' I said. And out loud I repeated: ' "Reddish in hue, the shell has not a whole-some aspect, but the snail itself is as a delicacy to the tainted palates of the Deep Ones." '

'Tainted, indeed!' Semple cut in, his voice slurred and deeper in pitch, it seemed to me in indignation or anger. 'Everything they don't understand has to be tainted. Man eats birds and beasts, aye, and shell-fish, too, but when it suits him he talks of the palates of others as being "tainted"!'

I was taken aback by the fervour in Semple's voice—by that and by his completely inexplicable outburst—and I turned to him to dis-cover what had prompted it. His eyes, large and round behind the lenses of his spectacles, stared fixedly at the open book with a look of . . . of outrage? But why? Then, seeing my look of astonishment, he immedi-ately pulled himself together.

'Forgive me, John. There are things you don't understand . . . yet.' Then he changed the subject completely: 'But listen: there's lots of time for you to look at this book—and the other books, too, if you wish—but let's first have a drink, yes?' He generously poured whisky over ice. 'Oh, and there's a young lady staying at the club who tells me she knows you. She and her father are engaged upon a project here which might interest you. And then there is our little collection—'

'Collection?' I sipped at my drink, pleased with its clean, familiar taste in this unfamiliar place.

'Oh, yes, very interesting. Several of our members are divers—that is to say they explore the ocean floor in one way or another—and they allow us to enhance the club with their finds.'

'Their finds?'

'Yes, they are displayed here. Fascinating! But why waste time talk-ing about what you may see for yourself? If you'll follow me, John?'

I finished my drink and went with him.

We turned right into the corridor and through the swing door into what I had taken to be the club room. If it was, then it doubled for a dining-room, for Sargent and two others were busy arranging chairs at a long table set for lunch. I followed Semple straight across this room to a third swing door. Passing through this and holding it open for me, he said:

'This is our display room. I'm sure you'll find it utterly engross-ing . . .'

And how right Semple was—and what an understatement.

Here and there about this fairly large room, which was at the land-side extreme of the building, were scattered easy chairs and divans, but all around the walls and displayed upon specially constructed room dividers similar to deep bookshelves were the very treasures of the oceans. Actual treasures: French, Spanish, and even Roman coins of gold—small bars of gold and silver, encrusted, discoloured, and welded together by action of the salts of the sea—amphorae and pottery which any museum in the world would be proud to display, alongside ancient bottles whose colours, shapes, and designs made them the very rarest of antiques.

And then there were models of ocean-going vessels of the early nineteenth century, of sailing ships large and small—vessels such as the barque *Sumatra Queen* and the brig *Hetty*, of which a brass plate on the base of their display cabinet gave details and a brief history—all constructed with loving care and in painstaking detail. I glanced at the brass plate for a moment longer, for something about it had caught my eye; but then, beckoned by Semple, I moved on.

'Come, John,' he said. 'I believe that's Mr Bishop over there, Sarah's father. Since you know her, I'm sure you'd like to meet him.'

At the far side of the room, hidden until now by ceiling-high display cabinets, seated at a large, heavy table and studying a number of fantastic models, a tiny hunched old man seemed quite oblivious to our presence. As we approached him, Semple cleared his throat.

'Ah—Mr Bishop?' The figure at the table turned, and Semple nodded a quick, respectful greeting. 'Mr Bishop, allow me to introduce John Vollister. This is the gentleman of whom Sarah has spoken. The, er, conchologist.'

'How do you do, sir?' I held out my hand.

The shrunken figure at the table made no attempt to stand; neither did he offer his hand, nor did he answer me immediately. Instead, he looked at me, and I in turn stared at him. I stared, yes, and yet was not conscious of the rudeness of my act, for this old man was indeed something at which anyone caught unawares might reasonably be expected to stare.

He wore what appeared to be a high-collared, yellow silk dressing-gown, buttoned up under the jaw, ancient pince-nez spectacles behind which eyes as big and bigger than Semple's stared fixedly, and a flesh-coloured skullcap which smoothly covered his scalp and ears. For a full minute the great eyes gazed into mine, then that small head turned and offered Semple the slightest of nods—a nod of approval, I thought—and finally Mr Bishop spoke:

'I hope you are well, Mr Vollister?' His lips, which were pale, thick, and fleshy, barely moved. His words, which came as the merest whisper, were yet harsh, as if forced from vocal chords almost atrophied by some cancerous wastage. Before I could answer him, he continued:

'Please sit. Look at the cities. Are they not beautiful?' As the old man turned back to the strange models on the table before him, so Semple drew up a chair for me. I sat down beside Mr Bishop, noting as I did a musty odour which seemed to emanate from him in heavy waves. Or was it simply the odour of the entire club house—the smell of deep seas—and particularly this room of treasures from the ocean floor? I tried to ignore the clamour of mental alarm bells, bells of warning at the edges of my subconscious, giving my attention instead to this eccentric old man's words.

Spread upon the table before us, three separate structures reared model towers and ziggurats from an undulating base made to resemble the seabed. They were remarkable models and intricately designed, and since patently they were meant to represent submarine realms, I hazarded a guess as to their names:

'Atlantis, perhaps? And this one could be Mu? Yes? And finally there's this one . . .'

Mr Bishop's wide mouth turned up at the corners in what I took to be a smile. 'No, no, Mr Vollister,' he whispered hoarsely, 'Atlantis and Mu were cities of men, gone down beneath the waves in vast seismic convulsions—and in geological terms gone down quite recently. R'lyeh, on the other hand, is a city as old as the moon—and it is not a city of men, though it has on occasion stood up out of the sea where it lies sunken once more. Look, this is R'lyeh.'

For a moment, as he pointed, I caught a glimpse of his shrivelled hand where it protruded from the wide sleeve of his silken gown. The man obviously suffered from some severe ichthyic disorder: his flesh was silvery-grey and scaled, his fingers webbed. Then I looked more closely at the model he had indicated.

So this was a miniature of R'lyeh, a name which—in connection with the New England conch—I already recognized from the *Cthaat Aquadingen*. Model though it was, nevertheless the thing was constructed to give an impression of unbelievable size, with vast green-slimed blocks of stone looming up dizzily to a monstrously carved monolith, about the base of which stood statues of loathsome krakens and squids poised in menacing attitudes.

Architecturally the city—if city it were, and not some mad builder's nightmare—was like nothing I had ever seen before. One looked upon the thing and received *impressions* rather than a true overall picture. Nothing specific fixed the eye at all, only *suggestions* of vastness and of queer angles that formed surfaces which were at one and the same time convex and concave. The geometry was dramatically out of touch with anything mundane, was blatantly alien, and over every senses-defying surface sprawled octopoid and piscine bas-reliefs of the most disturbing and unbalanced nature, and hieroglyphs that hinted of worlds and dimensions not only lost in vacuous abysses of time but separate from the clean world of Earth by countless light years.

Complemented in its hideousness by festoons of weed and oceanic incrustations, the thing *was* nothing less than a crazy nightmare. 'City' the old man may have termed it, but I saw it only as a monstrous necropolis, and I shuddered at the thought of any man, genius or lunatic, deliberately sitting down to construct the thing; and I wondered morbidly at the inspiration, real or imagined, from which this menacing model had sprung.

'Awesome, isn't it?' enquired the old man, as if reading my thoughts. 'Perhaps this other model, of Y'ha-Nthlei, will be less . . . confusing?—to your eyes and mind.' Again he pointed, and once more I saw that withered claw he wore for a hand, and again I looked at the object of his instruction.

It was the second of the submarine cities—Y'ha-Nthlei, he had called it—and, yes, it was more acceptable, far less intrinsically alien; and indeed certain of its lines were quite pleasing, designed with a flowing symmetry. In fact, the longer I looked the more I found myself imbued with a sensation of glory, of being uplifted, as if I gazed upon some shrine or holy place. For, layered as it was in every detail with a softly luminous mother-of-pearl, the model glowed with a chill internal fire, a cold fire that seemed to burn through weed and slime alike to set spark to memories that lingered, half-awake, in the back of my mind and being.

Blinking my eyes and shaking my head, I looked again. There was something Roman or Grecian about it: with balconies, great esplanades, and sweeping stairways; and then there were temples and amphitheatres, and everywhere columns and fluted pedestals and statues. But while the statuary and the titan idols of the temples were those same krakens of R'lyeh, still the place appeared to my eyes much as I might have expected to find Atlantis, a city drowned in prehistory. With but one exception.

As old Mr Bishop had pointed out to me, this was not a city of men sunken in some cataclysm of Earth, it was a city *built beneath the sea* in aeons lost to memory, built and inhabited by subaqueous beings—a city of the Deep Ones. And as such, Y'ha-Nthlei still lived!

'But what purpose do you have in—' I finally began, and paused uncertainly. 'I mean—why are these models here?'

The old man smiled at me with that queer turning-up of the corners of his too-wide mouth. 'Pardon?' he whispered. 'Our purpose in having the models here? The answer is simple: the real R'lyeh lies in the depth of the Pacific many thousands of miles away, and Y'ha-Nthlei is far away across the Atlantic. We cannot have the real thing, and so—'

'Sunken cities and lost races,' Semple abruptly, hurriedly cut in, 'are a hobby of Mr Bishop's, John. A hobby which almost entirely absorbs him. But come, they're serving lunch. You can come back in here later, if you wish.'

I stood up on legs which were unaccustomedly shaky, glancing down at Mr Bishop where he remained seated. For a moment more he gazed up at me, then turned his eyes back to the models on the table.

He reached out his hand and it trembled as it touched the skeletal frame of the third and last model, as yet incomplete, little more than minia-ture foundations. But as I began to turn away, I distinctly heard him whisper:

'Ah, yes, John Vollister, you may well wonder. But when Ahu-Y'hloa is finished out there in the sea, and when you yourself see her shining towers and temples and her myriad pillars, then—'

I would have turned back then to question him again, but Semple caught my shoulder and cautioned me with a finger to his lips. 'The old man,' he explained when we were out of earshot, 'is not quite right. It's his age and his condition, you understand.'

'Listen, David.' I drew him to one side as we went back through a swing door into the dining-room. 'There's an awful lot I don't under-stand here. A good many odd coincidences that don't quite seem to—'

'John!' came a girl's voice from behind me—a voice that sounded genuinely full of surprise and pleasure—driving all queries and doubts right out of my mind. 'There, didn't I say we'd meet again?'

I turned, and it was Sarah Bishop. Out of the corner of my eye I saw Semple make some sort of sign, a greeting perhaps, but I could sense that he was glad of Sarah's intrusion. 'I'll speak to you later, John,' he said as Sarah led me away to the table.

Seven or eight residents or club members were already seated, and I joined them, Sarah at my side, without formal introductions. Not wishing to seem gauche or ignorant, I none the less averted my eyes from them as best I could, but not before noting the fact that they all seemed cut in the same mould. Indeed, it was as if they were all mem-bers of the same family. With the exception of Sarah, Semple, and one or two others, all of them wore a peculiarly repellent, bulge-eyed, ich-thyic look, as if they were younger versions of old Mr Bishop.

I would have made conversation with Sarah, but we were no sooner seated than she struck up with a woman on her far side. I concentrated on an excellent prawn cocktail washed down with a glass of resinous yellow wine, then went on to the main course of boiled fish beautifully dressed. My own portion was excellently cooked, but I did little more than taste it. I had noticed that the others at the table, with the sole exception of Sarah, seemed to be enjoying portions which to all appearances were partly or wholly raw!

A queasy feeling which had been growing in the pit of my stomach since my arrival at the place—particularly since taking that glass of whisky in Semple's room—seemed suddenly to come to a head. My extremities became unmanageable in a moment, and unable to grip knife or fork I let both fall clatteringly to the table. As I struggled to my feet, Sarah took my arm, her strange eyes full of concern, her mouth, framing a question I could not hear. The room tilted and swam before me, and a roaring filled my head. I was conscious of bulging eyes staring curiously and fixedly at me where I swayed, my hands gripping the back of my chair in that gloomy and ominous room.

Later I was to remember thinking that this was the way I had felt as a small boy following a debilitating illness, when I had been prone to fainting spells—and also that whatever else happened *I must not faint here,* not in this strange place of strange people. Then my vision blurred over completely and in my whirling mind's eye I saw submarine visions of R'lyeh and Y'ha-Nthlei, and of finny shapes that swam in the shrouding weeds—and knew where I had seen those cities before: in my dreams on the first night after receiving the New England conch!

Finally, as I swayed and fell backwards into waiting arms, I saw again a mental picture of those sailing ships of old, the brig *Hetty* and the barque *Sumatra Queen.* The ships, yes, and the brass plaque beneath their case—which proudly described them as being '*Vessels of the Marsh Line, out of Innsmouth*'!

Then, for a while, I knew no more . . .

III

TIDE OF TERROR

I doubt if I could ever convey the wonderful feeling of relief that flooded over me upon awakening safe and sound in my own bed, after a period of unconsciousness full of indeterminate but extremely frightening dreams and nightmares. There was a dull ache at the back of my skull, and my vision was still blurred, but I knew my own room.

I was not alone; Sarah was with me. I heard her sharp intake of breath and sensed her movements as I began to move my limbs beneath the sheets. How I knew it was her I can't recall; perhaps her perfume, but something made me certain of her identity. Then, against a glow of late afternoon that penetrated the drawn curtains of my room, I saw her outlined as a silhouette. She was doing something . . . pulling on her sweater, I thought. I couldn't be sure. Things were still very hazy.

I closed my eyes against the sudden light, and a moment later felt her cool hand on my brow. Finally recovering my senses and orientation, I asked:

'What happened? I feel such a damned fool!' I opened my eyes again and her face swam into perspective. She wore a worried look, which gradually relaxed as I tried to smile at her.

'The doctor said it must have been something you ate,' she said. 'Probably the prawns. The reaction was so very quick! He said you'd probably been letting yourself go lately—not bothering greatly with yourself—that you were run down and in a state of nervous exhaustion.'

'Doctor?' I half propped myself up.

'One of the club members. He gave you a shot, said it would keep you asleep for a few hours. I have some pills for you, too. Here.' She took a glass of water from my bedside table and popped two yellow tablets on to my tongue. I swallowed them without thinking, then washed my mouth with water.

'They should put you down for a few hours more,' she added with satisfaction.

'Now wait a minute!' I protested too late. 'I have things to do, and—'

'You have nothing to do that won't wait,' she said.

'But how did I get back here—and who put me to bed?' Suddenly I was conscious of my nakedness.

'David Semple drove you back here and I followed behind on my scooter. But you have to stop worrying, John. Everything is all right, now.'

'But—'

'No buts! You rest now and I'll go into the village for some food. Did you know your icebox is almost empty? Later I'll make us a meal.'

Feeling a warm numbness creeping slowly up my body and wondering at the swift efficacy of the tablets, I let my head fall back on to the pillows and closed my eyes. Before sleeping, I turned on my side and was surprised to find a hollow beside me in the softness of my mattress, as if someone had lain there recently. The hollow was still warm and it smelled of a heady, musty perfume . . .

The next time I opened my eyes it was to find the room in darkness. Through a gap in partly-drawn curtains, stars showed in a clear night sky. I had been awakened by the clatter of crockery from the kitchen downstairs. Good as her word, Sarah was back and at work.

My headache had disappeared, and sleeping seemed to have done me good. Considering that my day had been extraordinary, and that my health had so recently been in jeopardy, I felt remarkably well. Nonetheless, I stayed right where I was, relaxing as the sweet smell of frying chicken came drifting upstairs to me. There was the sharp tang of coffee, too, and it seemed unlikely that I would be left alone much longer.

Very well. Now was my chance to think things out. In the space of the last few days, event had piled upon event thick and fast, and I had had little enough time to assimilate all of the details. It had all been very bewildering, and in retrospect unreal. Perhaps Sarah's 'doctor' had been right and I had let myself become run down, which might in turn explain why I was hallucinating or imagining the most peculiar things. Yet the strangeness had not been confined merely to the last few days, for the beginning of it all could be traced back to the arrival of the New England shell. The 'Innsmouth' conch . . .

Yes, it had started with that peculiar left-handed conch from unknown deeps; with that, and with my equally unknown benefactor, one William P. Marsh. And it had been a Marsh, too—an 'Innsmouth' Marsh—who had owned that line of sailing vessels back in the early nineteenth century. Coincidence, of course. After all, what's in a name?

. . . Marsh had sent me the conch, out of no apparent motive other than admiration for certain of my writings; I had been unable to trace the thing; it was to all intents and purposes a 'new' specimen. Ian Carling had seemed as much excited about it as I was, which to me had been ample proof of the thing's unique status. And yet it had been described in a book as old as the hills, and its picture had been drawn for that book God only knows how many years ago! I thought of the book.

The *Cthaat Aquadingen*: a strange title, I wondered what it meant. 'Aqua' must surely be 'water,' and 'dingen' was German for 'things.' Something about water-things? A passage from the book flashed suddenly before my mind's eye:

' . . . the snail itself is as a delicacy to the tainted palates of the Deep Ones.'

Just a few words, but for some as yet unfathomed reason they had angered David Semple inordinately. And how did the rest of it go? . . .

'Yet they crop the slug with care, for under their direction vast colonies of the creatures layer the pearly and subaqueous houses and temples of their cities!'

Their cities. Cities like R'lyeh and Y'ha-Nthlei, perhaps? I thought of the model I had seen of many-columned Y'ha-Nthlei—of the pearly, nacrous patina that glowed over its shrines, statues, and kraken-adorned columns—and my mind conjured up the vision of armies of conches and their snail inhabitants crawling over naked stone, building up a glistening surface of nacre to 'beautify' the houses of the Deep Ones.

And who in hell *were* the Deep Ones, anyway? Some secret society or other? Deep Ones: somehow the words had a familiar ring to them, but in what connection? R'lyeh—Y'ha-Nthlei—Deep Ones—Ahu-Y'hloa? What on earth was it all about, and how had I managed to get myself caught up in it?

Sarah's footsteps on the stairs put an abrupt end to my cogitations. She entered through the open door—a silhouette bearing a tray—moved over to the bed, and put the tray on my bedside table.

'I'm awake,' I told her, sitting up. 'And I'm feeling pretty good.'

'Fine!' she answered. 'Are you hungry?'

'For a bite of chicken and a mug of coffee? Yes, I am. What time is it?'

'Almost midnight. You began to stir about half an hour ago, so I got your meal going. I've eaten already. But I'll enjoy watching you. You don't mind?' She switched on the bedside lamp. The lamp had a red shade, and in its warm glow there was that about Sarah Bishop which fascinated me. Suddenly I remembered something, and secretly reached out my hand beneath the sheets to where the hollow had been—that warm, musty-smelling hollow. But it was no longer there. I had either destroyed it in my sleep, or . . . or it had not been there in the first place. Just a part of some forgotten dream.

While I ate, Sarah sat in a wicker chair and hugged her knees, watching me attentively and yet, paradoxically, in a strangely lazy manner. I could feel her eyes on me, but her half-pensive attentions caused me no great concern. I was very much at my ease with her, as I had felt with no other woman since losing my wife. As I finished eating, she said:

'Your pyjamas are under the pillow; dressing-gown behind the door. I'll go wash up, and you can stretch your legs. Then I suppose you'll want to talk.'

'There are things I'd like to ask you, Sarah, yes. But shouldn't you be getting back to your father? It's not that I'm ungrateful, but I'm sure he'll be worried about you.'

'He's in London—and in any case, I'm perfectly capable of looking after myself.' She smiled. 'Or is it that your English roses all turn into pumpkins when the clock strikes twelve? I can leave whenever I want to, or whenever you want me to. My 98cc carriage is right outside!'

'If I had neighbours,' I told her, 'you'd ruin my reputation—if I had a reputation!' Then I shrugged and added: 'All right, I'll dress and then we'll talk.'

She stood up and took my tray. Leaving the room, she looked back over her shoulder and asked: 'Five minutes?'

I nodded, and she closed the door behind her.

I dressed in my pyjamas and gown, splashed some water on my face in the bathroom, and generally tidied myself up. Then I went through into my study and put on the light. Something was missing.

The shell . . .

Damn and blast! Following my fainting fit, the New England conch had been left in Semple's room at the boat club. Angry at myself, I promised that I would pick it up at the first opportunity. Then, noticing that however good I felt my legs were still a bit shaky, I opened the French windows and went out on to the balcony. I aerated my lungs and looked out upon a calm night. A few minutes later, hearing Sarah mounting the stairs once more, I went back into the study and called out to let her know where I was.

She walked in, dressed as I had first seen her, and came straight over to me. She took my hands in hers. 'Are you sure you feel all right? I may tell you, you had me worried at the club.'

'My right arm stings a bit,' I answered, rubbing at the dull ache that I felt between elbow and shoulder. 'Other than that I seem to be okay.'

'Don't rub it,' she admonished. 'That's where the doctor stuck his needle in you.'

'Oh!' I frowned. 'Well, it seems I'm indebted to this doctor of yours, whoever he is. Nervous exhaustion, you say? Strange—but I suppose he must be right.'

'You were just a bit overwrought, that's all. Perhaps it was simply that you were in strange company, and that—'

'Strange company!' I rudely cut her off. 'You can certainly say that again!'

For a moment she looked hurt, and I quickly apologized. 'I'm sorry. I meant no offence. But there's a certain feeling about that place you're staying at, and I noticed a few things that didn't really seem, well, normal.'

She frowned and half turned away; then having obviously reached some decision or other, faced me once more. 'All right, John Vollister, I'll tell you what it's all about, but first you must promise me that it will go no further.' She saw the questioning look forming on my face and quickly added: 'Oh, don't concern yourself. There's nothing criminal about it.'

'Well, then,' I laughed, 'that settles it. I've always loved a mystery. Come on, tell me all about it.'

We seated ourselves in easy chairs before the open French windows, cool but comfortable in the almost unnoticeable breeze off the sea, watching for a while as the moon silvered a path from the horizon to the beach. The night was very calm.

'Do you have any idea,' Sarah began with a question, 'how much water there is in the world?'

'It covers sixty percent or more of the Earth's surface,' I answered.

'No, no, no!' she said. 'That's like looking at an apple and counting the drops of dew on its skin. It doesn't tell you how much juice there is inside.'

'Or how many worms,' I added.

For a moment she favoured me with that strange look of hers, half-searching, half-wondering, before continuing:

'Very well, let's look at it your way: mathematically. The Earth's surface is almost two hundred million square miles, of which one hundred and twenty million are water and another twenty million glacial ice. Agreed?'

I nodded. 'Knowing very little about it, I'll just have to accept your figures. You seem to know your subject well enough.'

'And so I ought to,' she answered, 'for I've studied little else for the last three years. You'll see why soon enough.'

I shrugged, settled back, gazed out over the sea, and listened to her,

wondering in the back of my mind what it was about her that so attracted me.

'So far we've only looked at the surface,' she went on, 'but what
about under the sea? The Altacama Trench in the East Pacific is over
two thousand miles long. You could drown all the British Isles in the
trench at least five times without raising a ripple on the surface. Similarly, you could take Everest, turn it upside down, and sink it in the
Marianas Deep—and its base would still be two miles underwater! Do
you begin to see what I'm getting at?'

'That there's an awful lot of water?'

She frowned impatiently. 'Well, you'll begin to take me seriously in
a moment—I hope! No, what I'm trying to say is this: that while man
has explored almost all of the surface of this planet, and while he has
even walked on the moon and looked hungrily at the other worlds of
the Solar system, he knows hardly anything about the deep oceans.'

'And what would you have him know?'

'Nothing, just yet, but I'll tell you what we've discovered . . . in a
moment. First, though, answer me this: why should intelligent life in
this world have confined itself to Man the Land-Dweller, when in fact
life began in the waters which form by far the greatest habitable mass
in the world as a whole? Why should Man, trapped in the two dimensions of dry land, be the dominant species?'

I shrugged again, trying to play down my increasing interest in
her subject. I had suspected her high intelligence, but already my es-
timate seemed in need of drastic upward adjustment. 'I suppose it
just happened that way,' I eventually answered. 'There is, of course,
the dolphin . . . '

'The dolphin? His brain is large, but he has no hands. Thus he's
limited in his use of tools. No, he befriends the Deep Ones just as he
occasionally befriends Man, but in no way can he be considered of the
same high order.'

'The Deep Ones!' I immediately sat up and took hold of her arm,
facing her squarely. 'I keep hearing mention of them, keep seeing them
named in print, but who or what on earth *are* the Deep Ones? And

what is it that you're driving at, Sarah? Can't you explain yourself more clearly?'

She climbed to her knees on her chair and threw an arm about my neck, her face close to mine, more serious than I had ever seen her before, but at the same time more childlike. 'All right, I'll tell you about . . . about the Deep Ones. The difficulty lies in knowing where to begin.'

'Try the beginning,' I advised.

'The beginning? I doubt if anyone could ever really fathom the beginning. But I can make a few educated guesses. . . .

'In the beginning there was a wonderful godlike being. His name was Cthulhu and he came down from the stars in Earth's prehistoric youth, when this world was the merest infant among worlds. He was old even then, but immortal—or very nearly so—and he built vast cities for his own kind in the steaming fens of pre-dawn Earth.

'Of his species, Cthulhu was the Father, the Great Old One, but many others came down out of the void with him. Among them there were Ithaqua the Wind-Walker; and Yog-Sothoth, the all-in-one and one-in-all; and Shudde-M'ell, the huge and subterranean burrower beneath; and many, many more. All of them were mighty in "magic," the magic of wonderful sciences which made their aeon-long voyage down countless light years possible, and they fled from the tyranny of other beings whose abhorrent laws they could never bring themselves to obey.

'Their oppressors followed them, and because they could not kill them imprisoned them here on Earth and in dim dimensions adjacent or parallel to this star system. Cthulhu was trapped in the vaults of R'lyeh and sent down beneath the deepest oceans to dream forever and yearn for the freedom which once was his.'

She paused, and I took the opportunity to ask: 'Then this Cthulhu—is that how you say it?—was a Deep One, as were all of the others trapped in the sea with him?'

'No, no. Cthulhu is the greatest of the Great Old Ones. The Deep Ones are merely his Earthly minions, his followers, his worshippers. He is the basis of their religion. They themselves are man's watery brothers, man's aquatic counterparts, the intelligent lords of the seas. They are a race of subaqueous beings for the large part unsuspected by Man. That is to say, they have in the main kept themselves to themselves. Only very occasionally, more often than not accidentally, has their existence been suspected.'

Again she paused, and once more, somewhat incredulously, I took the opportunity to put a question to her. At least, I tried:

'Are you seriously asking me to believe that—'

'That Man is not the sole master of this world?—that there are mermen and maids?—that in the countless millions of cubic miles of water surrounding this planet there is an intelligent manlike species whose origin, science, art, and religion predates Man? Yes, I am.' She paused briefly, then continued:

'Is it so hard to believe? Can you so easily discount all of the countless sightings of mermaids reported through the centuries? As long as Man has recorded curious stories and legends—which is to say since the first man learned how to write—he has been aware of the people that live in the sea. It's only recently, in the modern, so-called 'enlightened' world, that explanations have had to be devised to put aside what Man has chosen to consider a myth, a pipe dream of drunken old sea captains.

'Ah, but in the days of the old clippers, in the days of the Pacific and East Indies trading ships, then there were captains who discovered the truth! They discovered that the Deep Ones were real—that mermen and maids really did exist, and that mutually beneficial coexistence was possible with these their brothers in the sea.

'For make no mistake, John Vollister, the Deep Ones *are* our brothers and sisters. Indeed, in certain of their own legends they have it that land-going Man descended from them, that Man's 'missing link' was in fact a Deep One. And who is to say that they are wrong?

'Is it so very inconceivable that long ago, when the first lungfishes were floundering on the muddy shores of shrinking oceans, Man was already exploring the land? Amphibian, yes, but naturally bipedal. And perhaps when those primal Deep Ones returned to the sea some of them stayed behind, at the edge of the waters, later to lose their gills and evolve into true men.

'True men! Is there any such thing as a true man? The first men, the *original* men, were Deep Ones. And I for one am glad that my forebears came up from the deeps rather than swinging down from the trees! . . . But now, John, let's have it right out in the open:

'My father and his friends at the club are at present negotiating with just such beings, are actually in contact with the Atlantic Deep Ones, whose cousins in their Pacific cities—where still they worship Cthulhu, dreaming in his crypt in R'lyeh—were known to the old sea captains of Innsmouth in the first decades of the nineteenth century.'

She paused again and looked me straight in the eye, defying me to laugh, willing me to believe that what she had told me was true; and in her own eyes—which were huge, dark, and liquidly hypnotic—I could discern no spark of humour, no sign that she was anything other than deadly serious. When I said nothing, she asked, 'Well? What have you to say now?'

'What have I to say? What can I possibly say to all that?' I finally answered, starting to feel more than a little exasperated. 'Sarah, I like you—in the very short time I've known you I've come to like you very much—so much so that I really don't care to see you being made a fool of, or for that matter making a fool of yourself.

'Now, if as I believe you're one hundred percent serious about all this, then it can only be that someone else is pulling your leg, having a laugh at your expense. Why, the theories you're proposing are downright ludicrous! Mermaids; intelligent manlike amphibians; submarine cities and shrines to immemorial gods old as the Earth itself—utterly ludicrous!'

'Ludicrous?' she exploded, white with anger. 'Let me tell you something, Mr Marine Biologist—'

'No,' I sharply interrupted, angry in my turn, 'you listen to me. Why, you'll be asking me to believe in flying saucers next! Have these crackpots who've been filling your head with all this rubbish produced one single shred of evidence to support their crazy ideas?'

'Blind!' She spat the word at me. 'Completely blind—and probably deaf, too, if this conversation is anything to go by.' Then her anger melted away in a moment and she broke into a peal of laughter. 'Oh,

John Vollister, you fool! What an opportunity you've been given. You, a professional marine biologist—for which reason you were chosen to be their intermediary, their ambassador—and all you can do is ridicule what should by now be obvious to you.'

'Obvious to me? I don't see that anything is—'

'No, you don't see. But today you actually *have* seen. You've seen Deep Ones! You ask for evidence? Wasn't that evidence enough?'

At her words I found myself assailed by sudden, incredible doubts. 'I saw them? I saw Deep Ones? I don't—'

'You sat down at the same table with them!'

Something of the nausea I had experienced at the yacht club returned along with the memory of those repulsive people I had seen eating what I had taken to be raw fish, so that I could hardly restrain a grimace as I said: 'But those people were completely degenerate, or at least they looked so to me.'

'Degenerate?' She seemed hardly able to believe her own ears, and when next she spoke the anger was back in her voice with a vengeance. 'Would a visitor from another world be degenerate because he was different? Is the Chinaman, the pygmy, the Eskimo degenerate? Is "different" degenerate?' Suddenly blazing with fury, she sprang to her feet. Her small clenched fists trembled at her sides. 'Of all the pig-headed—'

'Now wait a minute,' I cut in, standing up and taking hold of her arms. 'A joke's a joke, but—'

'Joke!' She choked out the word. 'There's only one joke here, John Vollister, and you're it!' She pulled her arms free. 'Well, you'll know where to find me when you want to apologise.'

And with that she was gone, storming out of my study, down the stairs, slamming the door of the house behind her to make *me* wince at the sound, and so out into the night. A moment later, I heard the clatter of her machine's tiny engine, but even then I was too astonished at her exit to make a move.

Finally I thought to step out on to the balcony, from which I could see her in the beam of her headlight below. Half in shadow, she was putting on her crash-helmet. 'Sarah,' I called down. 'Sarah, listen to me.'

'Listen, nothing!' she shouted up at me. 'I'm different from your English women, John Vollister. I don't simply stand still and accept insults. Especially insults to my intelligence. Oh, yes, I'm different all right—"different," do you hear? Does that make *me* degenerate, too?'

And away she went, her headlight's beam cutting an erratic white swath through the darkness. I watched that shaky beam go out of sight, then went back inside and sat down. After cursing myself for a fool—and Sarah for a bigger fool, for it certainly appeared that she believed all the rubbish she'd been spouting—I poured myself a drink, then a second, and later a third . . .

After that, and after consuming a further half-bottle of whisky in extremely short order, I was too drunk to think at all (a condition I had not experienced since the frustrations of my courting years) and so put the whole thing out of my mind. I would deal with it in the morning. Fumblingly, I locked the French windows and made my way to the bedroom where I collapsed upon my bed.

For a while, the darkness was soothing, then the room began to spin, reminding me how much alcohol I had consumed. Mercifully I was not sick, but the day's events had hardly been such that I could hope to sleep peacefully on them. I remember cursing myself again for a fool before drifting into sleep . . .

And, of course, I dreamed.

It was the same dream as before: at first the gentle water sounds, gradually building to a storm, a tempest—and the sensation of nameless aeons of time passing in a chaos of primal ocean, geologic ages concentrated into mere moments, and the sepulchral sounds of alien prayers, of monstrous worship, throbbing hideously as a background to the storm's fury—until once more I was crushed in pounding surf, tossed unresisting from one giant wavecrest to the next, and gyrated madly on the glassy walls of dizzy whirlpools.

At this point, as in that other dream of mine, a week old now, I started awake. I awoke—but there came no surcease, no abatement of the crashing of waves and the hiss of flung spray. For a moment only,

I thought myself still dreaming; then, leaving my bed, I went shakily into the study and steadied myself at my desk.

There the storm sounded even louder, as though the waters dashed about the very feet of the cliffs below the house, and I knew then that the tide was in and the sea must be in an absolute tumult. A glance at my watch told me the time was 3.15—an unthinkable hour to be awake and suffering from a hangover in the middle of a storm!—and I had slept for only an hour or two.

I went unsteadily to the French windows and unlocked them, bracing my shoulder against them to stop them from flying open. The effort was wasted, for as I carefully drew the windows inward and stepped through them on to the balcony the pounding of the sea subsided, died away in a moment, *and I gazed out upon a scene of unbelievable calm!*

I frankly could not believe my eyes, and the shock of the sight beyond the balcony—the near-distant sea, flat and silvery in clear moonlight, the rippled sands stretching away beneath a night sky across which, diaphanous and eerily silent, scattered wisps of cloud slowly drifted—caused me to reel with its almost physical intensity following, as it did, so rapidly in the wake of the imagined storm.

For of course that tempest of my dreams had existed purely in my imagination, had carried over like an echo from the subconscious caverns of my mind into the waking world during the transitory phase between sleeping and waking proper. I had *not* been fully awake, even though I had left my bed to go into my study, and only the cold night air of the balcony had brought me to my senses.

It was the whisky, of course, only the whisky. That could be the only possible explanation. But following so closely on the events of the last twenty-four hours, and despite all rationalizations, the alcohol-inspired nightmare had left me utterly shaken. Trembling in every limb, I went back inside and began automatically to close the windows; and it was then that a terrifying thought came to me.

Wasn't there some sort of disease that started off with symptoms like mine? With wild imaginings and hallucinations? With fainting spells and giddy bouts, and periods of awful whirling and rushing sensations? Where the victim's sense of hearing becomes so acute that in the end he dies or goes mad from the sheer pressure of supposed or imagined noise? Or was this merely some theory I had read or heard of somewhere or other? It was all very worrying.

So worrying, indeed, that my sleeping was done with for the rest of that night. Instead I prowled the house through all the remaining dark hours, putting on the lights as I went pale and sickly from room to room, until dawn found me near-exhausted from a sort of frustrated fretting and the recounting over and over of all that had passed since first the New England conch came into my possession.

It was then that something Sarah had said came back to me, what she had reported some doctor or other as remarking of my condition: that I was close to being in a state of nervous exhaustion. Well, possibly, but frankly that was the *only* thing she said that had made any sort of sense. Nervous exhaustion? Much more of this and I might well begin to consider myself a candidate for the local asylum.

. . . Asylum?

I frowned as a new thought occurred to me. An asylum!

Could it possibly be that the club on the beach was some sort of sanatorium? Now, with dawn spreading bright fingers over the sky and the fears of the night receding along with my mood of alcoholic depression, it seemed to me that I might well have stumbled across the truth.

Was it possible that the 'club' was no club at all but a retreat from the rigours of a world too harsh for the delicate minds of certain persons—certain extremely well-to-do persons—whose 'eccentricities' had carried them over the edge? If so, then naturally the place would have its staff of attendants, one of whom had tended me when I had been taken ill on the premises.

The more I thought about it in the clear light of day, the more logically the pieces of the puzzle seemed to slip into place. The location of the refuge was certainly out of the way, as one might expect; its 'residents' patently were the owners and had a hand in the running of the place; but at the same time the staff—doubtless well-qualified and highly paid—must always be there in the background to ensure the safety of their charges, their employers.

How then would Sarah Bishop fit into this conjectural jigsaw I was constructing? Thinking of her father and what I had seen of him, I was more convinced than ever that I was on the right track, that indeed the Bishops fit in extremely well. The old man's case was plainly advanced, and doubtless complicated by an extreme physical disorder; but worse by far from my point of view was the fact that his mental condition must be hereditary. For surely Sarah, too, suffered those same delusions that obsessed her father, had absorbed and adopted his harmless but deranged opinions and concepts.

As for David Semple: had not my old friend Ian Carling warned me that Semple was 'a queer sort of chap,' however likeable he was in his own way? On the man's own admission he was a collector of all sorts of weird and wonderful books, specializing in volumes dealing with the occult and esoteric. And without a shadow of a doubt those books that he had showed me were strange enough.

Moreover (and as is often the case with deranged people), Semple had been remarkably quick off the mark to point out old man Bishop's much more obvious deterioration; the fact that he was 'not quite right,' and that it had to do with his 'age and condition.' But I knew that Mr Bishop was only sixty-seven years old; hardly an age at which advanced senility might normally be expected to take over or exact so drastic a toll . . .

Oh, to be sure, there were ambiguities and inconsistencies in my reasoning. There was, for instance, the question of the Innsmouth Marshes and their obscure connection with the club; and the fact that Semple had found a genuine reference to the New England conch in one of his many books; and the odd circumstance of my meeting with Sarah Bishop in the first place. But here I must surely make allowance for pure coincidence.

By this time I had convinced myself that I was right, and as additional proof I thought again of those strange and emotionless faces I had seen grouped about the great table where I had sat down to lunch with Sarah Bishop and the other members of . . . no, the other *inmates*. I thought of those faces and how similar they had seemed, as of a single family, the way the features of sufferers from mongolism appear similar, as self-identifying as any retarded group when seen against a normal background—as I had often seen them myself on outings in the streets of London and other cities, carefully shepherded and conducted by their attendants.

Yes, that must be the answer. The club was an asylum for a group of people who had themselves recognized and taken precautions against the encroachment of their own infirmities. They were in no way dangerous lunatics, merely sick people whose mental deterioration—probably a gradual process in most of them—had demanded a haven wherein they might periodically find respite when the going got too rough for them.

And Sarah, poor Sarah . . . No wonder she had felt outraged when I had called the others 'degenerate.' In her heart of hearts she must know well enough the truth, which she had tried, in her own way, to tell me: that they were merely 'different.' No wonder I had thought the girl strange and wondered at the way she looked at me! She had offered me friendship (and, I suspected, much more than friendship) which I had seemed so callously to throw back in her face. And yet, now that I had guessed the facts of the matter, perhaps my failure to accept her had been just as well at that . . .

Having thought the thing out more or less to my satisfaction, finally I was reminded of the conch. It must be in Semple's room where I had left it. Well, it was still my property, and I wanted it back. Not that I could see any sort of argument brewing over its possession, but the sooner it was returned to me the better. Then, for the first time, I noticed a scrap of paper tucked under the handset of my telephone. There was a number on it, and a bold signature reading 'Sarah Bishop.'

I nodded to myself in understanding: obviously she had foreseen the outcome of her telling me her 'story.' And she had said that I should know where to find her when I was ready to apologise. But it was too early in the day just yet, I fancied, to attempt to contact her. And in any case, having worked the nervous tension out of my system—not to mention a large overdose of alcohol—I now found myself inordinately weary. Easier in my mind, I decided to try for a few hours' sleep and speak to Sarah later.

I had not reckoned on sleeping any great length of time, but my exhaustion was such that it put me down well over the allowed-for period, with the result that I did not open my eyes again until early evening. On reflection, however, it was not difficult to see why I had needed to sleep my fill: the previous day's stresses and excitements— followed by periods of drug- and alcohol-induced unconsciousness of doubtful restorative value, and terminating in a nightmare and half a night spent in enervating prowling—had completely sapped my strength. Now, following a shower and a shave, a bite of food and glass of fruit juice, I felt up to just about anything . . .

The first problem came when I phoned the number Sarah had left for me and got Sargent on the other end of the wire. He was polite but almost completely inarticulate, and it was not without a deal of difficulty that I eventually discovered Sarah to be sleeping (she had left instructions that she was not to be roused until 9 P.M.) and Semple to be 'away on business but returning later.'

Then, when I would have put the phone down, the man surprised me by enquiring after my well-being, and by stating that 'the doctor' had asked that I be informed of his availability should I require any further attention. I answered that all now seemed perfectly well with me, but asked that the doctor be thanked for his kind offer anyway, and with that replaced the receiver.

I spent a further half hour at my desk, fidgeting and fiddling with an old, heavily corrected and interlineated manuscript, and only succeeded in ruining it completely, after which I threw down my pencil and resolved to return to the place on the beach at once. I had reasons enough, to be sure. I desired to retrieve the conch; I would welcome the opportunity to excuse my peculiar behaviour of yesterday before as many of the club's 'members' as possible; and last but not least I must certainly apologise to Sarah for my regrettable lack of manners, and any other 'offences' against her sensibilities of which she might consider me guilty.

Having made up my mind, I attempted to phone for Seaham's lone taxi, but after dialling for ten minutes gave it up for a bad job. Obviously, Sam Hadley, the owner of a battered old Ford of incredible mileage and stamina, was already out on a job. Since Sam never allowed himself to be engaged for long journeys (Newquay was about as far as he would go) I decided to walk into the village and try my luck at finding him in when I reached his cottage on the seafront.

It was not quite 6.30 P.M. when I set out, and while it was still broad daylight I noted that a pale sun was already slipping down towards the sea. The chill of evening was creeping in while the shadows of rocks and pebbles gradually lengthened on the beach. In less than two hours it would be quite dark.

Twenty minutes later, I was at Sam's place at the northern tip of the decaying concrete promenade. The old Ford was not in its accustomed place, and Sam, a bachelor, was not at home. The sign which he normally kept in his window, saying simply TAXI, was missing. I knocked at his door just to be sure, and as I was turning away Sam's ancient next-door neighbour, Jason Ridley, appeared at his door and called across to me:

'Um's gorn inter Newquay, Mr Vollister. Gettin' some repairs done to the old bus, I reckon. Be late in fer sure. Should I tell um you was 'ere?'

'No, don't bother yourself, Jason,' I answered. 'It's not important. I'm just out for a walk, that's all.'

'Walkin' is it? On the beach? Tide's cummin in. Are you goin' far, sir?'

'Oh, no—up the beach, that's all. As far as the, er, new place. The boat place, you know?' I started to walk away.

'That there queer place, d'you mean?'

Now I stopped and turned back towards the old man. 'Queer place, Jason? What do you mean?'

'Ar, um's a funny old place, um is. Bought the little bay outright, um did, an' dun't let no un near um along the beach. Private property, um says it is. Funny lot.'

'But you said "queer," Jason. Now what did you mean by that?'

'Well,' he drawled. 'You know, sir—kind of vacant, um be. Fishy-lookin' lot.'

'Vacant? You mean you think they're simple or something?'

'Simple? Like a bit balmy, d'you mean? Oh, I wouldn't go that far, sir. A bit queer, that's all. Still um's an out of the way place, an' um dun't seem ter bother no um. Sam Hadley does a fair bit o' trade wi um . . .'

But now it seemed that our brief chat had soured the old chap and he began to turn away from me. 'Yes,' I answered, nodding. 'Well, then—that's all right, then.'

He seemed not to have heard me, however, and went back into his cottage, mumbling to himself and shaking his head from side to side. Old Jason was a bit of a funny old duck himself, come to think of it. Still, he had more or less confirmed my own suspicions. 'A queer sort of place,' indeed.

That settled it; I couldn't leave the New England conch at the club, but must get it back immediately. It should take me no more than an hour or so to walk to the club, and with a bit of luck I might even get David Semple to drive me home again. Briskly I set out . . .

Thirty minutes later the shadows had lengthened appreciably. Already, in a sky which was slowly clouding over, I thought I could make out the first gleam of stars as the sun began to sink in the sea. There would be a thin moon tonight, but I should be at the club before dark.

Now the shadows of the cliffs on my right drove me farther down the beach until I walked on the high-water mark between sea and crags. The sea itself was fairly calm and would not be up for half an hour or more, and in any case there were few places where a man might find himself trapped by the water along this stretch of the coast.

Shortly, as I put on a little speed and lengthened my stride, I noticed that indeed the stars were fast appearing, and that the sun was now down beyond the sea's horizon. An aircraft, flying high over the ocean, was caught in the last rays of the sun and magically transformed into a silent, speeding silver dart. Then it passed behind a hummocked cloud formation and was gone.

Suddenly I felt a chill and shuddered—not alone, I fancied, from the effects of a freshening breeze off the sea. There was an eeriness about the sands at night, an aching loneliness. And the ocean's *hush, hush* where it rolled gently against the land was so regular as to be almost hypnotic. Too, it seemed to be growing dark far too early; or perhaps it was simply that the clouds were gathering and I had misjudged the distance between Seaham and the place on the beach.

Then, ahead, I spied the southernmost bay-arm where its outcrop jutted towards the slowly surging sea. Another ten minutes should see me rounding that natural breakwater, when I would be within a hundred yards of the . . . sanatorium? And now, too, at this late hour, I began to think of what I was doing in a different and somewhat morbid light.

For here was I alone on the beach, with night fast falling and the tide creeping ever closer, and just ahead lay my destination—a mental institution of sorts, however well-disguised—whose inmates were, to say the very least, disquieting. Oh, doubtless I would be attended to by one of the staff, a night nurse I supposed, and in all likelihood I would be on my way again within minutes, possibly in David Semple's car; but still I could not rid my mind's eye of a certain recurrent picture: that of a circle of staring, bulge-eyed, not quite vacant faces that gazed at one oddly, almost expectantly. And again, despite all rationalizations, I shuddered as I recalled those incidents which had led up to my fainting fit in the presence of the sanatorium's peculiar inhabitants.

So preoccupied was I with these recollections of mine that at first, as I turned my feet seaward in order to skirt the outcrop of rock which formed the arm of the bay, I almost failed to notice a movement in the shadows at the foot of the crags to my right. And although by now the moon was up, silvering the sea a little and casting some small illumination in previously stygian places, still I believe that it was pure intuition—or premonition—that brought the hackles upright at the base of my neck and made me look back.

Hadn't old Jason Ridley told me something about the people at the sanatorium not letting anyone near the place? Could it be that they had guards out? A sensible precaution, surely.

And yes, there was movement there, but not, I thought, the sort that a man might make. It was a strange slithering motion at the foot of the outcrop behind me, a humping of darkness that seemed to bulge threateningly in my direction. For a moment I paused, stopped breathing, and stared hard into the shadows, and in that same moment clouds passed over the moon and plunged the beach into darkness. Instantly the shadows of the cliffs and those of the sharp, weed-festooned rocks lengthened and seemed to leap at me across sands already dark, and I could sense a tensing in the night like a bunching of alien muscles.

Then the clouds passed, the moon's weak beam began to creep over the beach once more, the shadows retreated, and I knew that I had only been reacting to a bad attack of nerves, and that there was nothing there at the foot of the rocks after all—

—*except that there was!*

I thought at first it was a rock—a lone, bulky rock standing up from the sand taller than a man between me and the outcrop proper—and I had taken a deep, thankful breath of air and had started to turn away, to resume walking towards the point . . . when suddenly the thing moved! Its outline changed, seemed to flow; its base thickened, made a motion like the contraction of the foot of a slug, a movement that brought it closer to me; its lumpy surface glittered in the thin moonlight as if studded with a hundred shining eyes . . .

Great God in heaven, they *were* eyes!

This thing couldn't be, not possibly. And yet even as I stumbled away from it, backing across the sand, it made that motion again, and came closer. I heard a noise then—the sucking, squelching sound a seasquirt makes when probed with a finger until it ejects its juices, but magnified a hundred times—and at that precise moment the clouds obscured the moon once more.

My God! Was it those poor people at the place on the beach who were demented, or was it I? For this was surely the stuff of a madman's nightmare. But sane or mad as a hatter, I could not bear the sight of that blackly looming monstrosity coming at me out of the night, and I uttered a strangled scream—more the choked, inarticulate, rasping gasp of an animal half-crazed with fear—as I leapt backwards away from the horror.

Finally, volition returning more fully, I spun away from the thing, fell, scrambled to my feet, and fled towards the point of rocks with a pounding heart and lungs which already felt as if they were ready to burst. Nearing the point, I dared to look back, and saw the thing flowing after me, upright, leaning towards me, a column of lumpy loathsomeness.

A moment more, and my feet splashed in water, another and I tripped, flying forward into a deepening pool. This was a permanent pool about the rocks that formed the point, freshened and replenished with each tide, and it should not be too deep. Mercifully, my clothing was light and impeded me not at all. I swam like never before.

Drawing level with the last rock and beginning to swim round it to enter the bay proper, as I suddenly stumbled upright in water which had shallowed off to a depth of only a few feet, fearfully I looked back. At first I saw nothing, then a movement—a *flowing* as of a thick shadow at the far side of the pool—a shadow that lumped itself together and grew upright like a black stalagmite of hell at the water's edge. And again those myriad glittering eyes fixed me. Then I was round the point, plunging again into deeper water, feeling the slow surge and lift of a current that told me the sea had finally joined with and was filling the pool.

The lights of the sanatorium were ablaze and there was movement about its raised front, but I was far too winded to cry out for help. Lying partly between myself and the building, rolling gently where it was moored, the dark outline of a forty-foot craft lay low in the water, a dim cabin light burning with an orange glow. On the beach within the small bay itself, a tractor-like vehicle—by its appearance a dumper or loader of some sort—moved towards the building, headlights ablaze. I had no time to worry over this seemingly inordinate activity, however; I quickly swam to the boat and hauled myself aboard.

Tarpaulins had been folded back to uncover the well of the prow, where doubtless a cargo of sorts had lain. Perhaps something was even now in the process of being unloaded. Well, the vehicle moving up the beach had made its last run of the night, for plainly the water was now too deep for another load to be taken off the boat. The sea was pouring in now and quickly filling the pool.

Then, as the boat leaned over sharply in the strengthening surge of water, and the glowing cabin light cast its beam upon what was left of the cargo, I saw—

—an impossible sight!

I staggered—partly from the shock of what I believed I had seen, partly from the heaving of the boat's deck—stumbling across the planking and grasping at the ropes of the tarpaulins to steady myself as I fell heavily against the port side. There I crouched, waiting for the light to shine once more into the well of the deck, and all but forgotten, now, the horror on the beach.

For I had to see it again, the cargo of this lolling vessel whose captain, apparently, had gone ashore for the night. And again, obligingly, the boat leaned over to show me its secret: a shallow hold still half-full of wetly gleaming seashells. Ah, but these were not mussels, no, neither were they oysters nor whelks, nor any of the familiar, edible variety of molluscs one might expect to find in a vessel along this coast.

They were conches of the same species as my 'unique' New England specimen, and they lay in their thousands alive and sluggishly mobile in the well of this suddenly loathsome craft!

What happened next consists mainly of dim and fragmentary memories, which is perhaps as well. I turned my face over the side of the boat as a sudden bout of nausea filled me. The vessel lay so low in the water that for a moment my face was mirrored in the dark surface of the sea. It was the abrupt *parting* of that liquid mirror image that brought the single shriek of absolute terror bursting from my lips—

—that and the bulge-eyed, thick-lipped, scaled and monstrous head which emerged in a toss of spray—and the hand that reached up to grasp my shoulder, the *webbed* hand that jerked me irresistibly overboard and into the slowly heaving waters!

As I went, my head struck the side of the boat with a force which mercifully robbed me of the last vestige of an already reeling consciousness . . .

IV
THE TANK

Awakening from a submarine nightmare in which I fought desperately to control lungs which threatened to burst at every moment while being pursued through mazy, coral-incrusted deeps by both the horror from the beach and the batrachian *thing* that had dragged me overboard and into the sea, I found myself straining frantically against fetters which bound me hand and foot. I was on my back in an utterly lightless place, and a wide band of leather or some similar material had been fastened over my chest to restrict my movements further. While my head ached abominably and my limbs seemed a little cramped, doubtless as a result of their immobilization, I did not believe myself seriously injured in any way; and I satished myself in this respect by carefully moving my arms, legs, hands, and head as best I might within their limits. Whatever the monster had been which had dragged me into the water, obviously it had seen fit to drag me out again before I could drown. What had happened after that, where I was at the present time, and what my circumstances were *exactly* . . . these were things upon which I could not hazard even to speculate.

Of certain things, however, I could now be sure: that there was much more to Sarah Bishop's story—much more to the 'club' on the beach and to the whole chain of weird coincidences, if indeed they had been coincidences, which had led me to my present position—than ever I had suspected. And as for 'my present position' itself:

My clothes were not wet, but only slightly damp, which told me that I had been out of the water for some time. Nevertheless, I knew that I was not far removed from the sea, for I could still hear the *hush, hush* of its incursion on the land, though somehow the sound seemed strangely hollow and mechanical, as if I heard it through some amplifying medium, or as if I myself now occupied an enclosed space which gave the sound a metallically amplified ring. The surface on which I lay was not solid: that is to say it had a certain resilience, now stretched almost to its limits by my weight and the additional pressure of whichever appliance held me immobile. In short, I lay upon a fairly wide bed of one sort or another.

Sudden panic gripped me. A bed? It felt more like an operating table, or maybe a couch specially constructed to withstand the furious strength of a madman. And no sooner had this thought occurred to me than I further pictured myself in some sort of cell—a *padded* cell—in the sanatorium on the beach!

For a few moments I struggled wildly against my bonds, until a sort of cold and calculating calm began to creep over my mind and I forced myself to relax. Patently I was the captive of . . . someone. Of people or beings of some sort. Or, if not their captive, then . . . their ward? Inmate of some institute for the mentally deranged? The horrible fact of the matter was that the latter alternative was not at all out of the question. I had seen and experienced things which simply could not be in any sane or ordered universe; I had suffered subconscious hallucinations, nightmares which had carried over into my waking hours; and, finally, I had apparently become the victim or captive of beings which I had believed were born purely of the imaginings of others, themselves deranged.

Or could it be that all my previous conclusions were incorrect? That Sarah Bishop's story was a wholly true version of the way things were and that her friends and companions at the place on the beach were not mental patients at all but . . . something else? For surely the mere fact that I could now lie here and attempt some sort of rationalization was adequate proof of my own sanity; and yet, on the other hand, if I were sane how might I explain that living, sentient pile of sludge I had seen on the beach? Whatever other anomalies I might eventually find myself obliged to accept, *that* thing would never number amongst them!

Then, breaking in on my confused thoughts, from somewhere fairly close at hand there came the low mechanical cough of an engine starting up, followed by its steady purr as muffled pumps began to labour. Seconds later, I heard the gurgling of water and felt a dull vibration that reached me through the surface on which I lay. Before I could consider the meaning of these new sounds or return to my previous train of thought, a light went on immediately above me in the darkness, momentarily blinding me.

I closed my eyes at once, turning my head to one side and peering through shuttered lids until my eyes became accustomed to the glare. A little while later, I could see that I was in . . . some sort of tank?

A tank, yes, a metal room—a windowless room, the interior of which wore the dull grey sheen of metal—in the walls of which were rounded, protruding heads of rivets and thickly welded seams where panels had been joined. Apart from its cubical structure, the cell might well have been the interior of some great ship's boiler; plainly it had not been designed to house human beings.

Set flush in the far wall I saw an inlet pipe of at least nine inches in diameter from which, even as I watched, a trickle of water began to enter the tank. Rapidly the flow increased until the water actually gushed from this large inlet. Then, turning my head even further and craning my neck to stare at the metal floor, I saw that the water was filling a sunken area of the tank which was all of four or five feet deeper than the floor space where stood my bed or platform. As of yet, of course, the purpose of the whole setup completely escaped me, but it seemed unlikely that the intention was to drown me. That could have been achieved earlier and far more easily.

Turning my head in the other direction and avoiding the glare of the single bulb that hung unshaded from the 'ceiling,' I saw in the nearer wall an oval metal door similar to the type found below decks and between bulkheads in ocean-going vessels. On my side of the door, however, there did not appear to be any mechanism for opening it. A wooden chair stood beside my bed, and in one corner I could see a portable lavatory of the kind used in caravans. Other than these few items the tank was quite bare and empty. The ceiling was perhaps nine feet high (thirteen in the sunken area) and the walls were square in plan, about fifteen feet in length.

Having studied as much as I could of the tank, I next turned my attention to my bonds, and was in the futile process of once more trying my muscles against them when there came a grating sound that drew my eyes back to the oval door. The grating stopped, was followed by a loud clang as of metal against metal, and slowly the door began to open. Well oiled, the hinges were soundless as the heavy door swung inward to reveal—Sargent!

With surprising agility for one who had previously seemed little more than a shambling hulk, the man stepped over the raised portal into the tank. In his hand he carried a heavy flashlight, which he switched off before approaching me where I lay. He blinked his eyes in the glare of the single bulb. Wherever I was, it had to be dark outside. Sargent came closer, nodding, offering me his emotionless smile. Then the not-quite-vacant grin slipped from his face as he tested my bonds and checked to see that I was completely immobilized.

While he was engaged in this task, I took the opportunity to study him closely, looking particularly at his face (especially his eyes) and at his large, rough hands. What it was I sought I could not have said for a certainty at that time. I only knew that somewhere deep within me a seed of apprehension had blossomed into a loathing—a morbid dread—of certain types of human physiognomy.

Sargent had that look, or at least something of it, for in him it did not seem quite . . . complete. Semple had it, too, but again unfinished. Now my thoughts flashed back to the car park at the top of the cliffs above the club, to the American car which had pulled away as I had arrived with Semple. I saw again the lumpish, shadowy, pallid-faced figures whose round eyes had gazed at me in the moment that their car drove off, and I knew now what it was that had so disturbed me about them.

It was that look which all of these people shared, the one thing above all others that they had in common and *which had been carried to the ultimate degree in the monstrous form of the creature that snatched me from the boat!* Though I could not have known it then, these characteristics I had come to fear so greatly were known as the 'Innsmouth Look,' and they were a stigma born of a primal evil which—

But that is to go ahead of myself . . .

Apparently satisfied that I was well and truly tied down, Sargent offered me his simpleton's smile and said: 'The doctor is coming, Mr Vollister. No need to worry. You're one of the lucky ones.'

Until now, I had been silent, staring at him in a stony fashion, unwilling to display any sign of fear. His words, however incongruous, now broke my dam of silence and I railed at him:

'Doctor? I don't need a doctor, Sargent. I'm not a patient—I'm a prisoner! No need to worry, you say! And I'm one of the lucky ones, am I? Man, you'll know what the words lucky and unlucky mean before I'm through. I'll have the police down on this place quicker than you can say—'

'Police?' he cut me off, that hideous smile disappearing in a moment. 'No police, Mr Vollister. You're with friends.'

'*Friends?*' I exploded, gritting my teeth as I again strained at my bonds. 'Did you say friends, Sargent? What the hell are you? A pack of crazy people—or worse than crazy—to tie me down and lock me in this damned . . . *tank?* My friends, you say? When I get out of this place, I'll—'

'No.' Again he cut me off, shaking his scraggly head of hair slowly from side to side. 'No, you don't get out, Mr Vollister. Not for a long time. Before very long you won't *want* to get out, and that's best. You're with friends.'

I stared hard at him, trying to divine his expression, his meaning, but his face was now completely blank. No, there was an expression of sorts there, but I couldn't quite make it out. Could it possibly have been—envy? But how might anyone have envied me in my position? I might have questioned him then, or at least attempted to talk to him in a more reasonable manner, but even as I began to consider my approach there came the tread of feet on boards from beyond the oval metal door.

In another moment the darkness outside was slashed by the probing beam of a torch, following which a dark-suited figure appeared at the door, peering into the tank before entering. A squat man, froggish in figure but not (I was happy to note) in feature; his face, head, and hands looked normal, or at least comparatively so. In one hand he carried a bag—a doctor's bag—and certainly his manner was that of a professional physician.

'Ah, Mr Vollister,' he said. 'We meet again, and sooner than either of us had suspected, eh?' He chuckled, a perfectly normal chuckle, and reached to check the pulse in my wrist. Instinctively, I tried to pull back from him. He paused, pursed his lips, and made tut-tutting sounds. 'Nerves, Mr Vollister?'

I could stand no more of it. 'Look,' I almost shouted, 'what's going on here? For God's sake, what's it all about? You look normal enough—which is more than I can say for anyone else around here—so can't we just hold a normal conversation?'

He released my wrist. 'Of course we can,' he answered, beaming delightedly and seating himself on the wooden chair. 'Indeed, we've been waiting until you were more receptive. Now, at last, it seems you want to know about us. Fine! Do you have questions? If so, ask away.'

'All right,' I answered, feeling hysteria rising in me like a wind. 'Who the hell are "we," exactly, and what *is* this place? And for heaven's sake . . . I saw something on the beach—something horrible—a *Thing*! And the shells—those conches in their thousands!' Now I babbled unashamedly and struggled once more to break free of my bonds.

'Am I mad or something?' I yelled. 'I don't understand what's going on! Is this an asylum or isn't it? Damn you—damn you all!—what have I done to you? Who the devil are you, anyway?'

While I raved, the 'doctor' had taken a hypodermic from his bag. Now he tested it and, as I once more tried to shrink away from him, said: 'Calm yourself, Mr Vollister. All of your questions will be answered . . . soon. But at the present time you're simply too excitable. Of one thing, however, you may rest assured, which is that you *are* among friends. And you are most certainly *not* mad!' He nodded to Sargent, who came forward and quickly rolled up my sleeve.

I caught my breath as my eyes fixed upon the glinting needle the doctor held. Then I cried: 'Keep that filthy thing away from me!'

'A sedative, Mr Vollister.' He tried to calm me. 'Only a sedative. And when you wake up there'll be someone here to tell you all you want to know.'

'But how? . . . What? . . . *Who?*' I whispered, feeling the sting of the needle as it went home. He leaned closer, and in a matter of seconds his face became blurred and distorted. Through lips already numb I managed to ask: '*Who are you?*'

'We are your friends,' he answered from a million miles away, his voice echoing down a long, long tunnel. 'Your friends, the Deep Ones!'

Whatever the nature of the doctor's 'sedative,' its effect could not be denied. And yet it did not produce total unconsciousness in me, merely a sort of drowsy numbness through which I was dimly aware of my surroundings but incapable of any sort of movement or even of constructive thought. On the other hand, my memory was only marginally affected, so that later I was able to recall almost everything of visits made to the tank and of conversations held over me or in my presence.

I especially remembered Sarah coming to see me, but such was the erotic nature of her visit that I later assumed myself to have dreamed that particular episode. It was too absurd, I thought, to be anything other than a dream: that this young woman should come to me, alone, release my fetters and rouse me to a pitch of sexual desire in order to make love to me!—and all this while I was a prisoner, drugged, and only dimly aware of what she was about. Oh, yes, certainly a dream.

Of the other visits, however, I was less certain. There was inherent in them a certain stealth, and to the whispered conversations which accompanied them a sinister element that reached me even through the fog of drug-induced lethargy which deadened my senses and perceptions. I heard the peculiar and distinctive voice of Sarah's father, together with the unctuous tones of 'the doctor,' and felt hands upon me that turned me this way and that while examining me minutely.

During one such discussion I suffered a probing of expert fingers in the region of my neck, following which there was a mention of 'undeveloped buds' (which I took to be a reference to the subcutaneous nodules I have had since boyhood, produced by continuous gland troubles in my teens), while an examination of my hands and feet seemed to produce evidence of 'a retarded but not inconsiderable webbing.'

And that was not all. My eyes were subjected to bright lights and my skin to a certain abrasion—not to mention a series of punctures by needles whose purpose I was incapable even of trying to guess—following which a blood sample was taken and the initial phase of my ordeal was over. Then, over a period of what must have been several hours, slowly my body was allowed to fight off the gradually diminishing effects of whichever drugs I had been subjected to and I was allowed to surface to the grim reality of the tank. Conditions, however, seemed to have improved.

I was naked of clothing now, but warm, dry, and comfortable between clean sheets and beneath soft blankets. My clothes were folded neatly and lay in a small pile at the foot of my bed. The light was on, shaded now, and by its light I saw that Sarah was with me, sitting on the chair beside me.

I looked at her through half-lowered lids, noting the pensive look on her face and the tension in her hands where they held one of mine. She seemed lost in thought and was not aware of my return to consciousness until I withdrew my hand from hers. Whatever her feelings for me, and however real her concern, she was obviously in league with my gaolers and therefore an enemy. Surely she must know that I would reject any pretensions of friendship? If so, then the look of pain which crossed her face as I withdrew my hand was marvellously well feigned.

Then, as I opened my eyes fully to stare at her accusingly, she masked her feelings to ask: 'John Vollister, why on earth did you have to precipitate things by coming back here—along the beach and at that time of night?'

'I came to get my shell back,' I lamely answered, finding my throat dry and painful and my voice unexpectedly weak. 'And I came to offer my apologies, not only to you but to the others here, and also to . . . oh, there were reasons enough. But I certainly didn't expect to be taken prisoner and locked in this place!'

She gave me that curious look of hers. 'Why did you really come, John? Because of our argument, our quarrel? Did you come to see me?'

I grunted in answer, unwilling to admit that she had probably hit upon the truth. 'That was part of it, I suppose,' I eventually agreed. 'I wanted to make sure that you were, well, *all right*, here. I thought that—'

'That we were all mad?' Her voice, not unkind, was nevertheless full of barely restrained amusement. 'Doctor Waite said as much. He also said you had many questions to ask, and that he believed you would now be more receptive to the truth.'

'The truth?' I laughed hoarsely. 'But that's *all* I'm interested in!'

'John, why don't you just listen to me,' her tone changed, becoming almost pleading as she again took my hand and squeezed it, 'and this time try to accept what you're told. One way or the other, you *will* accept it in the end. So far, you've incurred no penalties, you owe us no penance, but if you persist in resisting our every—'

'Penance?' I broke in. 'Am I some sort of criminal, then? Have I broken the law? Funny, I was feeling more sinned against than sinner! As for my "resistance": does it really surprise you that I object to being kept in captivity?'

She pursed her lips. 'Why are you so stubborn? If only you'd *listen!*'

'I keep listening!' I almost shouted, trying to sit up and discovering that, while my bonds had been removed, my body was now as weak as my voice, far too drained of strength to effect any sudden or violent movement. 'I keep listening,' I repeated more quietly, collapsing back on to my pillows, 'but nothing I hear makes any sense. Why not just tell me where I fit into all of this—whatever it is you're doing—without any sort of embroidery?'

'You've already been told the truth—' she answered, 'or at least the basic facts—if only you would accept them . . .'

'You mean all of that . . . all you told me about a subaqueous race of—'

'Amphibious,' she quickly corrected me.

'Right, a race of amphibians, dwelling for the most part in the sea, with their own submarine cities and religions and—'

'All of that, yes,' she once more broke in. 'But listen, John, this is getting us nowhere. I'm not the best qualified person to explain everything. They tried to tell me that before, but I wouldn't listen. David Semple is the expert.'

'Semple? What about him?' I asked, revulsion flooding over me as I thought of the man and of my first impressions of him.

'He'll be coming to see you after I leave,' she told me, 'and you'll be able to study under him. As to why you're being kept here—"against your will," if you insist—it's simply that we can't afford to let the outside world know too much about us or get the wrong picture of us just yet. And you've already seen things you weren't supposed to know about until much later. In modern jargon, we're still very much a "minority group," and we know the sort of opposition we'd be up against. We just can't afford to let you go running free and perhaps bring all sorts of people down on us. Don't you see? They would be no more willing to understand, believe, or listen to us than you have been.'

'But—'

She shook her head, releasing my hand and standing up. 'My time's up, John. I'll be back—you know I will—but now it's David's turn.' The pleading look returned to her eyes. 'Only please, *please* try to help him as much as you can. Don't give us any more trouble. It will only rebound on you, and I couldn't bear that. Now I have to go . . .'

She turned away and went to the door, lifting her hand as if to rap upon its metal oval. Then she paused and turned to face me. She seemed about to say something, but no words came.

'Sarah,' I prompted her, 'what is it you want with me?'

She answered, 'You . . . remember, don't you, John?'

And at once I knew her meaning. Our eyes met, and it flashed between us like a spark of some weird energy, so that I immediately felt a longing in me. 'I thought it must be a dream,' I told her, then paused before asking: 'And before—at my house?'

She nodded. 'Then, too, yes.'

'Not that I'm not flattered,' I said, 'but why? I mean, I'm old enough to be your father.'

She gave me that curious look of hers yet again, and shook her head. 'That doesn't matter,' she answered. 'It doesn't matter now, and it will have no importance at all . . . later.'

'Oh? There's to be a "later," is there?'

'Yes, plenty of time later,' she answered with a strange little laugh. 'Years and years of it. Hundreds of them!' Then she rapped on the door, and when it opened she stepped through and was gone.

A moment later, Semple entered. In his arms he bore a dozen thick loose-leaf binders. Sargent came after him with a light folding table which he opened up before leaving, closing the door behind him. Placing his binders on the table, Semple drew up the chair and sat down. He nodded an almost perfunctory greeting, selected a binder, opened it, and began . . .

And so, without any further objection or resistance, I listened and learned. Before he began to instruct me in his main subject, however, Semple—whose presence now aroused in me an even greater revulsion—'put my mind at rest' by advising me in respect of one or two things which he suspected might have been bothering me.

Six days had gone by, he told me, since my lone and utterly stupid return to the place on the beach. That was where I was now, in one of three great tanks whose bases were buried in the rocks and sand of the beach, situated beneath and behind the concrete legs that supported the front of the building. Eventually, a channel would be cut from the pool-like basin in front of the club to the permanent natural pool at the mouth of the bay. At each tide, the huge containers would automatically flush and refill themselves with fresh sea water (a process whose purpose Semple did not see fit to explain, except to say that the tanks were 'storage and transfer chambers,' and that they had not been designed as prisons, though plainly they were ideally suited to such a use) which at present could only be accomplished by the use of pumps.

During my six days of captivity I had been kept sedated, washed, shaved, and fed, the latter minimally—only sufficient food and water to keep me alive, which explained my somewhat dehydrated condition—and I had undergone a series of 'tests.' Again, Semple did not attempt to explain the nature of these tests, nor did he mention the injections I had been given. I might have questioned him on these points, but Sarah had begged me not to hinder him or place any obstruction in his way . . . for my own sake. For the time being, I thought, it might be as well to follow her advice.

Semple had noted my interest when he mentioned how long I had

been a prisoner at the club—the 'headquarters,' as he referred to it—
and he had smiled as if he could read my thoughts. No, he assured me,
I would not be notified as missing, no matter how long I remained away
from the house. Notes had been left and telephone calls had been made
explaining my 'temporary absence,' messages which could later be mod-
ified to meet any situation as it arose. My newspaper had been cancelled,
and even a finished manuscript had been sent off on my behalf to a
publisher in London. I was simply holidaying somewhere in the north.
Certain 'friends' in the village would obligingly put it about that I was
considering a move to Scotland, so that even in the event of my complete vanishment only a modicum of curiosity would be aroused.

Then, with the preliminaries over and any hopes I might have entertained of outside intervention dashed, Semple got down to business;
and his business was to convince me, completely and irrevocably, of the
actuality of the Deep Ones and all Sarah Bishop had told me of them.
His method was simple, direct, and comparatively undramatic, though
the same could never be said of the effects of his disclosures on me. As
for proof: he had photographs, documents—literature I could study
with him or on my own—and, most convincing of all, he had himself,
his own body, his own person. The last, however, together with my final
acceptance of all I was to be told, did not come until the very end of
my period of instruction, and that was not to be for at least a further
three weeks. During that time I was to learn—and learn to believe—
many things.

Right from the start of my schooling my days were divided in the
following manner:

I would sleep (invariably under the influence of a combination of
drugs) and on waking would be given food. This was usually fish of one
sort or another, with water or occasionally wine to wash it down. Now
and then, Sarah would come and take the odd meal with me, but she
never stayed for long. Very infrequently I would wake to find her about
to take her departure, having obviously been to bed with me. Sargent
would also visit me periodically, presumably to ensure that all was well.
But for all this visiting, I did have a degree of privacy. After each period
of sleeping, and between visits, I would be left for several hours on my

own to read and study the literature Semple left for me, and to exercise as best I might in the small space available. Later, Semple himself would come in for two or three hours to continue with my instruction. And the more I listened to him, the more sure I was that this thing I was somehow involved in was more than merely some vast, crazy fantasy.

And so I began to learn of the Deep Ones: those amphibian dwellers in the deeps whose existence has always been suspected by men, hinted at in myths and legends of mermen and maids come down the centuries, but never proven. I learned how their race existed yet, in teeming thousands where their greatest cities stood, mere pockets or small submarine communities in other places, and discovered how, if only men knew exactly where to look, proof of their primordial existence as a high order of elder intellect predating Man could still be found.

I was told of sunken altars beneath the deep slime of Titicaca's inner cone where the batrachian Priests of Yatta-Uc once worshipped the Great Old Ones five hundred thousand years ago; and it was explained to me how, though the Deep Ones of Yatta-Uc are no more, still their small cousins the frogs swarm as of old in the great lake's marshy fringes. I learned of an ages-extinct branch of the Deep Ones in which alien reptilian strains had spread to bring about the final decay and doom of that branch; and of the buried Nameless City in the desert, wherein the sundered remains of their primal sarcophagi may still be found. It was explained to me why, long aeons ago, in the Nan-Matal of the Carolines, the Deep Ones built their greatest cities and raised towering submarine shrines to the mighty gods of a fantastic pantheon; and I was told the location of a place where even now a secret door leads down to subterranean lakes unsuspected, where near-blind cavernicolous Deep Ones live out their spans in a dedicated priesthood whose bleakness would seem hellish even to the most austere of Man's monkish orders.

All of this and much more, documented wherever possible and illustrated with incredibly detailed photographs, was made known to me; and as the days passed, I became heir to a veritable fund of lore lost to humanity for aeons—or, in the majority of cases, never even guessed at by the race of Man. I learned of R'lyeh, the mightiest fortress of indestructible stone whose drowned houses and temples were raised by neither men nor Deep Ones but by a race of beings come down from the stars when Earth was still partly plastic, and I gasped in awe of certain pictures of that massive necropolis from which, it was perfectly obvious, Mr Bishop's model had been constructed.

I saw immensely carved doors of fantastic proportions and dimensions, embossed with piscine and octopoid bas-reliefs and crusted with the oceanic debris of ages. I grew dizzy at elusive angles of architecture which formed surfaces at one and the same time convex and concave, or which changed from one to the other before one's eyes in the manner of optical illusions, from which I deduced that such photographs must in fact be real, for no ordinary photographic equipment could fake visual effects such as these. But over and above all else the most striking thing about R'lyeh—even more astounding and awesome than its utterly alien, non-Euclidean architecture—was its *sheer size*, which, even without a scale of comparison, must surely have been megalithic to dwarf the pyramids. And this, Semple told me without a trace of humour in his voice, in his most matter-of-fact manner, was the merest tip of the actual city, the peak of a sunken mountain range that went down thousands of fathoms to the roots of the Pacific–Antarctic Ridge itself—all of which was R'lyeh!

'Oh, yes,' he had asserted when I was unable to suppress an incredulous expression, 'there are many thousands of square miles of cities beneath the silt on the bed of the Pacific. Even the Deep Ones do not know their full extent, or what secrets are still hidden down there. For remember, they are not cities of the Deep Ones but those of the Gods they worship . . .'

At a later date we spoke of the locations of extant Deep One cities and colonies. There was, of course, Y'ha-Nthlei off the coast of New England; and quite separate from the prehistoric piles of the Pacific already mentioned, there were still several substantial colonies scattered about Ponape. There were, too, certain settlements in the region of the Tongatupo Hole whose origins were immemorial, while six thousand miles to the north there was an expansive outpost even in the frigid deeps of the Aleutian Trench. Another city lay at the edge of the south-eastern Atlantic Basin, and yet another off Sumatra in the Indian Ocean.

There hardly existed a body of water on the surface of the entire planet which did not know the presence of the Deep Ones, or had not known it at some time or other in the dim and abyssal past.

Even the comparatively shallow waters of the Mediterranean had their share of Deep Ones, in the form of a colony dwelling at the bottom of a hole unfathomed by men. 'Oh, yes,' Semple told me, 'and they have been there since the beginning. You may rest assured that when Venus rose up from the waters near Paphos in Cyprus, men gazed upon a Deep One! She was that Aphrodite whose name they applied to the drugs which she distilled from the juices of certain conches, an art in which Deep Ones excel to this very day . . .'

At about this stage of my 'education' (I would guess that a week to ten days had passed since first Semple started working on me), I began to notice a peculiar and disturbing change taking place in the food that I was eating. As I have said, my diet was mainly of fish prepared in a variety of ways, but the quality of the food's preparation had been gradually declining—or, rather, it was the *amount* of preparation that was in question. Quite simply, my food was uncooked and reaching me half raw. However much this fact was disguised in presentation, still I could tell from the texture and the taste of the stuff that only the merest pretence of cooking was being made.

When I protested to Semple, he replied: 'I shouldn't make too much fuss, John Vollister. Next week you'll be catching your own food, right here,' and he pointed to the sunken area of the tank, three-quarters full of sea water. 'Fresh from the sea, my friend, rich and sweet and salty—so you'd better get used to the idea now!'

V

THE SECOND PRISONER

When next he came to see me, Semple answered several questions that I had put to him from the first, all of which he had previously ignored. One of these was about the . . . creature? . . . I had seen on the nighted beach, which had pursued me like some gigantic, filthy slug on the night of my capture. It was, he told me, a shoggoth, a protomorphic slave of the Deep Ones, like a monstrous amoeba of tremendous strength and incredible adaptability, little more than a multipurpose 'engine' of the sort created in Predawn by the Great Old Ones to construct cities such as R'lyeh. According to Semple, several others of its kind were even now working in the Atlantic, building Ahu-Y'hloa in the depths of the ocean.

And I had been fortunate indeed, Semple further informed me, that the thing had not been given strict instructions in respect of unwanted visitors, for then I would most certainly have died, absorbed into the shoggoth, fuel for whichever alien fires drove the thing. As to why it had been there in the first place: that had been in the nature of an experiment, probably a mistake. Shoggoths did not make good watch-dogs where human beings were concerned; they were better at their tasks of guarding R'lyeh's sunken tombs or labouring beneath the sea under the direction of the Deep Ones.

As for the manlike batrachian who had dragged me into the sea: that had been my first meeting with an almost wholly aquatic Deep One, a being born, bred, and in the main confined to the sea. He was of that sort employed by the more truly amphibious Deep Ones as escorts to ocean-going vessels in their employ. As such and with several others of his kind, he had accompanied the boatload of conches during its voyage from 'somewhere off Innsmouth' where the shells had been taken aboard to its destination at the place on the beach. The cargo of conches from Y'ha-Nthlei could not simply be unloaded into the sea near Ahu-Y'hloa (where eventually they were to perform their functions of cementing, polishing, and finishing the new buildings of that city), for they first required a very delicate form of 'acclimatization.' This would involve their immersion in a special brine solution at a controlled temperature for some three weeks, after which they must be fed for a while with a variety of especially rich nutrients. That was why the shells had been unloaded from the boat to the building on the beach, where they now occupied the sunken area of one of the other tanks.

Furthermore, the molluscs had provided a delightful diversion in the diets of those at the beach headquarters, for they were indeed 'a delicacy to the palates of the Deep Ones,' though 'tainted' was a word which Semple was no longer willing to use even in a derisory context. And it transpired that I myself had eaten of the flesh of the snail in a number of 'salads,' but (as Semple pointed out) I had not seen fit to complain until recently, and even now not of the substance of my food but of its degree of preparation.

'Of course,' he had continued, 'the conch is what you might like to call 'a protected species,' for its reproductive cycle is very slow. But, as in the old times, still we 'crop the slug with care.' You must consider yourself honoured that already you have tasted of its delicate flesh . . .'

The one thing that Semple would not disclose, no matter how often I might broach the subject, was the nature of the drugs which were still being given to me. Of them he would tell me no more than that they were 'tranquillizers,' and that they were 'merely a safety measure' under the influence of which I would remain comparatively flexible and incapable of any foolish or violent action against my captors. This was how he explained the purpose of such drugs, but even at that time I had my doubts. I did not believe he told the whole truth.

But in any case, that was all there was of revelations at that time, for on his next visit Semple restricted himself to my instruction in matters concerning the Deep Ones.

This time his subject was the pantheon of their religion, a fascinating rigmarole of myths as fanciful as anything in classical mythology. The basic theme was simply a repetition of what Sarah had already told me, but Semple's version was so detailed as to preclude any possible suggestion of fakery. The thing had not been created for my benefit, but was obviously a cult of worship ancient as the hills. That is not to say that I was converted to the Cthulhu Mythos—on the contrary, I was not . . . not then—but while I myself did not believe, it was plain to me that my instructor did.

It is not my purpose to reproduce all of the details here; I could probably fill an entire book with such information as was made available to me, and time simply will not allow for that. Instead, I shall simply present an abbreviated version of most of what I was told, all of which and more, according to Semple, might be discovered in books written by men of the surface world. They were not books which could readily be found in common public libraries, however, but usually in private collections (such as Semple's own) or locked away in the more restricted archives of such institutions as the British Museum, the Widener Library, the Moscow State Hall of Antiquities, and the Bibliothèque Nationale.

Among many unlikely titles were several that stuck in my mind with an unshakeable persistence, and it later dawned on me that indeed I had seen one or two of them in Semple's room. I mean such volumes as the *Liber Ivonis*, and Le Fe's *Dwellers in the Depths*; but there were also many others with titles which were equally fascinating, such as Ludwig Prinn's *De Vermis Mysteriis*, the *Unaussprechlichen Kulten* of Von Junzt, and the Comte d'Erlette's *Cultes des Goules*. These books and others like them held the keys to the pantheon of the Great Old Ones myth cycle—that is, to the lists of gods attaching to it—or at least as much of the subject as had ever been known to land-dwelling man. They named Yog-Sothoth, 'the all-in-one and one-in-all,' a Supreme Being high in the ranks of the pantheon who was coexistent with all time and conterminous in all space; and Ithaqua the Wind-Walker, a marvellous creature of air and space with the power to walk on the winds that blow forever between the worlds; and Shudde-M'ell, Lord of the Cthonians or Earth-deities, who dwells in the very bowels of the Earth, and many others of equally fantastic attributes.

And here I discovered at least one peculiar parallel with Man's own mythologies; for among lesser gods there was one Dagon, who must surely be that same Dagon or Oannes of the Phoenicians and Philistines, shown on ancient coins and carvings as being half man, half fish! When I mentioned this to Semple, he seemed to lose patience with me, saying:

'Haven't you heard a single word I've said, John Vollister? Who do you think taught the early Phoenicians the art of extracting purple dye from the murex shell? The Deep Ones, of course! Yes, certainly they are one and the same, Dagon and Oannes: the Dagon of the Deep Ones and the Oannes of the Phoenicians. Why, it was their connection with the Mediterranean Deep Ones that brought about the rise of the Phoenicians in the first place, and it was the destruction of their temples to Dagon and the defection of his worshippers from the faith that brought them down.'

Along with Dagon (who was to the Deep Ones 'the Power, the Guide'), there was Hydra, apparently a female, Dagon's mate or wife, and a great list of lesser gods and elementals of one sort or another, including the Hounds of Tindalos, Nyogtha, Cthugha, Bugg-Shash, Yibb-Tstll, and Zhar, all of them holding places of significance and power in the overall myth cycle. Their servitors were many, and covered a wide range of mythological creatures as fantastic and more so than our own dragons, unicorns, nymphs, and satyrs. Indeed, they had their own Great Satyr, Shub-Niggurath, 'the Black Goat of the Woods with a Thousand Young,' to whom I could only liken the better known Pan of more popular legends.

Much was made of certain of these beings in the books, Semple told me, though rarely with any degree of accuracy, truth, or sympathy, for the authors of such works had almost universally chosen to set themselves against the principals of the mythos. Such misinterpretations were invariably the fault of bigoted, misguided, and self-centred Man, who never could see much past the end of his own nose; and since most of the books were several centuries old, this had been even more true at the time of their writing. Why, in those dark centuries of witch-hunts and trials, where every ancient crone or pseudo-chemist was seen to be a witch or diabolist of one sort or another, it must surely be a foregone conclusion that the Cthulhu Cycle and its devotees—however little or much had actually been known about them—would be written off as demons or the agents of 'dark forces.'

In point of fact, however, the truth was entirely the opposite, for with very few exceptions—chief among them Hastur, Cthulhu's half-brother, prisoned in the Lake of Hali in Carcosa—the deities of the mythology were benign beings who looked with kindly eyes upon the works of those who worshipped them. When the stars were right and

Great Cthulhu rose up again from the waves and came forth from his R'lyehan sepulchre, then would his followers reap the benefits of his almighty glory! As for those who opposed, scorned, or denied him . . . it were better for them had they never existed.

In so many words Semple contradicted himself, with offers of glorious fulfilment on the one hand and threats of monstrous dooms on the other. I made no attempt to query the ambiguity, but let him get on with it.

The real villains of the mythology (he continued) were the so-called 'Elder Gods,' whose place was in Orion. In a vastly remote epoch, the Great Old Ones had rebelled against the tyranny and oppressive laws of the Elder Gods and had fled down the spaces between the stars to the Solar System. The Elder Gods gave chase and, when they caught up with the interstellar rebels, imprisoned them wherever they found them. Cthulhu they bound with spells in his house in R'lyeh and sank it down into the Pacific; Ithaqua the Wind-Walker was prisoned on a world called Borea in a strange parallel dimension (from which he later broke free, only to find that the Elder Gods had robbed him of his previous freedom and that he was now condemned to wander for ever in the bitterly cold and frozen places of the universe); Yog-Sothoth and Yibb-Tstll were banished to chaotic continua beyond any knowable design of nature, and so forth.

But as slowly and surely as the stars wheel in the heavens and the aeons creep by, so Cthulhu's devotees—not only Deep Ones but, amongst certain backward peoples, human cults and covens also—were ever at work, patiently and persistently bent upon releasing their master from his immemorial prison, for the Deep Ones believed that Cthulhu was not dead but merely sleeping, and that in his long sleep the Great Old One sent out telepathic dreams from R'lyeh to guide his worshippers and show them the way to effect his release. Abdul Alhazred had known this when he wrote his enigmatic couplet:

> *That is not dead which can eternal lie,*
> *And with strange aeons even death may die.*

This, then, was the prime purpose of the Deep Ones: to spread the word of their god—however slowly, stealthily—and eventually to raise him up again to a glorious resurrection, so that he might once more rule the Earth as he had in aeons past before the evil Elder Gods had thrown him down.

In toto, the Cthulhu Mythology was an utterly fascinating thing, and despite my captivity and periods of enforced study it intrigued me enormously. Semple seemed pleased on the one hand when I told him of my interest, but on the other disappointed that I could not bring myself to accept the mythos as anything other than purely mythical.

'And yet you now accept everything else,' he said at the end of this latest session. 'You accept the Deep Ones, their submarine cities, even the shoggoths. Why not the Great Old Ones? It was our hope that you would find it possible to embrace the cult of Cthulhu without further persuasion.'

'Persuasion?' I looked at him sharply. 'I don't know what you mean. Of course I accept the Deep Ones—yes, and shoggoths, too—for after all I've seen living examples of both. But Cthulhu? Why is it so necessary that I "embrace" your god to become your ambassador? I assume that what Sarah told me was true: that ultimately I am to be an ambassador of sorts, between the Deep Ones and my own people?'

'Your own people?' For a moment he looked startled, then quickly composed himself. 'Ah, yes, she told you that, didn't she . . . ?'

'Well?'

'It should not be long now, John Vollister, before you begin to understand your future functions more clearly. To say any more now would be superfluous. In any case, it will all become clear without explanation. You'll see.'

'But surely,' I began to protest, 'you can tell me more than—'

'Not now, John,' he stopped me. 'Another week, and then we shall begin to see what we shall see.' And with that he quickly left.

I did not see Semple again for at least a week, but it was a week full of changes. For one thing, I was rapidly regaining my strength, mainly due to the fact that for the past five or six days I had not been taking the pills Semple gave me when each of his visits was at an end. I would place them under my tongue and pretend to wash them down with water, then get rid of them as soon as I was left alone.

I suspected that my food was drugged, too, but however distasteful that half-raw mulch of fish invariably was, still I could not go without sustenance. And, truth to tell, despite the fact that the food was raw, I was eating ravenously. This was wholly due (I told myself) to the fact that I was now being given less and less as the days went by, almost as if my captors were intent upon starving me.

Also, I was seeing much less of Sarah now, and when she did visit me there was something different in the way she looked at me. I would find her holding my hands and examining them minutely, or staring at my face as if seeking something in my eyes, something hidden there which she expected to find if only she looked deeply enough. Too, she would pretend to kiss me, but as she did so I would feel her fingers gently massaging the sides of my neck. It was as if she knew that I had developed a nagging sore throat and that the swollen glands of my boyhood had returned to trouble me again.

Then, on the ninth day, after Sargent had been in with fresh blankets and clean sheets (my linen had to be changed regularly due to the damp atmosphere of the tank), he returned with—of all things—a bucket of young, live mackerel! These he released into the water in the sunken area of the tank, telling me that they would live for two days . . . after which they would be no good for eating. And from then on there was no more food.

I slept, started awake from my now recurrent nightmare of pursuit through submarine caves of coral, nervously paced the confines of the tank for hours on end without receiving a single visitor, then kneeled to peer into the shallow water of the sunken area. The mackerel were there, their movement sluggish now, and my hunger was increasing with each passing moment.

Later I slept again—and awoke wondering what would be the difference between the taste and texture of fish fresh from the water and the uncooked food which until recently I had been receiving. One thing was certain: I must not starve myself, for then I would never be able to find the strength necessary to effect my escape.

My escape, yes, for that one thought was now uppermost in my mind: to get out of here and bring the existence of these creatures—of the Deep Ones—to the attention of the authorities. It could well be that eventually a time would come when Man and Deep One might meet on terms of mutual trust, friendship, and benefit, but not while groups such as this were capable of crimes against the person such as I had suffered. The sooner I got out of here the better, but to achieve that end I would have to be strong enough to tackle at least one of my captors. Which led me to the question: which one?

I couldn't picture Sarah or the doctor coming to see me without having someone close at hand to call upon if needs be; which left only Sargent or Semple. The former, while seeming somewhat retarded and slow, had impressed me as capable of great strength. But Semple was slim and small-framed; it would have to be him. As for when I would make my attempt . . . It might be one more day or ten before my chance came, and meanwhile . . . meanwhile I was hungry.

I hardly intend to go into the details of the meal I then made, when I had to strip off my clothes and go into the water after the mackerel. But I did eat, and after the first tentative taste, the first bite, I felt no further nausea but attacked the food with relish. For all said and done, that is all it was: food, sustenance; and my stomach welcomed it without the slightest qualm. Obviously, I was a harder man than I had previously suspected.

By the time I was done with eating, I was dry, and as I put on my clothes I found myself wondering why I had not felt the cold. It must surely be cold in the tank; indeed, I remembered feeling cold during my first few days of consciousness. And yet, while my throat was still very sore and my neck glands bothered me continuously, I now felt quite warm and comfortable. I was given no more time to think the matter out, however, for as I finished dressing there came the clatter of approaching feet and the sounds of a struggle growing louder outside my door.

The scuffling and kicking sounds, accompanied by grunts and thuds, moved past the tank and I heard the banging of a metal door being thrown open. Then, coming to me clearly, I heard the harsh sounds of voices raised in anger—and another voice almost shrill with fear. There were several heavy thumps against the wall of the tank, followed by a cry of pain, and finally I heard the metal door slammed shut and barred. Then, along with a string of low curses uttered in vicious and guttural tones, there came again the sound of feet, retreating this time, and at length silence.

It was only then that I thought to hammer on my own door and demand to know what was going on, which I would have done had not sounds of low moaning coming from close at hand checked me. I put my ear to the metal wall and listened. Yes, on the other side of that steel panel someone was hurt and groaning in his pain. A second prisoner? But whoever he was, how could I possibly help him?

In sudden desperation I cast about with my eyes until they lighted upon a small recessed ventilation grille which was fitted in the wall at a height of about eight feet. I had noticed it before, but had given it no great consideration. Only nine inches square, even if I had managed to remove the grille my case would not be improved any. Now, though, if I stood on my chair, I should at least be able to see into the adjacent tank.

I pulled the chair over to the wall and climbed up on to it, stretching myself to peer through the metal lattice of the grille. There on the narrow ledge of the recess, on my side of the grille, lay a small screwdriver, a little rusty but still serviceable. It must have been left there by a workman when the tanks were built. Making a mental note of this potential weapon, I looked beyond it through the grille and into the tank on the other side. This second tank, too, had a light which had been left on. I could see that the place was a duplicate of my own cell and that it appeared to be empty—

—Or was it? If I raised myself a few inches higher I should be able to look down through a fairly steep angle and . . . *yes!*

There on the floor, spread wide apart, I could see the lower half of a pair of trousers with projecting feet, one of which had lost its shoe. The feet moved jerkily even as I watched. A moment more and there came another groan as the feet tensed for a second or two before falling slack. The groaning stopped abruptly. Whoever he was, my colleague in the adjacent tank had passed out.

Either that, or he was dead . . .

For what must have been all of two hours I sat on my bed, my ear to the metal wall behind which lay the sleeping or dead stranger. Every so often I would climb on to my chair and peer through the grille, and at last I thought to take up the rusty screwdriver and begin working on the four screws which held the grille in place.

I managed to loosen three of the screws (no mean feat with a blade which was far too small for the task), but the fourth and last screw would not move. I felt like hammering at the stubborn screw with the hard plastic body of the screwdriver, but feared that the noise would bring someone to investigate. In the end I gave it up, placed the tool back on its ledge, got down, and dropped the three successfully removed screws into the water in the sunken area of the tank.

As I was doing this I noticed that the remaining three or four fish barely were moving, all of them on or close to the surface. I was poising my hand over the water, preparing to pluck out a fish as it swam slowly by, when there came a low, painful cough followed by a recurrence of the groaning. Immediately I stood up, climbed on to my chair, and peered through the grille.

I was in time to see the pair of feet withdrawn, to hear more groans and an uncertain fumbling at the metal wall, and then at last the stranger staggered into view with one hand held up to the side of his head. He was of medium build, blond with short-cropped hair, in his early forties at a guess. He moved over to the door, turned to scan the interior of the tank with pain-slitted eyes, then returned his attention to the door and lifted a fist as if to bang upon its metal oval.

'Don't!' I called out, keeping my voice low. 'You'll only bring them back down on us.'

'Wha—?' He started, spinning about to scan the interior of the tank once more. His face was bruised and bloodied, and as I tapped quietly on the grille with the screwdriver, so it seemed that his eyes met mine where I peered at him.

'Who—?' he began again, moving to stand uncertainly beneath the grille and squinting up at me. Perhaps he could make out the outline of my face, or at least my eyes through the bars of the grille. I studied his face for a moment, then breathed more easily at the discovery that it showed none of the now-familiar stigmata.

'I'm a prisoner, like yourself,' I told him. 'A prisoner of these . . . these madmen!'

'Madmen?' He laughed low and bitterly, then groaned and held his head, staggering slightly. 'Possibly they are mad. I don't know. But men?' He slowly shook his head.

'What do you know of them?' I eagerly asked as he sat down carefully on the metal floor, lowering his head to hold it in his hands. 'Why have they brought you here?'

He looked up again, sharply, and I thought I saw suspicion in his eyes. 'Who are you?' he asked. 'One of them, trying to find out just how much I know?'

'Vollister,' I told him. 'My name is John Vollister, and I assure you I am not—'

'John Vollister?' he cut in. 'The marine biologist? Yes, that would be right enough. I remember reading somewhere that you lived out this way.'

'Yes,' I answered, 'that's me, but I don't work a great deal these days. I live a few miles down the coast—or at least I did until I walked into this. But who are you that you know my name?'

'Oh, I know your name, all right. I've read your stuff—all of it. I've been reading everything I can find on the sea and its creatures for years now. My name's Belton—Jeremy Belton.'

In my turn I recognized his name immediately. 'Belton the journalist? Wasn't there something about you in the news quite recently? Something about "sensational revelations" or some such? A "cosmic threat" of some sort or other? I don't pay too much attention to the dailies. But what's brought you to this?'

'What brings me here?' Again he laughed his bitter laugh. 'Well,

Mr Vollister, if I may borrow a phrase from you, I also "walked into it." As neat a trap as ever was laid.'

'A trap?'

He nodded. 'I was contacted by "a friend" who told me he had definite proof of the existence of Deep Ones right here in England. A meeting was arranged at a quiet pub in London. There were drinks—which must have been drugged—and . . .'

'And they brought you here.'

Again he nodded. 'I woke up in a moving car and managed to catch sight of a signpost in Newquay. That told me where I was. And I feigned unconsciousness while they were carrying me down here from the car. So I'm at a place on the beach somewhere in Cornwall, right? I tried to make a run for it as they were bringing me into the building, but—' He shrugged, then thumped the metal floor with his clenched fist. 'What a damned fool I am!'

'Shh!' I cautioned him, then asked: 'But why have they done this to you?'

'Those "sensational revelations" you mentioned. You know what it was all about? No, of course you don't. No one knows, for I've kept it close to my chest for the last five years.'

'I think I do know,' I answered. 'You were going to reveal them to the world—the Deep Ones, I mean.'

His eyes widened momentarily in surprise. 'You're catching on,' he said. 'Yes, I had been promised a spot on television, a little space in the newspapers . . . if my story was hot enough. You see, I still have a lot of contacts from my days as a newshound. If I said I had something big, then they knew it was pretty big! But our friends got wind of it, and—'

'And here you are.'

He nodded yet again. 'The story was due to break in a week's time. But not now. Now I'm here—of all places.'

'Of all places? How do you mean?'

'Cornwall,' he answered. 'Mermaid country. Didn't you know that? Why, there are still people in these parts who claim they have mermaid ancestors. And, by God, they're probably right!'

'You really do know a lot about them, then?'

'The Deep Ones?' He squinted up at me. 'Do I know about them? I've devoted myself to tracking them down, finding out as much as it's humanly possible to know about them, everything. My one mistake lies in doing it on my own, I've kept it all to myself, told no one—but my trail must have looked a mile wide to the Deep Ones. I might have known they wouldn't let me get away with it.'

'But what will they do with you? They can't hold you here indefinitely. They've told me that they mean people no harm, that I myself am to be their ambassador, and that—'

'No harm!' he exclaimed, cutting me off. Then his voice became scornful. 'And you believe that! "Ambassador," you say? The first mankind will know of it is when they're crawling all over us!'

And suddenly I knew he was right, and that I was a bigger fool than I had previously been willing to admit. 'I've had my suspicions,' I answered. 'But if they've been lying to me . . . then what do they want with me?'

He shook his head and shivered. 'With you? I can't say. But I know what they want with me.' Behind the streaks of dried blood his face was pale. 'I doubt if I'll ever see the outside of this place.'

'Murder?' I said. 'You believe they'd go that far?'

Now he laughed, weary hysteria in his voice. 'Oh, you don't know them at all, do you, John? They'll go just as far as they need to. All of them—in all their many forms—they're bent on one thing and one thing only. One goal, and once they've achieved that, the next step will be the destruction of mankind, of the universe itself!'

There were so many questions I wanted to put to Belton, but I could only ask them one at a time. 'Their many forms?' I repeated him. 'What do you mean?'

'Well, there are those that remain landbound, who never fully take on the true form of the aquatic Deep Ones. They're sort of half-and-half. Then there are those that are born on dry land and go to the sea later. These are the real amphibians. Yes, and I guess there are other types. I've had a personal and very real experience with at least one more . . .' He paused.

I said nothing for a moment, but thought back on what Semple had told me about blind Deep Ones in subterranean lakes. Finally, I asked: 'What is this other type you mention?'

'It's a long story,' he answered. 'But since it looks like you're destined to be my one and only audience . . . ' He shrugged. 'It started with Haggopian.'

'Haggopian?' I repeated, frowning. 'Haggopian! But he's dead, or at least disappeared, five, six years ago. If ever a man was my idol, Richard Haggopian was that man. Wasn't there something odd about the way he vanished?'

'Something odd?' Again he uttered his hysterical laugh, finding great difficulty, I thought, in controlling it. 'Listen, I was with him at the end.'

'When he died?'

'Yes . . . no,' he said. He shivered again and hugged his coat closer. 'I was with him,' he repeated, his eyes searching the grille almost pleadingly. 'Listen, and I'll tell you about Haggopian.'

VI
HAGGOPIAN

'I'll never forget it,' Belton began. 'Richard Haggopian, perhaps the world's greatest authority in ichthyology and oceanography, to say nothing of all the many allied sciences and subjects, had at last agreed to an interview. I was jubilant. At least a dozen journalists before me, from as many parts of the world, had made the futile journey to Kletnos in the Aegean to seek out Haggopian the Armenian, but only my application had been accepted.

'It's not hard to say why Haggopian excited such interest among the world's foremost journalists. Any man with his scientific and literary talents, with a beautiful young wife, an island in the sun, and—perhaps most important of all—a blatantly negative attitude towards even the most beneficial publicity would certainly have attracted the same interest. And, of course, he was a millionaire.

'For eight frustrating days I had waited on the Armenian's return to Haggopiana—his tiny island hideaway two miles east of Kletnos and midway between Athens and Iraklion—and just when it seemed that my strictly limited funds must surely run out, then Haggopian's great silver hydrofoil, the *Echinoidea*, cut a white scar on the incredible blue to the southwest as it sped in to a mid-morning mooring.

'With binoculars from the flat white roof of my Kletnos—hotel?—I watched the hydrofoil circle the island until it disappeared behind Haggopiana's wedge of white rock. Two hours later the Armenian's man came across in a sleek motorboat to bring me news of my appointment. I was to attend Haggopian at three in the afternoon. A boat would be sent for me.

'At three I was ready, dressed in sandals, cool grey slacks, and a white T-shirt—civilized attire for a sunny afternoon in the Aegean— waiting for the motorboat when it returned to the natural rock wharf. On the way out to Haggopiana, as I gazed over the prow of the craft down through the crystal-clear water at the gliding, shadowy groupers and the clusters of black sea urchins, I did a mental check-up on what I knew of the elusive owner of the island ahead.

'Richard Hemeral Angelos Haggopian, born in 1919 of an illicit union between his penniless but beautiful half-breed Polynesian mother and millionaire Armenian-Cypriot father; author of three of the most fascinating books I had ever read, books for the layman, telling of the world's seas and all their multiform denizens in simple, uncomplicated language; discoverer of the Taumotu Trench, a previously unsuspected hole in the bed of the South Pacific almost seven thousand fathoms deep; benefactor of the world's greatest aquariums and museums, etc., etc., etc.

'Haggopian the much married—three times, in fact, and all since the age of thirty—an unfortunate man, apparently, where brides were concerned. His first wife (British) died at sea after nine years of wedded life, mysteriously disappearing overboard from her husband's yacht in calm seas on the shark-ridden Barrier Reef in 1958; number two (Greek-Cypriot) died in 1964 of some exotic wasting disease and was buried at sea; and number three—one Cleanthes Leonides, an Athenian model

of note, wed on her eighteenth birthday—had apparently turned re-
cluse, since she had not been seen publicly for more than two years.

'Cleanthes Haggopian—yes! Expecting to meet her I had checked
through dozens of old fashion magazines for her photographs. That had
been a few days ago in Athens, and now I recalled her face as I had seen
it in those pictures: young, natural, and beautiful in the Classic Greek
tradition. And again, despite rumours that she was no longer living with
her husband, I found myself anticipating our meeting.

'In no time at all the flat white rock of the island loomed to some
thirty feet out of the sea and my navigator swung his fast craft over to
starboard, passing between two jagged points of salt-encrusted rock
standing twenty yards or so out from Haggopiana's most northerly tip.
As we rounded the point I saw that the easterly face of the island was
formed of a white sand beach, with a pier at which the *Echinoidea* was
moored. Set back from the beach in a cluster of pomegranate, almond,
locust, and olive trees there sat an immense and sprawling flat-roofed
bungalow.

'At the dry end of the pier my quarry waited until, with the very
gentlest of bumps, the motorboat pulled in to mooring. He wore
grey flannels and a white shirt with the sleeves rolled down. A wide,
silken, scarlet cummerbund was bound about his waist. His thin nose
supported heavy, opaquely-lensed sunglasses. So this was the great
man—tall, awkward-seeming, bald, extremely intelligent, and very, very
rich—his hand outstretched in greeting.

'He was something of a shock. I had seen photographs of him, quite
a few, and had often wondered at the odd sheen such pictures had given
his features. I had always taken the quality of the shots as being simply
the result of poor photography. His rare appearances in public had
always been very short ones and unannounced, so that by the time
cameras were clicking or whirring he was usually making an exit.

'Now I could see that I had short-changed the photographers. He
did have a sheen to his skin, and there must also have been something
wrong with his eyes. Small tears glistened on his cheeks, rolling thinly
down from behind the dark lenses. In his left hand he carried a square

of silk with which, every now and then, he would dab at this telltale dampness.

' "How do you do, Mr Belton?" His voice was a thick, heavily accented rasp, conflicting with his polite enquiry and manner of expression. "I am sorry you have had to wait so long, but I am afraid I could not delay my work . . ."

' "Not at all, sir. I'm sure this meeting will amply repay my patience."

'His handshake was unpleasant, and I unobtrusively wiped my hand on my T-shirt. Patently, that sheen to the man's skin was the result of sun oil. His hand had seemed greasy. An allergy, perhaps, which might also explain the dark-tinted glasses.

'I had noticed from the boat a complex of pipes and valves between the sea and the house, and now, approaching that sprawling yellow building in Haggopian's wake, I could hear the muffled throb of pumps and the gush of water. Once inside the place it soon became apparent just what the sounds meant: the building was nothing less than a gigantic aquarium.

'Massive glass tanks lined the walls, so that the sunlight filtering through from exterior porthole-like windows entered the rooms in greenish shades that dappled the marble floors and gave the place an eerie, submarine aspect. There were no printed cards or boards to describe the finny dwellers in the huge tanks, and as he led me from room to room it became clear why such labels were unnecessary. Haggopian knew each specimen intimately, his rasping voice making a running commentary as we visited in turn the bungalow's many wings.

' "An unusual coelenterate, this one, from five hundred fathoms. Difficult to keep alive—pressure and so forth. I call it *Physalia haggopia*—quite deadly. Makes a waterbaby of the Portuguese man-of-war." (This of a great purplish mass with trailing, wispy-green tentacles undulating horribly through the water of a tank of huge proportions.)

'Haggopian, as he spoke, deftly plucked a small fish from an open tank on a nearby table, throwing it up over the lip of the greater tank to his "unusual coelenterate." In a frenzy, the fish swam straight into one of the green wisps—and instantly stiffened. A few seconds more, and the hideous jellyfish had commenced a languid ingestion.

' "Given time," Haggopian grated, "it would do the same to you." '

'In the largest room of all, I paused, literally astonished at the size of the tanks. Here, where sharks swam through brain and other coral formations, the glass of these miniature oceans must have been very thick. Backdrops had been arranged to give the impression of vastly sprawling submarine vistas.

'In one tank ugly-looking hammer-heads of over two metres in length were cruising slowly from side to side. Metal steps climbed up to and over this tank's rim, then down the other side and into the water itself. Haggopian explained: "This is where I used to feed my lampreys— they had to be handled carefully. I no longer have them; I returned the last of them to the sea three years ago."

'Three years? I peered closer as one of the hammerheads slid his belly along the glass. On the white and silver underside of the fish, between the gill slits and down the belly, numerous patches of raw red showed, many of them forming clearly defined circles where the close-packed scales had been recently removed and the sucker-like mouths of lampreys had been at work. Obviously a slip of the tongue—three days, more like.

'I stopped pondering my host's mistake as we passed into another room whose specimens must surely have delighted any conchologist. Again tanks lined the walls, smaller than the others I had so far seen but marvellously laid out to duplicate perfectly the natural environs of their inhabitants. And these were the living gems of every ocean on Earth. Great conches and clams from the South Pacific; tiny, beautifully marked cowries from the Great Barrier Reef; hundreds of weird uni- and bi-valves of every shape and size. Even the windows were of shell—great, translucent, pinkly glowing fan shells, porcelain thin but immensely strong, from very deep waters—suffusing the room in blood tints different again from the submarine dappling of the previous rooms.

'My tour was interrupted here when Costas, the Greek who had brought me from Kletnos, entered this fascinating room to murmur something of obvious importance to his employer. Haggopian nodded his head in agreement, and Costas left, returning a few moments later with half a dozen other Greeks, each of whom had a few words with Haggopian before departing. Eventually we were alone again.

' "They were my men," he told me, "some of them for almost twenty years, but now I have no further need of them. I have paid them their last wages; they have said their farewells; now they are going away. Costas will take them to Kletnos and return later for you. By then I should have finished my story."

' "I don't quite follow you, Mr Haggopian. You mean you're going into seclusion here? What you said just then sounded ominously final."

' "Seclusion? Here? No, Mr Belton—but final, yes! I have learned as much of the sea as I can from here; my education is almost complete."

'He saw the puzzled look on my face and smiled wryly. "You are at pains to understand, which is hardly surprising. Few men, if any, have known my circumstances before, of that I am certain. That is why I have chosen to speak now. You caught me at the right time, for I would never have taken it upon myself to tell my story had I not been so persistently pursued. Perhaps the telling will serve as a warning. It gives me pause, the number of students devoted to the lore of the sea who would emulate my works and discoveries." He frowned, pausing for a moment.

' "Tomorrow when the island is deserted, Costas will return and set all of the living specimens loose. Even the largest fishes will be returned to the sea. Then Haggopiana will truly be empty."

' "But to what end?" I asked. "And where do you intend to go? Surely this island is your base, your home and stronghold. It was here you wrote your wonderful books, and—"

' "My base and stronghold, yes," he harshly cut me off. "The island has been these things to me—but my home? No longer. When your interview is over I shall walk to the top of the rocks and look once more across the water to Kletnos. Then I will take my *Echinoidea* and guide her out through to Kasos Straits on a deliberate course until her fuel runs out. There can be no turning back. There is a place unsuspected in the Mediterranean, where the sea is so deep and cool, and where—"

'He broke off and turned his glistening face to me. "But there, at this rate the tale will never be told. Suffice to say that the last trip of the *Echinoidea* will be to the bottom—and that I shall be with her."

' "Suicide?" I gasped. "You intend to—drown yourself?"

'At that he laughed, a rasping cough of a laugh that jarred like chalk on a blackboard. "Drown myself? Is a watery grave so distasteful, then?" He laughed again.

'For a few moments I stared at him in dumb amazement and concern, uncertain as to whether I stood in the presence of a sane man or . . .

'He gazed at me intently through the dark lenses of his glasses, and under the scrutiny of those unseen eyes I slowly shook my head, backing off a step.

' "I'm sorry, Mr Haggopian, I just . . ."

' "Unpardonable!" he rasped as I struggled for words. "My behaviour is inexcusable! Come, Mr Belton. Perhaps we can be more comfortable out here."

'He led me through a doorway and out on to a patio surrounded by lemon and pomegranate trees. A white garden table with cane chairs stood in the shade. Haggopian clapped his hands sharply, then offered me a chair before seating himself opposite. Again I noticed that the man's movements seemed oddly awkward.

'An old woman, wrapped around Indian-fashion in white silk and with the lower half of her face veiled in a long shawl answered the Armenian's summons. He spoke a few guttural but gentle words to her in Greek. She went, to return shortly with a tray, two glasses, and (amazingly) an English beer with the chill still on the bottle.

'I saw that Haggopian's glass was already filled, but with no drink I could readily recognize. The liquid was greenly cloudy with sediment, yet the Armenian did not seem to notice. He touched glasses with me before drinking deeply. I, too, took a deep draught, for I was very dry; but as I placed my glass back on the table I saw that Haggopian was still drinking. He completely drained off the murky liquid, put down his glass, and again clapped his hands in summons.

'At this point I found myself wondering why the man did not remove his sunglasses. We were, after all, in the shade. A glance at the Armenian's face served to remind me that he must suffer from some allergy, for again I saw those thin trickles of liquid flowing down from behind the enigmatic lenses.

'The silence was broken when the old woman came back with a further glass of her master's drink. He spoke a few more words to her before she once more left us. I could not help but notice, though, as she bent over the table, how very dehydrated her face looked, with pinched nostrils, deeply wrinkled skin, and dull eyes sunk deep beneath the bony ridges of her eyebrows. An island peasant woman, obviously. She seemed to find a peculiar magnetism in Haggopian, leaning towards him noticeably, visibly fighting to control an apparent desire to *touch* him whenever she came near him.

' "She will leave with you when you go. Costas will take care of her."

' "Was I staring?" I started guiltily, aware suddenly of an odd feeling of unreality and discontinuity. "I'm sorry—I didn't intend to be rude."

' "No matter. What I have to tell you makes nonsense of all matters of sensibility. You strike me as a man not easily . . . frightened, Mr Belton?"

' "I can be surprised, sir—but frightened? Among other things, I've been a war correspondent, and—"

' "Of course, but there are worse things than the horrors of war."

' "That may be, but in any case I'm a journalist. I'll take a chance on being—frightened."

' "Good! And please put aside any doubts you may by now have conceived with regard to my sanity."

'I started to protest, but he quickly cut me off. "No, no, Mr Belton! You would have to be totally insensible not to perceive the strangeness here."

'He fell silent as for the fourth time the old woman appeared, placing a pitcher on the table before him. This time she almost fawned on him, and he jerked away from her, nearly upsetting his chair. He rasped a few harsh words in Greek, and I heard the strange, shrivelled creature sob as she turned to stumble away.

' "What on earth is *wrong* with the woman?"

' "In good time, Mr Belton." He held up his hand. "All in good time." Again he drained his glass, refilling it from the pitcher before commencing his tale proper.

' "My first ten years of life were spent in the Cook Islands, and the next five in Cyprus," Haggopian began, "always within shouting distance of the sea. My father died when I was sixteen, and willed to me two and one half millions of pounds Sterling. When I was twenty-one I came into this money and found that I could now devote myself utterly to the ocean—my one real love in life. By that I mean all oceans, all great waters . . .

' "At the end of the war I bought Haggopiana and began to build my collection here. I wrote about my work and was twenty-nine years old when I finished *The Cradle Sea*. It was my success with that book—I used to enjoy success—and with *The Sea: A New Frontier*, which prompted me to commence work upon *Denizens of the Deep*.

' "I had been married to my first wife for five years by the time I had the first rough manuscript of my work ready, and I could have published the book there and then but for the fact that I had become something of a perfectionist both in my writing and in my studies. In short, there were passages in the manuscript—whole chapters on certain species—with which I was not satisfied.

' "One of these chapters was devoted to the sirenians. The manatee in particular had fascinated me for a long time, in respect of its undeniable connections with the mermaid and siren legends of old renown; from which, of course, the order takes its name. However, it was more than merely this that took me off initially on my Manatee Survey, as I called those voyages, though at that time I could never have guessed at the importance of my quest. As it happened, my enquiries were to lead me to the first real pointer to my future—a frightful hint of my destination, though of course I never recognized it as such." He paused.

' "Destination?" I felt obliged to fill the silence. "Literary or scientific?"

' "My *ultimate* destination."

' "Oh!"

'After a moment, Haggopian continued, and as he spoke I could feel his eyes staring at me intently through the opaque lenses:

' "You are aware of the theories of continental drift, which have it that the continents are gradually floating apart and that they were once much closer to one another? Such theories are sound. Primal Pangaea did exist, trod by feet other than those of men. Indeed, that first great continent knew life long before the first man wondered at his place in the Universe.

' "But at any rate, it was partly to further the work of Wegener and the others that I decided upon my Manatee Survey—a comparison of the manatees of Liberia, Senegal, and the Gulf of Guinea with those of the Caribbean and the Gulf of Mexico. You see, Mr Belton, of all the shores of Earth these two are the only coastal stretches where manatees occur in their natural state: excellent zoological evidence for continental drift.

' "Well, eventually I found myself in Jacksonville on the East Coast of North America. There, by chance, I heard of certain strange stones taken out of the sea—stones bearing weathered hieroglyphs of fantastic antiquity, presumably washed ashore by the back currents of the Gulf Stream. Such was my interest in these stones and their possible source— you may recall that Mu, Atlantis, and other mythical sunken lands and cities have long been favourite themes of mine—that I quickly concluded my Manatee Survey to sail to Boston, Massachusetts, where I had heard that a collection of such oddities was kept in a private museum. There, when I saw those ancient stones bearing evidence of primal intelligence, I knew that I had conclusive proof of the floating continents theories. Why, I had seen evidence of that same intelligence in places as far apart as the Ivory Coast and the Islands of Polynesia!"

'For some time, Haggopian had been showing an increasing agitation, and now he sat wringing his hands and moving restlessly in his chair. "Ah, yes, Mr Belton, was it not a discovery? For as soon as I saw those basalt fragments I *recognized* them! They were small, those pieces, yes, but the inscriptions upon them were the same as I had seen cut in the great black Pillars of Geph in the coastal jungles of Liberia—pillars long uncovered by the sea and about which, on moonlight nights, the natives cavorted and chanted ancient liturgies. I had known those liturgies, too, Belton, from my childhood in the Cook Islands—*Ia-R'lyeh! Cthulhu fhtagn!*"

'With this last thoroughly alien gibberish fluting weirdly from his lips, the Armenian had risen suddenly to his feet, his head aggressively forward and his knuckles white where they pressed down on the table. Then, as I quickly leaned backwards away from him, he slowly relaxed and fell back into his chair as though exhausted. He let his hands hang limp and turned his face to one side.

'For at least three minutes, Haggopian sat like this before turning to me with a half-apologetic shrug of his shoulders. "You—you must excuse me, sir. I find myself very easily given to over-excitement."

'He took up his glass and drank, then dabbed again at the rivulets of liquid from his eyes before continuing. "But I digress. Mainly I wished to point out that once, long ago, the Americas and Africa were Siamese twins, joined at their middle by a lowland strip which sank as the continental drift began. There were cities in those lowlands, and suffice to say that the beings who built the ancient cities, beings who seeped down from the stars over inchoate aeons, once held dominion over all the world. But they left other traces, those beings, queer gods and cults and even stranger . . . residua.

' "However, quite apart from these vastly interesting geological discoveries, I had something of a *genealogical* interest in New England. My mother was Polynesian, you know, but she also had old New England blood in her. My great-great-grandmother was taken from the islands to New England by a deck hand on one of the old East India sailing ships in the late 1820s, and two generations later my grandmother returned to Polynesia after her American husband died in a fire. Until then the line had lived in Innsmouth, a decaying New England seaport of ill repute, where Polynesian women were anything but rare. My grandmother was pregnant when she returned to the islands, and the American blood came out strongly in my mother.

' "I mention all this because . . . because I cannot help but wonder if something in my genealogical background has to do with . . .

' "You see, I had heard many strange tales in Polynesia as a child—tales of *things* that come up out of the sea to mate with men, and of their terrible progeny!"

'For the second time a feverish excitement made itself apparent in Haggopian's voice and attitude, and his whole body trembled, seemingly in the grip of massive, barely repressed emotions.

' "*Ia-R'lyeh!*" he suddenly burst out again in that unknown tongue. "What monstrous things lurk even now in the ocean deeps, Belton, and what other things *return* to that cradle of earthly life?"

'Abruptly he stood up to begin pacing the patio in his swaying, clumsy lope, mumbling incoherently to himself and casting occasional glances in my direction where I sat, very disturbed now by his obviously aberrant condition. But at last he sat down again and continued:

' "Once more I ask you to accept my apologies, Mr Belton, and I crave your pardon for straying so wildly from the principal facts. I was speaking before of my book, *Denizens of the Deep*, and of my dissatisfaction with certain chapters.

' "Well, when finally my interest in New England's shores and mysteries waned, I returned to that book and especially to a chapter concerning ocean parasites. Of course I was limited by the fact that the sea cannot boast so large a number of parasitic or symbiotic creatures as the land; none the less I dealt of the hagfish and lamprey, of certain species of fish-leech, whale lice, and clinging weeds, and I compared them with fresh-water leeches, types of tapeworm, fungi, and so on. Now, you might be tempted to believe that there is too great a difference between sea- and land-dwellers, and of course in a way there is—but when one considers that all life as we know it sprang originally from the sea . . . ?

' "But to continue:

' "In 1956 I was exploring the oceans of the Solomon Islands in a yacht with a crew of seven. We had moored for the night on a beautiful uninhabited little island off San Cristobal, and the next morning, as my men were decamping and preparing the yacht for sea, I walked along the beach looking for conches.

' "Stranded in a pool by the tide I saw a great shark, its rough back and dorsal actually breaking the surface. I felt sorry for the creature, and even more so when I saw fastened to its belly one of those very bloodsuckers with which I was still concerned. Not only that, but the hagfish was a beauty! Four feet long if it was an inch, and definitely of a type I had never before seen. By that time, *Denizens of the Deep* was almost ready, and but for that chapter I have already mentioned the book would have been at the printers long since.

' "Well, I could not waste the time it would take to tow the shark to deeper waters, so I had one of my men put it out of its misery with a rifle. Goodness only knows how long the parasite had fed on its juices, gradually weakening it until it had become merely a toy of the tides. As for the hagfish: he was to come with us. Aboard my yacht I had plenty of tanks to take bigger fish than him, and of course I wanted to study him and include a mention of him in my book.

' "My men managed to net the strange fish without too much trouble and took it aboard, but they seemed to be having some difficulty getting it back out of the net and into a sunken tank. I went over to give a hand before the fish expired, and that was when the creature began thrashing about. It came out of the net with one great flexing of its body—and took me with it into the tank!

' "My men laughed at first, naturally, and I would have laughed with them—*had that awful fish not in an instant fastened itself on my body, its suction-pad mouth grinding high up on my chest and its eyes boring horribly into mine!*"

'After a short pause, during which Haggopian's face worked hideously, he continued:

' "I was delirious for three weeks after they dragged me out of the tank. Shock?—Poison? I did not know at the time. *Now* I know, but it is too late. Possibly it was too late even then.

' "My wife was with us as cook, and during my delirium, as I feverishly tossed and turned in my cabin bed, she tended me. Meanwhile, the crew kept the hagfish—a previously unknown species of Myxinoidea—well supplied with small sharks and other fish. They never allowed the cyclostome to drain its hosts completely, you understand, but they knew enough to keep the creature healthy for me.

' "My recovery, I remember, was plagued by recurrent dreams of monolithic submare cities. Cyclopean structures of basaltic stone peopled by strange hybrid beings: the amphibious Deep Ones, minions of Dagon and worshippers of dreaming Cthulhu. In these dreams eerie voices called out to me and whispered things of my forebears—things which made me moan through my fever at the hearing . . .

' "After I recovered the times were many when I would go below decks to study the hagfish through the glass sides of its tank. Have you ever seen a hagfish close up, Mr Belton? No? Consider yourself lucky. They are ugly, with looks to match their natures, eel-like and primitive. And their mouths—their horrible, rasplike, sucking mouths . . . !

' "Two months later, towards the end of the voyage, the horror really began. By then my wounds, the raw places on my chest where the thing had had me, were healed completely; but the memory of that first encounter was still terribly fresh in my mind, and—

' "I see the question written on your face, Mr Belton, but indeed you heard me correctly—I did say my *first* encounter. Oh, yes—there were more encounters to come."

'At this point in his remarkable narrative, Haggopian paused once more to dab at the rivulets of moisture seeping from behind his sunglasses and to drink yet again from the cloudy liquid in his glass. It gave me a chance covertly to look about me. The Armenian was seated with his back to the great bungalow, and as I glanced nervously in that direction I saw a face move quickly out of sight in one of the smaller porthole windows. Later, as Haggopian's story progressed, I was able to see that the face in the window belonged to the old servant woman and that her eyes were fixed firmly upon him in a kind of hungry fascination. Whenever she caught me looking at her, she would withdraw.

' "No," Haggopian finally went on, "the hagfish was far from finished with me. As the weeks went by, my interest in the creature grew into a sort of obsession, so that every spare moment found me staring into its tank or examining the curious marks and scars it left on the bodies of its unwilling hosts. And so it was that I discovered how those hosts were *not* unwilling. A peculiar fact, and yet—

' "Yes, I found that having once played host to the cyclostome, the fishes it fed upon were ever eager to resume such *liaisons*, even unto death! Later I was able to establish quite definitely that following the initial violation the hosts of the hagfish submitted to subsequent attacks with a kind of soporific pleasure. Apparently, Mr Belton, I had found in the sea the perfect parallel of the vampire of land-based legend. Just what this meant, the utter *horror* of my discovery, did not dawn on me until . . . until . . .

' "We were moored off Limassol prior to starting on the very last leg of our trip, the voyage back to Haggopiana. I had allowed the crew—all but one man, Costas, who had no desire to leave the yacht—ashore for a night out. My wife, too, had gone to visit friends in Famagusta. Myself: I was happy enough to stay aboard. I had known a tired feeling, a lethargy, for a number of days.

' "I went to bed early. From my cabin I could see the lights of the town and hear the gentle lap of water about the legs of the pier at which we were moored. Costas was drowsing aft with a fishing line dangling in the water. Before I dropped off to sleep I called out to him. He answered in a sleepy sort of way, saying that there was hardly a ripple on the sea and that already he had pulled in three fine mullets . . .

' "When I regained consciousness it was three weeks later and I was back here on Haggopiana. The hagfish had had me yet again. They told me how Costas had heard the splash and found me in the cyclostome's tank. He had managed to get me out of the water before I drowned, but had needed to fight like the very devil to get the monster off me—or, rather, *to get me off the monster!*

' "Do the implications begin to show, Mr Belton?

' "You see this?" He unbuttoned his shirt to show me the marks on his chest—circular scars of about three inches in diameter, like those I had seen on the hammerhead—and I stiffened in my chair as I saw their great number. Down to the silken cummerbund he unbuttoned his shirt, and barely an inch of his skin remained unblemished. A number of the scars even overlapped.

' "Good God!" I finally managed to gasp.

' "*Which god?*" Haggopian instantly rasped, his fingers trembling again in that strange passion. "Which god, Mr Belton? Jehova or Oannes—the Man-Christ or the Toad-Thing—god of earth, air or water? *Ia-R'lyeh, Cthulhu fhtagn, Yibb-Tstll, na Yot-Sottot!* I know many gods, sir!"

'Again, jerkily, he filled his glass from the pitcher, literally gulping at the sediment-loaded stuff until I thought he must choke. When finally he put down his empty glass, I could see that he had himself once more under a semblance of control.

' "That second time," he continued, "everyone believed I had fallen into the tank in my sleep; as a boy I had been something of a somnambulist. At first even I believed it was so, for at that time I was still blind to the creature's power over me. They say that the hagfish is blind, too, Mr Belton, and members of the better-known species certainly are—but my hag was not blind. Indeed, primitive or not, I believe that after the first three or four times he was actually able to recognize me!

' "I used to keep the creature in the tank where you saw the hammerheads. Forbidding anyone else entry, I would pay my visits at night, whenever the *mood* came on me; and he would be there, waiting for me, with his ugly mouth groping at the glass and his queer eyes peering out in awful anticipation. He would go straight to the steps as soon as I began to climb them, waiting for me in the water until I joined him there. I would wear a snorkel, so as to breathe while he—while it—"

'Haggopian was trembling all over now and dabbing angrily at his face. Glad of the chance to take my eyes off the man's oddly glistening features, I finished off my drink and refilled my glass with the remainder of the beer in the bottle. The chill was long off the beer by then, and it was flat. I drank solely to relieve my mouth of its clammy dryness.

' "The worst of it was," he went on after a while, "that what was happening to me was not against my will. As with the sharks and other host fish, so with me. I enjoyed each hideous liaison as the drug addict delights in his delusions, and the results of my addiction were no less destructive.

' "I experienced no more periods of delirium, such as I had known following my first two *meetings* with the creature, but I could feel that my strength was slowly but surely being sapped. My assistants knew that I was ill, naturally, but it was my wife who suffered the most. I could have little to do with her, do you see? If we had led any sort of normal life, then she must surely have seen the marks on my body. Oh, but I waxed cunning in my addiction, and no one guessed the truth behind the strange sickness which was slowly killing me, draining me of my life's blood.

' "A little over a year later, in 1958, when I knew I was on death's very doorstep, I allowed myself to be talked into undertaking another voyage. My wife loved me deeply still, and believed a prolonged trip might do me good. I think that Costas had begun to suspect the truth by then. I even caught him one day in the forbidden room, staring curiously at the cyclostome in its tank.

' "His suspicions became more obvious, however, when I told him that the creature was to go with us. He was against the idea from the start. I argued that my studies were incomplete and that when I was finished with the hag I intended to release it at sea. I intended no such thing. In fact, I did not believe I would last the voyage out. From fourteen stone in weight, I was down to less than eight.

' "We were anchored off the Great Barrier Reef the night my wife found me with the hagfish. The others were asleep after a party aboard. I had insisted that they all drink and make merry so that I could be sure not to be disturbed, but my wife had remained sober and I had not noticed. The first thing I knew of it was when I saw her standing at the side of the tank, looking down at me and the . . . *thing*!

' "I will always remember her face, the horror and awful knowledge written upon it—and her scream, the way it split the night!

' "By the time I got out of the tank, she was gone. She had fallen or thrown herself overboard. Her scream had roused the crew, and Costas was the first to be up and about. He saw me before I could cover myself. I took three of the men and went out in a little boat to look for my wife, to no avail. When we got back, Costas had finished off the hagfish. He had gaffed the thing to death. Its head was little more than a bloody pulp, but even in death its suctorial mouth continued to rasp away—at nothing.

' "After that, for a whole month, I would have Costas nowhere near me. I do not think he *wanted* to be near me. I believe that he knew my grief was not solely for my poor wife . . .

' "Well, that was the end of the first phase, Mr Belton. I rapidly regained my health, the years fell off my face and body, until I was almost the same man I had been. I could never be exactly the same, though. For one thing, I had lost all my hair. As I have said, the creature had taken me to death's very doorstep. Also, to remind me of the horror, there were the scars on my body and a greater scar on my mind: the look on my wife's face when last I had seen her.

' "During the next year I finished my book, mentioning nothing of my discoveries during the course of my Manatee Survey, nothing of my experiences with the awful fish. I dedicated the book to the memory of my poor wife, but yet another year was to pass before I could get the episode with the hagfish completely out of my system. From then on I could not bear even to think back on my terrible obsession.

' "It was shortly after I married for the second time that phase two began . . .

' "For some time, I had been experiencing a strange pain in my abdomen just above my navel, but had not troubled myself to see a doctor. I have an abhorrence of doctors. Within six months of the wedding, the pain had disappeared—to be replaced by something far worse.

' "Knowing my terror of medical men, my new wife kept my secret; and though we neither of us knew it, that was the worst thing we could have done. Perhaps if I had seen about the thing sooner—

' "You see, Mr Belton, I had developed—yes, an organ! An *appendage*, a snoutlike thing had grown out of my stomach, with a tiny hole at its tip like a second navel. Eventually, of course, I was obliged to see a doctor; and after he examined me and told me the worst, I swore him—or, rather, I paid him—to secrecy. The organ could not be removed, he said. It was part of me; it had its own blood vessels, a major artery, and connections with my lungs and stomach. It was not malignant in the sense of a morbid tumour.

' "Other than this, he was unable to explain the thing away. After an exhaustive series of tests, though, he was further able to say that my blood, too, had undergone a change. There seemed to be far too much salt in my system. The doctor told me then that by all rights I ought not to be alive.

' "Nor did it stop there, Mr Belton, for soon other changes started to take place—this time in the snoutlike organ itself—when the tiny navel began to open up at its tip!

' "And then . . . and then . . . my poor wife . . . *and my eyes!*"

'Once more, Haggopian had to stop. He sat there gulping like—like a fish out of water—with his whole body trembling violently and the thin streams of moisture trickling down his face. Again he filled his glass and drank deeply of the filthy liquid; and once more he wiped at his ghastly face. My own mouth had gone very dry again, and if I had had something to say, I very much doubt I could have managed it.

' "I—it seems—you—" the Armenian half-gulped, half-rasped, then uttered a weird, harshly choking bark before finally settling himself to finishing his unholy narrative. Now his voice was less human than any voice I had ever heard before:

' "You—have—more nerve than I thought, Mr Belton, and—you were right: indeed, you are not easily shocked or frightened. In the end, it is I who am the coward, for I cannot tell the rest of the tale. I can only—*show* you, and then you must leave. You may wait for Costas at the pier . . ."

'With that, Haggopian slowly stood up and peeled off his open shirt. Hypnotized, I watched as he began to unwind the cummerbund at his waist, watched as his *organ* came into view, as it blindly groped in the light like the snout of a rooting pig! But the thing was not a snout.

'*Its end was an open, gasping mouth—red and loathsome, with rows of rasp-like teeth—and in its sides breathing gill slits showed, moving in and out as the thing sucked at thin air!*

'Even then the horror was not at an end, for as I lurched reelingly to my feet, the Armenian took off those hellish sunglasses. For the first time, I saw his eyes: *his bulging fish eyes—without whites, like jet marbles, oozing painful tears in the constant ache of an alien environment—eyes adapted for the murky gloom of the deeps!*

'I remember how, as I fled blindly down the beach to the pier, Haggopian's last words rang in my ears; the words he rasped as he threw down the cummerbund and removed the dark-lensed sunglasses from his face:

' "Do not pity me, Mr Belton," he had said. "The sea was ever my first love and there is much I do not know of her even now—but I will, I will. And I shall not be alone of my kind among the Deep Ones. There is one I know to be waiting even now, and one other yet to come!"

'During the short trip back to Kletnos, numb though my mind ought to have been, the journalist in me took over and I thought back to Haggopian's hellish story and its equally hellish implications. I thought of his great love of the ocean, of the strangely cloudy liquid which helped to sustain him, and of the thin film of protective slime which glistened on his face and presumably covered the rest of his body. I thought of his weird forebears and the exotic gods they had worshipped, of *"things that came up out of the sea to mate with men!"*

'I thought of the fresh marks I had seen on the undersides of the sharks in the great tank, marks made by no ordinary parasite, for Haggopian had returned his lampreys to the sea all of three years earlier; and I thought of that second wife who, rumour had it, died of some "exotic wasting disease." Finally, I thought of those other rumours I had heard of his *third* wife; how she was no longer living with him—but of the latter, it was not until we docked at Kletnos proper that I learned how those rumours, understandable though the mistake was, were in fact mistaken.

'For it was then, as the faithful Costas helped the old woman from the boat, that she stepped on her trailing shawl. That shawl and her veil were one and the same garment, so that her clumsiness caused a momentary exposure of her face, neck, and one shoulder to a point just above her left breast. In that same instant of inadvertent unveiling, I saw the woman's face for the first time—and also the livid scars where they began just beneath her collarbone.

'At last I understood the strange magnetism Haggopian had held for her, that magnetism not unlike the unholy attraction between the morbid hagfish of his story and its all-too-willing hosts. I understood, too, my previous interest in her dehydrated face—which yet had classic features.

'For now I could see that it was the face of a certain Athenian model lately of note: Haggopian's third wife, wed to him on her eighteenth birthday! And then, as my whirling thoughts flashed back yet again to that second wife, "buried at sea," I knew finally, cataclysmically what the Armenian had meant when he said: "There is one I know to be waiting even now, and one other yet to come!" '

VII
ESCAPE!

Despite my personal problems—or perhaps more correctly because of them—the horror of Belton's tale reached out to me. And for all his journalistic background, I guessed that he had coloured the story not at all, that it had happened just the way he told it. But while during its telling there had been so much in the story I could relate to my own knowledge of the Deep Ones, still I had not in this instance found anything to prove conclusively their inimical nature. Instead, Haggopian's case had inspired in me a sort of pity; I had felt a definite empathy with the man in his extremes of horror. Oh, I myself could now testify to the fact that the Deep Ones were devious in their ways, no doubt of that—but deadly? A threat to the world? To the universe? That was something entirely different.

By now, however, my legs felt stiff from standing so awkwardly on the chair, and one of them was about to go to sleep on me. I told Belton

I would be back in a few minutes, and got painfully down. Pacing back and forth for a little while in the confines of my tank until my joints were eased, I found myself dwelling morbidly on Haggopian's dreams, which had seemed so reminiscent of my own, and on his peculiar genealogy. My background, too, had more than its fair share of anomalies, which I must certainly look into if ever my position permitted it.

Then, as I was about to climb back up on to my chair, there came the sound of unhurried feet outside, and a few seconds later I heard Belton's door once more thrown open. Almost immediately, the door was slammed shut and barred again, and the footsteps paused outside my own door. I heard Sarah's voice raised in what sounded like a request, and Semple's firm refusal before all sounds passed on and faded away.

After a little while, I got back up on my chair and tapped on the grille. Belton looked up and managed a wry smile. 'They don't intend to finish me just yet, at any rate,' he said. 'Look here, I've been given a blanket!' Then his face hardened. 'There were three of them—three Deep Ones.'

I nodded, though he could hardly have seen more than the merest movement of my head through the grille. 'You knew them by their looks?'

'By their looks, their smell, their damned fish-eyes. They're unmistakable. In New England it's called the "Innsmouth Look." Who is the big hulking one?'

'Sargent, you mean? He's some sort of servant around here.'

Belton nodded. 'A changeling who never quite made it. Faithful to the Deep Ones as a dog to its master.'

'How do you mean, "changeling"?' I asked. 'Not in Haggopian's way, surely?'

He shrugged. 'There are changelings and changelings. It was a long time after Haggopian that I started to look at the native legends and myth patterns of the Solomon Islands. You'll remember he found his hagfish off San Cristobal? Well, all anyone need do is pick up a book on Oceanic Mythology at any bookshop, and he'll find more than enough evidence of the Deep Ones and changelings. The natives out there know well enough of the *adaro*, "sea-sprites" who are part-human, part-fish. They visit men in their dreams and teach them strange songs and chants, and they call to them on conches and tempt them into the sea . . .' He paused for a moment, then continued:

'But no, the half-people here in this place are not of Haggopian's sort. I rather fancy that he was the first of his kind—"protogenus," you might say—and that his inherent Deep One genes were both activated and mutated by the advent of the hagfish. More than that I can't say. I'm no biologist.' He looked up at me strangely, quizzically, I thought; but before I could comment, he went quickly on. 'But as I was saying, these people are not Haggopian's sort.'

'Then just what sort are they?' I asked.

'I haven't seen them all,' he answered, 'but there are three types here, at least. Sargent is landborn and didn't make the change. One of his parents was a Deep One, but the human side was dominant. And for all their prowess with drugs, the true Deep Ones haven't been able to bring about the full change in him. Or perhaps they started on him too late, when he was too set in his human ways, or when his body was no longer able to accomplish the metamorphosis. Incidentally, one of the side-effects of their damned drugs when they don't work is to stunt the mind and retard its processes. That poor devil Sargent looks to me to be a classic example.

'Then there's the one called Semple. He's a half-breed, too, except that in his case the dominant side was all Deep One. He's just about ready to take to the water, maybe already has, in which case he's a true amphibian. And there was one in the car whose smell nearly turned my stomach. My guess is that he was an original Deep One, with no human blood in him at all. That type can't stay out of the sea very long.' He paused, then after a moment went on.

'Yes, it looks to me like they're after a setup here similar to what they once had in America. Back in the early 1920s, Innsmouth was crawling with all types of Deep Ones. It was one of their biggest strongholds, remote and decaying, and of course there was one of their submarine cities close by.'

'Y'ha-Nthlei?' I asked, knowing that I was right.

He frowned up at me. 'Hmm! You know a bit more than I thought. Yes, Y'ha-Nthlei, and they had been mingling the blood for ages. That part of the American coastline, just like this part here in England, has always been "mermaid country." You see what I mean? Anyway, in 1928, government agents got wind of what was going on and stepped in. They just about levelled half the place, but they in no way finished off the job . . . more's the pity. I don't suppose the government men really knew what they were dealing with . . .'

As he finished speaking, the scientist in me suddenly rebelled against all I had already more than half-accepted. 'Listen,' I began, with something of desperation in my voice, 'a moment ago you mentioned that you're not a biologist. Well, I *am* a biologist—a marine biologist— and I just can't make myself accept that there could ever be issue from this sort of union. It's just too fantas—'

'No,' he shook his head, 'it's not too fantastic at all. You yourself could mate with a pygmy girl and raise six-foot sons.'

'Of course I could,' I exploded. 'But not with a damned frog!'

'Oh?' He peered up at the grille. 'It's not so very long ago that they used to test a woman for pregnancy by injecting a female frog with her urine. If the frog spawned, the woman was pregnant. It actually works. Are you saying there's no link?'

'Oh, I know all about that,' I told him, 'and if there were enough time, I could even explain it to you, but—'

'But, but, *but!*' he cried out. 'There can be no argument. It's real, I tell you! Changelings? My God, just look at the life-cycle of the common frog! And as for why they want you—why, you've already answered that one yourself.'

'What? How do you mean?'

'You're a biologist, aren't you?'

'A marine biologist, yes.'

He nodded. 'Yes, and they've been recruiting all sorts to their cause. Doctors, scientists, biologists . . . men, yes, human beings. Every man has his price, they say—and the Deep Ones know it.'

'I still don't follow you.'

'Don't you? You must know what a clone is.'

'A clone? Of course I know what a—' I stopped short. 'What are you getting at?'

'Just this: I believe they're about ready to start cloning Deep Ones!'

'*What?*'

'I have evidence, I tell you! And something else: in all of the experiments performed so far in cloning, which do you suppose have been most effective? What type of creature may most readily be cloned?'

The short hairs rose of their own accord on the back of my neck, and I shuddered uncontrollably. 'The amphibia!' I answered in a whisper.

'Yes.' He vigorously nodded his head. 'Damn frogs! And that's what they're after: an entire submarine world full of Deep Ones—every body of water on Earth swarming with them—and when there are too many of them for us to handle . . .'

'Then?'

He hugged his blanket around his shoulders. 'We'll be herded, like cattle—and then they'll be able to concentrate on their main objective.'

'Which is?'

'To release Cthulhu, of course. To set that ageless monster free!'

'But surely Cthulhu is a purely mythical creature?' I argued. 'The "god" of their faith? And the way they tell it, he's benign And—'

'Benign?' He choked on the word. 'My God! Do you know what you're saying? Not only is Cthulhu real, he's responsible for half of this crazy world's madness! Those are not ordinary dreams he sends out from R'lyeh, but nightmares! Hideous visions to turn the minds of men and drive them mad!'

For a moment, I was gripped by the intensity of his belief—dragged by it to the rim of a chasm of utmost lunacy—but still something in me, some imp of the perverse, refused to let me finally accept the truth of his statements.

'No,' I said. 'I just can't believe it. The rest of it I'll allow, everything, but Cthulhu—'

'Listen, man,' he stopped me, 'I *know* he's real. Christ, if you'd read the *Johansen Narrative*—and I have—then you'd know it, too!'

'The *Johansen Narrative?*' I said. 'I never heard of it.'

'No,' Belton was suddenly calmer, resigned, 'and I don't suppose it makes much difference, really.' He shook his head disgustedly. 'If you did read it, you'd probably call it fiction. But let me tell you, anyway:

'In 1925, the bed of the Pacific buckled and tossed R'lyeh up to the surface. Johansen was the sole survivor of a ship that landed on that hellish upheaval. It was a crazy place, of monoliths and mad angles, all covered with monstrous carvings. Johansen's story, a tale he didn't long survive, is more terrifying than anything I've told you so far. But he *saw* Cthulhu, and his hair turned white at what he saw!'

'Go on,' I pressed him. 'What, exactly, did he see?'

Before he could answer, as I tried to ease my legs by changing my position, the chair rocked beneath me. I held tight to the corners of the grille to steady myself, and felt the metal plate move under the pressure exerted by my fingers. In another moment, I had managed to steady myself.

'Have you got that thing loose?' Belton asked, peering up at the grille. 'I thought I saw it move, then.'

'It did, yes,' I answered. 'Just let me get this last screw loose, and—'

I took up the screwdriver, turned its blade in the slot of the screw— and the grille moved. Three or four more turns of the blade, and it was almost loose. I forced the grille down until it hung from that single screw, then stared at the face of Belton through the small opening. He stared back—stared up at me—and in a moment his mouth fell open and his eyes went wide.

Then he stumbled back, away from the metal wall, away from me, arms wide and flailing, an inarticulate gurgle welling in his throat.

I was too amazed at Belton's inexplicable reaction to do or say anything on the spur of the moment, and only a second or so later it would have been impractical to try, for even as I heard the sound of muffled footsteps from outside and the grating of bars being removed— even as I fumblingly replaced the grille and stepped clumsily down from the chair—the door of my tank burst open and Sargent, the doctor, and one other entered single-file and in great haste. From the adjacent tank,

I heard Belton shouting something in a defiant voice, and the sound of vicious cursing and desperate activity, followed by a sickening thud of flesh against the wall as a human scream, rising, was cut short.

Caught red-handed, I faced the three who cautiously approached me. I had placed the screwdriver out of sight in my pocket; now I thought to reach for it, and only just managed to check myself. The tool would be of no use against the three of them. I needed to keep it until later, when there might be only one of these creatures to deal with.

As they backed me up against the wall, I merely glanced at Sargent, whose face was now puffed up in rage, and at the doctor, who bit his lip in annoyance—but as for the third one . . .

. . . him I could not take my eyes off!

For if he were not that same creature which had dragged me from the boat in the bay, then certainly he was its brother! The Deep One came closer, fish-eyes unblinking—approaching with movements which were half-slither, half-hop—and my instinctive reaction was to flee. Then I remembered how weak I was supposed to be, and backed along the wall until the back of my legs struck the edge of the bed. Down I fell on the bed, unresisting as the three closed with me and took hold of my arms.

While Sargent and the Deep One held me, the doctor produced a needle and hovered over me. 'So,' he said, 'we found a way to chat with our friend next door, did we?' He glanced up at the grille, which had fallen half open of its own accord, then at the chair where it stood close to the metal wall. 'And doubtless he told you many lies. Well, no matter—no matter at all.'

He slid the needle into my arm, and in the space of a few seconds I felt a numbness creeping over me. I closed my eyes, and the two who held me released their grip. Their voices came to me from far away.

I heard Sargent say: 'The fish—he's taken some of them. Bones over here.' And he was answered by another voice—that of the Deep One, whose *texture* and *tone* still do not bear detailed description—which seemed to concur with and approve of Sargent's observation.

Then the doctor said: 'Yes, he makes rapid progress. Sarah made a good choice. But it was a mistake to put Belton next door. Still, what's done is done.' I felt his fingers at my neck, probing gently in that area where the skin was rough through my constant chafing and rubbing. Then he lifted the lid of my right eye, and his face swam into view. He smiled, but his face was out of focus, so that his expression seemed to me like the grin of one of hell's own demons. 'Rapid progress, indeed!' he repeated, lowering my eyelid like a shutter and allowing me to slide down into the darkness of oblivion . . .

And again the nightmare—but this time more monstrous than anything I had dreamed so far.

. . . I swam in frozen, weed-shrouded deeps between basaltic towers of titanic proportions, and behind these massive stone facades I knew that somewhere the loathly Lord Cthulhu dreamed his own damnable dreams of dominion. I was searching for something, a door, yes, and at last I found it looming open behind a slab of coral-encrusted basalt fallen in ages past from the main structure.

Down into gloom I swam, in lightless vaults whose immeasurable antiquity numbed the mind, until finally I came to those inner chambers which housed the sleeping god. And, at last, glowing in fires of luminescent rottenness, I saw Cthulhu Himself!

But it was an unquiet sleep that the Great Old One slept, and his demon claws tightened threateningly on the sides of his great throne even as I watched, while his folded wings moved as if to open over his tentacled head and lift him up from the deeps to the unsuspecting world above! The eyes in his great face were closed—which I knew was a mercy—and the tentacles that fringed and bearded his head like the tendrils of some obscene anemone were almost, but not quite, still, so that I went carefully indeed, for fear of waking him.

Then, when I would have turned to steal silently away, he sensed me. His wings stopped their trembling; his fitfully scrabbling claws became purposeful and started to reach out towards me; his eyes became great slits which hideously, hypnotically began to open; and, horror of horrors, his face tentacles uncoiled like waking snakes, groping with unimaginable intent in my direction where I backed frantically away, stirring up the aeon-deposited silt and slime in my haste to be out of that place! And as I fled—

—So I awakened.

Sweat-soaked, I awakened to darkness. The light was out, and the tank was stifling as a tomb. As my dream receded, I remembered all that had gone before, and felt for the screwdriver where it lay in my pocket. Reassured, I listened to the pounding of my heart until it slowed and returned to normal. Not too far away, I could hear the gentle *hush* of the sea against the beach, and guessed that the tide was in and that it was night outside. Night, and the place was dark and silent—or was it?

From somewhere overhead, a muted creaking sounded, and the merest suspicion of voices told of life in the building above me. Anger—yes, and hatred, too—tightened my face as I determined to wait no longer, but make my escape at the very next opportunity.

And with the decision came pain, enough to make me put my hands up to my neck and feel tenderly the ruptured skin beneath my jaw on both sides. I felt ... and what I discovered brought instant panic! For the lesions beneath my unbelieving fingers were fresh and deep, regular slits that ran parallel to my jaw-bone and felt like flaps of raw flesh.

Sheer panic, but only for a moment, and then I knew a cold and calculating calm that should have frightened me almost as much as its cause—which was a sudden and shockingly illuminating knowledge of the truth!

The truth at last, yes, for of course I now *knew*. I knew what had frightened Belton when first he had seen my face through the open grille, knew also why I had been 'chosen' in the first place. Oh, there was much I still did not know, but these things I knew—in one cataclysmic moment I knew them—these and one other. That through no doing of my own, *I had acquired the Innsmouth Look*, and that one way or another I would make the Deep Ones pay!

A moment later, I slipped out of my clothes and into the water in the sunken area of the tank. Even in the dark the fish were easy to find; I seemed to sense their whereabouts. They were not yet dead, though very nearly so, but even had I found them floating belly up on the surface, still I would have eaten of them. Oh, yes, for I would need what strength I could muster now for what was next to come . . .

Semple did not come alone, but with Sargent. Lying on my bed in feigned sleep, I silently cursed my luck as the door opened with its customary clanging, and their voices reached me. My plan had depended upon only one of them coming to see me, for come he surely must, sooner or later, if only to replenish my 'food' and see how I was 'progressing.' I had not had to wait for very long, but now I was at a loss what to do; it fully appeared that I might have to put my plan back. Then I felt the light burn through my closed eyelids, and heard Semple step through the raised portal into the tank. As he did so, he said to Sargent, 'Here, take the flashlight.'

Sargent answered, 'Should I wait?'

'No need,' Semple answered. 'He'll be weak as a kitten. Shove the door to, but don't bar it. I'll let myself out.'

So, I was to be left alone with Semple, was I? My pulse quickened on the instant.

'Good-night, sir,' came Sargent's phlegmy reply, then the dull thump of the door closing, and finally the sound of slow footsteps retreating.

Now I had to fight to control my breathing, my pounding heart as Semple approached my bed to stand over me. What was he doing, standing so still? Did he suspect?

I was startled at what came next. I had been prepared for a hand on my arm, shaking me 'awake'—not the gentle tremor of Semple's fingers at the freshly opened gill-slits of my neck!

I started up, my hands reaching to close viciously on his own silk-covered throat before he could cry out, forcing him down to the metal floor and holding him there, motionless, until his eyes began to glaze and his fleshy lips started to tremble spasmodically. By now, Sargent would be well away, in his room up above in the main building. Still, best to be sure.

Gradually, I released my hold on Semple's neck, and he drew air— but only with difficulty. The silk scarf he still wore had been displaced, and beneath my fingers I could see his bruised and battered gills. Already I had done him grave injury. Not fatal, however, as yet, for he was an amphibian and could use his lungs like a normal human being.

'Fool!' he hoarsely croaked. 'You'll pay!'

'No, you'll pay, Semple—for what you've done to me. Now listen. This can be easy or hard—hard on you. I'm getting out of here, and I'm taking Belton with me. He's not in the next tank; I know because I've looked. You left the light on in there, and the place is empty. So the first thing you're going to do is tell me where he is.'

'You . . . can't help Belton,' he wheezed. 'Not now.' Then his voice became pleading. 'Listen, John, you don't know what you're doing. The penalties for—'

'Penalties? I'll pay no penalties, Semple. Not to you, or the Deep Ones, or anyone. You're coming with us—you, me, and Belton—and there's no chance my story won't be believed. Let's face it, there isn't a medical man in England who wouldn't know you for an alien on sight! Whatever you are—half fish, frog, whatever—they'll declare you in-human. And just suppose they do mistake you for some poor unfortunate freak . . . what about me? What you've done to me—or started to do—will be more than sufficient proof, even without Belton's word. I'll have the authorities down on this place before you can turn about!'

'Oh?' he croaked as I allowed him just sufficient air to keep talking. 'And how will all of this help you? What good will it do you? You're a Deep One, John. You always have been. The seeds were there all along, but they were dormant. We've only set them working—accelerated a natural process—to bring about the change. When it's complete, then you'll be an amphibian, a Deep One.'

'But I was a human being!' I hissed through clenched teeth, fighting the urge to throttle him there and then. 'I still am. What you've done to me will go no further. I haven't taken a single one of your damned pills for more than a week.'

'You *what*?' He choked the words out, stopped struggling, and gazed up at me in utter astonishment. 'Man, have you any idea just what those pills were?'

'Oh, I know what they were,' I answered. 'They did this to me—' and I inclined my head, showing him my neck.

'No,' he croaked, squirming beneath my grip. 'The drugs for the change—the hormones and catalysts—they were in your food, in the injections you've been given. You can't stop the change, John; it's irreversible. It's in you, working even now. But those other drugs, the pills, *they were to help you retain your sanity!*'

'What?'

'What have you done, you fool? You were a perfect subject!'

The wave of horror—horror and red rage—which his words conjured in me was almost too great to bear. I bit my tongue and felt tears of frustration wash down my face as I tightened my grip on him. 'You . . . you . . . *you!*' I hissed furiously. Then I threw back my head and screamed voicelessly, in my mind, screamed through a mist shot with blood as I applied still more pressure through my fingers and squeezed, squeezed, squeezed!

Gone now were all thoughts of preserving Semple's life, of keeping him as a *specimen* with which to alert the authorities. I myself should be evidence enough. My own person, coupled with what Belton had to tell, should satisfy even the most—

—Belton! I still didn't know where they had put him!

I released my grip on Semple's throat, and his head thumped on the metal floor like a lump of lead. His eyes had almost left their sockets, and his gills were crushed to pulp. He was stone dead.

All emotion left me in a moment. All horror, hatred, passion, drained from me in a split second. I had murdered a man!

Then—

No, I told myself, I was no murderer. I had merely killed a Deep One, destroyed an enemy of Man, crushed a scorpion. I shuddered in loathing of the thing on the floor, took out my screwdriver, glanced once more about the naked tank which had housed me for . . . how long?—then carefully pushed the door open and stepped through into a gloomy corridor.

It was not completely dark, though nearly so, and I could only just see to make my way to the door of the adjacent tank. It, too, was unbarred, and I managed to open it silently, sufficiently to peer inside. Momentarily the light blinded me, but then . . . I was correct: Belton had been taken elsewhere. His blanket lay on the floor, but otherwise the tank was quite empty. Then, remembering that Semple had told me there were three tanks, I moved cautiously along the corridor until I found the third door.

This door was also unbarred—which alone seemed to suggest that the prisoner was not to be found here—but I decided nevertheless to enter the tank and make sure. As I was about to do so, I became aware of a red, dimly glowing light behind me. My eyes were more accustomed to the gloom now, and as I turned I could make out the shape of a door in the wall of excavated rock directly opposite me across the wooden flooring of the corridor. The upper panel of the door—of conventional design, unlike the metal manholes of the tanks—was of frosted glass, behind which the red light burned.

For a moment I paused breathlessly. I still did not know how I would get out of the place, and what if there were Deep Ones behind the door? True, the place seemed silent enough, and even with my ear to the frosted glass panel I could hear nothing at all of voices or movements . . .

—Well, I must do something, for plainly I couldn't stay here much longer. For all I knew, Semple's companion of a few minutes ago might well be up above, even now waiting for him to put in an appearance. He would have to wait a long time.

Since it seemed unlikely that Belton could be in the unbarred third tank, perhaps he had been put in the room with the redly glowing light. In any case, my curiosity had been piqued. Despite my terrifically dangerous position, I had to know what lay behind that door.

Carefully, with each and every nerve in my body shrieking its tension, I turned the knob of the door and opened it, then entered silently and closed the door with the merest click behind me. The room was completely still, with only that single, dim red bulb glowing at some indeterminate distance from me. On the wall, my hand found a nest of light switches, one of which was depressed. I tripped this one switch and the red light went out. Immediately, my heart skipped a beat . . . but nothing else happened. I switched the light on again—and a second, a third. Three red lights, evenly spaced out, now lit the gloom, but their combined light gave little more illumination than one bulb on its own. I tripped a fourth switch . . . and was almost blinded as the white glare of a large industrial bulb blazed into life close to where I stood!

Wide-eyed in shock, I gritted my teeth, expecting . . . something!

But no, the seconds passed with the leaden thumping of my heart, and there was no sign of life. The place was still, and utterly silent. I started to breathe again, and began to take in the size of the subterranean room in which I now found myself. After spending so long in the tank, this place and its unexpected hugeness completely overawed me. Tiled walls stretched away for at least thirty yards or more, and the width of the room was only a little less than its length. The entire area beneath the place on the beach had been completely hollowed out.

A tiled walkway some ten feet wide surrounded a large sunken area six or seven feet deep, with metal steps leading into—or rather out of— the pool. Without the slightest shadow of a doubt, this was a pool, empty at the moment, but destined for a great deal of use. The unfinished pool which fronted the building up above was merely for show, an acceptable excuse for cutting a channel from the sea direct to the Deep Ones' headquarters; and this secret pool was where the Deep Ones would emerge, unseen by human eyes, whenever they came in from the ocean.

A pair of large pipes just big enough to take two swimmers abreast showed their shiny white mouths in one of the sunken walls, and in my mind's eye I could picture monstrous frog-shapes emerging, convening in the salty water of the pool and doing . . . what?

What in hell was this place really for? What did the Deep Ones plan? The pool was a big one; why did they need a pool so large? Was

Belton right in everything he suspected? Perhaps this was where I might find out.

There were doors in the tiled walls of the room, each one bearing a name or title on a plastic plate. Moving round the pool (apart from the comparatively low ceiling and the absence of diving boards, it was for all the world like being in a small, deserted swimming-bath after hours). I paused to peer at the first nameplate. It said PUTH'UUM-LAHOIE! Was this really someone's name? I tried the door, but it was locked. The next door, which had an as-yet-unmarked plate, stood slightly ajar. I entered a medium-sized room piled high with crates, boxes, and sections of metal shelving waiting for assembly. There was nothing there to interest me, however, so I quickly moved on.

Then, at the far end of the pool, I came to a door with Semple's name on it. I entered, put on the light . . . then stood gaping in astonishment at the veritable library of occult and esoteric literature contained within that small enclosed area. It would have been pointless even to attempt to remember more than half a dozen titles from those ceiling-high shelves, much less list them; they meant little enough to me, and would doubtless mean nothing at all to anyone but a student of such matters. While Semple had told me that he was just such a student, I had never thought of his obsession in terms of such magnitude. But, much as I would have liked to stay longer and look into some of these disquieting volumes, I still had to find Belton, and my position must surely have been growing more and more untenable by the minute.

Hurriedly, I moved on, trying doors and briefly entering those that stood open, discovering nothing of any great importance and growing ever more aware of a rapidly thickening aura of hideous danger. Then, when I had almost returned to my starting point, after examining the rooms of several unrecognized human names—and one at least which I did know, that of DR ABRAHAM WAITE, the same 'doctor' who had so misused me—and those of true Deep Ones with names every bit as unearthly as the almost unpronounceable 'Puth'uum-lahoie,' I was brought up short by a plate bearing a name which I immediately recognized.

The plate said simply: I. ZCHASKOV—but the Igor Zchaskov I knew of was a Russian biochemist whose work in certain areas of biology—including cloning—had made him a fairly famous (and, in other quarters more concerned with ethics than results, an unprincipled and *in*famous) name in his field. He had defected from the Soviet Union in 1964, since which time he had gradually faded from the limelight. And now . . . ?

The door of Zchaskov's room was open and I entered; and in less than a minute I had satisfied myself that indeed Belton was correct in all he suspected of Deep One ambitions and motivations. The room was nothing less than a small but extremely sophisticated and well-equipped laboratory, and to me it was abundantly clear what Zchaskov's work was to be. This was the room where eventually he would attempt to manufacture an army of identical Deep Ones!

I had seen enough. Now, without more ado, I must find Belton and get out of this monstrous place. I left Zchaskov's laboratory, went to the main door, switched off all the lights except for the one small red bulb whose glow had led me to the place, and silently slipped out into the corridor. The oval door of the third tank stood before me, my last shot before attempting to discover a way out of this nest of evil.

I stepped across the corridor, pulled the door open, and entered. The light was on, which was as well, for I would not have known where to locate the switch, and the tank was—empty?

No, not empty, for Belton's clothing lay in a disordered heap in one corner. Also, there were thick red smears on the metal floor . . .

My flesh crawled as I froze, turned to stone by a movement glimpsed in the corner of my eye, a movement so slight as to be almost unnoticeable. Something was coming up over the lip of the sunken area, following a scarlet smear where it had dripped over the edge: a conch, one of those 'unique' sinistral conches with which this entire nightmare had commenced.

On legs which were suddenly weak as columns of jelly I moved to the edge of the sunken area. It was half full of water that was alive with conches. Directly beneath where I stood, a barrel-shaped knot of the slugs bobbed gently in the water on something which slowly revolved beneath their moving weight. Even as I watched, a cluster of them fell from the half-submerged object, fell bloated and red and . . . *sated*!

'Acclimatization! . . . Immersion in a brine solution at a controlled temperature! . . . Fed with especially rich nutrients!'

As God is my witness—if God there ever was—the eyeless, half-devoured, bloody gobbet of flesh in the water was all that remained of Jeremy Belton!

VIII
CHANGELING

The rest of it is a blur, a frenzy of memories seen now in my mind's eye like a stroboscopic nightmare. I remember finding a metal staircase that led upward, and a door that opened on to the beach on the southern side of the main building. I remember hugging the shadows beneath leering, peeping stars as I fled to the rocks of the southern promontory, and how I made my way around that tall tumble of boulders until I waded, then swam in the cool waters of the pool as the sea receded. I recall the way the moon silvered the water as I swam, adding its lustre to a fire of morbid excitement that burned in my veins. And for all that a greater passion drove me, there was a lure in the nighted ocean that was near-hypnotic.

Then I remember stumbling from the water on the southern side of the bay arm, to be confronted by the *thing* which grew menacingly out of the shadows until it towered over me like a nodding stalagmite of sentient slime—the shoggoth, whose myriad eyes gazed at me, whose pseudopod arms reached out avidly to encircle me—before it shrank back in seeming consternation to stand mute and uncertain, though still vaguely threatening, beside an upright needlelike boulder large as itself. Then . . . a warning. As if to show me that my identity and loyalties remained in doubt, that the . . . creature . . . was far from satisfied with my authenticity, it turned on the rock standing up from the damp sands and enveloped it in an instant.

This *envelopment* was simply that: the shoggoth flowed forward and enclosed the rock. Then . . . there followed a hissing, slight at first but rapidly increasing to a subdued, contained roar. I stood, trembling, dripping salt water, frozen in my terror, watching as the shoggoth's outline seemed to vibrate where its protoplasmic body *crushed* the solid stone it enclosed.

In some inexplicable way I was given to know the creature's purpose: to demonstrate its power, its awesome strength. And like a whale blowing, suddenly the top of the shoggoth opened (I can explain it no other way: its upper surface developed an aperture or orifice) and from this palpitating opening reeking furnace gasses rushed upwards in a roaring jet, carrying with them small, charred, sticky fragments of stone which rained down spatteringly to steam and hiss upon the beach. I covered my head with my arms to avoid being struck by this super-heated debris and backed away; and as I retreated, so the shoggoth ended its display and flowed back into its original position. Now, where so recently the boulder had stood, a black circle of tarry liquid steamed and bubbled; and of the great rock in its original form, no slightest shadow remained.

Without more ado, as I continued to back away, the shoggoth melted back into the shadows of the beach and was gone. Just as poor Belton had done, this protoplasmic horror had finally accepted me for what I was rapidly becoming: a Deep One, and as such it could do me no harm.

Released from my paralysis of fright, at last I turned and ran; and there followed my long, loping, low-panting flight along the beach beneath the cliffs, until at last I climbed Seaham's old and crumbling seawall to the promenade, where I paused and drew breath as my eyes took in the silhouette of the seafront by night. I looked closer, staring into the darkness, unable to believe my good fortune. A light was on in Sam Hadley's window, and his battered old Ford stood on the pavement in front of his house.

My one thought now was to get as far away from Seaham as possible, give myself a little time to think things out, and work out a sure means of presenting my case to the authorities. A long taxi ride into Newquay would allow me sufficient time to compose myself, and once there I could go straight to the police. My best approach would be to report Jeremy Belton's death, which must surely be guaranteed to produce the desired result. Before morning, the place on the beach would be crawling with police, and the plans of the Deep Ones in England would be completely scotched, blown sky high!

As to what would then become of me . . . only time would tell. I was not without influential friends. What could be done for me would be done. I could not, dared not believe that what had been started in me was truly without remedy; I had to cling to the belief that whatever else happened, I myself could be . . . put right.

And so I walked unsteadily along the promenade to Sam's place, made my way down the garden path, and knocked on his door. There was movement within; the door opened, and Sam stood in the night-shadowed hall.

'Sam,' I said, 'you don't know how glad I am to find you up! I have a job for you that will pay four times your normal rate, if only you'll—' And there I paused as I noticed the way he silently regarded me, his face white in the moonlight that flooded his doorway. 'Sam?' I said. 'Is something—'

He stepped to one side, and a previously hidden form suddenly loomed in the darkness of the hall behind him. A great hand shot out, grabbed me by the shoulder, and jerked me forward. I threw up my own hands, but too late. In the moment before a massive, clublike fist struck me in the forehead, I recalled something old Jason Ridley had told me when last I had tried to enlist Sam Hadley's services: that the people from the club 'did a fair bit o' trade wi' um!' Then, as I reeled and fell into Hadley's garden, the owner of the sledgelike fists stepped into view: Sargent. And the way he and Hadley stood over me told me that indeed the latter was in league with the Deep Ones, and that once again I was in their power . . .

———

Somehow I held on to consciousness as I was picked up by Sargent and Hadley, carried down the garden path and out through the gate, to be bundled unceremoniously into the back of the old Ford. Then the car's doors slammed and the engine started into life. A moment more, and the car was making a three-point turn in the narrow roadway.

No need to wonder where I was being taken. Doubtless Semple's body had been discovered where I had left it, and the Deep Ones had sent Sargent after me. The trip was a matter of minutes by car. They had phoned Hadley; he had gone to the place on the beach to pick up Sargent; then, returning to Hadley's place, the two had simply waited for me.

As my head began to clear, I lay still and feigned unconsciousness, at the same time easing the rusty screwdriver out of my pocket. One thing was certain: come what may, I was *not* going back to Deep One headquarters. When the car turned left and picked up speed, I knew we were in Sea Lane, Seaham's 'main street' that led to the coastal trunk road, and so to Newquay. At the top of Sea Lane, two hundred yards beyond the village, there was a 'T' junction where the car would once again turn left. There, directly across the bar of the 'T,' was an old, deep, and derelict quarry whose fenced side ran parallel with the road for a distance of some thirty yards. Picturing the quarry as I remembered it from my many walks in the area, a desperate scheme began to form in my mind.

Carefully, moving my body as little and as slowly as possible, I eased myself up until I could see who was driving. It was Sargent, and that suited my scheme perfectly. I doubted if I could do what must be done to an entirely human person, no matter his affiliation with the horrors from the sea. Then I gathered my feet in beneath me and waited, crouching there in the dark interior of the car until Sargent began to apply the brakes as we approached the junction.

Just as the car turned left and started to accelerate, Hadley casually turned and looked directly into my face. His eyebrows shot up in shock, and he yelled: '*Sargent, he's—*'

But I had already looped my right arm round Sargent's neck, lifting his chin while I used my left hand to drive the blade of the screwdriver into his throat. Then, as he choked and grabbed with both hands at his spurting neck, I dropped the screwdriver, shoved him against the door, grabbed the steering wheel and jerked it to the right. The car careened across the road in a screeching of tyres, and mounted the kerb.

By now Hadley was trying to snatch my left hand away from the wheel. I obliged him, smashed the back of my fist into his face, and knew the satisfaction of feeling teeth give way under my knuckles. In the glare of the headlights as the car began to jounce on the uneven slope that formed the quarry's rim, I caught sight of a white wooden fence and knew that time had run out. Falling back, I yanked frenziedly at the door handle and hurled myself out into the night.

I bounced heavily through long grasses, tumbling half-winded into the fence at the quarry's very lip. As I grabbed wildly at an iron upright, the bottom rail of the fence gave way and my lower body slipped through into empty air. I hung on grimly as my arms took the full weight of my body. Below me there was only the darkness of the quarry's sheer depths—which suddenly erupted into a bright gout of fire as a loud explosion shook the night. My plan had worked: the car had plunged through the fence and fallen to the quarry's boulder-strewn floor. Pulling myself to safety, I looked down at the scene below.

The car was standing on its flattened nose in a sea of fire, its interior already a blazing inferno. Sam Hadley's ten-gallon tank must have been full to the brim. Even so, it was unlikely that anyone in the village had heard the crash. The nearest house was two hundred yards away, and the quarry's walls would have deadened the sound of exploding gasoline.

I fought my way through long grasses, gorse, and brambles to the road, crossed it, and started back down Sea Lane. My left ankle was sprained, causing me to limp badly, but other than that I seemed unhurt. For once, good fortune had been with me. I was thinking much more clearly now, and knew what I must do. The house of the village constable stood directly behind his tiny police station midway down Sea Lane. In this sleepy little village of less than six hundred inhabitants, there was no such thing as a twenty-four-hour watch. I would have to wake the elderly constable, William Hearst, and if I knew 'Billy' he'd be sleeping soundly.

In less than five minutes I was leaning against the wall of the police station and giving my ankle a moment's rest. The police station—humble symbol of sanity—I had thought never to see so glad a sight again. And still my luck was holding, for in all the village only one light shone out: a yellow ray of hope from the crack where the door stood ajar beneath the old blue lamp. Billy must be up working late on some report or other.

Then I remembered my last conversation with the ageing policeman: how he had told me he was due for retirement in only a few short weeks. There would be a new man in the job, now. But no matter; a policeman is a policeman . . .

Despite all I had been through, I was conscious of the hour and of my own wild appearance. But surely my condition would only substantiate what I had to say. So I entered that friendly building and crossed to the counter, behind which I knew stood an old oak desk. At the desk, his head bent low over a sheaf of papers, William Hearst's relief kept his lonely vigil. If he heard me enter, he gave no sign.

'Constable,' I said, my voice strange and strained even in my own ears. 'Constable, I wish to report—' And at last he looked up.

His eyes widened in surprise, and his mouth fell open. Then, slowly rising to his feet, he regained his composure. He was a big man of about my own age. I didn't recognize him, but I knew his looks at once!

'Wasn't really expectin' you, Mr Vollister,' the constable drawled. 'And you got somethin' or other to report, 'ave you?' His eyes bored into mine, unblinking eyes that were too big and round above a narrow nose and fleshy lips that curved upward now in an emotionless smile.

Another one of their 'friends' in the village—*a changeling who hadn't quite made it!*

I backed away, strangled noises rasping from a throat suddenly grown dry as a desert, groping behind me until I found the door where it stood open. Then I turned and leaped out into the street, bounding and floating in a mindless panic-flight over the ancient cobbles, down Sea Lane to Front Street and the promenade, leaping like a madman across the tumbled debris of the old sea wall, knowing the biting agony of my twisted ankle and caring not a bit, until I felt the soft sand of the beach beneath my flying feet and turned them homeward.

Homeward, yes, for there was nowhere else to run. How many more of the villagers were part of the Deep One plot to establish themselves in England? I had no way of knowing. And in any case, no matter whom I called on for help, once the 'constable' caught up with me he would soon put an end to any 'wild claims' I might make. And so I could only run.

Nor did I stop until I reached the foot of the steps where they zig-zagged up the cliff face, and only then because I feared that if I did not stop I must surely fall dead from my exertions. But even there, so close to home, still I was full of fear.

Gone now the man of action who had escaped in such spectacular fashion from Sam Hadley's taxi. Now I was in the grip of terror! Terror whispered in a thin wind that sprang up unbidden off the sea, gloomed from the shadows at the foot of the cliffs, stared blindly down from the pale face of the old moon.

Hopping where I could and trailing my injured foot, I somehow managed to climb the precipitous stairs and make my way to my lonely refuge. There I found my door key in its secret place and let myself in. There was evidence that the house had been visited, and I knew that the Deep Ones would not have found too much difficulty in gaining entry, but a quick search of the premises satisfied me that they were not there now. Then I went straight to the telephone . . . a futile hope.

The line must have been down. No, I was fooling myself; the line had been deliberately cut against just such an eventuality as my return to the house.

Now I looked about to see how best I might fortify the house, for I knew that it wouldn't be long before they came for me. Using hammer and nails and a stack of stout shelving from the garage, I set about systematically to barricade the ground-floor doors and windows. I worked all through what remained of the night, and at last, as dawn came up over the horizon, the task was completed to my satisfaction. Then, incapable of keeping my eyes open a second longer, I collapsed on my bed. My exhaustion was such that for once, mercifully, there were neither dreams nor nightmares; or, if there were, I could not re-member them. . . .

Something brought me awake.

I awoke with the sort of shock that often follows a heavy drinking bout—of which I had had my share after the death of my wife—when there is a feeling of dislocation and discontinuity: the sensation of having been stopped, like a timepiece, and then restarted. Then I recognized my own room, saw that I was still in my clothes (and noted how un-kempt and full of sand they were), and the rest of it came back to me as a hideous kaleidoscope of memories.

But what had awakened me?

I sprang from my bed, then reeled drunkenly and almost fell as the searing pain from my now badly swollen ankle washed over me. But I knew that there was much more than a mere sprain wrong with me—indeed, my entire metabolism was now out of order. My brain seemed to burn, my eyes were on fire, every muscle of my body ached as if shredded, and I felt completely dehydrated. I stumbled into my study, starting spastically as the telephone jangled for a second time.

The telephone? Perhaps the line had been down after all, and was now repaired. I snatched the handset from its cradle and said, 'Yes? John Vollister here. Who's calling?'

The shock of hearing my own voice, so guttural, altered, debased, almost made me drop the telephone. The change must be speeding up in me . . . and I had wasted so much time. Sunlight flooded my study, and the absence of shadows outside the balcony window told me that it must be around noon.

'John, is that you?' came Sarah's voice over the wire, a much deeper, coarser voice than I was used to. And, a moment later, there came a sound which at first I could not quite make out. Crying? She was crying! 'John, John—why did you do it? Everything was going so well, for both of us, and now—'

'Why did *I* do it?' I croaked, cutting her off, feeling rage rising in me at the thought of her treachery. 'Me? I did something? Why in hell did *you* do it, Sarah? You knew what they were doing to me, yet you lied to me all along, right from the start. "Ambassador to the Deep Ones," you said—but you didn't tell me that my duties would include this!'

'The change?' she sobbed. 'Is that what you mean? But that might have happened to you, anyway, John.'

'And it might not!' I shouted.

'But what if it had? What would you have done then, as a . . . a half-thing, like Sargent? Why, a man like you—you'd have gone mad!'

'Oh? Would I?' I asked through grinding teeth, wishing I had her there with me, my hands about her throat and not merely the neck of this plastic, impersonal thing that spoke to me now. 'I'd be like Sargent, would I? Oh, yes, I remember. He told me I was one of the lucky ones—and I didn't understand what he meant. Lucky—my God!'

'Listen, John,' her voice was calmer. 'It's not too late for you to square things, even now. There will be a penance, of course, but—'

I listened no further, but slammed the phone down into its cradle, cutting her off. I wondered if they had found Hadley's burned-out car yet; and, of course, they were totally ignorant of the fact that I had not taken the full course of the metamorphosis treatment. 'Not too late,' indeed. Little she knew of it! And yet still I dared hope that the . . . *damage* . . . I had suffered might be repaired.

Then, uselessly, I began soundly to curse the Deep Ones and all they stood for. Where had they been, I wondered, when the change began to affect my father? For surely there must have been far more of their tainted blood in him than there was in me.

It all made sense now—all of the genealogical anomalies in my recent family history, which had always puzzled me—the record of strange deteriorations, suicide, and sudden madness. And perhaps it was that very record which had led them to seek me out in the first place. Poor Belton had said they were recruiting doctors, and through them it was doubtless easy to acquire access to records. It could only have been recently, after all, that they had really started to organize their activities again following the big operation against them in Innsmouth in 1928.

Yes, and that was where it had all started for me, too: in New England . . .

It had been following a trip to America to visit a distant cousin that my grandmother, a young woman, had 'gone into seclusion.' She was still unwed when my father was born at the home, and she died giving him life. This was as much as I had ever known about her, told to me by my mother before her own decline. As for my father: I never knew him. He killed himself when I was a very small child: and that, too, had been following a brief period of severe mental and physical deterioration: 'the change,' of course. No wonder my poor mother, who had never been strong, had followed him in the space of so few years to the grave. She must have seen the horrible thing come over him.

But, damn it all, the blood of the Deep Ones had not been strong in me! I would have lived out my life in total ignorance of them but for their meddling. And now, here I was, with the morbid seeds they had awakened in me blossoming into hideous life, trapped like a rat in my own home. Trapped here, yes, for when I went out on to my balcony I could see them where they waited for me: the big American car along the track that led to the coast road, the little knot of 'picnickers' along the clifftop, the silent watcher who waited at the top of the stairs that wound down to the beach.

To venture outside now would be to give myself into their hands, when they would surely kill me rather than let me carry my story to the authorities. And yet somehow I *must* make the world aware of what was happening. And so my plan took shape and I started work on this manuscript, work which has been continually interrupted but which, nevertheless, I have now almost managed to complete. A few pages more, and . . . But that is to jump ahead of myself.

Scribbling desperately all through the afternoon, I first paused at around 6 P.M. to take a drink and a bite of food, and to tend to my ankle, which was now causing me constant pain and crippling my every movement. I did not want night to descend and find me completely immobilized.

It was then, as I searched for bandages for my sprained ankle, that I heard raised, angry voices from beneath my balcony windows. I had deliberately left the windows ajar in the forlorn hope that someone—some completely human person—might pass my way. Since my house is so out of the way, this was highly unlikely, but there was always a chance, however remote. Now it seemed that good fortune was with me. The male voice I heard was that of my newspaper delivery boy, Graham Lane, and I could only assume that the other voice, female, belonged to his fiancée.

I crept out on to the balcony, keeping well down and out of sight of who or whatever might be watching the house, and raised my head until I could look down. There stood Graham, his shoulders drooping, abjectly watching the haughtily retreating figure of a young woman who hurried back along the lane towards the main road. Twice he called after her, and twice her head lifted a little higher as she stalked jauntily off. Patently they had been out walking, there had been an argument—a lover's tiff—and now she was going off on her own.

'Graham!' I called down. And then, quickly, as he began to turn his head upward: 'No, don't look up. It's me, Mr Vollister. Now listen! Don't turn around. Just stand there, looking after your young lady. I'm being watched, Graham, and I need help. No! For God's sake, *don't look round!* Nod your head, just a little, if you can hear and understand. Good! Now listen:

'I'm in bad trouble, Graham, and it's government business. You see those people up the path there? In the big American car? Those are some of them. There's also a bunch of picnickers on the clifftop—except they're not picnickers. And there's a man at the top of the steps. Don't speak to anyone if you can possibly avoid it. There may well be others. Can you hear me?'

Again the slight nod of his head.

'Good! Now, Graham, there's a hundred pounds in this for you if you can get my message out. Use the public telephone in the village, or maybe the phone in your father's shop. Get the police, Graham, but whatever you do, *don't go to the police in Seaham!* I can't explain now, but the new constable's not to be trusted. Okay?'

Once again the nod. And his whisper, floating up to me: 'Did you say a hundred pounds, Mr Vollister?'

'Two hundred,' I answered, 'if you can pull it off. Make it as dramatic as you like. Counterfeiters, a drug ring—whatever you like. Only get the police here. As many as possible, and as quickly as you can.'

'But what is it?' he whispered. 'What's going on?'

I groped desperately in my mind for an answer he would be able to accept, finally saying: 'Atom spies—sabotage—the new power station at Gar Fell. But don't tell the police that. Tell them it's kidnapping or something. A drug ring would probably do the trick. You'd better get going now before they suspect. Call out after your girl, then run after her.'

He moved to obey as I whispered one last instruction. 'Tell no one else. And remember: don't go to the police in Seaham! Good luck, Graham. You're my one chance . . .

Then he was gone, down the lane, around a bend, disappearing in trees and hedgerows. Without more ado, I crept back into my study, moved away from the windows, and stood up. So far, so good. Providing the lad followed my instructions, I should be safely out of this in the space of a few hours. Perhaps by nightfall. Then—a doctor. The best doctors in the land. What drugs had done to me, perhaps other drugs might reverse. And, by God, wouldn't I have a story to tell when these vile creatures from the sea were brought to book? Indeed I would . . .

On the other hand . . . Suddenly it occurred to me that I might well have placed young Graham Lane in the most terrible danger. What if something should go wrong with my plan? But what could go wrong? Nothing, as long as he followed my instructions . . .

With all of these jumbled thoughts and worries revolving in my head, I removed my clothes to shower before tending to my ankle. It was then, in the clear light of day, that I noticed for the first time the alterations in my feet: the tough webbing of skin that now extended halfway down the length of my toes. This led me to an immediate examination of my hands, which in turn proved to be growing a webbing of toughly elastic skin between the fingers. The bathroom mirror, which until now I had avoided, showed all too clearly how quickly my metamorphosis was taking place: the ichthyic coarsening of the pores of my skin, the toughening of my now near-functional gills, my hideously enlarged eyes, and my rapidly receding hairline.

The sight of these monstrous changes and the knowledge of how they had been wrought in me brought on a seething rage that lasted until I took my shower. And only then did I realize the importance of water to my new state of being, for of course I was rapidly becoming one with the amphibia, beginning to share their traits and characteristics, and while certainly I might live on dry land, I now found the sheer joy of bathing almost unbearable! The water took away all my aches and pains, eased the constriction of my throat, softened my gills, and soaked into my skin, making it pliable and slick to the touch.

My God! At last the horrible implications of my position—my *condition*—drove stunningly home, particularly the inescapable fact that I was no longer completely human. I had known it for some time, of course, ever since discovering myself to be gilled in the cramped confines of the tank, but only now did the real horror of my position truly dawn on me. Even the strongest of men might weep in my predicament, and I am not ashamed to state that I, too, wept.

Afterwards, I sat for a while, and gradually my mood of utter hopelessness began to lift. I could still strike back—*must* strike back—before this thing went any further. And though I had already started to lose faith in my plan of escape (that rescue I had arranged through Graham Lane), still, even in the event that the worst should happen, I could at least leave a documentary warning behind me when finally *they* came for me.

For certainly to rely solely upon my secret messenger would be a great mistake. Graham might be stopped, might not even begin to carry out my instructions. What if he had reconsidered, perhaps suspecting himself to be the would-be victim of some sort of practical joke? In his place I myself would be extremely wary, cautious, suspicious. And what if he in some way attempted to verify the facts of what I had told him? Just suppose he completely ignored my warning and went straight to the police station in Seaham? The short hairs at the back of my neck stood up straight at the thought of *that*, then slowly subsided as I began to plot along the lines of Graham's possible failure to make my plight known to the authorities.

For if indeed anything should go disastrously wrong, still I could not simply let the Deep Ones win so easily. No, I must leave evidence against them, something which would be found after my passing, a clear indictment of their activities. And so it was that as the light began to fail and evening crept in I donned my dressing-gown and returned to working on my manuscript, writing as quickly as possible. It was imperative that the tale be told fully, that as much light as possible be shed upon the hellish activities of these invaders from the deep.

Twice when I paused to rest my eyes, I thought to try the telephone, but on both occasions, as soon as I picked up the handset, guttural enquiries made it obvious that I might only speak to the Deep Ones. Thus I learned to leave the telephone alone. Then, as evening deepened ...

IX
THE UNENDING NIGHTMARE

A sound outside brought me bolt upright from where I had slumped at my desk. I must have dozed off, for my study was now shadowed and gloomy, and the roll of the sea had grown quiet with the hush of encroaching night. Quietly I went out on to my balcony. Figures, looking human enough in the dusk, were down below me in the shadow of the house. If only I had a rifle ... whatever they were up to, I would soon put an end to it. I had no weapon, however, so I went back inside to find my flashlight. Its batteries were weak, but still it should give some light.

Armed with the flashlight, once more I crept out on to the balcony. There, aiming the light downward, I switched on its beam. For a moment, the uncertain shaft of light trapped a pair of startled round-eyed faces that stared up at me, then the furtive figures melted into shadows and moved away around the corner of the house. As they went, I heard a jingling of keys. Well, they'd have little luck in that direction; in addition to being boarded up, my doors were bolted on the inside. But at least this attempted intrusion illustrated the determination of the Deep Ones to get in at me, and I was glad I had taken the precaution of securely barricading the house.

Then, as I was about to return yet again from the balcony to my study, I heard my name softly called from below: 'John—John Vollister—why don't you give in, John Vollister? You can't win, you know.'

Though I had never heard this particular voice before, by its uneven texture I knew its owner for a Deep One. Flashing the beam of light into the shadows of trees that bordered the path to the cliffs, I dimly illuminated a small group of figures. There were four of them, one of whom was—Graham Lane!

His hands were bound behind him and his face seemed to be bloodied. A dark gag (dark with blood, I suspected) filled his mouth, and his hair was awry. His jacket was badly torn, and he stumbled weakly between the three Deep Ones where they kept him in their midst. How he had fallen into their hands I could not say, but certainly he had been badly beaten.

One of the three Deep Ones turned his face directly into the beam of my flashlight and, in that same previously unknown voice, said: 'You should come out now, John Vollister. Already you have incurred grave penalties—and there will be penances in plenty—but nothing you can't endure. If you continue to be awkward, however . . .' The figure shrugged.

'And what do you intend doing with . . . with him?' I finally, hoarsely answered, shining my beam on Graham where he staggered between them. 'He's of no use to you, and he's certainly no threat. Why don't you let him go?'

A chuckle, deep and evil, sounded in the night. 'Come now, John. We all know better than that, don't we? Now listen, it's high time we came to an understanding. You're fairly important to us, and that's why we've been lenient with you—so far. There will be penalties, however, as I've said, and the longer you defy us the worse it will be for you. Indeed, it's not entirely impossible that you might yet incur the ultimate penalty . . . which is why we've brought along young Mr Lane, here. After all, we can't allow him simply to sabotage our programme, now can we? So we've decided to make an example of him . . .' The voice faded into a hideously suggestive silence.

'What do you mean?' I croaked. 'Who the hell are you, to threaten and—'

'Be quiet!' the voice hissed, its feigned affability disappearing in a moment. 'Be quiet—*and watch!*'

The three Deep Ones stepped away from their stumbling captive and left him isolated on the path. My light faltered where it fell upon the bound, beaten youth, then strengthened momentarily as an over-whelming stench of seaweed and foulness welled up from the darkness. I nearly dropped the flashlight then, as I recognized that deep ocean smell. It was the monstrous stench of a shoggoth—and I immediately guessed what the 'ultimate penalty' would be!

Caught in the trembling beam of light, Graham Lane also smelled that fatal fetor and stumblingly turned towards its source. Swelling out of the shadows came a greater blackness glinting with myriad eyes, all of them fixed upon its victim as the shoggoth flowed and squelched with sea-squirt sounds along the path towards him. At first frozen to the spot, finally Graham turned to flee. He stumbled, fell, somehow struggled to his feet . . . and the thing was upon him!

Transfixed with horror, clutching at the balcony to maintain my balance, I could only watch. God help me, I *could not* turn away as the thing happened!

Graham's form, stumbling down the old path, hands tied behind him, had just started to topple forward into a second fall as the shoggoth enveloped him. One moment he was there—and in the next there was only the pulsing, blackly glistening distorted shape of the monstrosity from the sea. Gagged, he had not even been able to scream as the thing took him . . .

And now there came that subdued roar I remembered so well—

the firing of the shoggoth's internal engines—and the opening of its vile exhaust orifice, and then . . . then.

That fine, black jet of stinking mist that shot upward high into the air—a spray of human debris—the atomized essence of Graham Lane!

Finally, sufficient strength and movement returned to my nerveless fingers to enable me to switch off the beam from my flashlight, and then for a long while I tottered in dumb oblivion high above the scene of Graham's awful murder. Slowly, very slowly, my senses returned to me, by which time all was silent and the shoggoth stench had disappeared. The whole episode had been like a nightmare which was now ended, except that I knew it was no nightmare.

Staggering back inside and locking the windows, I felt a weird and utterly unnatural excitement rising in me: the crazy urge to tear down my sturdily erected defences, throw back the bolts, and rush outside to do battle with those who sought me. Rapidly, the wildest of schemes occurred to my fevered brain, insane urges that sent me raging through the house until, at the last, I recognized the source of this new threat and began to combat it.

This was surely a manifestation of my emerging madness, no doubt brought on by Graham Lane's hideous death, proof that my drug-damaged psyche was rapidly deteriorating. In just such a fury I had crushed the life out of Semple; and, when escaping from the place on the beach, I had also felt a lunatic urge to swim out to sea and give myself into the hands of the eternal tides. A similar madness had crept over me when I had spoken to Sarah on the telephone, which had made me lust after her life in a murderous fury. In short, the mad emotions I felt within me were a direct result of my metamorphosis—and of my failure to take the pills which alone might have saved my sanity.

When the truth dawned on me, I went straight to the bathroom and doused my throbbing head. And a few minutes later I was myself again. Then, putting to the back of my mind as best I might the death of the youth who had tried to help me, I returned to this, my manuscript, and scribbled frantically until well after midnight.

It was then, just as I was beginning to nod once more over my work, that I heard a peculiar sound issuing from somewhere below. My ears were, of course, attuned to the house, to each familiar creak of settling timbers and every quiet gurgle of the plumbing, so that any extraneous sound was immediately apparent to me. Quickly, I went down into the darkness of the ground floor, silently inspecting all my fortifications and listening for any repetition of the sound. I was in the library, checking my interior work on its tall, narrow-framed windows, when I was shocked into immobility by a recurrence of the sound, this time from close at hand. Someone was working on one of the windows beyond the barricade with a glass-cutter!

Silently I made my way to the kitchen, found a meat cleaver, and returned to the library. Knowing the house intimately, I had not once resorted to the use of lights. Only the light in my study continued to burn, and doubtless my adversaries believed me to be up there right now, fast asleep. Well, they were in for an unpleasant surprise. I seated myself, placed the cleaver in my lap, and waited.

The luminous dial of the library clock showed the hour to be just after 1 A.M. when the first board was sufficiently loose to be carefully removed out into the night. I stood up then and moved to one side, careful to keep out of sight as a light was flashed into the library from the darkness outside. A breeze was coming off the sea, and with it a powerful smell of deep ocean that was far from right. There were Deep Ones out there, for a certainty, and to prove the matter beyond dispute there came into view the hand that galvanized me into action. It was mottled and webbed, that hand, with a webbing far more pronounced than my own meagre growth, so that I knew its owner to be a fully developed Deep One.

In the hour or so that I had sat there in silence, the rage within me had once again reached terrifying proportions, so that I was no longer wholly in control of myself when I made my move. The hand had just commenced to explore the edge of the gap formed by the missing board, was groping and pushing here and there, when I chopped at the fingers with my cleaver. Immediately, there came an agonized howl of pain as the hand was withdrawn—but three fingers and the tip of the thumb stayed inside the house with me!

Then, laughing demoniacally and almost dancing with crazed glee, I tossed the grisly digits out after their owner before taking up an even stouter board and nailing it into place. This time I used long spikes of nails which nothing less than a large hammer would be able to dislodge. I had no fear that the Deep Ones would use a shoggoth's great strength to break in: that would have caused a great deal of damage which might not be too easy to explain away should anyone stumble upon the house in the near future, before repairs could be effected.

Finished at last with the work on my breached barricade, I put on the lights and spent a further hour nailing up more boards in the other lower-level rooms. Whatever else happened, I didn't intend the Deep Ones to take me until my work on my manuscript was done.

At some time during these frantic physical exertions of mine, the madness went out of me, so that as I finished I discovered myself sane once more and weary from exhaustion. But finally, satisfied at last that the house was once again as secure as I could make it, I left the ground floor lights on and returned silently to my study. Let them believe that I was still downstairs; perhaps it would keep them away from the house.

And so I spent the rest of the night writing—and often as not nodding—at my desk, until the early morning sun crept into my study to tell me that I had survived to face another day. I threw some water on my face to freshen up, then went out on to the balcony. They were still there: the big car, the picnickers, the watcher at the top of the steps. But none of them was near the house. That suited my purposes perfectly, and I made a quick breakfast before preparing to take a shower.

Then it was that I discovered a further development of the siege, one which would have very serious consequences for me. It was simply this: that the water from the shower was flowing with much less than its usual force.

I shut the water off at once, put on my dressing-gown, and went up into the attic. It was as I had feared: the Deep Ones had somehow contrived to shut off my water supply; no water was reaching the house from the outside. How long, then, before they also interfered with the electricity supply? My answer came at midday when I tried to make coffee. The game was over; now they were in earnest. And yet . . . if I could only make it through one more night, I knew I could finish my work. And indeed that work had now become an obsession with me, so that as the afternoon grew towards evening I worked ever faster.

I could not possibly hope to keep this up without sleep, however, and I found myself snatching the odd half hour now and then, always jerking into wakefulness at the slightest sound. Then I would get up from my desk, go to the bathroom, and thoroughly douse my face and gills, always carefully turning off my rapidly diminishing water supply when I was finished.

At about 6 P.M., I was startled from fitful sleep by the persistent ringing of my telephone. Not only that, but my study light was on. For some reason, the Deep Ones had temporarily restored my power—but not, I later discovered, my water. Before answering the phone, I had sufficient wit to dash downstairs and switch on my electric kettle. It had dawned on me that when the call was finished it might also signal the end of my electricity. So, if I could only keep the caller busy on the wire for a few minutes, I should have some coffee!

It was Sarah on the telephone, and her voice was now almost un-recognizable: 'John, listen—and please don't put the phone down—you *must* listen to me. The Deep Ones are very angry, John, and unless you'll see sense they intend to take you by force. Surely you must know by now that you can't win?'

'I can try,' I answered.

'John, don't be a fool! There's nothing left for you now among ordinary men. You're finished with all that. Now it's you and I—both of us together—and the Deep Ones forever!'

'I'll kill myself first,' I told her, fighting back the rage that was rapidly building in me.

'But why? We'll have each other, John, and even now it's not too late for—'

'Sarah,' I cut her off, forcing myself to maintain a semblance of sanity, 'it is too late. Much too late. I didn't take the pills.'

There was a long pause, then: 'Pills?' Her voice was hushed, a cracked whisper. 'What pills? Not the—'

'Yes, *those* pills—the ones that stop your poor damned victims from going mad. The ones that help them keep their mental equilibrium as the change accelerates. Semple told me all about them—but too late. I didn't take them.'

'John—I'll come to you,' she said, her altered voice full of desperation. 'I'll come!'

'Not now, Sarah,' I told her. 'Don't come tonight. Not in the dark—not with the lights out—with the stench of the Deep Ones on you! If you do, I'll kill you! I'll kill every damn one of you who puts his damn nose anywhere near me! Do you hear? *Do you hear?*' And I slammed the handset back into its cradle. Damn every last one of the stinking, Hell-spawned devils!

I went stumbling into the bathroom, my rage seething within me, caught my reflection in the mirror as I splashed my face with water—then ripped the mirror from the wall! And that was the signal for me to go on a rampage of destruction right through the house. I overturned chairs and tables, brought down shelves of cut crystal which had taken me years to collect, ripped pictures from walls, and tore down curtains until at last, as the mental fever began to burn itself out (at least for the moment), I found myself in the kitchen. The water in the kettle was still hot. Shaking like a leaf in a gale, dizzy and weak from my uncontrollable excesses, I made coffee and shakily carried the jug and a cup back upstairs to my study.

Then, as dusk began to settle in and the light started to grow dim, I remembered a box of candles long ago pushed to the back of a drawer in the kitchen. I had bought them in the village months ago when a fault had developed in the house's wiring. I went back downstairs and found them, eight of them, lighting two and placing them strategically in my study to give a maximum of light. At the same time, I primed and brought up a blowtorch I'd once used in paint-stripping; it might come in useful, if only as another source of light.

Having made what preparations I could before the onset of night, I decided to trust to luck and snatch an hour's sleep. I set the alarm clock and stretched out on my bed, where exhaustion soon overtook me . . .

Something woke me from a nightmare of sinking endlessly into black waters. Sweating profusely, remembering what had gone before, I started up and stared at the luminous dial of the alarm clock. 11.35? What had happened? I couldn't believe my eyes!

Snatching up the clock, I shook it angrily before noting that the alarm mechanism had jammed. Obviously, the fault was mine: I had overwound the thing! I tossed it down and went through to my study where one of the candles still guttered in its saucer. The tiny wick was floating in a little pool of wax. Immediately, I lit another candle, then sat down nervously to wait for a recurrence of whatever it was that had awakened me.

I didn't have long to wait.

No sooner was I seated than there came fumbling sounds from outside, small furtive noises that only just reached me from the other side of the house. I went to the bathroom, which is on that side, and carefully, quietly opened the window a few inches. An almost overpowering odour at once wafted up from below, driving me back from the window in horror and disgust! There must be an entire gang of Deep Ones out there to create a stench like that—but what were they up to?

I closed the window, took up my cleaver, and made my way silently downstairs to the kitchen. A side door led from the kitchen into the garage, and by my judgement that was where the Deep Ones had gathered. But what could they be doing? The garage had no windows, and its exterior door was of stout metal. Surely they would not be looking there for a way in?

I opened the door to the garage—and literally staggered in the hideous rush of vile gasses that immediately poured out to fill the kitchen! Although the batteries of my flashlight were almost exhausted, still I had thought to bring it with me. Holding my nose against the stench, I put down my cleaver, took the flashlight from the pocket of my dressing-gown, and flashed it briefly about the untidy interior of the disused room. It was exactly as I had last seen it, and—

No, not exactly the same, for there was a sound: a trickling as of some oily liquid. That monstrous stench—the trickling sound—and a *motion*! I had seen something move as I flashed my dim beam across the room. Holding the flashlight tightly, trembling so badly that I could barely control my movements, slowly I swung the beam back to the wide metal door. A slow, thickly glutinous trickle of dark—*substance*—was entering through the keyhole in the door and forming a small pool on the concrete floor.

Silently stepping over old boxes and cartons and skirting a pile of unused boards, I approached the door and knelt to watch this filthy stuff filter into the garage. It was shiny black and full of the same evil smell which so offended me; indeed, it was the source of that smell. Was it inflammable, I wondered? Did the Deep Ones intend to burn me out? I hadn't thought they would dare anything so extreme. Any subsequent investigation would surely lead to—

A hideous suspicion had entered my mind, and before I could consciously stop myself, I had put out a finger to dab it at the edge of the small puddle of goo. It was warm, sticky, and it clung to my finger as if . . . alive!

I snatched my finger back, saw that the outer layers of skin had been removed from it—dissolved away—and, mouth agape, turning my eyes once more to the pool of noxious matter, I saw . . . saw that it was forming a little hump, a gelatinous stalagmite that grew up inches from the floor even as I watched, and formed—formed—an eye!

Great God in heaven, it was a shoggoth they had out there, one of their protomorphic 'machines'! And it was pouring itself into my garage like pus from some cosmic sore!

For a moment the vile trickling paused as that single eye gazed at me, then the loathsome orb melted back into its elementary slime and the flow continued at a redoubled rate. I fled upstairs, uncaring now of any noise I might make, back to my lighted study where I cast about for a way to drive the shoggoth out into the night.

Almost at once my eyes lighted upon the primed blowtorch. Would that work, I wondered? God!—it must work! If there was one thing that the horror in the garage could not stand against, surely that thing would be heat. Oh, I knew well enough that these monsters could generate tremendous heat *within* themselves (they would need that facility, for it's an extremely cold world on the bed of the ocean), but this small pool, this tendril of living matter—it must surely be vulnerable.

I rushed back downstairs, through the kitchen and into the garage, crossing to the door and kneeling beside the now *rippling* and lumpy pool of loathsomeness. Quickly I struck a match to the blowtorch and pumped the flame to a roaring lance of invisible heat. Faster still the goo poured in, and more purposeful the agitation in the ever-widening pool. Two eyes formed this time, rearing up to peer at me—just as I turned the blowtorch on them!

Instantly a mephitic cloud of steam rose up from the pool, obscuring everything as I covered my nose and mouth with one hand while directing the blowtorch with the other. Suddenly I felt about my legs the whipping lash of something that burned like acid, and through a momentary gap in the shrivelling pool of shoggoth tissue I saw writhing pseudopods of frenziedly thrashing slime. Then, accompanied by an utterly unearthly shriek of agony from beyond the door—a sound which neither human nor any animal throat, nor any mechanical device known to man, might make—the remaining thread of tissue was withdrawn through the keyhole and I was left playing the blowtorch on an area of stained, scorched cement.

Once more I had won, and in so doing had given myself the time necessary for the completion of my manuscript. I went back upstairs and splashed myself all over with life-giving water; then, as soon as my nerves were sufficiently calmed, I returned to my desk and to this, my work, which was then well over three-quarters completed . . .

That was last night, almost twenty-four hours ago, and it was the last attempt of the Deep Ones to drive me from my home. In any case, they had probably known that I could not hold out much longer. My guess is that they were simply attempting to 'save me from myself,' from my threat to commit suicide. I had never intended to do so in the first place, but they didn't know that.

This morning, as the sun came up, I tried to doze a little, only to discover that my nightmares were now so monstrous that sleep was no longer possible. And later, Sarah phoned to tell me that she would come at noon.

She came, bringing with her the conch that had first introduced me to the horror. She brought both the shell and the answers, at last, to those few remaining questions which still baffled me; answers that now fit together to complete the puzzle.

I did not kill her as I had threatened, but instead put away my manuscript, took down the boards that barred her entry, and made her as welcome as I could. The madness was off me, and only a great weariness remained. It was the weariness of defeat, the knowledge that I could not possibly win the whole game, and that my only hope for personal survival lay with the Deep Ones.

Yes, she brought me my conch, a shell similar to the type used by the *adaro* of the Solomon Islands to call to their land-born brothers and lure them down to the sea. And indeed it was that conch which had first lured me, whose colours and contours had struck hidden chords of that ancestral memory which flows in the blood and lingers in the minds of all Deep Ones. That shell, and with it those dreams from R'lyeh with which I had been so singularly honoured, had been the triggers to quicken the seeds within me. The rest of it should have been a slow but certain process of indoctrination and preparation.

Sarah was to have helped, was the sweet worm with which they had baited their tender hook, and certainly I had taken the bait. Then, just as things were going exactly as they had planned, I had wrecked the entire scheme by returning to the place on the beach when they were not expecting me. The only course left open to them then had been to take me forcibly and process my metamorphosis as quickly as possible.

These things I already knew, but there were others I still did not understand. Sarah told me about them. For instance, there was her 'father.' He was not her father at all, but her *four-times-great-grandfather!* One of the benefits of being a Deep One is extreme longevity. And I, too, could be 'proud' of my genealogy, for my unknown grandfather had been an Innsmouth Marsh of the original Marsh line, which was one of the two reasons why I had been tracked down and singled out for . . . rehabilitation?

As for the other reason: Belton had been right. I was a marine biologist, and there was much I could teach the Deep Ones—and learn from them—there in the great deeps. There were problems to be overcome, though, for science in a submarine environment is no simple matter.

All of these things Sarah told me, and certain others, but when I felt the madness returning, I made her go. Then I boarded up the door again before taking a shower in the last of my water to cool and ease pains both mental and physical. As to what had set the rage burning in me once more—that vicious boiling of my blood and the hideous lusts it engenders—I think it was Sarah's face, no longer a wholly human face, and yet in no way as repulsive as I had thought I might find it. It was to me, with its bulging eyes and thickening lips, as a mirror of my own face, which no longer offends me but looks almost—natural? And, indeed, that was the paradox that sparked the rage in me . . . but only for a little while.

Since making her leave me, I have spent most of my time at my desk, tidying up this work as best I might, and at last I have brought it to a close. Now, as midnight approaches, there are strange shadows on the silver sands, and some of them tower and nod in an entirely monstrous fashion. For this is the hour appointed, when I swore to deliver to the Deep Ones my final word—which is that I shall join them there in the Deeps!

Except that—

Whoever you are, reading this, be certain of one thing: that even though I go to join them, still I loathe and detest them! But life is dear to me—even as a changeling, life is dear—and all the untold wonders of the oceans await me . . .

Yet still I say to you, *I will be avenged!* This I swear!

Whoever you are, and whenever you discover this manuscript locked in its metal box, do not delay, but ensure that it meets the eyes of the proper authorities immediately! *The continuity of your very world depends upon it!*

And whosoever doubts my word, only let him look beneath the waters, let him only walk along the shores of this world and listen to the songs of the sea. For in the end, if ever the Deep Ones are to be rooted out and destroyed, it must be you and not I who brings about that destruction. I cannot help you, for I can no longer help myself. Although I have sworn vengeance, such vengeance can strike only through you now.

For the madness is on me and the voice of the storm calls to me. I hear it raging from the mouth of my conch, see it foaming in the white-caps conjured in the contours of its whorl! And I must go where the octopus stares with cat's eyes and the squid silently starts on jets of ink, where the timeless tides tell stories of primal ocean, and coral labyrinths thrill to siren songs from abyssal caverns.

Ia-R'lyeh!

I am one with all the hosts of Dagon and Mother Hydra—one with the Deep Ones in the worship of the Great Father Kraken—and with them I shall make my home in vasty vaults of ocean . . .

Personal—by hand—for the attention of:
William P. Marsh, Esq.
c/o The Gilman Hotel
Innsmouth, Mass.
July 28

Venerable Brother—

Most humble greetings from England, where all pro-ceeds according to plan—except for that of which you were previously apprised. Ahu-Y'hloa grows apace, and already her columns take on a certain lustre—but more of that, and of the gains we have made and continue to make in Seaham at a later date.

With regard to the manuscript which accompanies this:

It was discovered hidden beneath some loose floor-boards in a ground-floor room of what was once your grandson's house. We have, of course, acquired the place in the furtherance of our plans, and the discovery of the manuscript was quite by chance.

In reading it I am sure you will note that under the precipitate circumstances all of our actions were fully warranted, and that if anyone is to blame for the outcome that one must surely be David Semple. As you are aware (and as the manuscript so graphically tells), he has already paid in full for his inefficiency.

As was your wish, no penance has been taken of your grandson, since it is deemed that by virtue of his own folly he has already paid enough. Despite his oath at the end of the manuscript, he no longer displays any hurtful tendencies towards us; at his best he is an avid student of the Lore.

Furthermore, he desires permission to undertake a pilgrimage—to R'lyeh! He wishes to enter that most sacred of doors and go down to the lower vaults, to the feet of dreaming Cthulhu Himself. Aye, for he has heard the call of Cthulhu in his dreams, wherefore we cannot deny him that most high audience.

The girl, Sarah, of my own flesh as you well know, would go with him on the journey. This will be an undertaking of several years' duration, during which they will visit and carry Cthulhu's word to many of the more remote settlements along the way. Of course, it is understood that she must first abide the time of her spawning. Since you have intimated your own desire that no further harm befall John Vollister, and since unfortunately he is no longer of any use for much else, the plan would seem a good one. His condition is quite irreversible, but the girl will be there to care for him when he is not himself . . .

Yrs. by the Sign of Ab-Hyth,
Ephraim Bishop